Swamp Story

"The funniest thing we've read in years, or maybe just since the last Dave Barry novel."

—*People*

"Before you open this book, ask yourself one important question: How hard do I want to laugh? Because (a) it's Dave Barry, and (b) it's Dave Freaking Barry. Of course *Swamp Story* is about greed, fraud, and viral fame, but there are also big-ass reptiles to keep the sketchiest characters on their toes. Everything that happens in this wild novel could easily happen in South Florida, and probably will. Read it here first. Dave's version is always the funniest."

—Carl Hiaasen

"With *Swamp Story*, Dave Barry combines two important elements of literature: a swamp and a story."

—Steve Martin

"Dave Barry continues his powerful, hypnotic sway over us readers with this latest, powerful, hypnotic work that is not only hilariously funny, but also powerful and hypnotic."

—ALSO Steve Martin

"I laughed out loud! (to think that Dave would dare publish a book). Yet, this book continues Dave's streak of humor writing that is the best in the country. Congratulations to Dave and all the lucky readers."

—AGAIN, Steve Martin

"I'm frankly tired of Dave Barry being so funny. Yet, he's done it again to the benefit and delight of all of us. A hilarious new work."

—STILL Steve Martin

"I haven't read it yet, but I love it!"

—YET AGAIN, Steve Martin

"An authentically rendered distillation of the Sunshine State's special sensibility. The novel is funny, ridiculous, and even moving—a typical Barry affair. . . . Barry's crew of misfits is a wild one, but the dual plots he sets in motion are why *Swamp Story* shines. . . . If you want to read about the state and have fun doing so . . . read *Swamp Story* and dive into the Floridian muck. It takes a Florida man to write a proper, ridiculous Florida novel."

—*Washington Examiner*

"If you are looking for a silly, inane, ridiculous, hysterically funny, and laugh-out-loud read for this summer, I have a book for you! . . . [O]ne heck of a yarn. Barry is a master of dialogue. . . . If you have ever lived in Florida, wintered in Florida, or even vacationed in Florida, you will appreciate the humor Barry finds in the state. And even if you haven't been there, you'll enjoy a good laugh at its expense."

—*Fredericksburg Free Lance-Star*

"Get ready to laugh out loud with Dave Barry's return to fiction, *Swamp Story*. It's a hilarious Sunshine-State caper. . . . The Pulitzer Prize winner and self-described 'Florida Man' always delivers the laughs, and *Swamp Story* is no exception."

—*Parade*

"Larger-than-life hijinks abound in *Swamp Story*, the zany thriller from Dave Barry. . . . [A] hilarious caper that could only happen in Florida. Fans of Barry and Carl Hiaasen will be on the edge of their seats— except when they're rolling on the floor."

—*Shelf Awareness*

"Florida's humorist laureate finds chaos and comedy in the Everglades. . . . Gold bars, pythons, and TikTok videos of swamp monsters add up to a hilarious Florida tale. . . . Barry makes mirth of all this mayhem with his usual aplomb."

—*Kirkus Reviews* (starred review)

"Crime fiction doesn't come much funnier than this Florida-set caper. . . . Barry conducts the hijinks like a maestro of comic suspense. Carl Hiaasen fans will be in heaven."

—*Publishers Weekly*

Also by Dave Barry

Homes and Other Black Holes

Dave Barry's Guide to Marriage and/or Sex

Claw Your Way to the Top

Dave Barry's Bad Habits

Stay Fit and Healthy Until You're Dead

Babies and Other Hazards of Sex

The Taming of the Screw

FICTION

The Worst Night Ever

The Worst Class Trip Ever

Insane City

Lunatics (with Alan Zweibel)

The Bridge to Never Land (with Ridley Pearson)

Peter and the Sword of Mercy (with Ridley Pearson)

Science Fair (with Ridley Pearson)

Peter and the Secret of Rundoon (with Ridley Pearson)

Cave of the Dark Wind (with Ridley Pearson)

The Shepherd, the Angel, and Walter the Christmas Miracle Dog

Escape from the Carnivale (with Ridley Pearson)

Peter and the Shadow Thieves (with Ridley Pearson)

Peter and the Starcatchers (with Ridley Pearson)

Tricky Business

Big Trouble

SWAMP STORY

A NOVEL

DAVE BARRY

Simon & Schuster Paperbacks

NEW YORK   LONDON   TORONTO
SYDNEY   NEW DELHI

An Imprint of Simon & Schuster, LLC
1230 Avenue of the Americas
New York, NY 10020

First Simon & Schuster trade paperback edition May 2024

SIMON & SCHUSTER PAPERBACKS and colophon are registered trademarks of Simon & Schuster, LLC

Simon & Schuster: Celebrating 100 Years of Publishing in 2024

For information about special discounts for bulk purchases, please contact Simon & Schuster Special Sales at 1-866-506-1949 or business@simonandschuster.com.

The Simon & Schuster Speakers Bureau can bring authors to your live event. For more information or to book an event, contact the Simon & Schuster Speakers Bureau at 1-866-248-3049 or visit our website at www.simonspeakers.com.

Interior design by Paul Dippolito

Manufactured in the United States of America

1   3   5   7   9   10   8   6   4   2

Library of Congress Cataloging-in-Publication Data has been applied for.

ISBN 978-1-9821-9133-7
ISBN 978-1-9821-9134-4 (pbk)
ISBN 978-1-9821-9135-1 (ebook)

This book is dedicated to the state of Florida,
which has its flaws, but which is never, ever boring.

Chapter 1

"Slater!" Jesse yelled. "Get out here! There's a snake!"

Jesse threw down her book and snatched Willa off the beach towel where she'd been dozing. The snake was maybe twenty-five feet away. It had slid silently around the side of the cabin. It looked huge to Jesse, its long, thick body covered with brown blotches, its triangular head an arrow pointing at her and her baby. Jesse knew it was a python. She'd seen pythons out here before. But none this big.

"SLATER!"

No answer from the cabin.

"Slater, there's a snake out here!"

Still no answer.

"SLATER! There's a very large snake! Please get out here right now!"

"Hang on." Slater's voice, drifting out through the open doorway, was hoarse, as if he had just taken a massive hit off a bong, which in fact he had.

The snake glided a few feet forward into the clearing, directly toward Jesse and Willa. Jesse wanted to run to the cabin, but that would mean running toward the snake. Clutching Willa, she backed up several steps, to the edge of the clearing, next to a live oak. If she stepped back any more, she'd be wading barefoot in the mucky, murky waters of the Everglades, which she knew contained both snakes *and* alligators, and God knew what else.

The snake slid a little closer.

"SLATER, GET OUT HERE RIGHT NOW!"

"Jesus Christ all RIGHT."

Slater appeared in the doorway, blinking, unsteady, clearly baked. His eyes were bright red; his hair, unwashed for weeks, hung in long greasy strands. He wore a filthy pair of cut-off University of Florida sweatpants, nothing else. Yet he still looked better than 99.999 percent of all human males who had ever walked the Earth. He was strikingly handsome in a classic Tom Cruise—in–his–prime way—thick, jet-black hair; brilliant green eyes; high cheekbones; square jaw. He was tall, a foot taller than Cruise, and his body, despite the fact that he never seemed to do anything for it, was spectacular—lean, muscular and sculpted, the body of an elite athlete in peak condition. Even in that moment, with a major snake threatening her and her baby, Jesse could not help but be aware, in some small sector of her consciousness, that Slater, sweaty, filthy and glassy-eyed from weed, was without question the hottest man she had ever seen.

Which is why she'd ended up out here in the Everglades with him and their baby. And ninety trillion mosquitoes. And no money.

And this snake.

"Where is it?" said Slater.

Jesse pointed.

"Jesus Christ," said Slater, eyes widening. He called back into the cabin. "Kark! You need to get this!"

"What?" said a voice, as hoarse as Slater's, maybe hoarser.

"Big fucking snake," said Slater. "I mean *big*."

The snake slid forward another two feet, directly toward Jesse and Willa. Jesse saw that she now no longer had the option of even trying to run past it.

"Slater!" she said, trying to keep the panic out of her voice, not wanting Willa to pick up on it.

Slater held up his hands in a *Calm down* gesture.

"It's cool," he said. "This'll be good. Good footage."

"Good *footage*?" said Jesse. "Are you—"

"Goddammit, Kark," yelled Slater, "get the camera out here!"

"OKOKOK," said Kark, emerging from the cabin, holding the video camera. He looked as bad as Slater looked good. He wore only boxer shorts, once white, now a multicolored mess of brownish-yellowish stains of God only knew what origin, the waistband hidden under the overhang of his vast, pasty, drooping belly. Kark's eyes—small bloodshot orbs in a big moon face—darted around the clearing.

"Where is it?" he said.

"There," said Slater, pointing.

"Holy shit," said Kark.

"I know!" said Slater. "You ready?"

"Yeah," said Kark, raising the camera to his face. "So what're you gonna do?"

Slater frowned, studying the snake. As he did, it glided another couple of feet closer to Jesse and Willa. It was now about ten feet away from them. Jesse inched back, her feet now in the water, sinking into the muck.

"Slater!" she shouted. "DO something!" Willa, startled by her mother's voice, began to cry.

"OKOK," said Slater. To Kark he said, "Make sure you get this." He took a cautious step toward the snake. Kark, with the camera to his eye, followed, belly jiggling as he moved.

The snake was still looking at Jesse and Willa.

Slater, with Kark right behind, took another small step. He was now about the same distance from the snake as it was from Jesse and Willa.

"Shoo," he said to the snake.

The snake did not appear to notice.

"Shoo?" said Jesse. "*Shoo?*"

"Fuck," said Kark, looking at the camera. "The battery's dead."

"You're kidding me," said Slater.

"Be right back," said Kark, waddling toward the cabin. "Don't do anything."

The snake slid forward another foot.

"SLATER!" yelled Jesse, stepping back, now up to her knees in the swamp. "YOU NEED TO DO SOMETHING ABOUT THIS SNAKE."

"Hang on," said Slater. "We have to change the battery."

"Where's the other battery?" yelled Kark, from inside the cabin.

"It was next to the cooler," said Slater.

"I don't see it."

"Jesus Christ," said Slater, heading back to the cabin.

"SLATER!" yelled Jesse.

"Just hold still," Slater answered. "I'll be right back." He disappeared through the doorway.

The snake slid forward. It was now less than five feet away from Jesse. Clutching Willa, she took another step back into the murky water, her legs sinking deeper into the muck. She realized she was about to become stuck there.

"SLATER!"

"One sec!"

The snake was at the edge of the water now, its massive body stretching halfway across the clearing behind it. Jesse tried to step back, struggling against the sucking swamp mud. She felt her right leg brush against something sharp. She glanced down, saw it was a fallen live oak branch, the tip sticking out of the water. She shifted Willa to her left arm, reached down, grabbed it and yanked. It didn't move.

"Dammit," she said. She shifted her weight and yanked the branch harder. It made a cracking sound and broke free. Jesse looked up and saw that the snake was close enough that she could touch it. She raised the branch and slammed it down as hard as she could on the snake's head.

"GO AWAY," she shouted.

"One sec!" Slater yelled from the cabin. "We found the battery."

"GO AWAY GO AWAY GO AWAY!" shouted Jesse, striking the snake's snout over and over. Willa was screaming now. Jesse braced herself, ready to dive backward into the swamp if the snake lunged at her.

But it didn't. Instead, it turned its head away from the pesky branch and glided, unhurriedly, to the side of the clearing, then disappeared into the tall sawgrass.

Jesse, struggling, pulled her feet from the sucking, stinking muck and stumbled forward onto firm ground. She fell to her knees, gasping and clutching her baby, who was still crying.

"It's OK, Willa," Jesse said, fighting her own tears.

As she knelt there, trying to calm herself and her baby, Slater emerged from the cabin, followed by Kark with the camera.

"Where is it?" said Slater, looking around. "Jess, where's the snake?"

Jesse, still trying to catch her breath, waved toward the edge of the clearing.

"Shit!" said Slater. He turned to Kark. "We finally get a fucking python and you have a dead fucking battery!"

Kark, from behind the camera, said, "Maybe it's still there."

Slater, with Kark trailing, walked across the clearing. He stopped at the edge and looked at the thick wall of sawgrass.

"Is this where it went?" he asked Jesse.

She glared at him. "Why don't you go in there and see?"

Slater looked back at Kark, who had the camera to his eye. "You getting this?"

Kark nodded.

Slater took a small step forward, parted the sawgrass with his arms and peered ahead for a few seconds.

"It's gone," he announced.

Jesse snorted.

Slater, ignoring her, faced the camera, frowning.

"We just missed it," he said. "A Burmese python, easily fifteen feet. A deadly predator, fully capable of killing a man and swallowing him whole. It could be anywhere out here. It's a risk we take every day, living the life of the Glades Guy."

"Man," said Kark.

"What?" said Slater.

"It's Glades *Man*," said Kark. "Not Glades Guy."

"You don't think Glades Guy sounds better? The two 'G' sounds?"

"Yeah, but they're called gladesmen."

"Who is?"

"The guys who live out here."

"Who calls them that?"

"They call themselves that. Everybody calls them that. That's how I pitched it to the network. If we sell the show it's gonna be called *Glades Man*."

Slater shrugged. "OK, then. Glades Man. You still recording?"

"Yeah."

"OK, we'll just pick it up from where I don't see the snake."

Slater faced the sawgrass, then turned dramatically back to the camera, frowning in an effort to convey disappointment. "We just missed it," he said. "A Burmese python, probably twenty feet long. A deadly predator that can kill a grown man and swallow him whole. It's just one of the dangers we . . . we *glades men* face every single day, out here in the wild and wide-open—"

"Look out!" shouted Jesse. "It's coming back!"

Slater, emitting a high, nonmasculine sound, jumped toward Kark, knocking him backward. The two of them fell to the dirt, Slater crawling on all fours away from the edge of the clearing.

"Where is it?" he shouted, looking around frantically, his voice still a good two octaves higher than usual.

Then he realized that Jesse was laughing.

And that there was no snake.

"Jesse, what the *fuck*," he said, scrambling to his feet. "That was not funny!"

"Oh, you're wrong there," said Jesse.

"Do we want to keep this footage?" said Kark, on his butt in the dirt but still holding the camera to his eye.

"No, we fucking don't want to keep it!" shouted Slater. "Turn it off!"

"OKOK," said Kark, hitting a button.

For a few seconds the only sound in the clearing was Willa's whimpering.

"Did you get anything we can use?" Slater asked Kark.

Kark frowned. "Just you looking at the grass where the snake went."

Slater shook his head. "We need to do better than that. We need something *real*. Something *dangerous*."

"Slater," said Jesse, "do you even understand what just happened here?"

"Yes, Jess, I do," he said. "What happened was, we had a chance to get some critical footage that could sell this reality show to the network, and we didn't get it."

Jesse shook her head. "No, what happened was, you were so concerned about getting your *footage* that you left me and your baby alone out here to get attacked by a gigantic snake."

"Jess, come on, it didn't attack you," said Slater. "It went away."

"IT WENT AWAY BECAUSE I HIT IT," shouted Jesse. Willa started crying again.

"You did?" said Kark. "You *hit* it?"

Jesse nodded. "With that." She pointed to the oak branch.

"Holy shit," said Kark.

"Jesus, Jess," said Slater. "Couldn't you have waited, like, thirty seconds?"

Jesse stared at him. "You're serious, aren't you?"

"Well, yeah," said Slater. "So we could have gotten footage of the snake. Maybe get a shot of me hitting it with the stick."

"Unbelievable," said Jesse.

"What?" said Slater.

Ignoring him, Jesse picked up the beach towel and book, then carried Willa to the other side of the clearing. She wished she could just keep walking, all the way out of this festering reptile-and-bug-infested swamp, away from this gorgeous asshole she had foolishly gotten stuck with, away from his idiotic schemes.

But at the moment she had nowhere to go, no money, no plan.

She spread the towel and sat down, comforting Willa.

"It's OK," she said, hugging her baby. "Don't cry. Mommy's gonna make it better."

She paused, watching Slater and Kark trudge back into the cabin, where they would undoubtedly spend the rest of the day as they spent every day, getting baked and talking about amazing things they would never actually do. Then she looked back down at her whimpering daughter.

"It's OK, Willa," she said. "Mommy's gonna get us out of here."

Chapter 2

At that moment, a little over fifty miles to the east, a sun-battered 2003 Hyundai Accent pulled up in front of the massively pretentious multi-columned entrance of a house much too large for its lot in an upscale Coral Gables community on the edge of Biscayne Bay named Moco del Mar.

The Hyundai's passenger door opened and Dora the Explorer stumbled out, falling to the sidewalk face-first.

"Fuck!" said Dora the Explorer.

"What happened?" said Elsa the *Frozen* princess, emerging from the driver's side.

"I can't fucking see," said Dora the Explorer, who, inside a football-shaped fiberglass costume head the size of a microwave oven, was a fifty-one-year-old unemployed journalist named Phil Teagler. "The eyeholes don't line up."

"Well just stay next to me," said Elsa, who, under an ill-fitting white wig with a long, thick braid, was Phil's neighbor Stu Krupp, a market-ing executive, age forty-eight, also unemployed. Stu's face was smeared with a thick coating of theatrical makeup, which failed to completely conceal his beard stubble.

"This is not good," said Phil, struggling to his feet. "Why couldn't I be, like, Spider-Man? Batman? Some kind of man?"

"I told you, the birthday girl wants Elsa from *Frozen*. You're sup-posed to be the sister. Whatshername. Emma?"

"But I'm *not* the sister. I'm Dora the fucking Explorer."

"I told you, they didn't have the sister costume. We'll just say Dora was another one of Elsa's sisters. The birthday girl is *four*, for chrissakes. At least you get to be inside a head. *I'm* the one wearing a fucking dress."

In fact Stu's original plan, since he was the one who had rented the costumes, was that Phil would wear the Elsa dress. But Phil, a big man—six-three and on the hefty side—couldn't begin to fit into it. Even Stu, despite being much smaller, was unable to zip the Elsa dress all the way up. His back—and it was a hairy back, for Stu was a hairy man—was clearly visible from the rear view, black tufts sprouting from the seam.

Phil, peering out through the right eyehole of the Dora head, looked at the birthday-party house, an $11.3 million modernistic white concrete turd, flanked by two equally ugly bloated insta-mansions, squatting shoulder to shoulder on canal-side lots. The street was lined with the party guests' cars, an armada of Land Rovers, the Official Vehicle of People Who Chauffeur Their Children to Their Expensive Private Schools in Land Rovers.

"I don't know about this," said Phil.

"It's *five hundred dollars*, Phil. Cash. Two fifty each."

"I know, but . . . I mean, *look* at us."

Phil gestured to his Dora costume, which, in addition to the giant head, consisted of a too-small purple T-shirt, stained orange gym shorts, old sneakers and yellow socks rising halfway up Phil's pale shins.

"Doesn't matter," said Stu. "The guy is desperate. He had a professional Elsa lined up, but she got sick. He *needs* us, Phil."

"I dunno, Stu."

"You better not back out on me now. I need the money. *You* need the money."

"I know, but—"

"Quiet," said Stu. "He's coming."

Phil aimed his eyehole at the front door, from which was emerging a tall, lean, balding hawk-faced man in tennis attire. This was the birthday girl's father, Andrew Pletzger, a prominent and influential commercial real estate developer, a man photographed smiling with his current wife, a former model, at every major charity event in Miami.

He was not smiling now.

"Oh shit," said Phil.

"What?"

"I know this guy. Pletzger. I broke a story about him illegally cutting down mangroves. I got him in trouble with the state. It cost him a shit ton of money. He fucking hates me."

"Jesus Christ," said Stu.

"We need to leave."

"No! Just keep the head on. Let me talk."

Pletzger was striding toward them, his face a furious red.

"Hi there!" said Stu, much too cheerfully. "Mr. Pletzger, right?"

"You're joking," Pletzger said. "Tell me this is a fucking joke."

"No!" said Stu, keeping it cheerful. "We're the entertainment! For the birthday girl. Kaitlyn, right? I'm Stu Krupp. We talked on the phone." Stu stuck out his hand.

Pletzger regarded the hand as he might a maggot-covered rat corpse, then fixed Stu with a stare that had radically contracted the sphincter of many a subcontractor.

"What we talked about," he said, "was Princess Elsa from *Frozen*, and her sister whatshername. Not a drag queen and"—he pointed at Phil—"whatever the hell *that's* supposed to be."

"That's Dora," said Stu. "The Explorer. She's very popular with the kids."

Phil, trying to appear popular, gave Pletzger a little wave.

This failed to soothe Pletzger, who said, "I want you assholes off my property right now."

"But, Mr. Pletzger, we—"

"RIGHT NOW," said Pletzger.

"Daddy! Is that Elsa?"

Pletzger, Stu and Phil turned toward the house. Four-year-old Kaitlyn Pletzger, wearing an Elsa dress much nicer than Stu's—it was custom-made, and cost $800—was running toward them, trailed by Pletzger's wife, Heidi, a tall, slim blond woman with perfect cheekbones who had recently completed her twenty-five hundredth Peloton ride.

"Kaitlyn, honey, go back in the house," said Pletzger. "Heidi, take her back in the house."

But it was too late. Kaitlyn had reached the sidewalk and was looking up at Stuart, wide-eyed.

"Elsa?" she said.

"Hi, Kaitlyn!" said Stu in a falsetto voice that he intended to sound feminine, although it came out as more of a squawk, like a rooster getting a rectal probe. "Happy birthday!"

Kaitlyn studied Stu for a few seconds. He was looking down at her, smiling desperately and sweating profusely. He did not look like a fairy-tale princess; he looked like the Joker in drag. His mouth was ineptly outlined by a smear of garish red lipstick; an oozing glob of white makeup formed a stalactite on his stubbled chin, then detached from his face and fell to the sidewalk with an audible splat.

"Princess Elsa was just leaving," said Pletzger. "She has to go . . . someplace else."

Kaitlyn's expression turned to one of horror.

"No!" she cried, lunging toward Stu. "Nooooo!" She wrapped her arms around Stuart's left dress-enclosed leg, sobbing.

Heidi shot her husband a warning look, then leaned down and gently put a hand on her daughter's shoulder.

"It's OK, Kaitlyn," she said. "Princess Elsa's not leaving. She's going to stay for your party! Aren't you, Princess Elsa?"

"Of course!" croaked Stu, patting the top of Kaitlyn's head. "And so is my sister Dora! Dora the Explorer!"

Dora gave Kaitlyn a little wave.

"Your sister is Anna," said Kaitlyn.

"Dora's my other sister."

Kaitlyn considered this new information.

"Can she talk?" she said.

Phil shook the Dora head so violently that it almost fell off.

"Dora doesn't talk," croaked Stu. "She's . . . she's shy."

"Let's all go inside for the party!" said Heidi. She took Kaitlyn's hand and started toward the house.

Pletzger blocked Stu and Phil from following.

"I don't like this," he said.

"Elsa!" Kaitlyn called from the doorway. "Come to the party!"

"I'll be right there!" Stu croaked. To Pletzger, he said, "She seems OK with it."

"Elsa!" Kaitlyn called again.

Pletzger looked back at his daughter, then turned a glare on Stu and Phil.

"If you assholes screw this up," he said, "I will kill you."

On that happy note they went into Kaitlyn's party.

Stu took Phil's arm, leading him through the pointlessly gigantic foyer and across the tennis-court-sized living room to the patio. The party guests were gathered next to the infinity pool, which overlooked the yacht-lined Coral Gables Waterway. Uniformed servants circulated with drinks and hors d'oeuvres. Hired teenagers were entertaining the children; a clown was making balloon animals. The patio was festooned with authentic Disney *Frozen* decorations; the centerpiece, on a low table, was a *Frozen*-themed cake the size of a Fiat. It was an exact replica of the *Frozen* castle, custom-made by the same baker patronized by Gloria Estefan. It had cost Andrew Pletzger $8,500 plus a hefty delivery charge.

For a half hour or so, Phil, his giant Dora head towering above the crowd, stood around sweating and feeling awkward. He could hear the adult guests laughing at him and Stu. He caught glimpses of them through his eyeholes—rich, fit, attractive, self-assured people, sipping wine, amused by this unexpected diversion, this pair of losers in pathetic costumes.

The children ignored Phil. Dora the Explorer was not the celebrity she once had been. She was Phil Collins at a rap concert.

Princess Elsa was a different story. It had been a few years, but she was still big. The kids swarmed Stu, grabbing at his dress, yelling, "Elsa! Elsa!" If they noticed that Elsa was a hairy, sweating middle-aged man, they chose to overlook it.

Stu handled the attention reasonably well until the birthday girl declared that she wanted him to sing "Let It Go," Princess Elsa's signature ballad. It had not occurred to Stu that he would have to sing. He had *heard* "Let It Go," of course—everyone on the planet had heard "Let It Go"—but the only lyrics he could remember for certain were "Let it go."

"Sing it, Elsa!" said Kaitlyn. "Sing 'Let It Go'!"

"Maybe later!" croaked Stu. "Why don't we—"

"Sing it!" said Kaitlyn, who was used to getting her way.

"Sing it! Sing it!" chorused the other children.

"Yes, sing it," said one of the adults, and then more of them, ready to be amused.

"I really think we should wait until . . . later," croaked Stu.

"No," said Pletzger, stepping close, glaring at Stu. "You'll sing it now."

"OK!" croaked Stu. He cleared his throat, looked around at the crowd of expectant faces, and, in a voice that quavered in the vicinity of several notes without actually hitting any single one, began to sing.

"Let it go," he sang. "Let it go . . ."

He paused for several seconds. The crowd waited. Then Stu sang:

"Let it go, in the . . . snow."

Kaitlyn was frowning.

"Let it go, in the snow, when it . . . snows."

"That's not the words," said Kaitlyn.

"When it snows . . . the, um, the wind blows . . ."

"Sing the right words!" said Kaitlyn, yanking on Stu's dress.

"I'm trying!" snapped Stu, in a voice far too deep for a Disney princess.

"Hey!" said Pletzger, grabbing Stu's arm.

"Mommy!" said Kaitlyn.

Heidi swooped in and took Kaitlyn's hand. "It's time to do the piñata!" she said, leading her daughter away.

The piñata was a staple of children's birthday parties in South Florida, a tradition imported by Hispanic immigrants but over the years embraced by Anglos as well. Most parties featured cheap piñatas from Party City filled with supermarket candy, but of course that would not do for the Pletzgers. The Pletzger piñata—a three-foot-high replica of Olaf, the comical snowman sidekick to Elsa the *Frozen* princess—had been custom-crafted by a premier Mexican piñata artisan and filled with truffles handmade by the same chocolatier patronized by both Martha Stewart and Jay-Z. Counting import duties, the Pletzgers had invested a bit more than $1,500 in this snowman. Anything for little Kaitlyn's special day.

At the moment Olaf, grinning goofily, clearly oblivious to the fate that awaited him, was dangling next to the massive castle cake, suspended from a rope tied to a nail in a roof overhang. Heidi, still holding Kaitlyn's hand, gathered the children around. The adults also drifted over to watch, as the piñata was usually the most entertaining element of South Florida birthday parties.

As the birthday girl, Kaitlyn would get the first whacks at Olaf. Heidi blindfolded her daughter, then handed her the whacking weapon. Ordinarily this would be a wooden stick, but Heidi had been concerned about splinters, so Andrew had reluctantly agreed to let the children use one of his backup golf clubs, a Callaway Epic Forged Star five-iron with a suspended tungsten core, for which Andrew had paid $325.

Kaitlyn gripped the club firmly with both hands as her mother positioned her in front of the dangling Olaf, who was still grinning obliviously.

"OK, baby!" Heidi said, stepping back quickly.

Kaitlyn swung the club hard, putting her whole body into it. The onlookers cheered as she made solid contact with Olaf, who gyrated wildly but remained intact. He had been solidly crafted by the Mexican artisan. He was no Party City piñata.

"Again!" shouted the crowd. "Harder!"

Little Kaitlyn took another big swing, which missed completely, then a third, even bigger swing, which landed with a solid *thump*, sending Olaf flying backward so hard that the rope yanked the nail out of the roof. Olaf went tumbling across the patio and came to rest on the lawn, still grinning.

Heidi was able to grab Kaitlyn before she could unleash another swing, potentially decapitating one of her playmates. Kaitlyn pushed up her blindfold and peered out, expecting to see scattered candy. Instead she saw Olaf in the distance, still intact, and burst into tears.

"It's OK, baby!" said Heidi, shooting a look at Andrew. "Daddy will fix it."

Andrew hustled out and carried Olaf back to the patio. The dads gathered around, men being manly, discussing how to rehang the snowman. They agreed that a ladder was needed, and a nail, and a hammer. The problem was, Andrew didn't have any of these things. Andrew did not do chores. He owned two Patek Philippe watches and one Vacheron Constantin—a combined value of about $235,000—but no hammer. Olaf had been suspended by the gardener that morning, and he was gone now, with his ladder.

While the men conferred around Olaf, the birthday girl grew increasingly distraught. Kaitlyn, having been denied nothing in her four years, was unaccustomed to disappointment. She wanted to hit the piñata, and she wanted to hit it *now*.

"Andrew," hissed Heidi, holding their sobbing child. "*Do* something."

At that moment one of the dads had an idea: "Somebody could hold it up by the rope, like at arm's length."

Andrew frowned, considering this idea. He decided it was worth a try. The question was, who would be the holder? Not him, of course.

He surveyed the crowd; his gaze stopped on the most disposable person at the party, who also happened to be the tallest.

"You!" he said, pointing at Phil. "Over here!"

Phil, oblivious inside the Dora head, did not realize he had been summoned. Stu hurried over and grabbed him.

"What?" said Phil, his voice muffled.

"Mr. Pletzger wants you to hold up the rope."

"What rope?"

"The rope attached to the snowman."

"What?"

"Get over here!" said Andrew.

Stu dragged Phil over to Andrew.

"Hold your arm out," said Andrew.

"What?" said Phil, trying to get a view of the situation through the eyeholes.

Andrew put Olaf's rope into Phil's right hand and said, "Hold this."

"What?" said Phil.

"HOLD THIS," said Andrew into the Dora head's left eyehole.

Phil gripped the rope, his arm dropping from Olaf's weight.

"HOLD YOUR ARM OUT," said Andrew.

Phil held his arm out, lifting Olaf, who dangled from the rope, still grinning.

"OK, Kaitlyn!" said Andrew, stepping briskly back.

Heidi slid the blindfold back over Kaitlyn's eyes and pressed the golf club into her hands.

Kaitlyn took a step toward Phil and drew the club back, a nice smooth backswing. She held the club still for a half second, then brought it forward hard. Really hard.

What happened next was captured on an iPhone by one of the parents and shortly thereafter uploaded to YouTube, where it ultimately, counting the various edits with added music soundtracks and commentaries, racked up 1.3 million views. The slo-mo version, set to the Richard Harris recording of "MacArthur Park" ("Someone left the cake out in the rain . . ."), provided the clearest picture of the sequence of events:

First, Kaitlyn executed a remarkably fluid golf swing. An average male amateur golfer swinging a driver generates a club head speed of a little over ninety miles an hour. Kaitlyn, at only forty-one pounds, did not possess that kind of power, but she had a beautiful natural motion—you can't teach it—and, according to a technical analysis of the video done later by a Golf.com writer, the head of the five iron was moving at close to fifty miles per hour when it collided with Phil's balls.

At this point the action froze for a fraction of a second—Kaitlyn holding one end of the club, the other end buried in Phil's crotch—as Phil's nervous system transmitted the unhappy news from his family jewels to his brain.

Then from inside the Dora head erupted an awful sound. At full speed, it was a chilling scream, sounding almost feminine despite being produced by a 237-pound adult male. In slow motion it was deeper in pitch but no less anguished, the sound that a large terrified animal such as a water buffalo might make as it was being pushed out of a helicopter.

As Phil emitted this noise he doubled over violently. The Dora the Explorer head catapulted forward off his shoulders and flew through the air directly into the face of Andrew Pletzger, breaking his nose. As Andrew yelped in pain, Phil, still doubled over, staggered sideways, directly toward . . .

"The cake!" shouted Heidi, realizing what was about to happen. "Andrew, the cake!"

Andrew, despite the fact that he had blood gushing from his nose onto his formerly immaculate tennis attire, lunged desperately toward Phil and managed to grab him, but Phil had too much mass and momentum to be stopped. The two of them—in slow motion, it was almost beautiful—fell hard into the $8,500 castle cake, sending a massive wave of white frosting exploding upward and outward onto the crowd.

Andrew and Phil, their legs cut out from under them by the table, rolled horizontally through the cake and fell out the other side onto the patio. Andrew, his nose still gushing blood, scrambled to his feet and, wiping white goo from his eyes, looked around at the devastation that had been visited upon the birthday party—the costly cake a massive mess, his wife enraged, his daughter sobbing, his guests spattered with big frosting gobs. He then looked down at Phil, writhing in pain on the patio. For the first time, Andrew got a good look at Phil's face.

"YOU!" he said, his frosting-and-blood-smeared face contorting with rage. "YOU!"

As several parents shouted in alarm, Andrew snatched the five iron from Kaitlyn's hands and turned toward Phil, raising the club overhead. Before he could bring it down on Phil—there was no question that he would have—Stu leapt forward and grabbed Andrew's arm. This led to another popular action sequence in the YouTube video, two middle-aged men, one bleeding and heavily frosted, the other wearing a bad wig and an ill-fitting princess dress, struggling desperately for control of a golf club.

Meanwhile, prominently visible in the video, and appearing vastly amused by the proceedings, was Olaf. Somehow, in all the commotion, he had managed to land upright. His carrot nose was gone, but he was grinning as brightly as ever.

Finally some of the parents stepped in and managed to separate Andrew, Stu and the five iron. Heidi gripped Andrew by the arm to restrain him. He was shaking with rage.

"I can't believe you came to my house!" he shouted at Phil, who had managed to sit up on the patio but was still in a lot of pain. "My house!"

Phil could only groan.

"GET OUT OF MY HOUSE, YOU FUCKING PIECE OF SHIT," bellowed Andrew.

"Andrew!" said Heidi, yanking his arm. "Language!" To Stu, she said, "You and your friend need to leave right now."

"Absolutely," said Stu, helping Phil to his feet. "If we could just collect, our, um, our fee, we'll be on our w—"

"YOU THINK I'M GOING TO *PAY* YOU?" screamed Andrew.

"I'M GOING TO FUCKING *KILL* YOU." He yanked his arm free from Heidi's grasp and stalked into the house.

Heidi turned to Phil and Stu. "Please," she said, "you need to leave right now. My husband has a very bad temper. Also a gun."

And so Stu and Phil left little Kaitlyn's birthday party, Stu carrying the Dora head—he'd put a deposit on it at the costume-rental place—and Phil walking very carefully, groaning with each step.

They didn't speak until they were back in the Hyundai, driving away.

"I don't believe it," said Stu.

Phil groaned.

"That prick owes us five hundred dollars!"

Phil groaned again.

Several minutes passed in silence, then Stu said, "I don't care who he is. He can't do this."

Phil said nothing.

"I got an idea," said Stu.

"No," said Phil.

"What do you mean, 'no'?"

"I mean, no to your idea."

"You didn't even hear it yet."

"I don't care. Thanks to your last idea, I'm a grown man dressed as a little girl cartoon character, I'm covered in cake frosting, and I feel like my balls went ten rounds with Mike Tyson. I'm done with your ideas."

"But we could—"

"Stu, NO."

"OK, then," said Stu. "Fine."

They rode the rest of the way in silence. Stu stopped in front of Phil's apartment complex. Phil opened the passenger door and gingerly started extricating himself from the seat.

"Listen," said Stu. "I'm sorry about your balls."

"Thank you," said Phil.

"Put some ice on that."

"I will."

"But about the money, I really think we should—"

"No," said Phil, groaning his way out of the car.

"Phil," said Stu, "at least listen to me. You still need money, right?"

Phil closed the car door without answering.

Stu, shaking his head, drove away.

Phil stood still for a few moments, steeling himself for the walk to his front door. He took a breath and sighed it out.

"Yeah," he said to himself. "I still need money."

Chapter 3

Ken Bortle looked out through the yellowed glass front door of Bortle Brothers Bait & Beer. A car was slowing down, turning off Route 41, also known as the Tamiami Trail, into the parking lot, which at one time had been asphalt but was now almost entirely dirt.

"Customer," said Ken.

Ken's brother, Brad, seated behind the counter, looked up from his iPhone, said, "Nope," and went back to playing Candy Crush, which was what he did for most of the working day.

"Well they're stopping," said Ken.

"Yeah, to use the toilet," said Brad.

"How do you know that?"

"That's a Tesla Model S. It costs seventy-five thousand minimum. Whoever bought that car isn't stopping here to shop." Brad gestured vaguely toward the wares on display in Bortle Brothers Bait & Beer. There were three bait tanks, one containing several dozen live and four dead floating pilchards, and two tanks containing only dark, dirty water dotted with floating scum; a wheezing beer cooler containing four and one-third six-packs of Bud Light; a cardboard display card that once had held an assortment of plastic bait worms but now was empty except for the words YUM DINGER; some dusty plastic alligators with FLORIDA printed on their backs and MADE IN CHINA printed in smaller letters on their bellies; and a stack of decades-old black T-shirts, all sized either extra small or XXXL, imprinted with BORTLE BROTHERS IN THE ♥ OF THE EVERGLADES (these were also made in China, where apparently nobody had noticed the "Y").

Ken watched as the Tesla stopped out front. A prosperous-looking family of four—mom, dad, daughter, son—emerged. The mom was eyeing the store unhappily, saying something to the dad, who shrugged. The son was reading the ancient weathered storefront sign, which said:

BAIT

BEER

LIVE GATOR SHOW

AIRBOAT RIDES

Dad pushed open the front door and stepped inside, followed by Mom and the kids. Mom wrinkled her nose at the smell, which was mostly a combination of mold and dead pilchards.

"Hi," said Dad.

Ken nodded. Brad looked up from Candy Crush.

"I was wondering if we could use your restroom," said Dad.

"Bingo," said Brad, looking back down.

"Yeah," sighed Ken, pointing. "Back there on the right."

Mom and the girl edged through the store, careful not to get near the bait tanks.

An awkward silence descended. Dad looked around for something he could pretend to be interested in. He settled on the YUM DINGER card, which he examined as though it were the *Mona Lisa*. The boy wandered over to the bait tanks and briefly watched the pilchards swim around, then said to Ken, "Where's the alligators?"

"The what?" said Ken.

"Alligators. The sign outside says there's a live gator show."

"He died," said Ken.

"Who did?"

"The gator," said Ken. "Also the guy who did the show."

"Oh," said the boy.

There actually had been a live gator show, back in the mid sixties, when Bortle Brothers Bait & Beer had been founded by Ken's and

Brad's father, the late Webster Bortle Jr., and his brother Canaan. They charged tourists fifty cents a head to watch Webster go into a pen out back and manhandle an eight-foot alligator named Rex for ten minutes. As was traditional in Florida gator shows, Webster would pretend that he was in grave danger of being injured or killed, but in fact Rex was well-fed and wanted nothing more than to resume lying inert in the muck.

Webster would heave Rex around for a while, then pry open the gator's jaws and exclaim, "Look at those teeth, folks! This big boy'll take your arm off in a second. One time I got careless with him and look what happened." Then he'd hold up his left hand, showing that the top joint of his forefinger was missing. The tourists would gasp.

In fact Webster had lost part of his finger one night when he was hammered (as he was every night) and he bet Canaan, who was equally drunk, five dollars that he could catch a ride aboard a moving truck. They staggered outside to Route 41, which at that time was the only route across the swamp between Miami and Naples, to settle the bet. Webster stood by the side of the road, letting a few trucks go past—most were doing sixty or better—before setting his sights on a somewhat slower-moving Southeastern Freight Lines tractor-trailer. He started running as it drew close and managed to get his left hand into the trailer undercarriage as the big rig roared past, but as he tried to get a better grip, he lost his footing and fell, the massive rear tires missing him by inches as the truck thundered past and disappeared into the steamy Everglades night.

Webster was still rolling on the roadside when Canaan caught up with him, demanding his money. It took Webster a minute or so to fully grasp that he'd lost part of a key digit. Both brothers found this hilarious. They considered driving to Miami for treatment but decided that it could wait until morning, being merely a small part of a finger. Canaan—after collecting his five bucks—bound his brother's wound with toilet paper and duct tape, and they resumed drinking.

The forefinger became the highlight of Webster's gator-wrestling act and remained so until 1987, when both Webster and Rex died just a few weeks apart, Rex from natural causes and Webster from cirrhosis of the liver. That was the end of gator wrestling at Bortle Brothers, but nobody had gotten around to editing the sign that the Tesla-family boy had noticed.

"What about the airboat rides?" the boy asked Ken.

"We don't do those anymore," said Ken.

"Why not?" asked the boy, a persistent lad.

The true reason was that in the late eighties Canaan, even more drunk than usual, had taken a group of tourists out for an airboat ride and hit a stump at forty miles per hour, stopping the boat cold and launching two elderly Belgians a good twenty-five feet into the swamp. There were multiple injuries. Since the accident occurred in the Big Cypress National Preserve, federal authorities got involved. Canaan wound up spending six months in prison, and the airboat was confiscated.

"Environmental impact," said Ken.

"Oh," said the boy.

The Tesla-family mom and her daughter emerged from the bathroom, noses still wrinkled from the stench, which was due to the fact that the toilet had not been cleaned since the Reagan administration.

"This place is gross," said the daughter, in a plainly audible whisper.

"Drew, let's go," Mom said to Dad.

"Right," said Dad. "Let me just get . . ."—he paused, looking around for something to buy, a mercy purchase in exchange for the bathroom stop—"one of these." He picked up a souvenir plastic Florida alligator from China and brought it over to Brad at the cash register.

"How much do I owe you?" he said.

Brad looked up from Candy Crush.

"Two hundred and fifty-seven dollars," he said.

Dad smiled uncomfortably and said, "Seriously, how much?"

Brad, not smiling, said, "Like I told you, two hundred fifty-seven dollars. It's imported."

"Very funny," said Dad. He dropped the alligator onto the counter, and the Tesla family exited the store. On his way out Dad paused in the doorway, turned back to Ken and Brad, and said, "I know you think you're funny. But I'm a business consultant, and I can tell you this: Your attitude is the reason this is a shithole and your business is a joke."

"Thanks," said Brad. "How much do we owe you for that?"

Dad shook his head and left.

The brothers watched the Tesla whir away.

Ken said, "Why'd you do that?"

"Because he's an asshole."

"An asshole who was about to give us money."

"Four dollars."

"Which is four more dollars than we got now." Ken paused, then said, "He's right, you know."

"About what?"

"Our attitude."

Brad snorted. "So if I smiled and sold him a plastic alligator, which he obviously didn't want, we'd be a booming business? Is that what you're saying?"

"I'm saying we're not even trying. We just sit here. Like we expect people to stop, when there's no *reason* for them to stop."

"So what're we supposed to do? Buy more stock? With what? Nobody'll give us credit. The beer truck doesn't even stop anymore. Pablo won't sell us any more bait. FP&L is about to shut off the electric. The only income we have is you selling the shit you get from Pinky, and aside from being sketchy, that's nowhere near enough. How're we gonna attitude our way out of that?"

"We need a new business model."

Brad snorted again. "*Business* model? You get that from *Shark Tank*?"

"Number one, you could learn something from that show. Number two, I'm serious. We need something besides bait and beer, which we don't really have anyways. We need like a . . . a hook."

"A hook."

"Yeah, a hook. Like those guys in Ochopee."

"The skunk ape guys? The 'Skunk Ape Research Headquarters'?" Brad made air quotes. "That's bullshit."

"It's bullshit but it *works*. They've been on TV, newspaper stories. People love that supernatural shit. They get tourists, Brad. People see that big skunk ape statue outside their store, they stop. They're selling mugs, T-shirts, all kinds of skunk ape souvenirs in there. They're selling that shit on the Internet. They got a *brand*, Brad. We need to do that."

"You want us to sell skunk ape souvenirs?"

"No, no, that's *their* brand. We need our own thing. Something new. Make people want to stop."

"Like what?"

"I dunno yet. I got some ideas. I'm gonna come up with something."

"Sure you will," said Brad, going back to Candy Crush.

Ken looked out the door. Another car whizzed past on Route 41, bound for somewhere else.

"I will," he said. "You'll see."

Chapter 4

"Where you going, Jess?"

Slater stood in the cabin doorway, shirtless as always, gripping the top of the doorframe, posed—to Slater, posing was as natural as breathing—to display his sculpted arms and bulging biceps, fully aware of how studly he looked.

"For a walk," said Jess. She had Willa in a baby carrier slung in front of her, a backpack behind her holding diapers, wipes, a water bottle, a towel and a book. She was wearing running shorts, a T-shirt, a red Miami Heat ball cap and filthy sneakers. She was holding a machete.

"Already?" said Slater, who'd just awakened.

"I've been up with Willa for three hours."

"Huh." Slater scratched his left armpit, studying Jesse. He called back into the cabin, "Kark, get out here. Bring the camera."

Kark appeared in the doorway, yawning, holding the camera. "What?"

"Get some footage of Jess," said Slater. "With the machete. Glades Woman."

"Slater," said Jesse, "I don't want to be on camera. I look like crap." Jesse hadn't shaved her legs or armpits in weeks. She hadn't washed her hair for four days. The cabin had a shower of sorts—a plastic water bag hung from an eave—but it was totally exposed, and Jesse was reluctant to use it; she didn't trust Kark, a lurker, not to watch—or worse, video her.

"You look hot, babe," said Slater. "Glades Woman! Doesn't she look hot, Kark?"

"She does," said Kark, his small red eyes taking in Jesse's body.

"Bye," Jesse said, starting around the cabin.

"Get this shot," Slater said to Kark. "Glades Woman setting off into the swamp."

Kark, eye to the viewfinder, waddled after Jesse.

"Make sure you get the machete!" said Slater. "Jess, turn around and show him the machete!"

Jesse turned around, showed Kark the finger, then turned back.

"We can edit that out," said Kark.

Jesse went around the side of the cabin and picked up the path, which wound through the swamp about fifty yards to the overgrown two-track dirt road where Slater kept the truck, a faded, battered old F-150 pickup.

Jesse sometimes thought about taking the truck. She knew where Slater kept the key. In her thoughts she'd drive into Miami; find a phone; call her parents in Greenwich, Connecticut; tell them they were right, she was a fool, please send her some money, let her come home to them with her baby. Every time she walked past the truck she thought about this. Every time she felt she was a little closer to actually doing it.

She stopped at the truck, looked inside, pictured herself at the wheel. Then she pictured her parents, seeing them again, them seeing their granddaughter for the first time, their joy . . .

But then, inevitably, their disapproval, their judgment, their I-told-you-sos. She knew her parents, and their friends. They wouldn't be able to help themselves, and the worst part of it would be knowing that they were right. They'd given her a good education, supported her, set her up with a generous trust. She had squandered it all. Or, more accurately, she'd decided—despite her parents' vehement objections—to trust Slater, and he had squandered it, all of it. When she'd gotten desperate, she'd begged her parents for more money, and they'd reluctantly given her some; Slater had squandered that, too. Slater had a black belt in squandering.

Jesse couldn't face her parents again, not like this. As much as she hated where she was now, she hated the idea of slinking home even more.

"Nope," she said, turning away from the truck. She looked down at Willa, who was looking up at her. "Baby girl, we gotta come up with something else."

She walked along the dirt track, no destination in mind, happy for the time away from Slater and Kark. She'd been taking more and more walks lately, wandering farther and farther, venturing off on old trails and footpaths that sometimes rose only inches above water, and sometimes were barely there at all. She carried the machete just in case but, aside from the occasional gator basking in the distance, hadn't encountered any worrisome critters.

She had come across a few dilapidated shacks, their roofs collapsed, their rotting walls overwhelmed by vegetation. Each time, she wondered who had lived in the isolated hovel. The Everglades, two million acres of wild wetland, had forever been a sanctuary, a hideout for hermits, moonshiners, drug runners, eccentrics, paramilitary wackos, lunatics, cultists, criminals and weirdos of every kind seeking refuge from society, or the law, or both. It was a perfect place to hide, this vast swamp. Or to hide things.

On this day Jesse's wanderings brought her to a weather-beaten dark-gray house she hadn't seen before. She almost missed it; it sat a dozen yards off the path, in the shadows, partly hidden by some cypress trees. Its windows were gone and its front door agape, but it was a bit bigger, a bit less overgrown and in slightly better shape than the other hovels she'd seen, as if it had been occupied more recently. She paused and thought about looking inside. But the dark doorway creeped her out.

Slater had told her a story he'd heard from some locals—who swore it was true—about a loner living out here somewhere, a few years back, who kept wolves as pets. The story went that the man would drive into Miami, pick up homeless people and prostitutes, bring them back to his house, and nobody would ever see them again. The locals claimed that at night they'd often heard the wolves howling. They said nobody went near the loner's place after dark.

Jesse, hearing Slater relate the story, had figured it was probably fiction, glades dwellers having some fun with a city boy. But she thought about it as she looked at the doorway, and she suddenly wanted to get away from there.

She hurried past the house and continued on the winding path a hundred yards or so. Willa, who did not complain without reason, started fussing a bit, her way of saying she was hungry. Jesse stopped in a small clearing, spread the towel on the ground and sat down cross-legged. She set down the machete, took Willa in her arms and lifted her T-shirt, helping her baby find her breast. She closed her eyes and leaned her head back, enjoying the sun on her face, the peace of the moment. Minutes passed. She could feel herself almost dozing off.

Something made her open her eyes. She blinked, adjusting to the light.

A man was watching her.

He was standing ten feet away, in the shadows at the edge of the clearing. He was stocky, round faced, with close-cropped black hair and a goatee. His eyes were hidden behind wraparound sunglasses. He wore camo pants and a tank top.

Jesse yanked her shirt down, upsetting Willa, who began to cry. Jesse scrambled to her feet.

The man had not moved.

"Who are you?" Jesse asked. "What are you doing?"

The man said nothing for a few seconds, then, "Just standing here."

"Were you watching me?"

The man smirked but said nothing.

"You're rude," said Jesse. "You're a rude person, sneaking up on me."

"I got a right to be here," said the man. "Don't I, bro?"

"Yep," said another male voice, from behind Jesse. She spun and saw a second man on the other side of the clearing. He was bigger than the other one and had a full-face beard, but otherwise they looked much alike. The full-bearded one wore camo head to toe, including a camo ball cap. He wore a belt with a pistol in a holster. He held a pole with a Frisbee-sized disc at the end—a metal detector, Jesse figured.

"Well, you shouldn't sneak up on people," said Jesse, trying to keep the fear out of her voice. Willa was still crying. "It's OK, baby," Jesse said. "We're leaving." Feeling the men's eyes on her, she put Willa back into the carrier, stuffed the towel into the backpack and picked up the machete. As she straightened up she saw that the full-bearded man had moved, and was now standing in the path where she had entered the clearing. The goateed man had also moved, stepping into the clearing, closer to her. Neither man had said anything.

"I'm not alone, you know," said Jesse. "My husband is with me." It sounded pathetic to her even as she said it.

"That right?" said the beard. He made an elaborate show of looking around, then turned toward the goatee. "You see anybody else out here?"

"Nope," said the goatee. "Just this pretty lady." He took a step closer.

Jesse gripped the machete tightly. She thought about trying to leave the way she'd come, but that would mean getting past the beard, who was blocking the path. She didn't like the way he was looking at her, as if inviting her closer. Out of the corner of her eye she saw the goatee take another step toward her.

She turned, raised the machete toward him and said, "You stay away from me!" She pivoted and left the clearing, picking up the path at the far end. She walked quickly, almost running, afraid to look back. She knew she was going the wrong way, farther from the cabin. But for the moment all she could think about was getting away from the men.

Fifty yards ahead the path veered right, around a thicket of tall bushes. As she reached them she looked back.

The men were following her.

They weren't hurrying, but they were keeping pace easily.

They saw her looking back, and they both smiled.

"No," she whispered. "Please no."

She rounded the thicket and, with the men temporarily out of sight, began running. She'd always been a fast runner, had played soft-ball and soccer for years. But since she'd had Willa she'd been out of shape. Clutching her baby tightly to her chest, she ran along the path, glancing back every few seconds. The men were still out of sight. She looked left and right for a way to escape the path, a place to hide, but on both sides lay nothing but sawgrass emerging from murky water.

She tried to run faster, but it was hard, carrying Willa, and she was getting tired. Ahead the path disappeared into the vast expanse of sawgrass, headed in the direction of some live oak trees in the distance, maybe a mile away. Beyond that she saw nothing but more grass, nowhere to escape. She looked around, desperate now. To her right, maybe one hundred feet away across an expanse of water, she saw a slight rise, a little island with a thick clump of bushes and a stunted gumbo-limbo tree. She looked back—still no sight of the two men—then ahead again at the trees in the distance. Then from behind her she heard a laugh; the men were close. She made a decision and left the path, plunging into the water to the right.

It wasn't as bad as she feared. The water was only knee-deep here, and the ground beneath it less mucky, more sandy than back at the cabin. She sloshed forward as quickly as she could through the sawgrass, constantly glancing back toward the path. She reached the rise just as the two men came into view. Finding firm ground, she dropped on her hands and knees and crawled into the bushes, grateful for Willa's silence.

She crouched, turned and peered toward the path. The two men apparently hadn't seen her. They were still on the path, looking ahead, not hurrying. They were talking, but she couldn't make out the words. Jesse figured that in a few minutes they'd be far enough into the sawgrass that she'd be able to get to the path unseen and head back the way she had come.

Staying low, she scuttled deeper into the bushes, which opened onto a clearing, the gumbo-limbo at the far end. She crouched at the edge of the clearing, listening for the men.

Willa whimpered.

"Oh, honey, not now," whispered Jesse. But she knew her baby; Willa was still hungry, and her next cry would be louder. Jesse sat cross-legged on the ground, pulled up her T-shirt again and brought Willa to her breast.

As the baby started feeding, Jesse felt something sharp poking her right hip. She shifted her weight and looked down. Something was sticking out of the ground; it glinted yellow in the sun. Holding Willa with her left hand, Jesse reached down with her right and brushed some dirt away. She uncovered the corner of something solid.

Something gold-colored.

As Willa fed, Jesse clawed at the soft dirt until she had uncovered a metal bar, roughly the same shape as a patio brick but about half the size. She tugged hard, pulled it out of the ground, hefted it. It was much heavier than it looked. She held it up. It reflected the sunlight with a lustrous golden glow.

"My God," whispered Jesse.

She looked down at the hole she'd dug to extract the bar. Clearly visible was the top of another one just like it. She dug her fingers into the ground and yanked it out; there was another bar below that, and the edges of more bars visible on the side of the hole.

"My God," she said again.

She was breathing hard now, both from the exertion of digging and from excitement. Willa was done feeding. She pulled her shirt down, rose and peeked through the bushes. There was no sign of the two men.

She put the first gold bar into her backpack. She returned the others to the hole and covered them with dirt.

Then she rose, settled Willa into the baby carrier and hurried back to the path.

Chapter 5

Phil was working on his second Moscow mule. For emotional reasons he wanted to guzzle it, but for financial reasons he needed to nurse it.

He was seated at the bar in the Gallo Grande, a seedy restaurant on the Tamiami Trail in far west Miami, almost to the Everglades. "Gallo Grande" means "big rooster," which explained the eight-foot-tall sun-bleached fiberglass rooster out front, listing at a steep angle ever since being almost blown over by Hurricane Irma. The rooster was one of the two things the Gallo Grande was known for, the other being that drugs could be purchased in the parking lot. It was not known for its food.

The Gallo Grande was Phil's regular hangout, because he could walk to it from his apartment complex, a clot of run-down buildings named Glades Falls, which did not have any waterfalls per se but did have, because of poor drainage, a semipermanent lagoon in the parking lot.

The other reason Phil patronized the Gallo Grande was that it had a three-for-the-price-of-one happy hour every weekday afternoon from two to five. Phil was pinching pennies. He was seriously broke, way behind on his rent and child support, living on credit card debt he currently had no way to repay.

He felt guilty, drinking when he should have been looking for work. But when he looked for work—which he'd been doing for seven straight months—he was repeatedly slapped in the face by the cold dead fish of rejection. Lately he'd decided that feeling guilty was slightly less awful than being rejected. So here he was, at 2:40 on a Monday afternoon, sitting at the bar of the Gallo Grande with the other happy hour losers.

"Another one?" asked the bartender.

Phil looked at his Moscow mule, which was down to ice water. He sighed and gestured for a third. At this rate, without some serious nursing, he'd be on his second three-for-one before three thirty. Not good.

His phone vibrated. He looked down and felt a tiny jolt of happiness when he saw it was a text from Stella, his sixteen-year-old daughter, who lived with his ex-wife.

r u busy?

No, he typed. *What's up?*

ummm

This was Stella letting him know it was going to be awkward.

What? he typed.

ok first heres some punctuation;;;;;;

Phil snorted, almost laughed out loud. As an old-fart newspaperman, he was always complaining about Stella's generation's aversion to punctuation, capitalization and grammar. So here she was softening him up with some semicolons.

He typed, *I'm surprised you could find that on your keyboard. Must be serious.*

it kind of is dad

Tell me.

i need some money

The bartender replaced Phil's dead mule with a new one. Phil stared at his phone, trying to think what to type. Stella, noticing the delay, typed another text.

im sorry dad i know its a bad time but theres a school trip

Don't be sorry! he typed. *I'm your dad.*

He felt foolish, typing that, and quickly added, *How much do you need?*

A longish pause from Stella, then: 235.

Phil picked up the mule and swallowed half in one gulp.

Stella typed, *i know its a lot dad im so sorry*

Phil stared at the screen.

Stella typed, *mom says she cant do it*

Phil stared at the screen.

if u cant dont worry i dont have to go

Phil typed, *When do you need it?*

friday

Phil took a deep breath and typed, *OK.*

Stella typed *really???* Suddenly, she was punctuating.

An image flashed in Phil's mind—Stella as a little girl, on a family trip to Disney World. She was wearing a princess costume, holding some kind of overpriced Disney princess wand Phil had just bought her at the overpriced Disney souvenir store just because she wanted it.

He used to buy her everything she wanted, his princess. He hadn't bought her anything nice since he'd lost his job. For her last birthday he'd taken her to lunch at Fridays; when he dropped her off at his ex-wife's house, he gave her, apologetically, her birthday gift, a $20 Amazon gift card. Stella, a good girl, did her best to act thrilled, hugged him and told him it was perfect, just what she wanted. He watched her walk to the house. She turned at the front door, gave him a wave and a smile, still his princess. He smiled and waved back, drove around the corner, pulled over to the curb and sobbed like a baby.

He was tearing up now, looking at his phone.

He typed: *Really.*

dad thank u SO MUCH i love u a million semicolons ;;;;;;;;;;

I love you a billion semicolons.

talk to u later bye xoxo

OK, baby girl. Bye.

Phil drank the rest of his mule, signaled for the bartender to start him on his second round of three. He was fully aware that getting drunk was going to make him even less capable than he already was of coming up with $235. But at the moment getting drunk was the only thing he could think of that would make him at least slightly less conscious of what an utterly worthless human he was.

"Shit," he said, aloud.

"I hear that," said a man sitting two stools over.

Phil glanced at him. "Sorry," he said.

"No problem," the man said. He pointed at Phil's phone. "Bad news, huh?"

Phil nodded. The bartender brought him his fourth Moscow mule.

"Lotta that going around," said the man.

Phil grunted and, not wanting to get into a conversation with another Gallo Grande loser, looked up at the TV over the bar, which was tuned to ESPN, one of those shows where middle-aged TV commentators pretended to find deep significance in the activities of twenty-four-year-old multimillionaire athletes. Phil stared at the screen, but he could feel the man still looking at him.

After a moment the man said, "You're the YouTube guy, right?"

Phil looked over. "What?"

"You're the guy from the YouTube video, with the big head, right? Got hit in the balls by that little girl? With the golf club? And fell on the cake? You're him, right?"

Phil sighed. "Yeah."

"I knew it! I saw you in here two days ago, and I said to myself, that looks like the guy from YouTube. I bet that hurt like hell, right? Your balls?"

"You have no idea," said Phil. "Listen, if you don't mind—"

"That was fucking hilarious," said the man. "I watched that like twenty times." He got up, grabbed a backpack off the floor and shifted over one stool, next to Phil. He stuck out his hand. Phil shook it reflexively.

"My name's Ken Bortle," said the man. "Of Bortle Brothers Bait & Beer? On the Tamiami Trail? You familiar with it?"

"Is that that one with the big thing out front?" said Phil. "Like a gorilla?"

Ken, disdainful, shook his head. "That's the skunk ape. That's our competition. So anyways . . . hold on, I don't even know your name."

"Phil," said Phil, reluctantly.

"Phil," said Ken. "Listen, Phil, I'll be honest, I was hoping I'd run into you here."

"Me? Why?"

"You in that video, first of all, hilarious. But also it fits so perfect with this concept I've been thinking about. It's like, boom, it just clicked in my mind. I swear to God it's fate, Phil, you being here."

"Listen," said Phil, "I'm not really—"

"You watch *Shark Tank*?" said Ken.

"No," said Phil. "Listen, whatever this is, I'm not—"

"Great show," said Ken. "Really, *really* great show. I watch every one. You know what I learned?"

"No," said Phil. He very much wanted to leave, but he had two more Moscow mules coming.

"What I learned, Phil, is if you want to make money, with a product, you need something different. Has to be unique. Has to grab their attention. That's what I'm focused on, Phil. Grab their attention. Make them pull off the road, instead of driving past. Now, here's where it gets a little weird."

"What does?" said Phil.

"Bear with me, Phil. You ever hear of the melon heads?"

"The what?"

"Melon heads."

"No."

"OK, bear with me on this, Phil. The melon heads are these legendary creatures, supposably they live in the forests of Michigan, according to the Internet. Also Ohio. They're some kind of whaddyacallit, genetic fuckup, kind of like a human, but they have these giant heads and sharp teeth. They avoid people, but anybody they see, they eat them. As a protective measure."

"They eat them?"

"Exactly. With their teeth. According to the Internet, the paranormal sites. Now, Phil, I'm gonna have to trust you on this. This is confidential."

"What is?"

"This concept."

"What concept?"

"Bear with me, Phil. What if the melon heads came here?"

Phil looked around the Gallo Grande. "Here?"

"Not *right* here. But Florida. The Everglades. It makes sense."

Phil, drawn in despite himself, said, "How does it make sense?"

"You look at the Gulf Coast, Naples, Fort Myers, all those places over there. Who lives there?"

"Retirees?" said Phil.

"Retirees from *Ohio and Michigan*," said Ken. "They come down from the Midwest on I-75, like a pipeline." Ken paused here to give Phil what he believed to be a meaningful look. "And who else is from Ohio and Michigan?"

"The melon heads?" said Phil.

"*Bingo*," said Ken, slapping the bar. He leaned close and lowered his voice to a whisper. "Now think about this. What if the melon heads came down here too?"

"Wait a minute," said Phil. "You're saying these . . . these melon heads are traveling on I-75?"

"Course not," said Ken. "They travel through the forests. At night."

"Ah," said Phil. "But why would they come?"

"Same reason as the retirees," said Ken.

"No income tax?"

"Very funny, Phil. I'm serious. They come for the climate."

"Ah," said Phil.

"And when they get here, they hide out in the Everglades. They're whaddyacallit, invasive. An invasive species. Like the pythons."

Phil finished his fourth mule, signaled for the fifth.

"So here's the thing," said Ken. He looked around the bar to make sure nobody was listening, which nobody was. "Suppose a melon head got sighted, out near the Trail. You follow me?"

"Not really."

"OK, suppose one got sighted, and I'm the guy who sighted it. Suppose I got a video of it. It gets on the TV news, YouTube, Instagram, all that social media. It goes viral. People are like, 'Holy shit, a melon head! Right here in Miami!' All of a sudden everybody wants to see this thing. Where do they go?"

"To the Everglades?"

"To Bortle Brothers Bait & Beer, Phil. Because that's where I am, and I'm the guy who saw the melon head. I'm the guy they all want to interview. I'm the guy the tourists want to talk to. And I'm the guy with the Everglades Melon Monster merchandise, which they can buy."

"Everglades Melon Monster?"

"The name I'm using for now," said Ken. "I'm still workshopping it."

"But you already have Melon Monster merchandise?"

"Not yet, Phil, but I will, once I get this thing rolling." Ken put his hand on Phil's arm. Phil immediately removed it. Ken did not appear to notice. "Phil," he said, "I'm trusting you here, OK? Because this is the meat of the whole thing, right here."

"What is?"

Ken lowered his voice again. "Do you still have the head? From the video?"

Phil frowned. "The Dora the Explorer head?"

Ken nodded rapidly. "The face is wrong, but we repaint it, make it a scary face, it's perfect. With that head, and your size, you'll be—"

"Waitwaitwait," said Phil, holding up both hands. "You want *me* to be the melon thing?"

"The Everglades Melon Monster," said Ken.

"Forget it," said Phil, his left hand involuntarily protecting his testicles, which were still in recovery. "I'm not wearing that head again."

Ken gave him an appraising look. "Not even for money?"

Phil started to say no. Then he looked at his phone. He stared at it for a few seconds, then turned back to Ken.

"How much money?" he said.

Ken leaned in. "A *lot* of money, Phil. Potentially. Sky's the fuckin' limit. This thing goes viral, we're selling Melon Monster T-shirts, hoodies, beer koozies, all kinds of Melon Monster shit. Possibly reality TV. You get a piece of that, Phil. A percentage. Every unit we sell. After costs."

Phil shook his head. "That doesn't work for me."

"Why not?"

"I need cash. Up front."

"Phil, this opportunity, I'm talking about a huge payoff. Potentially. You gotta think long-term on—"

"Nope. Cash. Up front."

Ken nodded. "You sure you never watched *Shark Tank*, Phil? And you negotiating like a hard-ass?"

"I'm not negotiating. I'm just telling you I'm not doing this unless I get paid cash up front."

"How much?"

Phil thought for a moment, then said, "Five hundred." The number just popped into his head. He was thinking $235 for Stella, plus whatever he could get from this lunatic.

Ken thought about it, nodded. "I can do that," he said.

"And what exactly do I have to do?"

"Simple, Phil. We meet here, you bring the head. We go to a location I got scouted out in the Everglades, it's maybe fifty miles. You put on the head, walk a little ways on the trail, we shoot some video, boom, you're done. The whole thing, round trip, you're back here in three, four hours max."

"And you'll pay me five hundred dollars. Cash."

"When we're done, yeah, absolutely."

"But right there. On the spot. You will give me five hundred dollars."

"Sure."

"And I'm gonna need to see the money before we go anywhere."

"I'll have the money, Phil."

"How soon do we do this? It has to be before Friday."

"I gotta set it up, but . . . OK, make it Wednesday. Say we meet here at four. That work for you?"

"That works."

Ken stuck out his hand. "So we got a deal?"

Phil shook the hand. "Deal."

"OK, then, Phil." Ken stood, picked up his backpack. "This thing is gonna be big, Phil. You'll see. And down the road, there's more opportunities. Win-win."

"Right," said Phil.

"Wednesday at four," said Ken.

"I'll be here."

Ken left the bar. Phil drained his fifth mule, signaled for the sixth.

"The Everglades Melon Monster," he muttered. "I am out of my fucking mind."

Chapter 6

Jesse was alone at the cabin with Kark. Slater was away—he'd been away a lot lately—telling Jesse he was going to Miami on business. She was pretty sure his business was screwing other women, but she was past caring about his infidelities.

Ordinarily when Slater was gone, Jesse took Willa and went for a walk. She disliked being alone with Kark, who was always trying, in what he believed to be subtle ways, to catch a glimpse of her breasts.

But today Jesse hung around. Kark was a creep, but he was a knowledgeable creep, and Jesse was looking for information.

"Hey, Kark," she called into the cabin, where he spent much of the day looking at his phone, presumably porn. "Can I ask you something?"

"Sure, Jess," said Kark. He appeared in the doorway, scratching his belly. "What's up?"

"Have you ever heard of, like, gold around here? In the Everglades?"

"You mean like buried treasure?"

"Yeah."

"Sure, there's stories. I read a bunch of 'em when I was researching *Glades Man.*"

"What kind of stories?"

"Well, there's a lot about criminals, drug runners, outlaws, hiding cash, drug stashes, stuff like that. And there's all kinds of stories about Indian artifacts out here, supposedly worth a lot of money to collectors."

"But what about gold? Are there any stories about that? Like bars of actual gold buried in the ground?"

Kark scratched some more. "There's one story I read about a few different places, supposedly it really happened. But I dunno. A lot of people looked for it and nobody ever found anything."

"What's the story?"

"OK, during the Civil War, supposedly these Confederate soldiers were transporting this big shipment of gold, like for a payroll. According to the story, the Yankees were chasing them, so they took the gold into the Everglades and buried it. And then the war ended, and everything was kind of crazy for a while, and nobody ever found the gold."

"Like where in the Everglades? Near here?"

"Some people say it was up in Broward. But some people say it's not up there, it's somewhere else. Nobody knows for sure. Nobody even knows if the gold really exists. Like I said, a lot of people have looked for it. I think some people are still looking for it. But nobody ever found it. Or if they did, they kept it secret."

"How much gold are we talking about?"

"I don't remember exactly. I think it was like half a ton."

"Half a ton? That's a lot of gold, right?"

"Oh yeah. A *lot* of gold. Today's prices, you're talking millions of dollars. Millions."

"Huh," said Jesse.

"Why're you asking about gold, Jess? You planning to go on a treasure hunt?"

"No, no, nothing like that. I was just . . . I was wondering, with all the, you know, weird stuff out here, all those, you know, old buildings and everything. I was just wondering what else might be out here."

"There's a *whole* lotta weird things out here," said Kark.

"Yeah."

A silence descended. Kark, still scratching himself, was staring at Jesse's body the way he usually did, as if he'd never before seen a live human female.

"OK, well," Jesse said, crossing her arms. "Thanks."

"No problem," said Kark. "Listen, if you ever, like, need anything, you know, with Slater not around . . ."

"Right, thanks," said Jesse. "So I'm gonna take a walk."

"You want company?"

"No thanks. I'm good." She picked Willa up off the towel where she'd been dozing, fitted her into the baby carrier and slid it over her shoulders. She could feel Kark's eyes on her. She grabbed her backpack, folded the towel and stuffed it inside. She picked up the machete.

"You and the baby gonna hunt for buried treasure?" said Kark.

Jesse forced a laugh. "Just taking a walk."

"Well, be careful," said Kark. "All kinds of weird shit in this swamp."

"Thanks," said Jesse. She turned and started walking. She could feel the hard weight in her backpack pressing against her hip.

Chapter 7

Ken Bortle was standing in the parking lot behind the Gallo Grande, waiting next to an overflowing dumpster baking in the late-afternoon Miami sun, emitting near-visible stench rays.

Ken was there for a meeting with a man known as Pinky. Pinky supplied Ken with drugs, mostly marijuana, which Ken then sold at a profit to residents of the Everglades who for various reasons did not wish to venture into civilization. This was essentially the current business model of Bortle Brothers Bait & Beer.

Pinky arrived punctually and silently in a highly modified Tesla equipped with bulletproof glass, a sound system that could liquefy granite and a front seat customized to accommodate Pinky's body, which weighed a tad over 430 pounds and measured nearly the same horizontally as vertically. Pinky, whose real name was Bob Kearful, had once been a standout nose tackle at the University of Florida and probably would have gone to the NFL had it not been for a crucial play in the Florida-Georgia game during which he bit off the little finger of a Georgia offensive guard and refused to spit it out. This conduct was deemed so unsportsmanlike that Pinky was permanently banned from the game, though it also earned him his nickname and the undying affection of Gator fans.

Pinky eased his massive bulk out of the Tesla and grunted himself to a standing position. He was wearing flip-flops, wraparound sunglasses in Day-Glo green, the world's largest pair of fire-engine-red Bermuda shorts and a tank top that said BUT FIRST ROO ROO.

"Hey, Pinky," said Ken.

Pinky, ignoring him, looked around the parking lot, which aside from Ken and himself was deserted. He popped the Tesla's front trunk, revealing four packages wrapped in black trash bags sealed with duct tape. He pointed to one. Ken grabbed it and stuffed it into his backpack.

Pinky closed the trunk. In a voice that seemed to originate from deep beneath the surface of the Earth, he said, "Saturday," meaning he would collect his money then. Pinky was willing to extend credit because Ken was a longtime customer who understood that if he failed to pay promptly, he would die.

"Right," said Ken. "So, Pinky, how you been? You like the Dolphins this year?"

It was like making small talk with a UPS truck. Pinky, his eyes still scanning the parking lot, turned, grunted his body back into the Tesla and whirred away.

"Good talk," said Ken.

Chapter 8

Phil rang Stu's doorbell. After a moment the door opened to reveal Stu's wife, Amy, who was the best friend of Phil's ex-wife, Laurie.

"Hello, Phil," she said. She did not invite him in.

"Hey, Amy," he said. "I called Stu before. I'm just here to pick up . . . something."

"The Dora the Explorer head," said Amy. She did not actually add the words "you pathetic loser," but Phil heard them clearly nonetheless.

"Right, the head."

"Stu!" she called over her shoulder. "Phil's here for the head."

Stu's voice came back: "Be right there."

Amy stood in the doorway, still not inviting Phil in.

"So," he said. "How're you doing?"

"Fine," said Amy.

"You talk to Laurie lately?"

"Yes," she said, conveying, in that single word, the message that of *course* she had talked to Laurie lately; she talked to Laurie, her best friend, all the time, thousands of words a day, many of them about Phil, none of which were complimentary, and none of which she would ever share with him.

"Well, tell her hi," said Phil.

"Right," said Amy, clearly meaning no.

Before the conversation could get even more awkward, Stu appeared behind Amy, holding the Dora the Explorer head, which was smeared with dried cake frosting. Amy, without saying goodbye to Phil, turned and went back into the house.

"Thanks, man," said Phil, reaching for the head.

Stu pulled it back. "I'm confused, Phil. Last time I talked to you, you're like, 'Get that thing away from me,' and now you want it?"

"I can explain."

"Good, because I'm really curious. Also, I had to pay seventy-five dollars for this thing because the rental place won't take it back because you got birthday cake all over it."

"OK, that's my bad. I'm sorry. I'll pay you the seventy-five. But I need the head."

"And I need to know why you need it before I let you have it."

"Seriously, Stu?"

"Seriously, Phil. The head is now my property. I'm legally responsible for it."

Phil sighed. "OK. I need it for a job."

"Like a birthday party? Do they need an Elsa?"

"No, it's not a party. It's . . . OK, it's really weird."

"I'm listening."

So Phil told him everything: how he'd promised $235 to Stella; how he'd been approached by Ken Bortle, of Bortle Brothers Bait & Beer, in the bar; how he'd agreed to be in the video for $500.

When Phil was done, Stu said, "The Everglades Melon Monster. Holy shit."

"I know," said Phil. "It's insane. But I'm desperate."

"No, I mean, holy shit, this could be really good."

Phil stared at him. "You don't really think—"

"I'm telling you, people love this stuff. The paranormal. This could be an opportunity, Phil."

"An opportunity to do what?"

"Get in on the ground floor."

"The ground floor of the Everglades Melon Monster?"

"You never know, Phil. Things go viral. People get rich. These kids on TikTok, you never heard of them, they do some stupid fucking dance, it takes off, they make millions of dollars."

"Well all I'm hoping to get out of this is five hundred. So if you'll please let me borrow your head, I'll give you the seventy-five when I get paid."

"I don't want the seventy-five," said Stu. "I want in."

"In *what*?"

"In on this project. I want a piece of it. In exchange for the use of my property. Also my marketing expertise."

"Stu, I don't think it's that kind of project. It's just this guy paying me to do this."

Stu shook his head. "You're not seeing the big picture. This is an opportunity, Phil. We missed a big one with that birthday-party video. That was gold, you taking that shot to the balls, landing in the cake. I'm still kicking myself. We should have monetized that."

"How the hell would we monetize that?"

Stu waved away the question. "Point is, this is an opportunity. I want in. I want to go with you."

"To the Everglades?"

"Yes. I want to talk to whatshisname, the bait and beer guy. As a marketing professional."

Phil hesitated. He thought Stu was delusional, but he liked the idea of having somebody with him when he went out into the swamp.

"OK," he said.

They agreed to meet at the Gallo Grande. Stu handed Phil the Dora head, making a gesture of it, the way a high school principal presents the plaque for Best Grade Point Average.

"See you Wednesday," said Phil, turning to go.

"This could be big," Stu said. "You'll see."

"Sure," said Phil, not looking back as he trudged, head in hand, to his car.

Chapter 9

Jesse knelt on the damp ground in the clearing, staring at the gold bar she'd just dug up, glinting in the late-afternoon sun, heavy in her hands.

She'd made her way back to this spot because she'd had trouble convincing herself, despite the weight of the bar in her backpack, that it was real—that there was as much gold as she thought she'd seen. She feared that it would somehow be gone.

But it was still here. The gold was real. And there was a lot of it. She'd walked around the clearing, probing the ground with the machete; over and over she felt it strike metal. There were many bars, dozens at least. This had to be the legendary shipment Kark had read about. He'd said it could be half a ton of gold. Worth millions of dollars.

Millions of dollars.

In the baby carrier, Willa whimpered. Jesse set down the gold bar, repositioned the carrier and pulled up her shirt so Willa could latch on. As her baby fed, Jesse tried to think of a plan of action, but all that came to her mind was questions. What was the legal status of the gold? Could she claim it as hers? Should she move it to a safe place? Where would that be? And *how* would she move it? She'd need somebody to help her, but who could she trust?

Not Slater. He'd already taken every cent she had. And definitely not Kark. Maybe a friend . . . She had friends, or she used to, before she'd met Slater and gotten swept into his weird world. But she doubted any of her friends had the kind of expertise she'd need to deal with this. Her parents, maybe, if she could swallow her pride and call them. And if they believed her.

Maybe she should tell the authorities about the gold. But which ones? And if she told them, would she be giving up any claim to what she'd found? She didn't know who owned this ground, didn't know what her rights were.

She was also worried about the two camo creeps she'd run into out here. One of them had been carrying a metal detector. And they'd been close to where she was now. Were they looking for the gold? Were they still out here? What if they found it? All the more reason for Jesse to move it as soon as possible. But that brought her back to the question of where to move it, and how, and who to ask for help . . .

No answers came. Willa finished feeding. Jesse repositioned the baby carrier. She pondered the gold bar she'd just dug up. She decided, since she already had a bar in her backpack, to leave this one here. She covered it with dirt, grabbed the machete and rose. She surveyed the area, looking over the tops of the bushes surrounding the clearing. Seeing no one, she sloshed back through the knee-deep water to the path. She turned back toward the cabin, still pondering what to do, whom she could trust. Her parents? A lawyer? The police?

Definitely not Slater. If he found out about the gold, he'd try to take it, or he'd come up with some unworkable, illegal scheme. Whatever he did, he'd think only of himself, and he'd screw everything up. He always did.

That thought got Jesse thinking about the bar in her backpack. Maybe she shouldn't keep it with her. Slater might go through her backpack; he'd done it before. Until she had a plan, maybe it was better to keep the bar hidden in a safe place, away from the cabin.

Up ahead, sitting in the tree shadows a dozen yards off the path, was the run-down dark-gray house that had spooked her the first time she'd come this way. It still spooked her, but it was a landmark she knew she could find.

She looked around to make sure she wasn't being watched, then left the path and walked through the tall grass to the house. A rickety-looking wooden staircase rose to a front porch that was missing half its planks. The front door, connected by just one hinge, hung open at an angle; inside, in the shadowy half-light, Jesse saw garbage and debris strewn across the filthy floor. She didn't want to go in there.

She studied the staircase. It had four steps, made of warped planks. She bent down and tugged upward on the lowest one. It gave a bit. She slid the machete blade between the step and the vertical riser supporting it, then lifted up on the handle. With a creak the step came loose on the left side, three rusted nails popping up. Jesse lifted the step and peered into the opening underneath. She saw only dirt.

She looked around again, then unslung the backpack. She dug out the gold bar and slid it into the opening. She pressed the step back into place and, using the butt of the machete, hammered the three nails down into the riser. She stood back. To her eye, the step looked undisturbed.

She returned to the path. Before starting for the cabin, she looked around one more time to make sure nobody was watching her.

She didn't see the two men in camo.

But they saw her.

Chapter 10

"Where's Jess?" asked Slater, looking around the cabin.

"She went for a walk," said Kark. "How was Miami?"

"Profitable," said Slater. He held up a wad of cash.

"Excellent," said Kark. "You hit the ATM, huh?"

"Oh yes," said Slater. "I hit her several times."

He was referring to the wife of a Miami-based Brazilian importer who traveled often. She was one of several wealthy Miami women who employed Slater as a "personal trainer."

"Where's the weed?" said Slater, rummaging through the mess of dirty dishes and empty food containers on the counter by the sink.

"We're out," said Kark.

"Shit, seriously? Can we get our guy out here?"

Kark held up his phone. "Just texted him. He's on his way. In fact, I thought you were him."

Slater nodded. "How's *Glades Guy* coming?"

"It's *Man. Glades Man.*"

"Whatever. How's the pilot coming?"

"Being honest? Not great."

"Why not? What you showed me looked pretty good."

"Well, yeah, *you* look good. But we can't just have shots of you standing around looking at shit with your shirt off. There has to be some kind of story."

"There *is* a story, Kark. I'm out here, alone, with my hot wife and cute little baby. Surviving in the swamp. With alligators and shit. Survival. That's your story right there."

Kark shook his head. "Not really. You guys are *characters*, and you're both hot, which is good visually. But the characters have to have a story with an arc. This is Screenwriting 101. Something bad happens, some kind of danger, you're in trouble, you get out of it. Or there's conflict, and you resolve it. Or there's a mystery, and you figure it out. Every episode, some shit has to *happen*. Story arcs. That's what the network wants."

"Like when the big-ass snake came."

"Exactly. That would've been perfect. We could've built a whole episode around that. Snake threatens Glades Man's family, Glades Man fights back, dramatic music, snake goes away, family saved, boom, there's your story arc. Except we got no video."

"I know, Jess fucked that up."

A voice came from outside: "Hello?"

"In here!" called Slater.

Ken Bortle appeared in the doorway. "Hey," he said.

"Just in time," said Slater.

"Call me FedEx," said Ken, opening his backpack. He pulled out a bulging baggie and handed it to Slater, who hefted it, nodded and tossed it to Kark. Slater counted off some bills and handed them to Ken.

Kark, packing the bong bowl, looked up at Ken. "Want to join us?"

"Don't mind if I do," said Ken, stepping inside. "You guys're my last stop, and I want to talk to you anyway. I got a business proposal for you."

"Then let's talk business," said Kark.

The three of them settled around the bong. Kark fired it up and they passed it around a few times, nobody talking, the cabin filling with smoke.

"So," said Kark, exhaling. "What kind of business proposal?"

"OK," said Ken. "You guys're making a movie, right?"

"TV pilot," said Slater. "It's a reality show. *Glades Guy*."

"*Glades MAN*," said Kark.

"*Glades MAN*," said Slater. "That's me. I'm the Glades Man. In the pilot."

"OK," said Ken. "But you have, like, professional equipment? For the video?"

"Yup," said Kark. He pointed to his camera.

Ken nodded. "OK, good. So here's my proposal. This could be a win-win. You guys ever hear of the melon heads?"

Slater, who'd just taken another hit, shook his head.

"Melon?" said Kark. "Like, honeydew melon?"

"No," said Ken. "Like watermelons. They live in Michigan."

Slater, exhaling, said, "Watermelons live in Michigan?"

"No," said Ken. "Melon *heads*."

"Wait," said Kark. "Just the heads of the watermelons?"

"Nonono," said Ken. "The whole creature. They live in Michigan."

"Who does?" said Slater.

"The melon heads," said Ken. "Also Ohio."

"I don't know what the fuck you're talking about," said Slater.

"OK, bear with me," said Ken. "Supposably, there's these creatures, the melon heads. They have these huge heads. They're mutants. They live in Michigan and Ohio. In the forest. Anybody sees them, they eat them."

"People eat the melon heads?" said Kark.

"No, the melon heads eat the people."

"Is this a movie?" said Slater.

"No. It's like a legend. It's on the Internet, the paranormal sites. It's a mythical creature. Like the whaddyacallit, yeti."

"Or that thing," said Kark. "At that place on the highway. With the gorilla statue. The swamp ape."

Ken made a face. "Skunk ape. That's the competition."

"What the fuck are we talking about?" said Slater.

"Competition for what?" said Kark.

"Bear with me," said Ken. "My idea is, what if the melon heads show up here? In the Everglades?"

Kark frowned. "But they're like, not real, right?"

"Prolly not. But let's say, hypothetical, there's a sighting around here. Say somebody gets video of this thing, puts it on YouTube, Tik-Tok, whatever. It goes viral. Gets on the TV news. CNN. Everybody's talking about it. They call it the Everglades Melon Monster."

"Who calls it that?" said Kark.

"Whoever puts it on the Internet," said Ken. "Which is me."

"Wait a minute," said Kark. "You have video of the melon thing?"

"Not yet," said Ken. "That's where you come in."

"Ohhh," said Kark.

"Now you're starting to see it," said Ken.

"Wow," said Kark.

"What the *fuck* are we talking about?" said Slater.

"But what am I shooting video of?" said Kark.

"I got somebody lined up," said Ken.

"Who looks like the . . . melon thing?"

"Everglades Melon Monster. Yes. He's big, and he has this giant head."

"You mean like a birth defect?" said Kark.

"No, not like that," said Ken. "It's not, like, attached to him."

"His head's not attached to him?"

"Can somebody explain to me what the fuck we're talking about?" said Slater.

"It's a costume head. Dora the Explorer," said Ken. "He puts it on."

Kark sat up straight, snapped his fingers. "Wait a minute! Is this the same guy who's on YouTube? At the birthday party? Takes a golf club to the balls and falls in a cake?"

"Bingo," said Ken.

"Holy fuck!" said Kark. "You *know* that guy?"

Kark nodded. "I got him all lined up. He's coming out here Wednesday. With the head."

"Holy fuck," said Kark. "That is *excellent*. That guy was hilarious."

"Right," said Ken. "But what I'm looking for, in the video, is more of a spooky effect. Paranormal. Mysterious."

Kark nodded. "Low light. Grainy. Ominous. You're not sure what you're seeing."

"Exactly," said Ken. "Like, 'What the fuck *is* that thing?' " He paused. "So, down to business, what would that cost me? For the video?"

"What video?" said Slater.

Kark, ignoring Slater, said, "How about nothing?"

"Seriously?" said Ken.

"Yeah. But here's the deal. We also get to use the video."

"Use it how?"

"For the pilot. *Glades Man.*"

Ken thought about it. "So, like, how would that work? Because I want to be who puts it on YouTube. I want people coming to my store. I mean, this is my fucking idea."

"Rightrightright," said Kark. "Totally, I get that. You're the man. You are Mr. Melon Guy. But what I'm thinking is, you have a sidekick. A Glades Man." He nodded toward Slater. "He's with you when you see the monster. He's in the video, reacting. Maybe with his shirt off. Then after it goes viral, we use the video in our pilot, maybe with some other stuff we shoot. Never-before-seen video of the creature, like that. Giving you full credit."

"So we both use the video," said Ken.

"Right. It helps your store, and it helps our pilot."

"Win-win," said Ken. "I like it." He stuck out his hand.

Kark shook it. "Deal."

"You ever watch *Shark Tank*?" said Ken.

"I love that show!" said Kark.

"So I'm the guy with his shirt off?" said Slater. "In the video?"

"Right," said Kark. "And now we got ourselves a real story arc. Glades Man meets the Melon Monster."

"I'll smoke to that," said Slater.

Chapter 11

The two camo creeps were brothers, last name Campbell, given names Donald and William, although they had been known to everyone since childhood as Duck and Billy. Duck was the older, taller one with the full beard; Billy was the shorter one with the goatee. They were equally mean. It could be argued that they were born mean, but abusive parents, foster homes, the juvenile-justice system, a lot of crystal meth and a stretch in Apalachee Correctional Institution for armed robbery had definitely made them meaner.

It was at Apalachee where they first heard about the Everglades treasure. The source was a fellow inmate known as J-Dog, who had hit it off with the Campbells because the three of them had nearly identical neck swastikas.

J-Dog had been born and raised in Ochopee, a dot on the map on Route 41, best known as the site of the nation's smallest post office building. J-Dog's father was an old-time gladesman, an alligator hunter who'd become friends over the years with some members of the Miccosukee Indian tribe.

One night, after some serious drinking, the Miccosukees told J-Dog's father a story about a place in the swamp where gold bars had been buried. He'd pressed them on the location, but their answers were vague. They'd never seen it themselves, only heard about it from older tribe members. But they were certain that the gold was real, and J-Dog's father believed them. He spent his last few years looking for it but died of cancer without finding it.

"He told me, at the end, he was close," J-Dog said. "Said he could feel it."

The Campbell brothers were skeptical.

"If the gold was real," said Duck, "why didn't the Indians take it? Not the ones who told your daddy about it. The ones who had actually seen it. Why didn't they just take it?"

"I dunno," said J-Dog. "Miccosukees are weird that way. Some things, they stay away from. Places in the swamp they won't go. They got their reasons. But I'm telling you, they don't make shit like this up. I know them. They say something's out there, it's out there."

"So why didn't *you* look for it?" said Billy.

"Oh, I was gonna," said J-Dog. "But I ended up in here." J-Dog was serving a life sentence for murdering a bartender he suspected was screwing his wife. J-Dog had waited in his truck outside the bar until closing time, then ran over the bartender six times, the last five being what convinced the jury that the act was premeditated. Mrs. J-Dog, who had in fact been screwing the bartender, divorced J-Dog and got everything, including the truck.

Duck and Billy were intrigued enough by J-Dog's treasure story to do some research in the prison library. The Everglades legends they read about intrigued them more. They went back to J-Dog, pressed him for specifics. He was cagey, but in the end they made a deal. He'd tell them what he knew, even draw them a map showing the general area where his father believed the gold was. In return the brothers would split any money they found fifty-fifty with J-Dog's only child, a teenage daughter he'd had with his ex-wife.

The deal was consummated by a blood oath, the three men slicing their palms, the brothers solemnly swearing to J-Dog that they would take care of his girl. They of course were lying. As Billy put it to Duck later: "I ain't givin' that girl *nothin'*, less she's hot, and then it won't be gold I'll be givin' her."

When the brothers were released after serving their sentences for armed robbery, they decided they needed money to pursue their new life as treasure hunters. So they committed more armed robberies. When they had enough of a stake, they bought a Jeep, a camper trailer, a metal detector and some supplies, then found an abandoned home-site to squat on deep in the Everglades.

Armed with J-Dog's crude map, they started searching for the gold. They'd been searching for four months now, and they were running low on both money and patience. They were close to giving up treasure hunting and returning to the less romantic but more reliable career path of holding up liquor stores.

And then, for the second time, they saw the woman.

They'd talked about her a lot since the first time they'd seen her—this super-hot woman, out here on her own with a baby. They'd talked about what they'd have done if they hadn't lost her, what they'd do if they saw her again. The baby was a problem, they agreed.

And now they'd found her again, near where they'd seen her the first time. They'd come up behind her on the path; she hadn't seen them. Billy wanted to go after her right away, but Duck held him back, put his finger to his lips to keep his brother quiet.

"Let's see what she's up to," he whispered.

They stayed well back, following her quietly. They saw her stop next to a run-down abandoned house.

"Down," whispered Duck, and the brothers flattened themselves on the ground. Through the tall grass they saw her look around. They watched as she approached the house, stopping in front of it, then dropping down, out of sight.

"What's she doin'?" whispered Billy.

"Quiet," whispered Duck.

After a few minutes the woman rose and walked back to the path. Billy started to get up, but Duck held him down. The woman looked around again, then started walking away.

"C'mon," whispered Billy, starting to rise.

"No," whispered Duck, grabbing Billy's arm.

"She'll get away," whispered Billy.

"We'll catch up."

They waited until the woman was out of sight, then rose and trotted to the house, stopping in front of it, where the woman had dropped from view.

"What'd she do here?" said Duck, looking at the ground, the stairs, the porch. "She did something here."

Billy put a foot on the bottom step, felt it move.

"This is loose," he said. He bent, grabbed the board and pulled. It came away from the riser on the left side.

Duck crouched and peered into the opening.

"Holy fuck," he said. "*Holy fuck*."

"What?" said Billy.

Instead of answering, Duck grabbed the board, yanked it free and tossed it aside.

The gold bar glinted in the sunlight.

"Holy *fuck*," said Billy.

Duck grabbed the bar, hefted it, feeling the weight. He handed it to Billy, who did the same.

For ten seconds the brothers just stared at it.

"It's real," said Billy. "The treasure's real."

"And she knows where it is," said Duck. "She found it around here somewhere."

They stared at the bar some more.

"I wonder why she put it here," said Billy.

"She was hiding it," said Duck.

"Hiding it from who?" said Billy.

"I don't know," said Duck. "But that bitch is gonna tell us exactly where she found it."

Chapter 12

Ken pulled up in front of Bortle Brothers Bait & Beer but kept the truck running so he could finish listening to Hank Williams Jr. sing what Ken considered to be his personal anthem, "A Country Boy Can Survive." On the last chorus Ken cranked the sound all the way up, raised his head and, nowhere near on key, belted out the ending along with Hank:

> ... *country boy can survive*
> *Country folks can surVIIIIIIIIIIIIVE!*

Ken shut down the truck and went into the store, where Brad, as usual, was behind the counter playing Candy Crush on his phone.

"Busy day?" said Ken.

"Crazy busy," said Brad, not looking up. "We're gonna have to hire some help, handle these crowds."

"Maybe soon we will," said Ken. He slapped a stack of bills on the counter.

Brad looked at the money, nodded. "How much?" he said.

"Twelve fifty," said Ken.

"How much you owe Pinky?"

"Five."

"Leaving seven fifty. OK, that's a start. We have to pay FP&L at least three hundred right away, or they're gonna cut off the electric. So that leaves, what, four fifty. Then we gotta pay—"

"Waitwaitwait," said Ken, putting his hand over the stack. "I got plans for this money."

Brad frowned. "Plans?"

"OK, I didn't want to tell you until I had it all lined up. But this is gonna be good, Brad. I can feel it. This is really gonna work."

Brad's frown deepened. "What's really gonna work?"

"OK, here goes. You ever hear of the melon heads?"

"No."

"OK, bear with me."

For the next ten minutes Ken laid out, in detail, his master plan to launch the viral Internet campaign that would have the world beating a path to the door of Bortle Brothers Bait & Beer.

Brad listened to the presentation stone-faced.

Ken finished and said, "Well?"

"OK," said Brad. "I want to make sure I got this right. You're gonna pay five hundred dollars to a guy you don't know to—"

"I don't *know* him," said Ken. "But I know who he *is*, from YouTube. He's totally legit. Viral."

"OK, you're gonna pay this totally legit viral guy from YouTube five hundred dollars to walk around in his giant head, while this *other* guy you don't know makes a video—"

"I *do* know him. He's a customer."

"OK, while this pothead makes a video, which you're gonna try to convince people is this Everglades . . . thing."

"Everglades Melon Monster."

"And then people will see this thing on the Internet, see you talking about it, and they're gonna come here and buy shit? That's your business plan?"

"Right. But not the shit we have here now. New shit. I already ordered T-shirts."

Brad rubbed his face with both hands.

"Ken," he said, "you remember the Gator Giveaway?"

"OK, that was a mistake, I admit it."

"You didn't think so at the time. I tried to tell you, but you were sure it was a killer idea. Give customers a live alligator for every purchase over twenty-five dollars. Remember how that worked out?"

"It might've worked out good, if some asshole didn't call Fish and Wildlife."

"Because it was *illegal*, Ken. Also, it was not a great idea to be giving people an eighty-pound gator to take home in their Dodge Caravan with their three kids and their Yorkshire terrier."

"Well I ran out of the smaller gators."

"It *ate their dog*, Ken. Which we had to pay for. A purebred dog. We were lucky they didn't sue our asses off."

"OKOK, I told you, that was a mistake. But this is different."

"I agree," said Brad. "This is different."

Ken looked at him. "You mean that?"

"Yup. The Gator Giveaway was very stupid. But *this*, this Everglades . . . thing—"

"Melon Monster."

"Whatever. This isn't stupid."

"It's not?"

"No, Ken. It's way, way past stupid. It can't even see stupid from where it is. It's the Super Bowl MVP of stupid ideas. We're in serious trouble here, Ken. We're dying. We can't be pissing away our money on this bullshit when we got bills to pay."

Brad reached for the stack of money.

Ken covered it with his hand. "No," he said. "I'm doing this, Brad."

"We're gonna lose the store."

"We're gonna lose it anyway, the way it's going."

Brad had no answer for that.

"Listen," said Ken. "*I* brought in this money. *I'm* the one out there hustling while you diddle on your phone."

Brad had no answer for that, either.

The brothers were silent for a few moments.

"Look," said Ken, "I know I fucked up a bunch of times before. And I know this idea sounds crazy."

"It doesn't just *sound* crazy, Ken. It *is* crazy. It is totally, one hundred percent, batshit crazy."

Ken smiled. "OK, maybe it is. But we tried sane, Brad. Sane ain't working for us anymore. It's time to try crazy. That's what we do out here." He waved his arm at the store, and the Everglades in general. "People said Daddy and Uncle Canaan were crazy when they started this business in the first place."

"They *were* crazy," said Brad.

"I know! That's my point. Crazy *worked* for them, putting on shows, talking bullshit to tourists, Daddy pretending Rex was this scary alligator about to bite his head off any second, showing the crowd his finger . . ."

Brad, now smiling despite himself, said, "Which he did to himself, trying to catch a moving semi."

The brothers laughed together, remembering. After a moment Brad sighed and pointed at the money.

"OK," he said. "You're right. You earned it. Take it. We're fucked anyway."

"You mean it?"

"Yeah."

"Thanks," said Ken. "I really think this could actually—"

"Whatever," said Brad, cutting him off. "Just make sure you keep enough to pay Pinky, OK? We do *not* need Pinky coming after us."

"Right," said Ken. "So, one more thing . . ."

Brad arched his eyebrows.

"Could you come with me?" said Ken. "To the video shoot?"

"Why? You don't trust these people?"

"No, they're OK. I just want to make sure they understand who's in charge of this thing. This is a Bortle Brothers production."

Brad laughed. "Seriously? We're producers now?"

"Why not? We're paying for it."

"OK," said Brad. "What the hell, I'll go with you." He shook his head, still smiling. "A Bortle Brothers production."

"Sounds good, right?" said Ken.

"Sounds insane," said Brad.

"Like I said," said Ken, "sometimes insane is the way to go."

Chapter 13

The Campbell brothers, high on adrenaline, ran hard along the path in the direction the woman had taken, Duck carrying the gold bar. The woman had a head start, but she was walking, and carrying a baby. They'd only been at the cabin for a few minutes; they figured they'd catch up to her quickly if they could follow the route she'd taken.

At one point the footpath was joined by a lesser-used path, coming in from the left. They hesitated, wondering if the woman had veered off here. They decided to keep going straight, on the more beaten path. When they reached the two-track dirt road, they knew they'd guessed right.

"There she is," said Duck.

The woman was about fifty yards down the road, passing an old pickup parked off to the side. She hadn't seen them. Duck turned to Bill and held a finger to his lips. *Keep quiet.*

They took off running toward the woman.

A few yards past the truck she turned right, off the road, onto a path. Duck and Billy lost sight of her. They were sprinting now.

Duck reached the path first. He veered onto the path and kept running, Billy close behind. The path wound through thick vegetation. After a minute Duck caught a glimpse through the bushes of the woman ahead. They were getting close. She had not noticed them.

They ran a few more yards, then Duck stopped so suddenly that Billy almost ran into him. Duck made a *Get down* gesture. The two men dropped into a crouch, both breathing hard.

"What?" whispered Billy.

"*Shh,*" whispered Duck. Keeping low, he crept forward, Billy following. Through a narrow opening in the bushes Duck could make out the cabin ahead. He saw the woman was talking to two men, one short and fat, one tall and ripped.

"Shit," whispered Duck. "*Shit.*"

He turned around.

"Go back," he whispered.

"Why?" said Billy.

"Just *go back*," said Duck.

They crawled back a few yards. Duck made sure they were well out of sight, then the two men stood.

"What is it?" said Billy.

"She's with two guys," said Duck. "At a cabin."

"What guys?"

"I dunno. Guys. One's pretty big."

"So what? You got a gun."

Duck held up his hand. "Lemme think a minute."

"Duck, she knows where the gold's at. We got to—"

"I said *lemme think a fucking minute.*"

Duck thought about it, then said, "OK, here's what we're gonna do. We're gonna keep a watch on her, twenty-four/seven. When she leaves, we're gonna follow her."

"Why'n't we just go in there now? You got a gun."

"Two reasons. One, there's at least two guys there. Could be more. They could have guns, too."

"Yeah, but maybe they don't, and if we leave, what's gonna stop them from getting to the gold first?"

"Because they don't know where the gold is, and that bitch ain't gonna tell 'em."

"How the fuck you know that?"

"Think about it, Billy. What'd she do with this?" He hefted the gold bar.

Billy frowned. "She hid it. Under the steps."

"And why'd she hide it? Why'n't she just take it back to those guys?"

Billy nodded, getting it. "She didn't want them to know about it."

"That's right. Bitch wants to keep the gold all to herself."

Billy shook his head at the dishonesty of it. "That bitch."

"So here's what we do," said Duck. "First, we put this"—he hefted the bar again—"back under the steps."

"*What?* Why we gonna do that?"

"So she don't know we know about it. I don't wanna spook her. This bitch is tricky."

"Can't we just, like, grab her when she comes out, mess her up a little 'til she talks? Or how about we take her baby away? I bet that'll make her talk."

Duck nodded. "Yeah, we can do that, if we have to. But I wanna keep our options open. For now we let her think nobody knows. Easiest thing for us, we just follow her, she takes us right to the gold."

"Then what happens to her?" said Billy.

"We'll see," said Duck.

"I wouldn't mind messing her up," said Billy.

Duck nodded. "OK, but first we get the gold."

"Right," said Billy. "Gold first."

"OK," said Duck. "Far as I can tell, this path ends at the cabin. Past there is open swamp. Sooner or later she'll come back up this path. So we set up back at the road where their truck is, out of sight in the bushes. We wait 'til she comes back out. I'll take the first watch." He handed the gold bar to Billy. "Put this back under them steps exactly the way it was, OK? Then go on back to the trailer and get some sleep. Keep your phone on loud. I'll call you when it's your turn to stand watch. Or if she comes out. Got it?"

Billy nodded.

"We're close," said Duck. "Real close. It's right around here someplace, and she's gonna show us where. One way or another, she's gonna show us."

Chapter 14

When Jesse got back to the cabin, Slater and Kark were baked, which was normal. What was abnormal was that instead of lying around the cabin, they were outside holding an animated conversation, the two of them striding around the clearing, gesturing and babbling excitedly about a video shoot.

They tried to explain it to Jesse, but the more they talked, the less coherent they were.

"So wait," she said. "Now you're making a video with your weed dealer?"

"In partnership," said Kark. "We're gonna use the footage for *Glades Man*. He's gonna use it to promote his store as the headquarters of the whaddyacallit. Melon thing."

"The melon thing?" said Jesse.

"It's gonna be our story arch," said Slater.

"Your what?" said Jesse.

"He means arc," said Kark. "For the pilot."

"The melon thing is?" said Jesse.

"Right," said Slater. "It's like this mystery. It's out in the swamp and I'm reacting to it, like, 'What the fuck is *that*?'" He turned to Kark. "You said I should have my shirt off, right?"

"Definitely," said Kark.

"And the melon thing is . . . what?" said Jesse.

"A guy from YouTube," said Kark. "With this giant head. He's gonna walk around in the head, and Ken, the weed guy, is gonna 'discover' him." Kark put air quotes around "discover."

"About that," said Slater. "Shouldn't it be me? Who discovers it?"

Kark frowned. "Well, what we told Ken was, he gets credit for the video. It was his idea. He wants to put it on social media, drive traffic to his store."

"So where do I come in?"

"Well, like I told Ken, you're like a sidekick. You're with him when he sees the melon thing, and there's a shot of you reacting. Like, 'Holy shit! A melon thing!'"

"Maybe I'm running toward it," said Slater. "Like I'm trying to catch it."

"The way you tried to catch that python?" said Jesse.

Slater ignored her. "My point," he told Kark, "is I'm the Glades Guy—"

"Glades *Man*," said Kark.

"Right, I'm the Glades Man, so seems to me I need to have, like, a bigger role in this. Not just sidekick to the weed guy."

"Definitely," said Kark, "in the pilot, you're totally the main character. Lots of shots of you looking around, tracking the melon thing, et cetera. We'll shoot all that later. But for tomorrow we mainly shoot the YouTube guy."

"With me reacting."

"Right, we'll get some reaction shots of you."

"Shirtless."

"Right."

"Or how about I start with my shirt on, then take it off?"

"That might be tricky, in a reaction shot. The motivation. Like, why would seeing the melon thing make you take your shirt off?"

Slater thought about that. "OK, maybe I'm getting ready to swim after it."

"Like you swam after the python?" said Jesse.

Slater glared at her. "Jess, this is serious."

"I see that!" she said. "So when are you guys shooting this video?"

"Tomorrow," said Kark. "At dusk. We want low light. Ominous."

"How long is the shooting gonna take?" said Jesse.

Kark shrugged. "Couple hours."

"OK," said Slater, "how about, I'm sweating a lot, because of the tension, seeing this melon thing, so I take off my shirt and wipe my forehead."

"That might work," said Kark. "If you do it fast."

"What time is dusk?" said Jesse.

"Around seven," said Kark.

"Maybe I should just, like, have my shirt off from the start," said Slater. "Keep it simple."

"That's probably the way to go," said Kark.

"So, like, what are my lines?" said Slater.

"Lines?" said Kark.

"Yeah, like when I'm reacting, I need to say something, right? Like 'Look at that!' Or 'Holy shit!' Can I say 'shit'?"

"I think so, yeah."

"What about 'fuck'?"

Jesse walked away, leaving them to continue their discussion. She went to the other side of the cabin and spread her towel on the ground. She carefully removed Willa, who was sound asleep, from the baby carrier and laid her gently on the towel. Jesse sat down next to her daughter and thought about her next move.

A plan was forming in her mind, inspired by Kark's and Slater's moronic video idea. Kark had said they'd be busy for a couple of hours. Jesse would take advantage of the distraction to take Slater's truck into Miami and see a lawyer.

The only local lawyer she knew personally was a guy she'd dated, very briefly, before she met Slater. The lawyer, Erik Turpake, had turned out to be an arrogant asshole, but he seemed successful. Ideally she'd have called or texted him, but her phone, like Slater's, was useless, because Slater had long ago stopped paying the bills. Kark's phone still worked, but she didn't see how she could get it away from him and use it undetected. She'd just have to hope she could track Erik down. She'd also have to hope he'd believe her story about the gold. It still seemed wildly improbable to Jesse, and she *knew* it was real.

Willa woke and started crying, her *I'm hungry* cry.

"It's OK, baby girl," said Jesse, picking her up, lifting her T-shirt. "Mommy's here."

As Willa fed, Jesse's thoughts went back to what she'd tell Erik. She decided her best shot at convincing him would be to show him the gold bar she'd hidden under the steps of the creepy cabin. That meant she'd have to spend time retrieving the bar before she could take the truck. But it seemed like her best hope of being believed. And right now she desperately wanted somebody to believe her, somebody she could trust.

She hugged Willa closer.

"Tomorrow, baby girl," she whispered. "We're gonna take a ride."

Chapter 15

Stu walked into the Gallo Grande, hesitating by the door, his eyes struggling to adapt to the dim light after the white-hot glare of the late-afternoon South Florida sun.

After a few seconds he saw Phil seated at the bar. He was wearing ratty gray sweatpants and a faded blue Duke sweatshirt. In front of him were two empty glasses and a full Moscow mule. Overhead a TV screen was showing a man with a serious expression tossing what appeared to be a beanbag.

Stu walked over and tapped Phil's shoulder, getting a nod in return.

"What the hell is that?" said Stu, pointing up at the TV.

"That," said Phil, "is a cornhole tournament."

"Seriously?"

"Yup," said Phil. "Not only that, but it's *professional* cornhole. These guys are getting paid to play cornhole. And that's not the worst part."

"What's the worst part?"

"I'm watching them."

Stu took a seat next to Phil. He gestured to the glasses. "Looks like you're also doing some pregaming. As the kids say."

Phil lifted his mule, drained half, set it down. "If I have to run around the Everglades wearing this stupid head"—he pointed to a black garbage bag at his feet—"I am not about to do it sober."

"Apparently not," said Stu.

"It's happy hour," said Phil. "You get three for one."

"I'm good," said Stu.

"You say that now."

"So," said Stu, "when's this guy supposed to be here?"

Phil looked at the neon Coors Light wall clock. "Any minute. If he shows."

"You think he might not show?"

"I don't know. I don't really know the guy. He seemed serious, but let's face it, this whole thing is insane. Maybe he'll figure that out, say the hell with it. I hope not, though. I really need the money."

"I don't think it's insane," said Stu. "I think it could work."

"Right, but you're also insane."

Stu laughed. "True."

The door opened. Ken and Brad entered, blinking.

Phil looked over. "That's my guy, the one in front."

"Who's the other one?"

"No idea." Phil waved to Ken, who waved back and came over, followed by Brad.

"Hey," said Ken.

"Hey," said Phil. He pointed to Brad. "Who's this?"

"My brother, Brad. He's coming with us."

Phil nodded at Brad, who was a taller and better-looking version of Ken. Brad nodded back. Phil got the impression he was not thrilled to be there.

Phil gestured toward Stu and said, "This is Stu. He's, uh—"

"I'm Phil's agent," said Stu.

Phil rolled his eyes.

"Agent?" said Ken. "You going Hollywood on me, Phil?"

"Oh yeah," said Phil. "I'm living the Hollywood dream."

Stu, sticking his hand out at Ken, said, "I'm very excited about this project."

"Really?" said Ken, shaking Stu's hand.

"Really. I think it could be big."

"So are you, like, a real agent?" said Ken.

"Absolutely," said Stu.

Phil rolled his eyes again.

"Like, what kind of agent stuff do you do?" said Ken.

Stu made a vague gesture. "Various projects. Marketing, PR, social, et cetera. Phil's a new client, but I'm very excited about this project. The, uh, melon."

"Everglades Melon Monster," said Ken.

"Right," said Stu. "Very exciting. I see an opportunity here for—"

"So, Ken," interrupted Phil. "You bring the money?"

"Yup," said Ken. "You bring the big head?"

"Right there," said Phil, pointing to the garbage bag. "Can I see the money?"

"What, you don't trust me?"

"I absolutely one hundred percent trust you. Can I see the money?"

Ken pulled a wad of fifties out of his pocket, counted them out on the bar in front of Phil. This drew the attention of the bartender, a former Miami police officer named Merrett Stierheim, who drifted over.

"Hey," he said. "Not inside."

"It's OK," said Phil. Meaning it was not a drug deal. The protocol at the Gallo Grande was that it was fine to discuss business at the bar, but physical transactions had to take place outside.

"Whatever it is," said Stierheim. "Not inside."

Ken repocketed the cash. Stierheim drifted away.

"So," said Ken. "We ready to do this?"

"I guess," said Phil, draining his third mule.

"I'm excited," said Stu.

"Me too," said Ken.

They both looked at Phil, who stood, picked up the garbage bag and emitted a burp lasting a solid five seconds.

On that note, they walked out of the Gallo Grande, into the glare.

Chapter 16

The sun was beginning to set on the Everglades, and a hint of a breeze was starting to take the edge off the hot afternoon. Jesse was outside the cabin, sitting on one of the folding lawn chairs, watching Willa move around on a towel spread on the ground. Willa had figured out how to roll from her back to her stomach and then back again. She was delighting in this new ability.

Jesse was enjoying it, too, but her thoughts kept going to the evening ahead, and her plan to go to Miami. She'd changed out of her shorts and T-shirt, into a dress. She wasn't thrilled about the dress: It was too short and clingy, dating from her clubbing days, a million years ago. But it was the only clean garment she had, and she wanted to look at least vaguely presentable for her lawyer ex-boyfriend Erik.

"Damn, girl, you look hot," said Slater, coming out of the cabin, followed by Kark. "Don't she look hot, Kark?"

"She does," said Kark, staring at her breasts.

"You got a date, Jess?" said Slater. "You going somewhere?"

"Just for a walk with Willa," said Jesse, getting up. "Unless you want to take your daughter for a while."

"Busy right now," said Slater. "We got this video shoot tonight." Jesse hadn't expected him to take Willa. Slater paid virtually no attention to their daughter—never played with her, never changed her diaper, never talked baby-talk to her. Never even held her, this beautiful little girl, his blood.

Of course these days he didn't pay any attention to Jesse, either. To Slater, both Willa and Jesse were props for the camera, extras in his idiotic fantasy of reality-show stardom. She asked herself often—she had plenty of time to think about this—how she had allowed herself to be trapped in this absurd situation, how she had not realized sooner what a shallow, narcissistic buffoon Slater was. She'd been the golden girl; she'd had her pick of suitors, good guys, stable guys, guys with real jobs. Yet she'd allowed herself to be swept away by Slater, who was none of those things.

One reason, of course, was how he looked, and the way every woman who saw Jesse with him looked at her—the jealousy in their eyes, the grudging respect. She was ashamed, thinking back on it, how much she had enjoyed that, how much validation she'd felt. But she had.

Another reason—again, not a good one, she saw now—was that her parents had immediately detested Slater, which led her to see him as a means to escape their dominance in her life, their well-intended but suffocating need to control her. *I sure showed them*, she thought bitterly. *Out here in the swamp with this jerk.*

The thing was, Slater hadn't always been a jerk to her. In the beginning he'd been charming and thoughtful. Or at least he was capable of acting thoughtful. He could even be funny. She remembered their first date: They'd left a loud South Beach club at two a.m. and crossed Ocean Drive to take a walk on the beach. It was a splendid, romantic Miami night, clear sky, full-moon reflection rippling on the glistening ocean. They walked barefoot on the damp seaside sand, holding their shoes in one hand and each other's hand in the other. It was a beautiful scene, and they were tipsy and happy and well aware of how perfect they looked together.

They walked in silence for a while, enjoying the night, then Slater stopped. He turned to face her, and he was, in the moonlight, the most knee-weakeningly gorgeous man she had ever seen. In that moment she was glad she'd worn her red thong.

"Listen," he said. "I know we haven't known each other very long, but I have to tell you something."

"Okay," said Jesse.

"It's something I've never said to a woman before. But I want to say it to you now."

"What is it?" said Jesse, barely breathing.

Slater put his hands on her shoulders, pulled her close, his face just inches from hers. Looking into her eyes, he said, "I really have to pee."

Jesse burst out laughing, so hard that suddenly she, too, really had to pee. And so they both peed, ladies first, under a lifeguard station, taking turns standing lookout for each other.

Bonded by that experience, they walked and talked some more, and as night was turning into dawn Jesse went back with Slater to his apartment and broke her previously inviolable absolutely-no-sex-on-the-first-date rule. And it was wonderful.

That was the beginning, and the wonderfulness continued for quite a while. Jesse had pictured herself ending up with a more intellectual guy—she knew, in her heart, that she was a lot smarter than Slater—but he won her over, and not only with his looks. He was attentive; he was charming; he was romantic; he was passionate; he was sweet. And he had fallen in love with Jesse, or at least he thought he had. He was talking about marriage far before she felt anywhere near ready. He said he wanted to have children with her, raise a family with her, take care of her. "You're all I'll ever want," he told her, over and over. In time she believed him. He probably believed himself.

But that was the thing about Slater, she now knew: When he was into something, he was all in. But only for a while. In time, inevitably, he started looking for something new to be into.

She knew that now.

Jesse's pregnancy had been unplanned, a slipup on her part. After a lot of conversation—with Slater, with her friends and with herself—she decided to keep the baby. Her parents were furious; her mother stopped talking to her. Slater was thrilled. Said he was ready to be a dad. Said she should quit her job, take it easy, rest up for motherhood. Said they would get married. Said he would take care of everything.

Jesse believed these things.

Then the pandemic hit, and the world was suddenly scary. Slater had this idea that the safest place for them and their baby would be out in the Everglades. He'd become infatuated with the fantasy that he'd be some kind of brave survivalist, out in the wilderness. He found a cabin on a nice piece of land, going for what he said was a great price. He told Jesse they could build a good life out there. They'd be happy and safe, he said. They'd get married.

Jesse believed this.

By then she'd allowed her financial affairs to become merged with his, though it wasn't much of a merger, since virtually all the money was hers. She knew now that giving Slater access to her money had been a terrible mistake. But in the worrisome confusion of the early COVID days, she'd been glad to turn over the decision-making to Slater, who seemed so confident, so reliable.

By the time she started asking questions, it was too late: All the money was gone. A big chunk of it went to buy this stupid cabin—with the deed in Slater's name—but Jesse could only guess where the rest of the money had gone. Drugs, for sure, and gambling, and "loans" to Slater's bro friends, and nights at South Beach clubs where table service started at $1,000. And of course, women. There were always women around Slater.

By the time Jesse's belly was big, Slater's interest in her was zero. He wanted nothing to do with the pregnancy or the birth. The night she delivered Willa, he'd dropped her off at the hospital and disappeared; he showed up late the next day in the same clothes, reeking of booze, pot and perfume. Jesse had hated the idea of going back to the cabin with him. But she had nowhere else to go.

It got worse from there, Slater often leaving her and the baby alone at the cabin, sometimes overnight, Jesse unable to sleep, listening for hours to the strange sounds coming from the pitch-blackness outside. She was almost glad when, without consulting her, Slater invited Kark, his partner in their insane reality TV scheme, to move in with them. At least, she thought, she'd have company. That was before she found out what a creep Kark was.

It had happened so fast. A year ago she'd been happily in love, ready to become a mom and build a new life with a man she thought was as beautiful on the inside as he was on the outside. And now . . .

. . . Now, thanks to foolish choices she'd made, her life was a wretched, pathetic mess. The only good thing in it was Willa—happy little Willa, joyfully rolling over and back on the towel, giggling with delight, oblivious to her mother's worries. Looking down at her daughter, Jesse thought maybe it would turn out to be worth it, all the misery and humiliation, if that was the price of having this perfect little person in her life. But she couldn't let Willa grow up like this. She had to do better for her baby.

Jesse fitted Willa into the baby carrier and adjusted the strap. She put the machete in the tote bag; she'd already stashed the key to the truck in there. She went over the plan in her mind. *Get the gold bar. Drive to Miami. Find Erik. Figure out a way to get out of here.*

She took a deep breath, let it out, and started up the path toward the road. It was time to take back her life.

Chapter 17

Ken was leading the way on the path to the cabin, followed by Stu, Phil and Brad. They stopped when they saw Jesse coming toward them, all four of them staring at this improbable vision approaching, this beautiful woman in a short tight black dress, carrying a baby, holding a tote bag. They stepped aside, giving her room to pass. Jesse, who was used to being stared at by men, nodded briefly in their direction but didn't speak or make eye contact as she walked past.

The men watched her disappear around a curve in the path.

"Holy shit," said Stu. "Who was *that*?"

"Slater's girlfriend," said Ken, who'd encountered Jesse on previous weed-delivery runs. "Slater's the guy who owns the cabin."

"Slater is one lucky man," said Stu.

"I dunno," said Ken. "She's kind of a bitch, you ask me."

"A woman who looks like that doesn't need to be friendly," said Stu.

"They married?" said Brad.

"I dunno," said Ken. "Why?"

"No reason," said Brad, his eyes still on the path where Jesse had disappeared.

Chapter 18

Billy had been jolted awake by the sound of the truck doors slamming. He'd been on surveillance duty all day, having relieved Duck at dawn. He was concealed, miserably, in some thick bushes near Slater's pickup truck parked by the side of the road. It had been hour after sweltering hour of swatting at bugs and watching absolutely nothing happen on the path leading to the cabin. He'd fought the heat, boredom and drowsiness as long as he could, but as the sky started to redden toward sunset he'd finally dozed off. He was sound asleep when the slamming doors woke him.

Peering through the bushes, he saw that a second truck had parked next to Slater's. Four men got out and started down the path.

Billy picked up his phone and called Duck, back at their camper.

"What?" said Duck, half-asleep.

"Four guys in a truck," whispered Billy. "They're headed toward the cabin."

"You recognize any?"

"Two of them are the brothers from that old bait shop. Two I don't recognize. One's a big guy. He's carrying a trash bag."

Duck thought a moment. "OK," he said. "Just—"

"Hang on," whispered Billy. "She's coming."

"The girl?" Duck was wide awake now.

"Yeah. She's coming up the path."

"She alone?"

"Yeah, she's alone. Jesus, Duck, you wouldn't believe the dress she's—"

"Shut up and listen. Don't let her see you. Follow her and let me know where you are. I'm on my way. Stay with her."

"OK," whispered Billy.

"Don't lose her," said Duck, ending the call.

Chapter 19

Phil, Stu, Brad and Ken found Slater and Kark waiting outside the cabin, Kark holding the camera, Slater shirtless, flexing reflexively.

Ken, the only one who knew everybody, made the introductions, the men nodding to each other.

Kark said to Phil, "Dude, that YouTube video, with the cake—"

"Don't remind me," said Phil.

"Funniest fucking thing I ever saw," said Kark. "The little girl with the golf club. I bet that hurt like a mother, am I right? Your balls?"

"I'm serious," said Phil. "Don't remind me."

"Anyway," said Kark, "so you're gonna be our guy in the video, the melon thing?"

"Everglades Melon Monster," said Ken.

"That's me," said Phil. He burped. "'Scuse me."

"You definitely have the size," said Kark. "Plus you're gonna wear the head, right?"

"Right here," said Phil, pulling the Dora head out of the garbage bag. It was smeared with dried cake frosting, dented and misshapen, as though Dora had been involved in a crowbar fight. But she was still cheerfully wide-eyed, smiling spunkily through the frosting and the pain.

Brad snorted. "That's your monster?" he said to Ken.

"I gotta agree," said Kark. "I mean, we're shooting low light, from a distance. But that thing's pretty cartoony looking."

"I know that," said Ken. "That's why I'm gonna paint it." He took off his backpack and pulled out two cans of Rust-Oleum spray paint, one semigloss black and the other flat white. He shook the white can vigorously and began spraying the Dora head.

"How long's this gonna take?" said Kark, looking at the reddening sky. "We should start shooting in like fifteen minutes."

"No problem," said Ken, spraying vigorously.

Slater reached into the pocket of his shorts and produced a joint. "Might as well pass the time," he said. He lit the joint, took a long hit, held it out to Brad.

"No thanks," said Brad.

"You sure?" said Slater. "It's good shit. Got it from your brother."

"No thanks," said Brad again.

Slater extended the joint to Phil. "How about you, Mr. Monster? You want a hit?"

"Absolutely," said Phil, taking the joint.

"Phil," said Stu, "you think that's a good idea?"

"I do," said Phil. "I think it's a fine idea." He took a hit, his first one in over a decade. Fighting back a cough, he passed the joint to Stu.

Stu looked at it for a moment, said, "What the hell," and took a hit. It had been a long time for him as well. He passed the joint to Kark, who took a hit and handed it down to Ken, who paused from spraying to inhale it along with a cloud of paint fumes, then handed it back to Slater, who finished it with one final massive drag.

The Dora head was now totally white. As Ken shook the black-paint can, Slater fired up a second joint. It made the rounds twice—everybody toking except Brad—as Ken sprayed facial features on the head. He made a long curving line for the mouth, then, for the eyes, added two fat Xs. He stood and displayed the finished work to the others.

"What do you think?" he said.

"Seriously?" said Brad.

"What?" said Ken.

"I mean, look at it," said Brad.

"What's wrong with it?" said Ken.

"You know what it looks like?" said Kark. "It looks like Marshmello."

"Marshmallow?" said Stu.

"Marshmello," said Kark. "M-E-L-L-O."

"What the fuck is Marshmello?" said Phil.

"A deejay," said Kark. "He performs with a bucket over his head, looks kinda like that. He's huge."

"It does look like him," said Slater. "Only with a bigger head. Stretched out."

"So is this gonna work?" said Stu. "As a monster?"

Kark considered it. "If I do a little post-production, I think I can make it work."

"OK then," said Ken, handing Phil the head. "Go time."

Phil took the head and said, "The second I'm done, you give me the five hundred, correct?"

"That's the deal," said Ken.

Phil put the head on. Inside it reeked of paint fumes. The eyeholes still did not line up with his actual eyes; that, and the dwindling daylight, left him with almost no visibility.

"I can't see shit," he said, his voice muffled by the head.

"What?" said Stu.

"I SAID I CAN'T SEE SHIT."

"That's all right," said Kark, getting the camera ready. "Just follow my directions."

"WHAT?" said Phil.

"JUST FOLLOW MY DIRECTIONS."

Phil nodded the big head. The effort made him stagger a little. He was starting to feel quite dizzy from the paint fumes, or the pot, or both.

"OK," said Kark, assuming the role of director. "Let's start with him walking on the path. When we get out to the road I'll shoot some other angles."

"WHAT?" said Phil.

"START WALKING," said Stu, taking Phil by the arm and giving him a little pull along the path. Phil began making his way unsteadily forward. Kark brought the camera to his eye and followed, with the others behind him.

"So when do I get in the video?" said Ken.

"Not yet," said Kark. "I need to get some good video of him first."

"But soon, right?" said Ken. "I could say something like, 'What the fuck is THAT?' And then the camera goes on me, looking at the Melon Monster."

"You should say that to me," said Slater.

"Say what to you?" said Kark.

"'What the fuck is THAT,'" said Slater. "You should say that to me."

"Why would I say that to you?" said Kark.

"Because I'm your sidekick, remember? The Glades Guy."

"Glades MAN," said Kark from behind the camera.

"Right, the Glades Man," said Slater.

Brad snorted. Slater turned to him and said, "What's so funny?"

Brad shook his head. "Nothing really," he said. "Just, I dunno, you're supposed to be a gladesman?"

"That's right," said Slater, flexing. "You think that's funny?"

"Not at all," said Brad. "You totally got the build for it."

Slater frowned, trying to decide whether he'd just been insulted.

Ahead, Phil blundered blindly over a root and, with a muffled "FUCK," pitched face-forward onto the path. His head flew off and rolled ahead a few yards. It came to rest grinning back at him.

Stu trotted up and got Phil back, unsteadily, on his feet.

"You OK?" said Stu.

"I think I messed up my knee," said Phil.

"Can you walk?" said Stu.

Phil tried a few gimpy steps. "It's pretty bad," he said.

"Here," said Ken, digging a gel capsule out of his pocket and handing it to Phil. It was large and crudely made, a pharmaceutical do-it-yourself project. "This'll fix you up."

"What is it?" said Phil.

"Painkiller," said Ken. "Prescription." In fact, Ken had no idea what was in the capsule; he had taken it as partial payment from one of his weed customers who was short of cash.

"I don't think that's a good idea," said Stu, eyeing the capsule warily.

"I need the money," said Phil.

"We're losing the light," said Kark.

"Fuck it," said Phil, putting the capsule in his mouth and forcing it down. He picked up the head, put it back on and resumed walking, now with a pronounced limp.

"And, action," said Kark, unnecessarily. The little group fell in behind the blind, deaf, gimpy and now heavily medicated Everglades Melon Monster as, with night falling, it made its unsteady way along the path toward the road.

Chapter 20

Billy had been following Jesse, keeping well back, although she wasn't looking around. She was walking fast, almost trotting, taking the dirt road to where it turned into a footpath, then entered some trees. She came to the place where the footpath forked, with a lesser-used path going to the right. When she took the left fork, Billy was pretty sure where she was going. He called Duck.

"You close?" Billy whispered.

"I just passed the trucks," answered Duck, panting hard from running. "Where's she at?"

"On that path, the one that goes by the cabin where she hid the gold. I think she's going back there."

"OK, stay with her. I'm coming. Don't lose her." Duck ended the call.

The sun had set. Billy strained his eyes to find the woman ahead in the deepening dusk. He trotted forward a few steps, then stopped suddenly as he caught sight of her. She had stopped on the path next to the cabin. Billy dropped to a crouch, watching her.

* * *

About a minute after Duck ran past the trucks, Phil the Everglades Melon Monster blundered blindly up the path and onto the road. Kark, camera to eye, was a few yards behind, followed closely by Stu, Ken and Slater, and more distantly by Brad.

Phil tripped in the road rut and stumbled forward, almost falling.

Stu ran up and grabbed Phil's arm, steadying him.

"You OK?" he said.

"WHAT?" said Phil, his voice muffled by the head.

"I need him to go that way," said Kark, pointing down the road.

"WHAT?" said Phil.

"HE SAYS GO THAT WAY," said Stu, giving Phil a shove.

"I CAN'T SEE," said Phil.

"JUST TRY AND STAY ON THE ROAD," said Stu.

Phil started walking, the others trailing, Kark filming, occasionally trotting alongside to get shots of the monster from different angles, waving the others back to keep them from getting in the shot.

Phil could see nothing but found he could navigate by feeling the rut in the road with his feet. As he walked, his mood, inside the head, was transforming radically. He noticed the throbbing in his knee less and less, and soon not at all. In fact after a few minutes, he began to feel—between the Moscow mules, the pot, the paint fumes and Ken's capsule—quite good, even euphoric, inside his personal sensory-deprivation chamber, his bubble of solitude.

A song came into Phil's brain. It was the Beach Boys singing "Don't Worry Baby," about a guy who's worried about driving in a car race but is reassured by his woman that everything will turn out all right. Phil had always loved that song and was happy that his brain had decided to play it for him now. He began to hum along with it and was surprised by how awesome his humming sounded, thanks to the acoustics inside the head. He began to sing.

"Don't worry baby..."

It sounded amazing. Phil had never heard his voice sound this good. And he felt terrific! His knee didn't hurt at all! Suddenly, spontaneously, he broke into a trot. He had no idea where he was going, but he didn't care. He felt *fantastic*. Still singing, really belting it out now— *"Everything will turn out all right"*—he picked up his pace, galumphing blindly along the road.

"That's good! Keep running!" puffed Kark, trotting behind with the camera, unaware that Phil could not hear him.

Ken, with Slater close behind, ran forward and caught up with Kark.

"When do I say my line?" Ken said.

"What?" said Kark, puffing hard now, having trouble keeping up with Phil.

"My line," said Ken. "Where I say, 'What is that thing?' When do you want to do that?"

"Oh yeah," said Kark, grateful for the excuse to stop. "Let's do that real quick."

"Now?" said Ken.

"Now," said Kark, aiming the camera at Ken.

Ken, looking directly at the camera, said, "What the heck IS that thing?"

"Not into the camera," said Kark.

"What?" said Ken.

"Don't talk straight into the camera," said Kark. "It looks fake."

"So how do I say it?" said Ken.

"You say it to me," said Slater. "We talked about this."

"That's right," said Kark. "Say it to Slater."

"Am I looking at him when I say it?" said Ken.

Kark thought about it, then said, "Look down the road first, like you're seeing the monster. Then you turn and say your line to Slater."

"Got it," said Ken, nodding.

Kark aimed the lens at Ken and said, "And . . . action."

Ken pretended to peer into the distance. He frowned, then turned to Slater and said, dramatically, "What in the heck IS that thing?"

Kark swung the lens toward Slater.

"I don't know!" said Slater, also dramatically. "Looks to me like it could be some kind of a monster!"

"Wait, cut," said Ken.

"You don't say cut," said Kark, bringing the camera down. "I say cut."

"OKOK," said Ken. "My bad. But should he be saying all those words?"

"Well I gotta say *something*," said Slater. "You asked me a question, so I'm answering it."

"All I'm saying," said Ken, "is it seems like a lot of words, for the sidekick."

"But I'm also the Glades Man," said Slater.

Brad, watching this, snorted.

"What's so fucking funny?" said Slater.

"Nothing," said Brad. "Not a thing."

Slater was about to say something more to Brad, but Stu broke in.

"Guys," he said. "Where's Phil?"

The five men looked in the direction Phil had been running. The road dwindled to a footpath, disappearing into the deep gloom of the trees. They did not see Phil.

"Shit," said Kark. "We lost him."

"Shit," agreed Stu.

They took off running down the road under the rapidly darkening sky, on the trail of the Everglades Melon Monster.

* * *

For a few moments Jesse stood on the path looking at the cabin, reluctant to approach, creeped out by the gaping black doorway.

"Come on," she told herself. She took a breath, let it out and left the path, picking her way through the tall grass to the staircase. She avoided looking at the doorway as she bent down, grabbed the lowest step and pulled. It came up easily. The gold bar was where she'd left it. She picked it up and put it into the tote bag. She made her way back to the path and started walking out the way she'd come in.

* * *

"She's coming back my way," Bill whispered into the phone. "You close?"

"Almost there," panted Duck.

"Should I grab her?"

Duck thought for a few seconds. "No, stay out of sight. Let her pass, then follow her."

"Got it," said Billy. He ducked quickly into some bushes beside the path and crouched, waiting. Less than a minute later, the woman walked past.

Billy let her get well past, then crept back out of the bushes. Night had fallen; he could barely see the woman on the path ahead. She was heading straight toward Duck. Billy started following. They had her now.

* * *

Phil lumbered forward, still running, stumbling at times but managing somehow to stay upright. He wasn't sure he was still on the road—the footing felt different—but he didn't care. He was feeling great in his own world, the world inside the head, the happiest place Phil had been in a long while.

He had run through several impassioned renditions of "Don't Worry Baby" and was now working his way through the rest of his Beach Boys repertoire, which was extensive—not just the famous ones, like "Fun, Fun, Fun" and "Shut Down," but also the obscure car songs that never got played on the radio. He had just finished "Our Car Club"—*We'll be the fastest at the drags, man, we'll really cut some low ETs*—and was currently singing "Custom Machine."

"Naugahyde bucket seats in front and back, check my custom machine!"

Phil veered blindly off course, sideswiped a tree and staggered a few steps. Recovering his balance, he got back on track and resumed singing and running deeper into the swamp, utterly unaware of his surroundings, with not a care in the world.

* * *

"Which way do we go?" said Stu.

The little posse pursuing Phil had stopped at the fork in the footpath. They peered down both paths, but it was too dark to see more than a few yards.

"Maybe the gladesman here can pick up his tracks," said Brad, nodding toward Slater.

"You trying to be funny again?" said Slater.

"Not at all," said Brad.

"PHIL!" shouted Stu into the darkness. "PHIL, YOU THERE?"

No answer from the swamp.

"I'm guessing he went this way," said Ken, pointing at the left-hand path. "It's a little straighter, and he can't see shit where he's going."

"All right," said Stu. "Let's try left, then."

Single-file, with Stu in the lead, they trotted down the left-hand path, a posse in pursuit of the elusive Everglades Melon Monster.

* * *

Jesse was talking to Willa, not because Willa could hear her—Willa was asleep—but because Jesse was feeling very alone, trying to pick her way along the shadowy path by the barely-there glow of the night sky.

"Mommy should've brought a flashlight," Jesse said to her sleeping baby. "But we'll be out of here soon."

The path passed beneath some trees, the branches cutting off most of what little light there was. Jesse focused on the ground right in front of her, worried about falling.

"Next time," she told Willa, "Mommy will *definitely* remember the flashlight."

"Who you talkin' to, sweets?"

Duck's voice came from right in front of her. Jesse froze, stifled a scream.

He was just a few feet away, a big silhouette blocking her path.

Jesse turned to run. She took a few steps, tripped on a root, stumbled forward.

Into Billy.

He grabbed her roughly, pinning her arms at her sides, pulling her against him. He reeked of body odor. She struggled to get away, but he was too strong. Willa, startled awake, was crying.

"Where you goin', pretty lady?" said Billy, pulling Jesse in tighter, rubbing his body against her, his face an inch from hers. His breath stank worse than his BO.

"Let me GO," Jesse gasped.

"You don't wanna cuddle?" said Billy.

"Please," said Jesse. "Please don't."

"Let her go," said Duck.

Reluctantly Billy loosened his grip. Jesse backed away from him, set down the tote bag and unfastened the carrier so she could comfort her baby.

"It's OK, Willa," she whispered. "It's OK."

"Maybe you need to feed that baby," said Billy. "I think we'd enjoy that, right, Duck?"

Jesse held Willa close to her chest. "Please," she said. "Please, whoever you are, just let us go."

"Sure," said Duck. "We'll let you go. Soon as you show us where it is."

"Where what is?" said Jesse.

Jesse didn't see him move, but suddenly Duck had a fistful of her hair in his hand. She whimpered in pain as he yanked her head toward him.

"Don't try that shit with me," he said. "You hear me?" He gave her hair a vicious yank. "I said *you hear me, bitch*?"

Jesse tried to nod, but, caught in his grip, she couldn't move her head.

"What'd you say?" Duck said.

"Yes," Jesse gasped. "I hear you."

"Good," said Duck, letting go of her hair.

Jesse staggered, caught herself. Willa was crying again. Jesse, fighting her own tears, sought to comfort her daughter.

"Now, here's what's gonna happen," said Duck. "You're gonna take us to the gold."

"Now?" said Jesse.

"Right now," said Duck.

"But it's dark. I don't know if I can find—NO! Please!"

Duck—the man was quick as a snake—had her by the hair again, pulling her face close to his.

"You can find it," he said. He pulled a flashlight from his pocket, turned it on, aimed the beam at her face, blinding her. "See? We got a light. So you'll take us to it *right now*. You understand?"

"Yes," said Jesse, squinting.

"Good," said Duck, turning off the flashlight. He released Jesse with a shove that sent her to her knees.

Willa was bawling now. As Jesse, on the ground, comforted her baby, she fought to control her panic, forcing herself to think. If she refused to take the men to the gold, they would hurt her. She had no doubt about that. But if she took them to the gold, then what? Would they simply let her go?

"Get up, bitch," said Billy, shoving her from behind with his foot.

"Just a second," said Jesse. She crouched, adjusting the baby carrier so that Willa, who was still unhappy, was behind her. Reaching out for balance, her hand fell on the tote bag she'd dropped, unnoticed, in the dark. Her mind was racing. These were violent men. She'd seen their faces.

They're not going to let me go.

"I said GET UP, BITCH," said Billy, kicking her.

"OK, OK, please," said Jesse, reaching into the tote, finding the machete handle with her right hand. With her left hand she grabbed the tote straps.

She braced herself, sensing that Billy was about to kick her again. When she heard him grunt she swung the machete backhanded as hard as she could. She felt it hit his leg, heard a *thunk* and Billy's scream. She was rising now, bringing the machete forward as quickly as she could to swing it at Duck.

He was quicker. He grabbed her wrist, yanked it hard, trying to make her drop it. She held on to it but couldn't swing her arm; Duck was much too strong.

"You fucking *bitch*," he said, drawing back his free hand to hit her.

He didn't see the tote bag coming.

Jesse swung it with all her strength, felt the heavy gold bar connect with the side of Duck's face. He staggered backward, groaning, and went down hard on his back.

Jesse, still holding the machete and the tote, stumbled over Duck, found the path and started to run.

She got two steps.

She felt the grip on the baby carrier, felt herself yanked violently backward, felt herself falling. She desperately twisted sideways, terrified that her weight would land on Willa.

As she turned she saw it was Billy who was pulling her down. She smelled his stench as she landed on him. She tried to scramble away but Billy had her, rolling over on top of her, pinning her and her baby. She struggled but could not move.

"Got you now, bitch," he said.

Willa was screaming.

"Please," she said. "My baby."

"Fuck your baby," said Billy.

Next to them, Duck was struggling to his feet, groaning. Billy looked up at his brother. "Bitch cut my leg," he said. "Bad. I'm bleeding, Duck."

"She got me too," said Duck, rubbing his head.

"I'm gonna hurt her," said Billy.

"First things first," said Duck. He turned on the flashlight, shone the beam in Jesse's eyes. "She's gonna show us where the gold's at. She's gonna take us right to it. And she ain't gonna fuck with us no more because I'm gonna hold her kid."

"No!" said Jesse.

"Shut up, bitch," said Duck. He bent down toward Willa.

"No, please!" said Jesse, struggling but unable to move, pinned by Billy.

Duck put his hands on Willa.

Then his head jerked up as he heard the noise on the path—the thumping of heavy footsteps, a large body crashing through the vegetation, a muffled moaning sound.

Duck aimed the flashlight up the path. The beam landed on a strange grinning face, coming straight at them out of the dark.

"What the fuck is THAT?" said Billy.

* * *

Inside the head, Phil was feeling good. Really, *really* good.

He had moved on from car songs and was now in Anthem Mode, belting out "Be True to Your School." This was tricky because on the chorus he needed to sing both the lyrics (*Be true to your school*) and the semi-simultaneous cheer refrain (*Rah rah rah rah sis boom BAH*). But Phil was doing it, and in his opinion he was doing it beautifully. He could not remember feeling this sharp, this happy, this vibrant, this *alive*. He had been running and running, bouncing off bushes and trees, but his body felt wonderful, and he wasn't tired at all. He could run for days!

He was in full stride, singing a refrain-ending "*BAH*" at the instant he collided with Duck. Duck was a big man, but he was unsteady from being clobbered in the head, and Phil was an even bigger man running full speed. The collision, accompanied by a loud *WHUMPF*, drove Duck backward hard into Billy, who, responding to the weird onrushing apparition, was struggling to rise from his crouch atop Jesse. Phil's momentum carried all three men beyond her and sent them sprawling in a grunting tangle on the ground, Duck's flashlight sailing into the bushes, Phil's head coming off and rolling to a stop several yards away.

Jesse, seeing her chance, grabbed Willa and started to get up.

"No, you don't," said Duck as he and Billy struggled to free themselves from under the inert, moaning form of Phil.

Jesse managed to get to her feet, but before she could get even a few steps Duck was on his feet and staggering toward her, Billy right behind. She couldn't outrun them with her baby. In a few seconds Duck grabbed her by the arm, yanked her to a stop. They had her.

Then they heard a man's voice shouting from the darkness.

"PHIL!"

Before Duck could stop her, Jesse screamed, "HELP! OVER HERE! HELP ME!"

"*Shut up*, bitch," hissed Duck, yanking her arm again.

"PHIL! IS THAT YOU?" More voices, coming toward them on the path. Men's voices, a bunch of them.

Duck and Billy looked at each other.

"Shit," said Duck.

Pulling Jesse by the arm, he started on the path away from the voices.

Jesse, clinging to Willa, went limp, dropping to the ground. Duck, grunting, dragged her a few feet.

"HELP!" she screamed.

"PHIL!" The answering voices were close now.

"*Shit*," said Duck, letting go of Jesse's arm. He took off running on the path, Billy limping after him, the two of them disappearing into the darkness.

Seconds later the posse arrived. Stu, in the lead, almost tripped on Jesse before he stopped. Behind him were Kark, Slater, Ken and Brad.

"Jess!" said Slater. "You OK?"

"No," she said, sitting up, holding Willa, who was squalling.

"What happened?" said Slater. "What're you doing out here?"

"There's two men," said Jesse. "They—"

"Phil!" said Stu, seeing Phil lying on the ground, facedown, groaning. The posse, except for Brad, left Jesse and gathered around Phil.

Stu, helping Phil sit up, said, "What happened?"

"I don't know," said Phil, groaning. "I was running, and I ran into somebody, and next thing I know I'm lying here."

"You must've run into her," said Stu, pointing toward Jesse.

"I dunno," said Phil. "I couldn't see shit."

"Where's your head?" said Kark.

"My head?" said Phil, concerned, his hands going to his head.

"No, the big head," said Kark. "The one you were wearing."

"I dunno," said Phil.

"Over here," said Ken, finding it on the ground. "You think we can still shoot some more?"

"Too dark," said Kark. "But I think I got enough, back on the road."

"You sure?" said Ken. "What about the part where I discover the monster?"

"And he tells me about it," added Slater.

"We'll see," said Kark. "Let's take a look at what we got, back at the cabin. If we have to, we can reshoot that, like a cutaway, you two talking."

"Maybe we should rehearse our lines," said Slater.

"So you're done with Phil, right?" said Stu.

"Yeah, I think so," said Kark.

Stu turned to Ken. "So you owe him five hundred."

"OK," said Ken, digging into his pocket.

"That's right," said Phil, who had temporarily forgotten why he'd been running blindly through the swamp at night wearing a giant fake head. He stood, groaning from the throb in his knee, which had returned. Ken handed him a wad of bills, which made him feel a little better.

The posse started walking back, Stu helping Phil, who was limping a lot now, followed by Kark, Ken and Slater, exchanging ideas for the video, debating what the dialogue should be for the big discovery moment. As they passed Jesse, who was still sitting on the ground, quieting Willa, Slater glanced at her, but he kept walking with the group.

Brad stayed behind.

"You OK?" he said to Jesse.

"I'm OK, thanks," she said.

He looked around, found the baby carrier and handed it to her. "Here you go."

"Thanks," she said, carefully putting the now-quiet Willa into the carrier and slipping it on. She stood, Brad helping her up.

"I'm Brad," he said. "I'm Ken's brother, but don't hold that against me."

"I'm Jesse," she said. "I . . . I live in the cabin with them." She nodded ahead.

"The Glades Man," said Brad.

Jesse snorted.

They started walking. After a few steps Jesse stopped, remembering the tote bag.

"Hang on," she said, turning around. "I dropped something back there."

They walked back, looking down.

"This it?" said Brad, picking up the tote.

"Yes, thanks," said Jesse, reaching for it.

"Want me to carry it? Kinda heavy."

"No, I'll carry it," she said, taking it from him. "It's . . . baby stuff."

Brad frowned but said nothing. They started walking again.

"So," Brad said. "Back there, when your husband asked you—"

"He's not my husband," said Jesse. "He's the father of my baby, but we're not married."

"Oh, OK, sorry."

"Don't be sorry," said Jesse. "I'm not."

"OK. Anyway, back there, when the father of your baby asked you if you were OK, you said something about two men."

Jesse was silent for a moment. She'd decided not to talk about the two men if she didn't have to, because they were after the gold, and she didn't want to run the risk that more people would find out about the gold. At the moment she didn't trust anybody.

"I was confused," she said. "That guy with the weird mask ran into me, and it was dark, and I guess I just . . . I got confused."

"That big guy ran into you?" said Brad.

"Yeah."

"Huh," said Brad. "You must be tougher than you look."

"That's me," said Jesse. "Glades Woman."

Brad laughed. He wished he could think of something equally funny to say in response, but nothing came to mind.

They walked in silence for a while, thinking their separate thoughts.

Jesse was thinking about her next move. She needed to get to Erik the lawyer as soon as possible. And she needed to get out of this swamp, away from the two men. They would come looking for her. She was sure of that.

Brad was thinking two things. One was that Jesse wasn't telling him the truth about what was in the tote bag, or about what had happened back there on the path. The other was that she was the most beautiful woman he'd ever seen in actual life, let alone stood next to. Brad wasn't big on small talk, but he decided he'd attempt some now.

"What's your baby's name?" he said.

"Willa," said Jesse.

Brad thought hard, trying to come up with something to say about that. The best he could come up with was: "That's a nice name." He immediately decided he sounded like an idiot.

"Thanks," said Jesse absently. She went back to thinking about her predicament. Brad concluded that she wasn't interested in talking to him, which made sense to him, since she was a spectacularly beautiful woman and he was an idiot with nothing interesting to say.

Chapter 21

"Goddammit, hold your leg still," said Duck.

"Is this gonna hurt?" said Billy, eyeing the white plastic bottle in Duck's hand.

"Hell yes, it's gonna hurt," said Duck. "It's Clorox."

They were in the parking lot of the Publix supermarket on the Tamiami Trail. Billy was sitting on the Jeep tailgate, his wounded right leg bleeding from a deep, ugly gash. Duck had gone into the store and come back with a bottle of bleach, some gauze pads and a roll of duct tape.

"Maybe I should go to the urgent care," said Billy.

Duck spat in disgust, the gob barely missing Billy's wound. "Fuck the urgent care," he said. "Charge you five hundred just to walk in."

"But what if it, like, gets infected?" said Billy.

"It won't," said Duck. He held up the bottle. "I got you the real Clorox, not the genetic. This kills everything, including the COVID, 'cept your drug companies don't want nobody to know that. Now hold still."

Billy was about to say something, but what came out was an agonized yelp as Duck splashed half the contents of the bleach bottle onto the wound. A passing shopper looked at them, then quickly looked away and hurried past with her grocery cart. "Don't be a pussy," said Duck, setting down the Clorox bottle and unwrapping the gauze pads.

"It hurts like a motherfucker," said Billy, tearing up.

"That's how you know it's working," said Duck. "That's your immune system kicking in." He set to work taping a wad of pads over the wound.

"I'm gonna kill that bitch," said Billy. "I'm gonna cut off her tits with her own fucking machete."

"First we get the gold," said Duck. "Then you do her whatever way you want."

"So what's our plan? We go back there with guns? Grab the bitch?"

Duck frowned. "I gotta think about it. For one thing, I wanna know who that big guy was, with the mask, ran me over. How'd he just show up like that, middle of nowhere?"

Billy nodded. "Yeah, what the fuck *was* that?"

"And those other guys, I wanna know how many, what their deal is."

"You think they know about the gold?"

"That's the thing," said Duck. "I don't think they do. The bitch was out there on her own, like she don't want nobody to know what she's up to. I think she's holding out on them. Which is good for us."

"So what do we do?"

"I dunno yet. But I'm thinking we gotta get the bitch alone again."

"Good," said Billy. "Because she's gonna pay for my leg."

"Oh yes," said Duck, touching the painful lump on the side of his head. "She is definitely gonna pay."

Chapter 22

Brad and Jesse walked back to the cabin in silence. Brad spent the time trying, with no success, to think of something clever or interesting or at least not idiotic to say. Jesse wasn't thinking much about Brad, beyond feeling somewhat reassured by his presence. What she was thinking about was the two men. She knew that sooner or later, probably sooner, they'd come looking for her. They knew about the gold, and they knew, somehow, that she knew where it was. She couldn't let them catch her alone again.

She still wanted to see Erik the lawyer but decided it was too late to try to get to Miami tonight. In the morning she'd try to figure out some way to take Slater's truck. For now she and Willa needed to rest.

When they got back to the cabin they found Phil sitting outside on one of the lawn chairs, unhappily examining his knee. He looked up as Jesse approached.

"Listen," he said. "I am really, really sorry about running you over. I'm Phil, by the way."

"Jesse," said Jesse, pointing to herself. "It's OK, Phil, really. I'm fine."

"That's what's weird," said Phil. "You're fine, and I got knocked out. It felt like I hit somebody a lot bigger than you."

Brad looked at Jesse, frowning.

"I'm tougher than I look," she said.

"I guess you are," said Phil. "The other weird thing is, when I was lying there, I thought I heard men's voices."

Brad's frown deepened.

"That was Slater and the others," said Jesse. "They came running down the path yelling for you."

"I guess that's what it was," said Phil. "I was pretty out of it."

"Are you OK?" said Jesse.

"No," said Phil. "I'd like to go back to my place and lie down for maybe a week, but my ride's in there." He nodded toward the cabin. "They decided they have to edit the video right now. They're very excited about this."

"They're easily excited," said Jesse.

"Let me ask you," said Phil. "Do you think this whole thing, with the swamp monster, is . . ."

"Stupid?" said Jesse. "Yes."

"What about you?" said Phil, looking at Brad. "It's your brother's idea, right?"

"Yeah," said Brad. "But it's totally stupid."

* * *

Inside the cabin, Kark, Ken, Slater and Stu were passing a joint around, discussing their various visions for the video, which Kark was preparing to edit on his laptop.

"It needs to look shaky," Stu was saying.

"A handheld feel," said Kark.

"Exactly," said Stu. "Like *The Blair Witch Project*."

"The what?" said Slater.

"You never saw *The Blair Witch Project*?" said Stu.

"Nope," said Slater.

"Classic horror movie," said Stu. "Huge box office. They shot the whole thing for like eight dollars. Really shaky video, camera waving all over the place. Half the time you had no idea what you were looking at. People in the theaters were literally puking into their popcorn."

"Huh," said Slater, impressed.

"OK," said Kark, pointing at the screen. "Here we go."

The group gathered around to watch. Phil appeared on the screen, looking very much like a man in a Duke sweatshirt wearing a large fake painted head.

Ken frowned. "That's not super scary, bro."

"This is the raw video," said Kark, tapping keys. "Gimme a couple minutes."

As he worked, the figure on the screen darkened; the Duke lettering was no longer visible. Kark tapped some more and the figure became blurrier, the head looking more like it was part of the body.

"Now you're talking," said Ken.

"Wait," said Kark. As the other three passed the joint around, he worked for another ten minutes, adding more effects and slowing the figure's motion down.

"OK," he said. "Take a look."

He showed them a ten-second segment. The figure was now a dark, vaguely humanoid shape moving through an ominous-looking landscape with an unnatural, strangely disturbing gait. At the end of the clip its huge, ghostly gray head briefly turned toward the camera and there was just enough illumination to show the slightest suggestion— it almost wasn't there at all—of big black eyes and a wide grinning mouth. Then the screen went black.

The other three, now thoroughly baked, were silent for a few seconds.

"Holy shit," said Ken. "That's it. That's the fucking Everglades Melon Monster."

"You, my man, are a genius," said Stu, patting Kark on the shoulder.

"Thank you," said Kark.

"So where's the part where we talk?" said Slater.

"That's right," said Ken. "Our lines. When I see the monster."

"And he tells me about it," said Slater. "And I react."

"I'll add that now," said Kark, turning back to the keyboard. "I need to change the lighting so it matches." After a few minutes he said, "OK, try this."

Ken, Slater and Stu gathered around the screen, which again showed the shadowy shape walking, then turning toward the camera. Then Ken's face appeared, saying, "What the heck IS that thing?" The camera swung to Slater, who said, "I don't know! Looks to me like it could be some kind of a monster!" Then the screen went black.

"Well?" said Kark.

Stu nodded. "I like it."

"Yeah," said Slater. "Me too."

"Play it again," said Ken.

Kark played it again, looked at Ken.

"Should I maybe say more words?" said Ken.

"Like what?" said Kark.

"I dunno," said Ken. "But it's like, I'm the one discovering this thing, and"—he nodded toward Slater—"he's saying more total words about it."

"I'm just reacting," said Slater. "It's like a natural reaction."

"Right," said Ken. "But it's a long reaction. I say just the one sentence, 'What is that thing,' and you're saying two sentences of reaction."

"It's really just one sentence," said Slater. "I'm like, 'I don't know, looks like some kind of monster.'"

"That's two sentences," said Ken.

"Not really," said Slater.

"Yeah, really," said Ken. "Also I think we need to get the word 'melon' in there. Like a branding thing. I got Everglades Melon Monster T-shirts coming."

Stu, who had been following the debate closely, said, "How about this. After Slater says his lines, we have Ken saying another line, to even things out word-wise. Can we do that, Kark?"

"Like tack it on at the end?" said Kark.

"Right," said Stu.

Kark nodded. "We can do that. We can shoot it outside right now."

The four men went outside, where Jesse, Brad and Phil were sitting in lawn chairs—Phil dozing; Jesse feeding Willa and thinking; Brad still trying without success to come up with something to say to Jesse.

Stu prodded Phil awake. "You OK, big guy?"

"Not really," said Phil. "You guys done?"

"Almost," said Stu. "Phil, this video, it's fucking fantastic." He looked at Jesse. "'Scuse my French."

Jesse waved it away.

"Seriously, Phil," said Stu, "you wouldn't believe how good you look."

Phil sat up. "I'm not recognizable, am I?"

"Not at all," said Stu. "You look like this weird . . . blob thing."

"Thank God," said Phil.

"We're just shooting a little more dialogue now," said Stu.

"There's dialogue?" said Phil.

"A little. Between Ken and Slater, when they see the monster, the two gladesmen reacting."

"Gladesmen," muttered Brad, shaking his head. Jesse looked over and gave him a smile that made his stomach turn over.

Stu wandered over to the edge of the clearing, where Kark, with Slater watching closely, was positioning Ken for his line.

"OK," said Kark. "I'll count down, and you say your line." He put the camera to his eye and said, "Three, two . . ." He pointed a finger at Ken.

"It's a melon monster, all right!" said Ken, staring into the lens. "And it's—"

"Cut," said Kark.

"What's wrong?" said Ken.

"Don't say it into the camera," said Kark. "You're saying it to Slater."

"Oh right," said Ken. "OK."

"All right," said Kark. "In three, two . . ."

"It's a melon monster, all right!" said Ken dramatically, looking at Slater. "And it's heading in the direction of Bortle Brothers Bait & Beer!"

"Cut," said Slater.

Kark pulled the camera down. "You don't say cut," he said. "I say cut."

"OK," said Slater, "but that was two sentences."

"No, it wasn't," said Ken. "I said it's a melon monster, and it's heading toward Bortle Brothers Bait & Beer."

"Which is two sentences," said Slater. "Plus, why're you mentioning your store?"

"It's called product placement," said Ken. "Which I paid five hundred fucking dollars for."

"He has a point," said Kark.

"OK," said Slater, "but maybe I should say one more sentence. Even up the word count. Maybe I say something about Glades Guy, for the branding."

"Glades *Man*," said Kark. "We can put that in another video. I think this one has enough dialogue. We don't want to turn it into *Citizen Kane*."

"Who?" said Slater.

"Never mind," said Kark. "Look, lemme just edit Ken in and we can get this out on social media."

"Like tonight?" said Ken.

"Absolutely, tonight," said Kark. "You have a YouTube account?"

"Not yet. I was gonna—"

"What about TikTok or Instagram?"

"Not yet. I think I'm on whaddyacallit. MySpace."

"Seriously?" said Kark. "MySpace?"

"Yeah, but I don't remember my password."

"Never mind," said Kark. "I'll create some Bortle Brothers accounts. We'll put it up, send links out to some people, see if we can make this thing go viral."

"You think it could?" said Stu.

"Only one way to find out," said Kark. "Upload it and see what happens."

He headed back to the cabin, trailed by Ken, Stu and Slater.

Meanwhile Phil had fallen asleep in his lawn chair. Brad and Jesse sat in silence for a few minutes, listening to Phil snore. Then Jesse said, "So this whole swamp monster thing was your brother's idea?"

"Afraid so," he said.

"And you guys have a store out here?"

"Yeah. Bortle Brothers Bait & Beer. We sell bait. Also, beer."

She smiled again, and Brad's stomach turned over again. "So you guys are the Bortle brothers?" she said.

"Actually, it was our dad and our uncle. They were the original Bortle brothers."

"But you grew up out here."

"Born and raised."

"So you're an actual gladesman."

"I guess I am."

"You know the swamp."

"I do."

Jesse looked at him for a few seconds. "There's some . . . There's some weird people out here," she said.

Brad nodded. "Definitely. Any particular ones you're referring to?"

Jesse started to answer, stopped. She wanted, very much, to talk to somebody about her situation, and Brad seemed like a nice enough guy. But most guys were nice to her, at least at first. She decided she really didn't know him.

Finally, she said, "Nobody in particular."

Brad nodded, waiting for her to say more, but she didn't. They sat in silence for a while. Then Brad said, "Look, you don't know me, but if you need anything . . . I'm not saying you do, but if you do, if there's . . . if I can help with anything . . ." He pulled out his wallet and extracted a stained BORTLE BROTHERS BAIT & BEER business card and handed it to Jesse.

"Wow," she said. "Professional."

Brad smiled. "My brother had these printed up. He gets these ideas, like we're a real company. He watches *Shark Tank.* Anyway, if you need to call me, the first number's disconnected, but the bottom number's my cell."

"Thanks," said Jesse.

Stu had drifted back over to the lawn chairs. He prodded Phil awake.

"Can we go now?" said Phil.

"Yeah," said Stu. "They're almost done in there. Where's the head?"

"Over there," said Phil, nodding toward where the head lay in the dirt, grinning at the night sky. "But I never want to see it again."

Stu walked over and picked it up, handed it to Phil. "You never know," he said.

"Oh, I think I know," said Phil, taking the head anyway. He rose, painfully, and nodded goodbye to Brad and Jesse.

"Sorry again for running you over," he said to Jesse.

"I'm fine," she said. "Really."

He shook his head. "I still can't get over that. You could play offensive tackle for the Dolphins."

"Why thank you," she said.

Stu and Phil left. A minute later Ken emerged from the cabin.

"OK," he said. "It's uploaded. You ready, Brad?"

"Yeah," said Brad, getting up. He turned to Jesse. "So . . . good night."

"Good night," she said. "Thanks for walking me back."

"Anytime," he said. "Really." He immediately regretted the "really," which he thought sounded desperate, although in fact he really did hope she would call him, although he couldn't imagine why she would, based on the impression he believed he was making on her. He hated it, this yawning gap between what he wanted to say to this woman and the words that actually came out of his mouth. At the moment, what he found himself saying to her—his parting words, following up on "really"—were: "OK, then." Having expressed that deep thought, he turned and followed Ken, moving quickly before he could blurt out something even stupider.

When they reached the path, Ken said, "You got no shot, you know."

"What?" said Brad.

"With her," said Ken, nodding back toward the cabin. "She is *way* out of your league, no offense."

"I don't know what you're talking about," said Brad. "I'm not trying to . . . I'm not interested."

"Really," said Ken. "Could've fooled me."

"Well I'm not interested in her."

"That's good, bro, because like I said, you got no shot."

"That's fine with me," said Brad.

Chapter 23

The final edit of the Everglades Melon Monster video had a running time of sixteen seconds. Kark uploaded it to TikTok shortly before midnight.

By 9:53 a.m. the next day, it had been viewed 3,247 times.

The 3,248th viewer was a twenty-seven-year-old Brooklyn deejay and social media influencer known as Lemons Rockwell, who had 8.3 million TikTok followers. He was very, very high when the TikTok algorithm chose to show him the Melon Monster video. It instantly resonated with him. He decided to use it in a TikTok "duet," meaning he created a split-screen video with the Melon Monster video running on the right side of the screen, and a video of himself reacting on the left side.

For the first two-thirds of the video—the Melon Monster walking, then turning toward the camera—Lemons Rockwell merely stared into the camera with a puzzled frown. When Ken appeared onscreen and said, "What the heck IS that thing?" Lemons Rockwell arched his right eyebrow quizzically. When Slater appeared and said, "I don't know! Looks to me like it could be some kind of a monster!" Lemons Rockwell's left eyebrow went up, joining the right one. When Ken said, "It's a Melon Monster, all right! And it's heading in the direction of Bortle Brothers Bait & Beer!" Lemons Rockwell smiled and nodded, as if the mystery had been solved.

That was it. That was the entirety of the Lemons Rockwell contribution to the original Everglades Melon Monster video: sixteen seconds of Lemons Rockwell reacting. He did not say a word. He spent less than three minutes on his duet, from conception to execution.

He posted it to TikTok at 10:17 a.m.

By eleven a.m. it had been viewed 238,436 times.

By noon it had nearly reached a million.

By two p.m. it was approaching five million, with no sign of slowing down.

It was also inspiring a wide variety of variations and riffs. People were posting duets of themselves reacting to the Melon Monster, or with Ken and Slater replaced by celebrities, including Pat Sajak, Homer Simpson, Adele, Barry Manilow, Jay-Z, and Margaret Thatcher. People were adding dubbed music to the video, and splicing in scenes from TV shows and movies, including *The Godfather*. People were inserting snippets of the Melon Monster into other videos, including a particularly sophisticated mashup with a grainy 1945 black-and-white newsreel in which the Melon Monster appears to be wading ashore with the Allied troops at Normandy Beach. In another the Melon Monster was dancing with a young John Travolta in a disco scene from *Saturday Night Fever*.

By the end of the day the phrase "It's a melon monster, all right!" was everywhere on the Internet, and there had been hundreds of thousands of Google searches involving the phrases "Melon Monster" and "Bortle Brothers Bait & Beer." Several Internet communities were engaged in intensive efforts to determine the identities of Ken and Slater, especially Slater, who suddenly had many ardent fans, mostly, but not all, female.

There was also a great deal of speculation about the original video. Many saw it as a joke or prank, but some saw it as a brilliant, so-bad-it's-good marketing ploy—for a movie, perhaps, or a yet-to-be-revealed product, or Lemons Rockwell.

Still other people—a minority, but a highly motivated minority—took the Melon Monster seriously. These people were mostly members of a subculture known as cryptozoologists, who believed in what they called cryptids—creatures such as Bigfoot, the yeti and the Loch Ness Monster whose existence was not recognized by traditional scientists. The cryptozoologists were excited by the original Melon Monster video, which they analyzed, frame by frame, as though it were the Zapruder film. Some were skeptical, but some respected members of the cryptozoology community were convinced it was real, and possibly related to the skunk ape.

By midnight, tens of millions of people had seen some version of the Melon Monster. People in Taiwan were lip-syncing Ken and Slater. Less than twenty-four hours after Kark had posted the original video, more people—*far* more people—were aware of the Melon Monster than could name the current vice president of the United States.

And it was just getting started.

Chapter 24

"Wake up, Ken."

Brad poked his brother, who had passed out on the couch in the cramped living room of the little wooden house behind Bortle Brothers Bait & Beer, the house they'd grown up in.

"Fuck off," said Ken, shoving Brad's hand away.

"No," said Brad, poking him again. "You gotta get up right now."

Ken rolled over, grabbed his phone, looked at it.

"Why?" he said. "It's seven fucking thirty." They usually opened the store at nine, sometimes later. It didn't seem to matter.

"Just get up," said Brad.

Muttering, Ken rose, staggered into the bathroom, urinated, staggered back out.

"What?" he said.

"Take a look out front," said Brad, opening the door. Ken went out and walked around the side of the store.

"Holy fuck," he said.

The Bortle Brothers parking lot, normally an empty expanse of rutted dirt, had a dozen cars parked in it. Two more were pulling in off the highway at that moment. A crowd of maybe twenty people—they all looked to be in their teens or early twenties—had gathered in front of the store. One of them, a scraggly bearded kid in a T-shirt that said LUKE, I AM YOUR UNCLE—spotted Ken and said, "That's him! The guy from the video!"

The crowd surged toward Ken.

"Holy fuck," he said again.

Chapter 25

Phil knocked on the door of the West Kendall condo and waited, steeling himself for the worst. This was the right move, because the worst was exactly what happened: His ex-wife, Laurie, opened the door.

"Hello, Laurie," he said.

"What do you want," she said.

"I, uh, I texted Stella. She said she was here."

"Yes. She lives here."

"Right. I have something to give her. The money for her school trip."

Laurie stared at him for a few seconds, during which Phil was pretty sure she was thinking about unpaid child support. Then she said, "She's in the kitchen." She turned and walked away, leaving the door open.

Phil took this as an invitation, or at least permission, to enter the condo. He was surprised, because Laurie had never invited him in before. Laurie loathed him.

Not that he blamed her. He had, as Laurie's husband, done a loathsome thing: He had cheated on her, and he had done it while she was undergoing treatment for breast cancer.

It could be said, in Phil's defense—although nobody, including Phil, defended Phil—that there were extenuating circumstances. His marriage with Laurie had been on shaky ground for several years, and the original cause of that shakiness had been Phil's discovery that Laurie was exchanging suggestive, sometimes borderline-explicit, texts with an old boyfriend. When Phil confronted her, she was ashamed and remorseful; she swore, sobbing, that nothing physical had happened, that she deeply regretted it, that it would never happen again.

Phil believed her, but the delicate balance of their marriage had been disturbed; there were nagging suspicions, a subtle undercurrent of tension. Phil, who had always been a drinker, dealt with the situation by drinking more, telling himself that it was Laurie's fault, although the real reason was that he really liked to drink. His drinking got worse when Laurie was diagnosed with cancer—another good excuse for him—and he was very drunk when, after a late night with some newspaper colleagues in a bar, he had hasty, blundering sex in his car with a digital content provider he didn't actually like at all when he was sober.

Word of this event got around quickly; these were, after all, journalists. Laurie confronted Phil and demanded that he do something about his alcohol problem. Phil, like most people with alcohol problems, insisted that he did not have an alcohol problem—that, yes, he had made a mistake, but he was under a lot of stress, and besides, hadn't Laurie made a mistake too?

Laurie, sick and weak and scared, was not receptive to this argument. She kicked Phil out of the house and filed for divorce. This was traumatic for Phil, but it also gave him yet another solid reason, and more free time, to drink. He started showing up at the newspaper drunk, blowing deadlines and getting into vicious shouting arguments with editors. Eventually he managed to get himself fired. Which of course warranted more drinking.

Thus Phil transformed himself, in the opinion of everyone who knew him, from a likable family man and award-winning reporter into an asshole drunk who had cheated on his sick wife and lost his job. In time, as he descended deeper and deeper into loserhood, Phil came to agree with this unflattering assessment. He was not ready to give up drinking; it was the only way he knew to make himself feel better, or at least less bad. But he understood now that the cause of his problems was himself.

By the time he figured this out, his bridges had burned. His divorce was final, and Laurie made it clear that, despite his groveling apologies, she wanted nothing more to do with him. He was down to one friend, Stu. His default mood was depression; he lived inside a thick, perpetually dark cloud of self-doubt and shame. The only ray of light was Stella. She had, naturally, sided with her mom in the breakup, but she never shut Phil out completely. And now that Laurie's cancer was in remission, with the doctors saying hopeful things, Stella was allowing her dad more and more back into her life.

Phil was grateful to her for that. And right now, as he headed for Laurie's kitchen with cash for Stella's class trip in his pocket, he was happier than he'd been in a long time. It was the same happiness he'd felt when he used to buy her whatever overpriced thing she wanted from the Disney gift shop. A dad making a dream come true for his princess.

Stella was sitting at the kitchen table, eating an Eggo smothered in Nutella and looking at her phone.

"Hey, baby girl," he said.

Stella looked up, gave him a heart-melting smile.

"Hi, Daddy," she said, offering her cheek to accept his kiss. Then she frowned. "Does Mom know you're here?"

"Yeah, she let me in. I brought you this." He handed her an envelope. "For your class trip, plus some extra." He'd put $300 in the envelope, leaving himself $200 from the money Ken had given him. He couldn't really spare the extra he'd given Stella; as it was, he had no way of paying his rent, among other overdue bills. But he'd worry about that later. At the moment the look on Stella's face was all he cared about.

"Thank you SO much, Daddy!" she said, getting up, giving him a hug. "Are you sure you can do this? I mean are you . . . are you OK?"

"I'm fine," he said. "Don't worry about me."

On the table, a voice spoke from Stella's phone. It was a voice Phil recognized.

It said: "What the heck IS that thing?"

"I don't know!" answered another voice, which Phil also recognized. "Looks to me like it could be some kind of a mon—"

The voices stopped; Stella had muted her phone.

"Sorry," she said.

"What was that?" said Phil.

"It's just a TikTok thing," she said.

"And it's on your phone because . . ."

"Oh, it's everywhere. Like three hundred people have sent it to me already."

"And what does the . . . the TikTok thing show?"

"It's really stupid. It's like this supposed monster walking around the Everglades, and these two morons talking about it."

"So why is it viral?"

"I dunno. It's just so stupid, I guess. And one of the morons is kinda hot. Also Lemons Rockwell dueted it."

"Who did what to it?"

"This DJ, he's a big influencer, and he . . . Never mind. It's just this stupid TikTok thing."

"But there's a monster in it?"

"Supposedly. Some people think it's pretty creepy."

"What do you think?"

"I think it's some moron in a stupid costume."

Phil nodded. "Sounds about right," he said.

Chapter 26

Patsy Hartmann, Channel 8 PeoplePower News reporter, looked at her phone and said, "Shit."

"What is it?" said Bruce Morris, cameraman.

"Jennifer," said Patsy. "She hates me."

Jennifer was Jennifer Taylor, the Channel 8 PeoplePower News director. When she had started at the station as a smart, ambitious and attractive college intern, Patsy—also smart, ambitious and attractive, but twenty years older—was the lead anchor on the six p.m. local news.

In those days Patsy dominated in the ratings. People asked for her autograph in Publix; she could walk into Joe's Stone Crab at eight thirty on a Saturday night, stroll past the hundreds of tourists who'd been waiting for hours and be whisked directly to a table by the maître d'. She was a celebrity in a city that loved celebrity.

That was then. Over the next decade, Patsy's ratings, as ratings will do, declined. She found that she could shop unnoticed in Publix. The last time she'd been to Joe's, the maître d', a new guy, had not recognized her.

"It's a two-hour wait," he said, looking behind her in case somebody important had arrived.

Meanwhile Jennifer had soared, rocketlike, into the Channel 8 management ionosphere. When she took over the news operation, her first move was to partner Patsy with a new, younger coanchor, who happened to look a lot like Jennifer but with bigger boobs, and who before long was getting most of the lines on the teleprompter. Patsy had been in the biz long enough to not be surprised when Jennifer called her into her office and told her she'd decided to take the six p.m. broadcast in "a new direction." Meaning the same direction, but without Patsy.

Jennifer offered Patsy a choice: take a semigenerous retirement package, or take a salary cut and become a field reporter. Jennifer obviously expected Patsy to retire. Patsy, mainly to piss off Jennifer, decided to stay.

Now, as she and Bruce the cameraman sat in the Channel 8 van in near-motionless traffic—this was how Patsy often spent her day—she was wondering if she'd made a mistake.

"Jennifer doesn't hate you," said Bruce. "She's a bitch to everybody."

"No," said Patsy. "It's personal with me. Look at the assignments I'm getting."

Bruce frowned, thinking about the stories he'd done with Patsy recently. These included a personal trainer on Miami Beach who was attempting to set a Guinness world record for crushing mangoes with her thighs; an elderly couple in Hallandale who believed their deceased son had been reincarnated as an iguana; and—this was the story they had just finished—a utility shed in Hialeah that was drawing crowds because it had a rust stain that many people thought looked like Jesus, although a substantial minority insisted it was Celia Cruz.

"You're right," said Bruce. "Jennifer hates you."

"Right?" said Patsy. "So get this." She held up her phone. "Now she's sending us to the Everglades to look for a swamp monster."

"A what?"

"A swamp monster. Apparently, it's all over the Internet."

"You're kidding."

"If only. We're supposed to go to some place on the Tamiami Trail called"—she squinted at her phone—"Bortle Brothers Bait & Beer."

"Because . . ."

"Supposedly this swamp monster thing was seen around there."

"Seen by who?"

Patsy shrugged. "Lunatics, probably. Anyway, Jennifer wants us out there right now."

Bruce shook his head. "She really does hate you."

Chapter 27

Kark was awakened by the sound of farting. It was his phone, alerting him to an incoming call. He looked at the screen, saw that the caller was Ken, tapped the answer button.

"Yo," he said.

"You gotta get over here," said Ken. "It's unbelievable."

Kark could hear excited voices in the background. "What is?" he said, sitting up on the air mattress he slept on.

"The video, man. The TikTok. It's all over the place. We got a line out the door, people buying T-shirts, everything we got. We're running out of shit to sell."

"Seriously? From the video?"

"It's huge, man. They *love* the Everglades Melon Monster. People're taking selfies with me, dude, people are asking for my fucking *autograph*."

"Holy shit."

"I know, right? You gotta get over here now. This is big, man. This is *huge*. We gotta jump on it, figure out our next move."

"What're you thinking?"

Ken lowered his voice. "Number one, I'm ordering more merch. Number two, I'm thinking we need to do another video. Build on the excitement, you know?"

"Another monster video."

"Yeah," said Ken, keeping his voice low. "Maybe me stalking him, something like that."

"You and Slater," said Kark. "The Glades Man."

"I guess," said Ken. "Look, I gotta go, there's like a million people here. I'm gonna call Phil and Stu. Get your ass over here. We can make money off this, dude."

Ken disconnected. Kark tapped his phone screen for several minutes, his eyes widening as he saw his video, in many mutant forms, all over social media.

"Holy shit," he said. He stood and went to the battered couch Slater had been sleeping on since Jesse kicked him out of the lone bedroom.

"Slater," he said, nudging him with his foot. "Wake up."

"Fuck off," said Slater.

"Look at this," said Kark, thrusting his phone in front of Slater's face.

Slater looked at the screen, frowned, sat up. "Is that . . . holy shit, that's Cardi B and me!"

Technically it was Cardi B twerking, via video manipulation, with the Everglades Melon Monster. But Ken and Slater did in fact appear at the end.

"Yup," said Kark.

"Where is that?" said Slater.

"TikTok," said Kark. "But we're all over. Take a look."

He handed the phone to Slater, who spent several minutes on it, shaking his head and saying "holy shit," pausing the video each time he appeared onscreen.

"This is incredible," he said. "Dude, I'm like, *famous*."

"We gotta get over to Bortle Brothers," said Kark. "Ken says there's a huge crowd, people buying shit, asking for his autograph."

"Seriously?" said Slater. "His *autograph*?"

"Yup. We need to get over there right away. We're gonna jump on this, do another video. Tracking the Melon Monster."

Slater nodded. "Great idea. The Glades Guy on the trail."

"Glades *Man*."

"Right, the Glades Man, on the trail of the monster, picking up clues. Shirtless."

"I like it," said Kark.

The bedroom door opened. Jesse stepped out, holding Willa.

"You're up," said Slater.

"You're loud," said Jesse.

"We got a reason to be loud," said Slater. "The video we made? It's huge."

"Seriously?" said Jesse.

"You wouldn't believe it," said Kark, holding up his phone. "We're talking millions of views. Literally millions."

"Good for you," said Jesse. "Listen, Slater, I need to use the truck."

Slater shook his head. "Sorry, babe. We need the truck."

"Slater, it's important. I have a . . . a doctor appointment."

Slater shook his head. "You'll hafta reschedule. We need to get to Bortle Brothers. We're gonna shoot another video ASAP."

"You think that's more important than a doctor appointment?"

Slater shrugged. "Not my call, babe. Other people are involved in this thing. This thing is big."

"OK, how about I drop you two off at Bortle Brothers, then I take the truck to Miami and pick you up later?"

Slater shook his head. "Sorry, babe. We might need the truck for the shoot."

"The shoot? Are you serious? The *shoot*? You're talking like it's a freaking Avengers movie, instead of a bunch of idiots running around the swamp chasing a guy wearing a fake head."

"Oh really?" said Slater. "Suppose I told you one of the people involved in this project was Cardi B?"

"It's true," said Kark. "Also Lemons Rockwell."

Jesse was about to say something heated, but then she remembered Brad handing her his business card.

"OK," she said. "But you have to give me a ride to Bortle Brothers. I'll get to Miami from there."

"With who?" said Slater.

"I'll ask Brad for a ride."

"Ken's brother?" said Slater. "He's an asshole. Thinks he's funny."

"I don't know about funny," said Jesse. "But he's nice."

Slater snorted. "He just wants to get in your pants."

"Does that bother you?" said Jesse.

"Course not," said Slater.

"Then we're good," said Jesse.

Ten minutes later they were in the truck, Slater at the wheel, Kark by the passenger window, Jesse, next to Willa in her car seat, jammed between them. On her lap sat the backpack, with the heavy mass of the gold bar sitting beneath the baby supplies.

After two miles of rutted dirt roads the truck reached the highway and headed for Bortle Brothers.

Nobody in the truck noticed the mud-covered, camo-painted Jeep following them.

Chapter 28

"Where you think they're going?" said Billy, squinting ahead at Slater's pickup.

"How the fuck do I know?" said Duck.

"So what's our plan?"

"Depends what they do. Best case, they drop her off somewhere, we grab her."

"What if they stay with her?"

"Then we get rid of them," said Duck, nodding toward the Glock pistol in the center console. "Either way she's ours."

In a few miles the pickup slowed. Ahead, dozens of cars were parked on the highway shoulder.

"What's that about?" said Billy.

"Looks like something at the bait store," said Duck.

"Seriously? That dump?"

Duck nodded toward Slater's truck. "That's where they're going."

Slater was turning into the Bortle Brothers Bait & Beer parking lot. Duck slowed the Jeep and cruised past, the brothers scoping out the scene.

"Jesus," said Billy.

The parking lot was jammed with vehicles, including a Channel 8 news van. Hundreds of people were wandering around, with dozens crowded by the front door of the store.

"What the fuck is going on?" said Billy. "Why's the TV van here?"

"No idea," said Duck.

"So what do we do?"

"We stay here," said Duck, pulling into a space on the shoulder. "Sooner or later she has to come back out. When she does, we'll be waiting."

Chapter 29

Slater nosed the truck through the crowd and stopped it next to the Channel 8 van.

"You believe this?" he said. "TV is here!"

"Where did all these people come from?" said Jesse.

"The Internet," said Kark.

Jesse shook her head. "This is insane."

"It's huge, is what it is," said Slater.

He opened the truck door, got out and was spotted immediately by a husky bearded man in a vast Hawaiian shirt.

"That's the other one!" the man shouted. Mimicking Slater, he added: "'Looks to me like it could be some kind of a monster!'"

In seconds Slater was surrounded by people taking selfies with him. A few were wearing cheap white cotton T-shirts that said EVER-GLADES MELLON MONSTER, illustrated with a crude drawing of a stick-figure man with a huge head. Others had faded old black T-shirts that said BORTLE BROTHERS IN THE ♥ OF THE EVERYGLADES. The crowd around Slater grew quickly, its membership dominated by women, some of them squealing.

Kark dismounted from the other side of the truck, followed by Jesse, wearing the backpack and holding Willa, who'd fallen asleep on the ride over.

"Slater!" Kark yelled. "I'm going inside to find Ken."

Slater, from inside his dense fan clot, gave a happy little "OK" wave and resumed participating in selfies.

Kark, with Jesse trailing, pushed his way through the crowd into the store. They found Brad next to the cash register, telling a disappointed crowd that there were no more T-shirts. Spotting Kark and Jesse, he beckoned them to join him behind the counter, out of the mob.

"This is nuts," he said, shaking his head. "They're buying everything. They're buying *pilchards*, for God's sake."

"What's a pilchard?" said Kark.

"A fish. For bait."

"Seriously?" said Jesse. "They're buying souvenir *bait*?"

"Yup," said Brad. "And it's not always alive."

"What are they going to do with it?"

"I don't know, and I don't want to know," said Brad. "All I know is, we sold everything we had, and people keep coming. What they really want is monster stuff, but we ran out of T-shirts fast. They even took the old Bortle Brothers ones we had sitting around for like twenty years. Ken ordered more shirts, but they won't be here for another couple days."

"Did he design that shirt?" said Jesse, pointing to a woman in the crowd wearing the white shirt with the stick-figure monster.

"He did," said Brad, laughing. "Drew the artwork all by himself. Never took a lesson, believe it or not."

"Did he think about looking up how to spell 'melon'?"

Brad shook his head. "Ken's a big-picture guy," he said. "He's got no time for the little details."

"Speaking of Ken," said Kark. "Where is he?"

Brad pointed into the crowd. "He's in there somewhere with the TV people . . . OK, here he comes."

Ken, preceded by backward-walking cameraman Bruce Morris, was working his way toward the counter, talking with Channel 8 People-Power reporter Patsy Hartmann, surrounded by gawkers. Seeing Kark, Ken lifted his chin in acknowledgment but kept talking to Patsy.

"Bottom line," he was saying, "it's a mystery. Lotta mysteries out here in the Everglades. We plan to do more research on it, working from Bortle Brothers, which is our research headquarters."

Brad caught Jesse's eye, the two of them sharing a silent laugh.

Kark stepped around the counter, blocked Ken's path.

"Ken, yo," he said.

"Not now," said Ken. "I'm doing an interview."

"I'm just letting you know Slater's here," said Kark. To Patsy, he said, "Slater's the other guy in the monster video."

"Really?" said Patsy. "The, uh, tall one? He's here?"

"The Glades Man," said Kark. "He's right outside."

Patsy turned to Ken and said, "How about we talk to both of you outside."

"I guess," said Ken.

Kark, Ken and the Channel 8 team went out, leaving Brad and Jesse behind the counter.

"So," he said. "You OK?"

"I guess," she said, shifting the still-sleeping Willa from her right arm to her left. "Listen, I . . ." She hesitated.

"What?" said Brad.

"When you offered to help me out . . . I mean, I realize this is a pretty big ask, but . . . do you think you could give me a ride into Miami?"

"Absolutely. I'd love to." Brad winced inside, thinking "I'd love to" sounded too eager.

"Seriously?" Jesse smiled a smile that momentarily shut down Brad's central nervous system.

"Sure, no problem. When do you need to go?"

"Whenever's good for you. I mean, I know you're busy right now."

"No, I can go now. We're out of everything." Brad gestured around the store, which was emptying as people followed the TV camera outside.

"You really don't mind?" said Jesse.

"Happy to do it," said Brad.

They went into the parking lot, where the crowd had gathered in a semicircle to watch the TV interview. Patsy, standing between Ken and Slater, looked down at her notes, then into the camera.

"I'm here with Ken Bortle and Michael Slater, the two men who claim they saw the swamp monster," she said. Turning to Ken, then Slater, she said, "Who wants to tell me what happened?"

Slater started to speak, but Ken beat him to it.

"Well, Patsy," he said, "we were hiking right near here at Bortle Brothers Bait & Beer, when I saw something weird in the distance. So I—"

"We both saw it," interjected Slater. "In the distance."

"Right," said Ken. "We saw it in the distance, and I was like, what the heck is THAT? And then—"

"And then I said, 'Whoa, that looks like some kind of a monster,'" said Slater. "I never saw anything like it in all my time out here in the Everglades."

Off to the side, both Brad and Jesse snorted.

"So you live out here?" Patsy asked Slater.

"Yes, ma'am," said Slater, suddenly developing a Southern accent. "I'm a glades guy." Off-camera, Kark cleared his throat loudly. "I mean *man*," said Slater. "I'm a glades*man*."

"Anyway," said Ken, getting Patsy's attention back, "soon as I saw this melon monster I knew it was some kind of an unexplained phenomena. So we're definitely gonna research it. This'll be our research headquarters. Bortle Brothers Bait & Beer."

"What kind of research will you be doing?" said Patsy.

"You know," said Ken. "Like . . . studying it."

"What do you say to people who claim the video's fake?" said Patsy.

"They can say what they want," said Ken. "I know what I saw."

"Me too," said Slater. "I know what I saw also."

"So this isn't just some kind of publicity stunt?" said Patsy.

"Absolutely not," said Ken. "This is a scientific research effort about a phenomena, based out of Bortle Brothers Bait & Beer."

"I notice you're selling T-shirts," said Patsy.

"Yup," said Ken. "We ran out, but we got more coming."

Bruce the cameraman panned the crowd; people waved their EVERGLADES MELLON MONSTER shirts.

"Want me to try one on?" said Slater.

"What?" said Patsy, surprised.

"Want me to try on a T-shirt?" said Slater.

Before Patsy could respond, Slater had his shirt off. Some women in the crowd whooped and hooted.

Watching this, Brad said to Jesse, "Why'd he take off his shirt?"

"That's what he does," said Jesse.

Slater, flexing, called out, "Anybody got a shirt I can borrow?"

A young woman in very short cut-off shorts, holding a MELLON MONSTER T-shirt, stepped forward and, giggling, handed it to Slater. He made a show of trying to put it on, flexing his massive biceps and rippling pecs, then said, "Nah, I'd just rip it." He handed the T-shirt back to the young woman but kept his own shirt off.

"So," said Patsy, attempting to resume the interview. "Do you think this monster, whatever it is—"

"The Everglades Melon Monster," said Ken.

"Right. Do you think it's still out there?"

"Absolutely," said Ken. "It's somewhere around Bortle Brothers Bait & Beer."

"And we're gonna see it again," said Slater, giving Kark a nonsubtle look.

"Why do you say that?" asked Patsy.

"Instinct," said Slater.

"Huh," said Patsy. Turning back to Bruce the cameraman, she said, "So there you have it, straight from the two men who claim to have seen the Everglades Melon Monster. For Channel 8 PeoplePower News, this is Patsy Hartmann, reporting from the Everglades, where—"

"At Bortle Brothers Bait & Beer," interjected Ken.

"—where monster mania is in full swing," said Patsy as Bruce panned the happy, T-shirt–waving crowd. He finished panning and signaled to Patsy that he'd stopped recording.

"And there it is," said Patsy, switching off her microphone. "Another steaming pile of journalism."

"That was great!" said Ken. "When will it be on TV?"

"Never, I hope," said Patsy.

"What?" said Ken.

"Just kidding," said Patsy. "It'll air tonight. By the way, you're aware that 'melon' has only one 'L,' right?"

"It does?" said Ken.

"The part with me and the T-shirt," said Slater. "You think that'll stay in?"

"I'd be very shocked if it didn't," said Patsy.

"All *right*," said Slater, pumping a fist.

Patsy and Bruce began packing up. Slater, still shirtless, resumed taking selfies with his growing, 100 percent female crowd of fans. Ken and Kark, heads together, voices low, discussed their next move. Brad and Jesse got Willa's car seat out of Slater's truck and headed for Brad's.

Out on Route 41, a steadily growing line of cars waited to get into the Bortle Brothers Bait & Beer parking lot, carrying people glued to their phone screens and eager to be at the epicenter of the viral sensation that was the Everglades Melon Monster.

Duck and Billy sat in the Jeep, watching, waiting.

Chapter 30

Phil was at his usual seat at the bar of the Gallo Grande, drinking his usual Moscow mule and feeling his usual guilt about it, when his phone buzzed, the screen saying it was Stu. Phil thought about sending Stu to voicemail—he'd had a lot of Stu lately—but decided to answer.

"Hello," he said.

"So whaddya think?" said Stu.

"About what?"

"You don't know?"

"I don't know what?"

"You're a star, dude. You're a fucking *superstar.*"

"What're you talking about?"

"Your video, Phil. It's huge. You didn't know this?"

"I know it's on TikTok, if that's what you're talking about. I saw it on Stella's—"

"No, Phil. It's not just TikTok. It's *everywhere.* It's on the TV news, Phil."

"OK, well, great. As long as nobody sees my face, I don't give a shit."

"You still have the head, right?"

"Why do you wanna know?"

"Because we're gonna do another shoot."

"No." Phil's free hand went reflexively to his sore knee. "I'm not doing that again."

"Phil, if you don't do it, they're gonna get somebody else."

"Fine with me."

"So you don't need a thousand dollars?"

Phil sat up. "What?"

"Possibly more," said Stu. "We're in negotiations."

"Negotiations with who?"

"Ken. At Bortle Brothers. I just got off the phone with him. He's raking it in, Phil. He sold all his T-shirts and everything else in the store. It's insane out there, all these people wanting to buy Melon Monster shit. Ken ordered a ton more merch, and he wants to keep this thing going. He wants to shoot another video right away."

"And he'll pay me a thousand dollars? Cash? You know this for a fact?"

Technically, Stu did not know this for fact. His conversation with Ken had been rushed, consisting mainly of Ken, calling from inside the mob at Bortle Brothers, whispering that they needed to make another video ASAP. They had not discussed payment at all. But Stu did not see the need to burden Phil with this information at the moment.

"It's absolutely a fact," he said. "So, you still have the head?"

Phil stared at his drink. A thousand dollars wouldn't get him out of debt—far from it—but it would allow him to avoid eviction a little longer. He picked up the drink, drained it, set it down, signaled the bartender for another.

"Yeah," he said, finally. "I still have the head."

Chapter 31

"You mind holding her?" said Jesse, handing Willa to Brad. "I need to attach her car seat."

"Sure," said Brad, taking Willa and holding her in front of him with both hands, the way a person might hold a fragile vase, Willa's little legs dangling, she and Brad eyeing each other warily.

Jesse smiled. "You ever hold a baby before?"

"Not a human baby, no," said Brad. "Am I doing it right?"

"Long as she's not crying," said Jesse.

When Willa was safely installed Brad and Jesse got into the truck on opposite sides of the carrier. Brad eased the truck through the crowd onto the highway, heading toward Miami, passing a line of cars waiting to turn into the Bortle Brothers parking lot.

Brad shook his head. "I know I said this whole thing is stupid—"

"It is stupid," said Jesse. "These people are insane."

"I know, but there's a *lot* of them, you know? I hate to admit my brother was right about something, but . . . maybe he was right about this. I hope he was, anyway. He ordered all this monster crap for the store, and I'm not sure how we're paying for it. He thinks it's gonna get even bigger. He thinks he's gonna get rich."

Jesse nodded. "And Slater thinks he's gonna be famous."

"The Glades Man."

"Yup. The Glades Man, with all his glades experience."

Brad glanced over at her. "Was he always . . . ah . . ."

"A conceited asshole?" said Jesse. "Yes, he was."

"So, uh . . ."

"So how did I end up having his child?"

"Yeah," said Brad. "If you don't mind me asking . . ."

"OK, did you see him, back there? When he took his shirt off? And a bunch of women basically ovulated right there in the parking lot?"

"Yeah."

"That's how it happened."

"So it was a purely physical thing, you and him?"

"Not *purely* purely, no. Believe it or not, he's not always a total idiot. He can be charming. He can even be thoughtful, when he wants to. Or at least he can *seem* thoughtful. But yeah, the physical part, that was pretty strong. Plus my parents hated him, which was a big plus for me. Plus there was COVID, and the whole world seemed crazy, and I got a little crazy, too. But those are excuses. If I'm being honest, the big reason was, just *look* at him."

"Not my type," said Brad.

Jesse laughed. "I guess not. What about you? You have a wife? Girlfriend?"

"Wife, no. Girlfriends, I've had some, but none at the moment."

"A bachelor," said Jesse.

"Yep," said Brad. "Leading a wild bachelor lifestyle at Bortle Brothers Bait & Beer in the heart of the Everglades." He glanced at the rearview mirror, frowned and said, "Huh."

"What?" said Jesse.

"Guy behind me, he's right on my tail, like he wants to pass, but he's not passing."

Jesse looked back, saw the camo Jeep following, way too close.

Saw the two bearded faces.

"Oh no," she said.

"What?" said Brad, his eyes flicking to her, then back to the mirror.

"Those men," she said. "I know them. I mean, I don't know who they are, but I know what they want."

"What do they want?"

"They want me. Not me, but something . . . something I know. Those are bad men." She looked back, locked eyes with Duck, who was driving the Jeep. He smiled at her. She turned away quickly. "Oh God," she said. "Oh God this is bad."

"You want me to call the police?" said Brad.

"No," said Jesse.

Brad glanced at her, then back at the road. "OK," he said. "No police."

They were about forty-five miles west of Miami, doing sixty-five miles per hour in light traffic, the road ahead straight as far as the eye could see, nothing on either side except sawgrass swamp. Brad sped up a bit; the Jeep sped up, too. They felt a jolt as the Jeep's front bumper tapped the truck.

"Oh God," said Jesse. "What's he doing?" She put a hand on Willa's car seat.

"It's OK," said Brad. "Once we get to Miami there'll be people around, and they can't . . ."

His voice trailed off as he saw the Jeep pulling alongside. Billy, in the passenger seat, was holding up a pistol, showing it to Brad. He pointed toward the roadside, signaling *pull over*, then pointed the pistol at Brad.

"He has a gun!" shouted Jesse, unnecessarily.

Brad stomped the gas and the truck shot ahead. The Jeep swerved back into their lane and came up fast behind them. Again they felt it bump the truck's rear bumper, harder this time. Brad hit the brakes and the truck fishtailed, as did the Jeep behind it. Brad regained control and mashed the accelerator again, the truck shooting forward, gaining a few yards of separation. But the Jeep straightened out and was coming again.

"We're not gonna make it to Miami like this," said Brad, eyes on the rearview.

"So what do we do?"

Brad returned his eyes to the road ahead, getting his bearings. "OK," he said. "I got an idea."

"What?" said Jesse, looking back at the approaching Jeep.

"Up ahead there's a—"

He was interrupted by the Jeep ramming them again, hard, on the left side of the bumper, spinning the truck clockwise so it swerved onto the shoulder. Brad fought the wheel, got the truck back onto the highway. Jesse's left hand gripped Willa's car seat, her right hand bracing her against the dashboard. Brad had the accelerator floored, the truck engine roaring, the speedometer needle quivering near ninety. The Jeep was still right behind them.

Brad, staring straight ahead, saw what he'd been looking for, a mile or so ahead on the right: a stand of trees and, just beyond it, an old, faded billboard advertising airboat rides. He lifted his foot from the accelerator. Immediately the truck slowed. Brad punched a button on his dashboard, turning on the truck's emergency flashers.

"What are you doing?" said Jesse.

"Hold on," he answered.

The Jeep pulled alongside. Billy showed the gun again. Brad lifted his hands off the wheel for a second and raised them in an *I give up* gesture. Billy waved the gun toward the side of the road. Brad nodded and, following the Jeep, guided the truck onto the shoulder.

"What are you doing?" Jesse said again.

"It's OK," said Brad. "Hang on."

A few yards ahead, the Jeep stopped, the doors immediately opening on both sides, Duck and Billy getting out fast, Jesse staring at them in terror. As their feet hit the ground Brad stomped on the accelerator and spun the wheel to the left, the truck surging forward, forcing Duck to jump back into the Jeep as the pickup shot past, clipping the Jeep's driver's-side door, which broke off and went tumbling onto the road. Jesse saw Duck's face, red and contorted with rage. He screamed something at her as she went past, but Jesse couldn't make it out over the roar of the engine.

She turned her head, looking back. Duck and Billy, now fifty yards behind them, were back in the Jeep, pulling back out onto the road.

"They're coming again," she said to Brad.

"I know," he said. "I just wanted to get us a little space."

Looming ahead was the stand of trees, and just beyond it the billboard. As they reached the trees Brad hit the brakes hard and made a squealing right turn, blasting by some bushes onto a narrow, rutted dirt road that was almost invisible from the highway. To the right were more trees; to the left, a four-foot drop down a steep embankment into a weed-clogged canal. The truck jounced violently on the uneven road; Willa, miraculously placid until now, started crying. Jesse rummaged through her backpack, found the emergency bottle and put it into Willa's mouth, quieting her. She looked back but saw only a thick cloud of dust kicked up by the truck.

"Where does this road go?" she said.

"Nowhere, really," said Brad. "It ends up ahead."

"But won't they follow us?"

"Yeah," said Brad.

"So what're you gonna do?"

"I got an idea," said Brad.

The dirt road, following the canal, curved right. Brad rounded the curve and braked to a skidding stop. He jammed the truck into reverse and quickly backed into an opening among the trees. He put the truck back in drive and gripped the wheel, breathing hard, staring at the dust cloud hovering over the road.

In thirty seconds they heard the sound of the Jeep roaring toward them.

"Hold on," said Brad.

Jesse braced herself against the dashboard. The roar grew louder, and then the Jeep rounded the curve, suddenly visible through the dust cloud. Jesse could see Duck and Billy, both looking forward.

Brad stomped the accelerator and the truck shot out from the trees. Jesse saw the shock on Billy's face as he turned and spotted the truck. She saw him shouting something to Duck as the pickup bumper rammed into the side of the Jeep, turning the front end violently left, sending it hurtling down the embankment, into the canal.

Brad hit the brakes hard, slammed the truck into reverse, spinning the steering wheel. He slammed it into drive and the truck shot back up the road toward the highway.

"You OK?" he asked Jesse.

"I think so," she said. "Jesus."

"Yeah," he said.

She looked back. "How deep is that canal?"

"Not deep enough, unfortunately," he said. "Maybe three, four feet. Gators in there, though, so there's that."

"So you just . . . you just knew about this road?"

"Yup." He glanced at her. "Used to come here with girls."

"Well it came in handy," she said.

"Yup."

"But I'm afraid you messed up your truck."

Brad shook his head. "It's a reinforced bumper. This truck's seen worse."

"Well, I really appreciate it."

"No problem."

"No, seriously, I'm grateful to you. You didn't have to do any of this, and I'm *very* grateful. I mean it. Thank you."

"You're welcome."

They reached the highway. Brad turned right, toward Miami. They rode in silence for a while. Then Jesse said, "Don't you want to know?"

"Want to know what?"

"You know what. Who those men are, why they're after me. I almost got you killed. I got your truck messed up. Don't you want to know what this is about?"

Brad looked at her, then back at the road. "I can't say I'm not curious. But I figure if you want me to know, you'll tell me."

Jesse put her hand on her backpack, felt the solid mass of the gold bar. She was about to say something but changed her mind.

"Well, thanks again," she said.

"No problem," said Brad.

They continued on to Miami in silence.

Chapter 32

The Jeep rolled as it plunged into the canal, coming to rest with its left side on the muck bottom and its right side barely sticking up above the canal surface. As the Jeep's interior flooded with warm, soupy, algae-green water, Billy, on the passenger side, managed to find the door handle. Pushing up hard, he got the door open, then he scrambled up and heaved himself out of the Jeep, gasping and sputtering. Flailing his arms, he half-swam, half-waded to the edge of the canal, where he stood, dripping, in knee-deep water. Supporting himself with a hand on the bank, he turned back toward the Jeep and yelled, "Duck! You OK? Duck?"

No answer.

"DUCK!"

Nothing.

"Shit," said Billy. He thought about swimming back to the Jeep, diving down inside, trying to rescue his brother. But he was a poor swimmer, and he was afraid of getting trapped down there, in the dark water. He was also worried about alligators.

"Shit," he said again. He took a half step toward the Jeep but could not force himself to go deeper.

He heard a splash and, to his great relief, saw Duck's head appear in the Jeep doorway.

"Duck!" yelled Billy. "Over here!"

Duck hauled himself up, supporting himself with his elbows on the side of the tipped-over Jeep. He vomited, then looked at Billy.

"You left me down there," he gasped.

"No!" said Billy. "I was just coming back for you."

"Like fuck you were. You kicked me in the fucking head getting your own ass out."

"Duck, I swear I—"

"Shut the fuck up," said Duck. He vomited again, then clambered out of the Jeep and made his way to the shore, struggling in the muck. When he neared the bank, Billy held out his right hand to help him. Duck grabbed it with his left hand, yanked Billy toward him and punched him hard in the face with his right. Billy went down like a bag of rocks. Duck grabbed his neck and plunged Billy's head underwater. He straddled Billy's body, using his weight to hold him under. Billy struggled, but he was stunned by the punch, and Duck was stronger. Thirty seconds went by. Billy's struggles grew more frantic, but he could not free himself from Duck's powerful legs clamped around him. Forty seconds. Fifty. Billy emitted a burst of bubbles that reached the surface with a muffled sound, a desperate cry for mercy. Still Duck stood over his submerged brother. Sixty seconds. Ninety. Billy was weakening, his body going limp.

Finally, Duck stepped off. He grabbed his brother's hair and yanked his head out of the water. He shoved Billy to the bank, watched as he gasped and heaved and puked, blood flowing from his damaged nose. It was five minutes before he could speak.

"Jesus, Duck," he gasped, his voice hoarse. "You could've killed me."

"I *should've* killed you," said Duck.

"Duck, I swear I tried to—"

"Shut the fuck up," said Duck. He turned and started climbing up the bank.

It was a few more minutes before Billy was able to join Duck on the road. The two brothers stood together, looking down at the submerged Jeep.

Billy said, "I really was gonna try to pull you out."

Duck looked at him, spat out a greenish glob that just missed Billy's feet. He turned and started walking back toward the highway. Billy, limping on his machete-gashed right leg and still bleeding from his nose, walked behind, following his big brother, as he always did.

Chapter 33

Erik Turpake, attorney at law and Jesse's former boyfriend, worked for a firm with offices in a tall, sleek, modern building on Brickell Avenue in Miami. Brad and Jesse spent fifteen minutes working their way up the maze of ramps in the vast parking garage, where it seemed as if every spot that wasn't occupied by a Mercedes had a RESERVED sign. Roughly every ninety seconds Jesse said, "I am so sorry"; each time Brad said, "No problem."

Finally, on the ninth parking level, they found a space. Jesse disconnected Willa's car seat and converted it to a carrier, which Brad insisted on lugging. They took an elevator down to the building's sleek, modern lobby, where they found a directory informing them that Erik Turpake's office was on the twenty-third floor. They took another elevator up, the doors opening to the law firm's sleek, modern reception area.

Jesse, acutely aware that her tiny nightclub dress was wildly inappropriate for the setting, approached the sleek, modern receptionist and said she was there to see Erik Turpake.

"Do you have an appointment?" said the receptionist.

"No, but he knows me," said Jesse. "Please tell him it's Jesse Braddock."

The receptionist looked doubtful but picked up the phone. She spoke quietly with someone, hung up and said, "Mr. Turpake will be out in five minutes."

"Thanks," said Jesse. She sat with Brad and Willa on a sleek, modern couch, trying to look ladylike, which was not easy in that dress.

Ten minutes passed, then a deep, confident male voice called out, "Jesse!" and Erik Turpake appeared. He was a sleek, modern man in a sleek, modern suit—tall, fit, tan, impeccably groomed, sincere smile, great teeth. Brad hated him instantly.

Erik crossed the reception area as Jesse stood, tugging her dress down. They hugged, then he held her at arms' length, looking her up and down.

"Still the hottest woman in Miami," he said. "Where you been, girl?"

"The Everglades."

"Seriously?"

"Yup."

Erik looked at down Brad, still seated. He was wearing jeans, work boots and a deeply faded ZZ Top T-shirt from the 2008 In Your Face tour.

"So," said Erik, "is this the lucky guy who finally got you to settle down?"

"No," said Jesse and Brad, simultaneously.

"I'm just driving her," added Brad.

"He's a . . . a friend," said Jesse.

"Brad," said Brad, giving a little wave.

"Great to meet you," said Erik. "And who's this cute little baby?"

"She's mine," said Jesse. "Her name's Willa."

"Congratulations! So are you . . ."

"Married? No," said Jesse. "Listen, I'm really sorry for barging in on you like this . . ."

Erik waved the apology away. "No worries. What's up?"

"I need to ask you about something," Jesse said. She looked around the reception area. "I was hoping we could talk somewhere private."

"Of course," he said. He looked at his massive, multidial $37,000 watch. "I have a few minutes now. Let's go into my office."

"Great," said Jesse. She leaned down to pick up Willa's carrier.

"I can watch her," said Brad. "You go on ahead."

"You sure?" said Jesse.

"Yeah," said Brad.

"Well, thanks," said Jesse. "If she cries, she's hungry, so you can give her this." She rummaged in her backpack and handed Brad a baby bottle. "If she keeps crying, she needs to be changed, in which case, come get me."

"Got it," said Brad, nervously eyeing Willa, who was awake now, looking around.

"Listen, Brett," said Erik, "if you need anything, just ask Vicki." He gestured toward the receptionist. "She's a mom. Right, Vicki?"

"No," said Vicki, although Erik did not appear to notice.

"It's Brad," said Brad.

"What?" said Erik.

"My name's Brad," said Brad.

"Of course it is," said Erik. "Good luck with little Willow."

Erik led Jesse into his office, which was sleek and modern and the size of a regulation squash court. It had a spectacular view of Biscayne Bay. Erik closed the door and gestured toward the sleek, modern sofa. Jesse sat, tugging her dress down. Erik sat next to her, put his left hand on her right knee and said, "So, Jess, how're you doing?"

"Not great, to be honest," she said.

The hand moved two inches higher on her leg, the fingers sliding down to her inner thigh. "How can I help?" he said.

You can take your fucking hand off my leg, she thought, although she did not say it aloud. She didn't want to piss Erik off, and she knew from experience that he was easily pissed off. His temper was one of the three reasons she'd broken up with him. Another was that her parents adored him. The third was that, while he'd been telling Jesse, with tears in his ice-blue eyes, that he loved her and only her, he had been regularly screwing at least two other women.

So Erik was an asshole. But he was also—not that this was contradictory—a highly successful lawyer. And right now Jesse desperately wanted sound, and free, legal advice. So she ignored the hand on her leg and said, "I found something. And I need to know what to do about it."

"What'd you find?"

Jesse reached into her backpack, pulled out the gold bar and handed it to Erik. He took it in both hands, suddenly no longer interested in Jesse's leg.

"Where did you get this?" he said, staring at it.

"In the Everglades."

"Where in the Everglades?"

"It's not really a place. I mean, it's a place, but it's kind of in the middle of nowhere. I just, like, stumbled into it."

"Just you."

"Just me."

"And this was just lying on the ground?"

"It was like half-buried. But there were more."

"How much more?"

"A lot."

"How much is a lot?"

"I don't know the exact number."

"Like dozens? Of these?" He hefted the gold bar.

"At least dozens. I think more."

"Like hundreds?"

"It could be hundreds. There's a lot."

Erik nodded, thinking. Then: "Who else knows about this?"

"Nobody."

"Not even whatshisname, out in reception?"

Jesse shook her head. "Brad. He doesn't know. But there's these two guys . . ."

"What two guys?"

"Two creeps, out in the Everglades. They're after me, trying to get me to show them where it is."

"How do they know you know where it is?"

"I don't know, but they know. These're bad guys, Erik. They tried to hurt me."

"Do you know who they are?"

"No idea."

"But you're sure they don't know where the gold is?"

"Yeah. Because they're still after me." She considered telling him about the Jeep going into the canal, decided against it for now.

"OK," said Erik, nodding. "And you came to me because ..."

"Because I want to know what my rights are."

"To the gold."

"Right. I found it, and I want to know if that means I can keep it."

Erik smiled. "Finders keepers," he said.

"Yeah, I guess so. Is that a real thing? Legally?"

"It's complicated."

Jesse made a face. "Why do lawyers always say that?"

Erik laughed. "Because it's almost always true. I know a little about this. When I was a new associate I was assigned to a case, pretty big case, involving an undersea salvage company that found a nineteenth-century shipwreck off Key West. Ship went down with a valuable treasure, a *very* valuable treasure, and a lot of parties were interested—the salvage company, the state of Florida, the feds, France, Spain. My firm ended up playing only a small part, but I spent a lot of time researching treasure and salvage law, antiquities, stuff like that."

"So what can you tell me about the gold I found?" said Jesse.

"OK, first thing, is it on your property?"

"No. I don't own any property."

"Do you know whose property it is?"

"No. It's the Everglades, you know? It's just like, swamp. The middle of nowhere."

"Right, but even in the Everglades, the land still belongs to somebody. There's federal land, there's state land, there's Miccosukee tribal land, there's private owners ..."

Jesse shrugged. "I dunno. There's no signs or anything. Like I said, it's just in this random part of the swamp. Obviously nobody goes there much, you know? Because all that gold is just sitting there."

"Right," said Erik.

"And it must have been sitting there for a long time. It'd probably sit there forever if I didn't find it."

"Right."

"So I should be able to keep it, right? Minus taxes or whatever."

Erik shook his head. "It doesn't work that way."

"Why not?"

"Because whoever's land it's on—and I guarantee you it's on somebody's land—whoever that is, they're gonna claim it's theirs."

"All of it? Even though they didn't find it?"

"Yup."

"They wouldn't like, split it with me or something, as the finder? A finder's fee? They'd want all of it?"

"All of it. And they'd win in court."

"But that's not fair!"

Erik smiled. "Jess, we're talking about the law here. Fairness has nothing to do with it."

Jesse stared at the gold bar, glinting in Erik's hands.

"So you're telling me that this gold, which I found, which probably nobody else would ever find, which has been sitting there for like a hundred years, which two psycho assholes tried to kill me *and* my baby over, you're telling me that after all that, somebody who didn't even *know* about the gold is gonna get rich off it, and I'm gonna get *nothing*?"

Erik nodded. "Pretty much, that's what I'm telling you, as a lawyer."

"Well that *sucks*."

"Yup, it does."

"And you're absolutely sure about this."

"Absolutely."

Jesse stared at the gold bar a little longer, then sighed and stood. "OK," she said, tugging her dress down. "I guess that's that. Thanks for your time, anyway."

"So what're you gonna do?" said Erik.

"I dunno. I have to think about it."

She reached down for the gold bar. Erik put his hand on hers.

"Hang on a sec," he said. "Let's talk about this."

"What's there to talk about? You said I can't keep the gold."

"I did say that. Speaking as a lawyer."

Jesse frowned. "Meaning what?"

"I might have more to say to you if I was speaking as a friend."

Jesse sat back down. "Like what?" she said.

"This is just between us, OK? I am not speaking to you as a lawyer or a representative of this law firm, and you are not my client, understood?"

Jesse nodded. "Understood."

"And if you repeat to anyone any part of this conversation, I will not only deny it, but I will make your life very difficult, which I can definitely do, understood?"

Jesse nodded again.

"OK," said Erik. "I think there might be a way to arrange things so that you get the . . . the benefit of your discovery."

"Arrange things how?"

He hesitated. "I want to do some research first, before we talk details."

"But whatever it is, it would be legal?"

"I think it could be done without any legal repercussions."

"OK, but does that mean it's legal?"

He smiled. "It means it's complicated. Listen, do you want the gold or not?"

She thought about it. "Yeah, I do," she said. "If there's an OK way for me to get it."

"I think maybe there is. For right now, you're just going to have to trust me."

Jesse paused, then said, "Why're you doing this?"

"You mean what's in it for me?"

"Yeah."

"What, you don't think I'd do it out of friendship?"

"No."

Erik laughed. "OK, yes, if I help you out on this, I think it's only fair that I be compensated. A contingency. Say a third. Does that sound reasonable?"

"You get a third?"

"Right. But only if you get the gold."

Jesse thought about it. "OK," she said.

"Great!" said Erik, putting his hand on her leg again, this time upper midthigh. "You know, you really do look fantastic, Jess."

"Didn't you get married?" she said, removing the hand.

"Yeah, but, I mean, it's really great to see you again." The hand was back. "I've missed you, Jess."

Jesse removed the hand again, more firmly this time. "Erik, please don't take this wrong, but go fuck yourself."

He laughed. "So I guess this is strictly business."

"Correct," she said.

"OK, then, getting back to business. The gold, you know exactly where it is, right?"

"Yes. I mean, I couldn't give directions to it, but I know how to find it."

"So you could lead somebody to it."

"Yeah, I could, but . . ." Jesse hesitated.

"Is there a problem?" Erik said.

"Kind of, yes," she said.

"What is it?"

"The way I see it, I'm the only one who knows where the gold is. That's all I have. That's my leverage. As soon as I show somebody else where it is, my leverage is gone."

"But at some point you're gonna have to show somebody."

"I know. I'm just telling you, I want to be very sure I'm protected before I show anybody, including you, no offense."

Erik grinned. "None taken. I totally understand. I'll figure out a way to handle this so you feel protected."

"Thank you."

"OK, so I need to do some research, figure this thing out. Give me a day. I'll be in touch. What's your number?"

"I don't have a phone."

Erik arched his eyebrows. "Seriously? Jesse Braddock without a phone?"

"It's a long story."

"Well you're gonna need a phone, so we can stay in touch." He set the gold bar down on the sofa, rose and went to his sleek, modern desk. He opened a drawer, took out an iPhone and charger.

"You can have these," he said, handing them to Jesse.

"Are you sure?" she said. "I can't pay for it."

"Don't worry about that." He produced his own phone and tapped the screen. "I'm sending you a text so you have my number."

She looked at the screen. "Got it."

"Great. OK then, I'll be in touch soon. Meanwhile, don't say anything about any of this to anybody, including whatshisname out there, OK?"

Jesse nodded. "OK." She reached for the gold bar on the sofa. Erik reached out his hand, stopping her.

"I need to hang on to that," he said.

"Why?"

"Just trust me, OK?"

Jesse looked doubtful.

"Look," he said, "we need to trust each other on this. I'm trusting you. And I'm giving you the phone."

Jesse hesitated, then said, "OK."

"Great."

They went back out into the reception area. Brad was cradling Willa in his left arm, feeding her the bottle with his right. He looked extremely relieved to see Jesse.

"I think maybe she pooped," he said.

Jesse came over, took a whiff and said, "Oh yes, she definitely did."

"On that note," said Erik, "I'm out. Jess, I'll be in touch. Nice meeting you, Brett."

"It's Brad," said Brad, but Erik was already headed back to his office.

Jesse, taking Willa back from Brad, said, "I'll go change her in the ladies' room. Thanks for watching her."

"No problem," said Brad.

"I'm afraid there's poop on your shirt," said Jesse.

* * *

Erik closed the door, picked up the gold bar, walked across the office and thumped it down on his desk. He sat in his desk chair, pulled out his cell phone, pressed a speed-dial number, waited.

"Yes?" said a man's voice.

"It's me," said Erik, looking at the gold. "I have something for you."

Chapter 34

Frank Wallner, chief press aide to the United States secretary of the interior, heard his computer make the special chime it made when he got an email from his boss. He looked at the screen and sighed. The email subject line read *URGENT!!*

The interior secretary was a man named Whitt Chastain, who had served four terms in the US House of Representatives. During his time in Congress he had never introduced a single piece of legislation but had raised his national stature to cabinet level by making 638 guest appearances on cable-TV news shows. This was believed to be a congressional record.

On a typical day Secretary Chastain sent Frank at least ten emails. The subject line on every one read *URGENT!!*

Frank read the email, then did some googling. Then he called in his assistant, Jacky Ramos.

"Yes?" she said.

"He wants to go to the Everglades."

Jacky frowned. "Is he aware that the Everglades is outdoors?"

Frank laughed. It was well-known among Interior Department staffers that the secretary detested nature and avoided it whenever he could. He would have much preferred, and had lobbied hard, to be secretary of state—he loved formal dinners—but he had zero qualifications for that post. He also had zero qualifications to be secretary of the interior, but the feeling in the administration was that this was not a major problem because, in the words of one presidential advisor, "It's Interior. Nobody gives a shit who the secretary is."

"Yeah," said Frank. "He knows the Everglades is outdoors. He also knows that it's located in a swing state with twenty-nine electoral votes."

Jacky nodded. As everyone in Washington knew, Whitt Chastain was planning to run for president sooner or later, probably sooner.

"So what does he want to do in the Everglades?" she said.

"Press conference," said Frank. "He's gonna formally kick off the Python Challenge."

"The *what*?"

"Python Challenge." Frank gestured at his computer screen. "It's this annual contest, they invite people to come to the Everglades and kill the Burmese pythons, which are an invasive species. There's prizes for who catches the longest python, the most pythons, like that. It's a state thing, so usually the governor kicks it off, but he can't make it this year. So the Everglades National Park people invited the secretary, and he was like, 'Hell yes.' "

"I hate snakes," said Jacky.

"Then you're gonna hate this, because these are *large* snakes. And do I have a fun assignment for you!"

Jacky frowned. "What?"

"Take a look." Frank turned to his computer and opened a file. On the screen appeared a photo of a large, sweaty, barefoot man with a moon-shaped face radiating beard in all directions. The man was smiling an alarming all-gums smile and holding up a massive snake, apparently dead.

"Who's that?" said Jacky.

"That," said Frank, "is your defending Python Challenge champion. His name is DeWayne Toobs, although he goes by Skeeter."

"You made that up."

"Nope. This is Skeeter Toobs, and your mission, whether or not you choose to accept it, is to get in touch with him and make sure he attends the secretary's press event."

"Really? Why?"

"Because the secretary saw this picture, and he loved it. He wants

Skeeter there. He doesn't want just a bunch of politicians and people in ranger uniforms. He wants, and this is a direct quote, 'a real person.'"

"And he thinks Skeeter here represents real people?"

"Apparently, he does."

Jacky stared at the photo, shaking her head. "Whitt Chastain standing next to this guy. The meme people are gonna kill us. Should we maybe try to talk him out of this?"

"You want to try?"

Jacky shuddered. "No." Nobody ever talked Whitt Chastain out of anything.

"OK then," said Frank. "See if you can track Skeeter down."

"You think he has a phone?"

"No idea."

"You think he has teeth?"

Frank laughed. "Maybe in his pocket."

Jacky stared at the photo for a moment longer.

"I hate snakes," she said, and left.

Chapter 35

Brad and Jesse were back in Brad's truck, with Willa buckled between them.

"So," said Brad. "Am I taking you back?"

"I guess," said Jesse. She didn't really want to go back to the cabin, but she didn't know where else she could go.

Brad, seeing her hesitation, said, "You hungry?"

"To be honest, I'm starving," she said. "But I've taken too much of your time already."

"You like barbecue?"

Jesse smiled. "I love barbecue."

"It's a little out of the way, but it's good."

"I'd go way out of the way for good barbecue."

So instead of heading back west, Brad drove south along the coast, through Coconut Grove and Coral Gables, past dozens of insanely expensive waterfront mansions, down Old Cutler Road to a funky outdoor barbecue joint called Pig Floyd. While Brad waited in line to order, Jesse went to one of the picnic tables. She discreetly breastfed Willa, then put a towel down on the grass and put Willa on it with a teething toy. A few minutes later Brad brought over a mound of meat, with some paper plates and plastic utensils.

"I didn't know if you wanted brisket or pork," he said, "so I got 'em both."

"Good, 'cause I like 'em both." Jesse piled some meat on her plate and dug in. "Ohmigod," she mumbled through a mouthful of brisket. "This is amazing."

"Local guys," he said, nodding toward the men tending the smoker. "Old-school."

They ate without talking for a while, Jesse occasionally emitting groans of pleasure. When they were done they sat back and watched Willa amusing herself with the toy on the towel.

"This is really nice," said Jesse. "Thanks so much for doing this."

"No problem," said Brad.

"It feels so good to feel . . . normal," said Jesse. "At least for a little while."

"So back there, with the lawyer," said Brad. "That went OK? I don't mean to pry."

Jesse nodded. "I think so. Erik's a smart guy."

"Yeah, he seems real smart."

Jesse, catching his tone, said, "You don't like him, do you."

He smiled, shook his head. "Not really. But I'm sure he's a good lawyer, based on the size of his watch."

"I hope he's a good lawyer," said Jesse.

"You think he's a good guy?"

Jesse paused, then said, "No. But he's the only lawyer I know."

They were silent for a few seconds, then Brad said, "Well, if there's anything I can do to help with . . . with whatever's going on, I'm here."

"Thanks. I mean it. But you've already done way too much." She stood. "It's getting late. I probably should be getting back."

Brad stared at her for a few seconds.

"Those assholes in the Jeep," he said. "If they didn't drown, which unfortunately they probably didn't, they're gonna come after you again."

She nodded. "I know."

"Do they know where you live?"

"I don't know."

"They were following you. They might've figured out where you live."

"I guess, yeah."

"So it's probably not a good idea for you to go back there."

"I don't have anywhere else to go."

"You can stay at the store. I mean, in the house behind it. We got an extra bedroom. It's nothing great, but it's a room."

"I appreciate that, but . . . I mean, I've already dragged you into this thing way more than I should've."

"It's no problem, really."

"You're sweet. Let me think about it, OK?"

"Sure."

She packed up Willa, now asleep. They drove back to the Everglades without saying much. Jesse stared out the window, pondering whether to take Brad up on his offer to stay at his place. She felt guilty about not confiding in him. He had, after all, saved her from the Jeep creeps, at considerable risk to himself. He had been incredibly nice to her. She wanted to trust him.

The problem was that men were always nice to her, at least at first, because, in her experience, roughly 100 percent of the straight men she met wanted to sleep with her. This did not mean they were trustworthy, Slater being Exhibit A. She liked Brad, as far as she knew him, but Erik had cautioned her not to trust anyone. For now, she decided, she wouldn't tell Brad any more than she had to. It was too bad, she thought, staring out the window. He really did seem like a good guy, and he was sort of cute, in an unkempt way.

For his part, Brad spent the drive mainly wondering how much he could read into the fact that she'd called him "sweet."

As they drove west out of Miami on the Tamiami Trail, they passed the Gallo Grande. Preoccupied with their separate thoughts, neither Brad nor Jesse noticed Slater's pickup truck, with Slater, Kark and Ken inside, coming the other way, pulling into the bar's parking lot.

Chapter 36

The Everglades Melon Monster steering committee—Kark, Slater, Ken, Stu and, reluctantly, Phil—had decided to meet in the bar of the Gallo Grande because (a) Stu and Phil were already there, and (b) Bortle Brothers Bait & Beer was overrun with people.

"It's insane," Ken was saying. "I put up a sign, 'Closed 'til tomorrow,' but they keep showing up, pounding on the door. There's people all over the place, taking selfies, making videos, looking for the monster."

"That's excellent!" said Stu.

"It'd be more excellent if I had shit to sell them," said Ken. "I'm supposed to get a big T-shirt shipment in soon."

Phil looked up from his Moscow mule. "How many 'L's?" he said.

"What?" said Ken.

"On the T-shirts," said Phil. "How many 'L's did you put in 'melon'?"

"One," said Ken. He frowned. "No, two. I think. Which one is right?"

"Jesus," said Phil, turning back to his drink.

"Irregardless of that," said Stu, "we need to keep this thing going, agreed?"

"Totally," said Ken.

"Like make a sequel," said Slater.

"I'm thinking another video," said Ken.

"That's what 'sequel' means," said Slater.

"I know that," said Ken.

"So what're we thinking about, specifically?" said Stu, looking at Kark.

"OK," said Kark. "Here's a scenario. In the first video we established that the monster is out there. It's walking around in the Everglades. It's mysterious, right? We don't know what its motivation is."

Phil looked up from his drink again. "Its *motivation*?" he said.

"Yes," said Kark.

"Jesus Christ," said Phil, looking back down at his drink.

"So anyway," continued Kark, "what I'm thinking is, our guys"—he gestured toward Ken and Slater—"have discovered this thing, and now they want to know more about it. So in the next video, they're out hunting for it."

"Near Bortle Brothers Bait & Beer," said Ken.

"OK, sure," said Kark. "It could be in the general vicinity."

"Maybe the Bortle Brothers sign is in the background," said Ken.

"Well, that would put us pretty close to the highway," said Kark.

"What's wrong with that?" said Ken.

"It's a *swamp* monster," said Slater. "Why the fuck would it be hanging around a highway?"

"Because it's curious," said Ken. "It hears car motors and it's like, 'What the fuck is *that*?' So it decides to take a look."

"That's not what it's gonna do if it hears a car," said Slater. "It's gonna be like, 'I need to get outta here.'"

"How do you know that?" said Ken.

"Logic," said Slater.

"So you're saying the Everglades Melon Monster has logic?" said Ken.

"That's exactly what I'm saying," said Slater.

"Do you assholes even hear yourselves?" said Phil, but nobody paid attention.

"OK," said Kark, trying to regain control of the discussion, "maybe we can have it be near the highway. That might work. We can figure out the specific location later. But my idea is, you guys are hunting for the monster. It's getting late. You're frustrated. You're hot."

"So my shirt would be off," said Slater.

"Seriously?" said Ken.

"What?" said Slater.

"Sure," said Kark, intervening. "Your shirt could be off, and it's getting late and you're frustrated because you can't find this monster."

"Instead of having shirts off," said Ken, "we could be wearing Everglades Melon Monster T-shirts."

"How many 'L's"? said Phil, but nobody paid attention.

"I'm not wearing a shirt," said Slater.

"Why, you need to show off your muscles?" said Ken.

"At least I have muscles," said Slater.

"I got muscles," said Ken.

"You think so?" said Slater.

"We can compare muscles any time you want," said Ken.

"Right now is good," said Slater.

"So, Kark," said Stu, stepping in. "You were saying? About the video?"

"Right," said Kark. "So you guys are hunting the monster, you can't find it, it's getting late. You're about to give up. And you're worried. Maybe you'll never see the monster again. Maybe people will start saying you never really saw it in the first place. And then, suddenly, you realize what's happening." He paused dramatically.

"What?" said both Ken and Slater.

Kark lowered his voice to a whisper. "The monster is stalking you."

"Wow," said Stu. "That's good."

"Thank you," said Kark.

"Wait," said Ken. "How do we realize this?"

"You hear a noise behind you," said Kark. "You say, 'What was that?' You spin around. Actually, the camera spins around, it's handheld, unsteady. You catch just the barest glimpse of the monster, maybe it's in some shadows, you just barely see the shape, this big scary head, coming toward you. You say something like, 'It's after us!' and start running. Now the camera's jouncing around and pointing all over the place, there's heavy breathing in the background. And then it goes black. End of scene. Cliffhanger."

"Wow," said Stu.

Kark nodded in modest acknowledgment.

"So wait," said Slater. "We're running away?"

"Right," said Kark.

"Like we're scared of it?" said Ken.

"More like startled," said Kark. "You didn't expect it."

"Right," said Slater, "but wouldn't the Glades Guy want—"

"Glades Man," said Kark.

"Right, Glades Man, wouldn't he want to fight it?"

"You're gonna fight it with your muscles?" said Ken.

Slater turned to Ken. "You seem really interested in my muscles."

"Guys," said Kark. "Can we for—"

"I'm not interested in your muscles," said Ken.

"So why do you keep talking about them?" said Slater.

"I don't keep talking about them," said Ken.

"You just did," said Slater. "You just now did."

"I don't fucking believe this," said Phil, to his drink.

"Guys," said Kark, "can we focus on the video?"

"OK," said Slater, turning back to Kark. "My problem is, if I'm running away from the monster, it looks like I'm scared of it."

"I actually agree with him on that," said Ken.

"I hear you," said Kark. "But here's the thing. If you're gonna *fight* the monster, we have to *show* the monster, and then it'll be obvious"—he paused to look around the bar to see if anybody was listening, which nobody was—"it'll be obvious that it's a guy wearing a fake head. Bang, game over."

"He's right," said Stu.

"If we want to keep this going," said Kark, "we need to keep the mystery, keep the monster at a distance. That's why the cliffhanger ending. People see it and they think, *Jesus, what happened next? Are those guys OK?* You leave 'em wanting more."

"Brilliant," said Stu.

"Thank you," said Kark.

Slater looked doubtful. "OK, I get that, but don't we look like pussies? Running away?"

"Yeah," said Ken.

"You're not pussies," said Kark. "You're *human*. You're two guys out in a swamp, facing the unknown, you're hot, you're tired, you're *vulnerable*. When you see this thing, you're startled, and you have a normal human reaction that anybody would have. People will relate to you. Plus now we've set the stage for a third video, where the hunted become the hunters."

"The hunters meaning us?" said Slater. "We go after the monster?"

"Exactly," said Kark. "It's called the third act."

"That's fucking brilliant," said Stu.

"Thank you," said Kark.

Slater and Ken were both nodding.

"So, like, for the second video," said Slater, "what are our lines?"

"I think the best thing is to improvise during the shoot," said Kark. "We've done pretty well with that so far."

Slater and Ken continued to nod.

"So," said Stu. "We're agreed on the second video, with plans for a third." He turned to Ken. "I think now's a good time to talk about the financial arrangements."

"What financial arrangements?" said Ken.

"The talent," said Stu, putting a hand on Phil's shoulder. "He'll of course need to be paid."

"I already paid him five hundred," said Ken.

Phil jerked his head up, looked at Stu. "I thought you already negotiated this."

"Bear with me," said Stu. To Ken, he said, "You paid him for the first video, which I think we can all agree he did a superb job on, despite suffering a potentially career-ending injury."

"Career?" said Phil. "This is *not* my fucking career."

"Be that as it may," said Stu, still looking at Ken. "The talent was paid for one video. But now we're talking about a second video, and

possibly a third. He's going to have to be compensated, as a professional."

"How much?" said Ken.

"OK," said Stu. "The way I see it, your store has benefited quite a
bit, financially, from this enterprise, correct?"

"Well, we sold our T-shirts, yeah," said Ken. "But I ordered more,
and I gotta pay for them."

"Right, but my point is, you're making money, and you expect to
make more, correct? Potentially quite a bit more?"

"I guess," said Ken.

"So taking that into consideration—the financial upside for you as
a result of the work performed by Phil here as the talent, the star of the
show if you will, not to mention his pain and suffering—I'd say a very
reasonable figure for the second video would be fifteen hundred."

"Dollars?" said Ken.

"No, kilometers," said Phil, to his drink.

"Yes," said Stu, ignoring Phil. "I think it's more than fair. And remember, you're not just getting Phil. You're also getting Phil's head."

Ken thought about it for a few seconds, then pointed to Kark and
Slater. "What about them?" he said. "Why don't they pay something?"

"I'm supplying the camera," said Kark. "I'm also doing all the camera work, the post-production, the social media outreach. Not to mention I'm directing. You're the only one making any money off this."

"What about your show?" said Ken. "*Glades Guy*. Aren't you
planning—"

"It's *Glades MAN*," said Slater, getting an appreciative nod from
Kark.

"Whatever," said Ken. "Aren't you planning to use the video for
your show?"

"If we ever sell it, yeah," said Kark. "Right now we're losing money.
We're doing this project totally on spec."

Ken thought some more. "Thing is," he said, "I don't think I can
swing fifteen hundred." In fact he had more than that in his pocket at

the moment, as a result of the locustlike buying spree of the voracious crowd at Bortle Brothers.

"Tell you what," said Stu. "Because Phil and I believe in the future of this project"—he put a restraining hand on Phil, who was about to say something—"and because we want to be in this with you for the long haul, partners if you will, we're willing to do it for twelve fifty."

Everyone looked at Ken.

"Twelve fifty," he said.

"Cash," said Phil. He stuck out his hand. "Up front."

Ken looked at the hand, hesitating.

"Think of it this way," said Stu. "We have a hit video series on our hands. A worldwide, international hit. Millions of viewers. *Millions.* And you're the producer."

"That's true," said Kark. "You'd get the producer credit."

"OK," said Ken.

"Excellent!" said Stu.

Ken, as producer, pulled a wad of cash out of his jeans and started counting out bills into Phil's hand. When he was done everyone shook hands, except Phil, who signaled the bartender for another Moscow mule.

The creative team talked a bit longer, forming a rough plan for shooting *Everglades Melon Monster Part II: The Sequel.* Ken, Kark and Slater then left.

When they were gone, Stu said, "You owe me two fifty."

Phil counted it out, handed it over, then said, "Partners? Seriously?"

Stu shrugged. "Who knows? This thing is big, Phil. And I think it's gonna get much bigger. We need to be part of it."

"This *thing*," said Phil, "is the single stupidest thing that ever happened in South Florida, if not the world. I don't want to be partners with those assholes."

"Let me ask you something," said Stu.

"What."

"Did you take the money just now?"

Phil looked down.

"Answer me," said Stu. "Is there, or is there not, one thousand American dollars in your pocket that wasn't there ten minutes ago."

"Yes," said Phil.

"OK then," said Stu. "Then stop pretending you're Stephen smarter-than-everybody-else fucking Hawking. We are partners with those assholes."

Phil took a swig of his Moscow mule, put it down. "I used to be an award-winning journalist," he said.

"That was then," said Stu.

* * *

Slater's truck, carrying Slater, Kark and Ken back to the Everglades, pulled out of the Gallo Grande parking lot thirty seconds before the highly modified Tesla pulled in.

The Tesla stopped in the far corner of the lot, near the dumpster. The entire car rocked as Pinky heaved his bulk out and stood. His eyes swept the empty parking lot. He frowned, his massive forehead forming wrinkles deep enough for a small rodent to hide in.

He looked at his Apple Watch. He was, as always, exactly on time. He frowned some more.

He waited for five minutes in the baking heat, sweat streaming from his massive body and puddling on the hot asphalt.

Then he left, still very much frowning.

Chapter 37

Erik picked his way through the sweaty, swarming Ocean Drive throng of tourists in bathing suits and flip-flops, trying not to let them brush against his suit, which was custom-made in Italy and cost $8,000. Erik was obsessed with high-end Italian fashion; except for betting on sports, buying expensive Italian clothes and accessories was his greatest passion. His shoes, also custom-made, were Italian leather and cost $11,500. His briefcase, Italian leather, cost $26,000. Erik had a stronger emotional attachment to this briefcase than he did to any human being, including his mother. Sometimes, when he was alone in his office and feeling stressed, he would calm himself by stroking its supple surface.

Erik did not want his briefcase, or any of his other possessions, to come into contact with the dripping, staggering, drink-sloshing, sunscreen-smeared Ocean Drive party herd. Like many Miamians, Erik hated South Beach and came here only when he had to.

His destination now was Bongo Mongo, one of the interchangeable sidewalk cafés that lined Ocean Drive, each sprawling in front of a renovated art deco hotel. The Bongo Mongo hostess, a part-time lingerie model whose dress clearly revealed that she was not wearing any lingerie, was holding a menu and trying to entice passersby to stop and try their "signature drink special." This was the Bongo Mongo Humongo, a sixty-four-ounce concoction of reconstituted fruit juice and enough off-brand vodka, gin and tequila to anesthetize a water buffalo, topped off with a generous floater of paint-thinner-grade rum. The Humongo was served in what was basically a small plastic aquarium, which, as the hostess pointed out, you could take home as a souvenir. It was especially popular with underage college students.

Technically the Humongo cost $49, but what with the various taxes, service charges and traditional South Beach mystery add-ons, the bill could easily be double that. The Bongo Mongo business model was built on the assumption that by the time the customers were handed the check, they would be too wasted to read it.

Erik brushed past the hostess and walked into the hotel, past the front desk and down a hallway leading toward the back of the building. At the end of the hallway was a door marked PRIVATE, blocked by a man with roughly the same physical dimensions as a commercial refrigerator, wearing what had to be the world's largest tracksuit. His name was Tenklo Jzerbak and he had once, during his friskier days back in his home country, single-handedly turned over a police car.

Tenklo was the hotel's director of security. He was also the person who was summoned by the server if Bongo Mongo customers wished to dispute the charges on their bill. These disputes almost always ended the instant Tenklo loomed into view.

Erik nodded at Tenklo. Tenklo did not nod back, partly because he was not a friendly individual by nature, and partly because he had no neck.

"He's expecting me," Erik said, pointing at the door.

Tenklo did nothing for a few seconds, establishing, in case there was any doubt, that he did not take orders from the likes of Erik. He then shifted his massive bulk ever so slightly, creating a small space between himself and the wall. Erik edged through this space, taking great care not to touch Tenklo, who reeked of garlic and Axe body spray.

Erik knocked on the PRIVATE door.

"Come in," said a voice.

Erik opened the door, went inside, closed the door behind him. He was in a small windowless office, fluorescent lit, with bare floors and walls; the only furnishings were a battered metal filing cabinet and a matching— not in a good way—metal desk with an old wooden swivel chair. Seated on the chair, tapping on the keyboard of a twelve-year-old Dell laptop running Windows 95, was a small, wiry, gray-haired man wearing a faded polo shirt tucked into khaki pants. The man's only remarkable physical feature was his eyes, which were coal-black, a shark's eyes.

The man's name was Kristov Berliuz. Erik owed him $173,400.

Berliuz was originally from Eastern Europe, where, during the chaos following the collapse of the Soviet Union, he became involved in trading arms and uranium. He was extraordinarily successful, thanks to shrewd business acumen, rigorous attention to detail and a willingness to shoot competitors in the head.

In the late nineties Berliuz had relocated with his fortune and a small cadre of henchpersons to Miami, where he bought the Bongo Mongo and the hotel behind it. He also purchased a number of other small businesses, including a tanning salon, an auto-body shop, a Pilates studio, an art gallery, two tattoo parlors and a reptile store.

Most of these businesses lost money, which was fine with Berliuz, as their real function was to launder the profits of his illegal enterprises. He was still involved in arms trafficking, but over time his biggest moneymaker had become a specialized bookmaking operation catering to an exclusive, high-end clientele—wealthy men (they were all men) who liked to be able to bet any sum of money on any sporting event, anytime, with no fuss and zero traceability.

Once Berliuz accepted you as a client, the arrangement was simple: If you won your bet, you were paid promptly; if you lost, you were expected to pay promptly. If you could not pay promptly, Berliuz might extend credit to you, but only at a nonnegotiable interest rate of 10 percent per week, and only for a strictly limited time. It was understood that if you failed to pay the full amount due, including interest, within that time, bad things—potentially *very* bad things, including, if the rumors were true, crucifixion—would happen to you.

It did not matter if you were a prominent member of the community, a person with clout; it did not matter if you were friends with powerful politicians, or business leaders, or violent criminals, or even rap musicians. None of these friends could protect you. None of them would even want to try, once they found out who was after you.

Nobody fucked with Kristov Berliuz.

Which was why Erik and his briefcase were here.

To say that Erik had a gambling problem was like saying that Hitler had an empathy problem. Erik was a consistently, at times spectacularly, unsuccessful bettor, the kind of overconfident, underinformed bettor who values intuition and hunches over actual information. Erik would bet on any sporting event, whether he had researched it or not; he had once lost $25,000 on an English Premier League soccer match because he was not aware that Manchester City was a different team entirely from Manchester United.

Like most gambling addicts, Erik believed that the problem was not his inability to make sound wagering decisions, but bad luck. He simply could not entertain the possibility that a man on his intellectual plane—a graduate of *Cornell Law*, for God's sake—was being consistently bested by a bunch of lowlife immigrant bookies who never even finished high school.

And like most gambling addicts, Erik believed that the way to compensate for his betting losses was to win the money back by making more bets, larger bets. Using this strategy, he had plunged deeper and deeper into debt, ultimately maxing out his home equity and every other form of credit he had access to. He had no liquidity left, and nobody left to borrow from.

And now he owed the scariest person in Miami, if not the entire world, $173,400, with the full amount due tomorrow, in cash, no extensions, no excuses.

Which is why he was here in this dingy little office with his supple Italian briefcase.

"Hi," he said to Berliuz, who was still tapping on his keyboard. "Thanks for agreeing to see me."

Berliuz, not looking up, continued to tap. Erik waited, shifting from foot to foot. There was nowhere to sit.

After two minutes, which felt much longer to Erik, Berliuz stopped tapping and looked up. His eyes were black holes.

"You have the money?" he said. He spoke with a thick accent, but his English was precise.

"I have something for you," said Erik.

Berliuz's eyes narrowed slightly. Erik felt his sphincter clench.

"Does that mean you do not have the money?" Berliuz said.

"I have something better," said Erik. He lifted his briefcase and pointed to it. "Can I show you?"

Berliuz stared at Erik for a few moments, during which Erik did not breathe. Then Berliuz gave a small nod.

Quickly Erik opened the briefcase and took out the gold bar. He set it on the desk. Berliuz picked it up, hefted it, studied it for a minute, two minutes. Erik waited.

Berliuz put the bar back down. "This is not enough," he said.

"Right, of course not," said Erik. "But there's more. A lot more."

"How much more?"

"Dozens," said Erik. "Maybe hundreds."

"Hundreds?"

"I think so."

"But you do not know?"

"I don't know exactly. But there's a lot."

"And you can bring them to me?"

"OK, that's the thing."

Berliuz's eyes narrowed again. "You cannot bring them to me?"

"I can definitely get you the gold," Erik said quickly. "If you'll permit me to explain."

Berliuz nodded.

Erik told him about Jesse's visit, her story about finding the gold, the two creeps who'd been after her, the agreement they'd reached, her promise not to tell anyone.

When he was done, Berliuz said, "So your arrangement is that this woman gets two-thirds, and you get one-third."

"Right, that's what she thinks," said Erik. "But what I'm proposing here is, you would get the two-thirds, which I'm sure will be far more than what I owe you."

"And who would get the other third?"

Erik hesitated, then said, "Well, I'm thinking I would. As the finder."

"And the woman?"

"I'd give her something, enough to make her happy, keep her quiet. The thing is, she doesn't really understand any of this. She doesn't know what the gold's worth, how to cash it in, what the law says. She thinks we have to keep everything secret or she won't get any money. She's totally relying on me for advice on this. To be honest, she's not particularly bright. She won't be a problem."

"And she will tell us the location of the gold?"

"She says she can't give directions to it, but she knows where it is."

"So she will lead us to it?"

"That's the thing," said Erik. "She's suspicious. She doesn't want to reveal the location to someone she doesn't know."

"She knows you."

"Right, but she doesn't totally trust me. At least not yet."

Berliuz was silent for a moment, staring at Erik, his shark eyes unblinking. Then, in a quiet voice that froze Erik's blood, he said, "I will talk to her."

"No!" said Erik quickly. "We can do this without . . . I mean, I think I have a better solution."

"I am listening."

"I gave her an iPhone," Erik said. "I'm tracking that phone on an iPad, but she doesn't know." He produced an iPad from his briefcase, turned it on and handed it to Berliuz. "All I need to do is give her a reason why she needs to bring me another gold bar. I'll come up with something she'll believe. When she goes to get the gold, we can track her on the iPad. She'll lead us right to it."

Berliuz thought about it, then nodded. "All right," he said. "But if your way does not work, we do it my way."

"Right, sure," said Erik. "But just so we're clear, after we get the gold and split it up, the woman will be OK, right? I mean, we won't need her anymore, so she can . . . she'll be free to go, right?"

"You are getting too far ahead," said Berliuz. "I do not have the gold yet. I do not know if the gold exists. And if it does, I do not know if there is enough to satisfy your debt to me."

"There will be. I'm sure."

"But I will not be sure until the gold is in my possession. Until it is, your debt to me is not satisfied, do you understand?"

"I understand."

Berliuz put the iPad into a drawer. He pointed to the gold bar on his desk. "I will keep this."

"Of course."

They talked for a few more minutes, working out some details. When Berliuz had what he wanted, he abruptly said, "Goodbye," and returned his attention to the laptop screen.

Erik started to open the door, then stopped and turned back.

"About the woman," he said. "Once we have the gold, will she . . . I mean, will she be OK?"

"Goodbye," said Berliuz.

Chapter 38

Jesse decided to take Brad up on his offer for her to spend the night at the house behind Bortle Brothers Bait & Beer. This was partly because she'd concluded that Brad was a good guy—Willa seemed to like him, too—but mainly because she was afraid that if she went back to the cabin, she'd run into the camo creeps.

Brad showed her to the musty bedroom that had once belonged to his parents—a metal-framed bed with a faded flower-patterned bedspread, two fake–French country nightstands from Sears, Roebuck with a matching bureau, everything the way it had been thirty-four years ago, when Ken and Brad were toddlers, and their mother died of cancer, and their father started sleeping on a cot in the store, surrounded by empty beer bottles, never to sleep in this bedroom again.

"Sorry about the smell," said Brad.

"Are you kidding?" she said. "I've been living in a tiny cabin with two world-class farters. This is like the Four Seasons."

Brad, standing in the doorway, said, "Is there anything I can get you?"

"No," she said, looking around. "This is great, thanks."

They stood facing each other for a few awkward seconds, Brad trying to work up the courage to deliver a speech he'd been composing in his mind during the mostly silent drive back from Miami. It went something like: *Look, I know you don't really know me. And I know you've heard a million speeches from guys like your pretty-boy lawyer friend who just wanted to impress you because you're beautiful. And don't get me wrong, I think you're beautiful too, and I want to impress you. But I also like you a lot, and I like Willa, and I want to help you, and I'd want to help you even if there was absolutely no chance I could ever be your boyfriend or anything, which I'm sure there isn't. But please just know you can trust me.*

That's what Brad wanted to say. What he said was: "Well, if you need anything, I'm right down the hall."

"Thanks," said Jesse. "Look, I'm exhausted, and it's past Willa's bedtime, so . . ." She put her hand on the door.

"Sure, of course," said Brad, stepping back.

"Good night," said Jesse, closing the door.

"Good night," said Brad, to the door.

* * *

At that moment, as night was falling, Slater and Kark were dropping Ken off at Bortle Brothers. It had been a tense ride back from Miami—Kark, seated in the middle, trying to keep the peace between Ken and Slater, who were having major creative differences about their visions for the next day's video shoot.

Currently the issue was whether the improvised dialogue should include the words "Bortle Brothers Bait & Beer."

"How's it gonna come up?" Slater was saying. "We're being chased by a monster. Why would we be talking about a fucking bait store?"

"Two reasons," said Ken. "One, the fucking bait store is paying for this, in case you forgot."

"I can't forget, since you remind us every five seconds," said Slater.

"Two," said Ken, "maybe it comes up because it's where we're running for safety. Like you could say, 'The Melon Monster is after us! What do we do now?' And I could say, 'Let's head for Bortle Brothers Bait & Beer!' "

"Nobody would say that," said Slater. He appealed to Kark. "Would anybody say that? Running away from a monster? 'Let's head for Bortle Brothers Bait & Beer'?"

"What I think," said Kark, "is that instead of trying to script it, we should just—"

"They'd say it if there was a bait store nearby," said Ken. "Why wouldn't they say it?"

"Because it sounds fake!" said Slater. "It sounds like a TV commercial, where they bring some product up for no reason. Like those commercials for whaddyacallit, Liberty Mutual, where that douchebag, for no reason, keeps talking about Liberty Mutual. Nobody's talking about car insurance, and suddenly this douchebag is going, 'Liberty Mutual blah blah blah.'"

"Guys," said Kark, "why don't we—"

"That's exactly my point!" said Ken. "You're proving my point!"

"What point?" said Slater.

"My point is, you remember the name of the product. Name recognition. Because the commercial is effective. It gets the message across."

"What message? That Liberty Mutual is a bunch of douchebags?"

"So you think you're smarter than TV advertising executives?" said Ken. "Who make millions of dollars?"

"I guess I am," said Slater.

"Talk about douchebags," said Ken quietly.

"What'd you say?" said Slater.

"You heard me," said Ken.

"You want to say it again?" said Slater, leaning forward, looking across Kark to glare at Ken.

"I'll say it again," said Ken, also leaning forward to return the glare.

"Go ahead, say it again," said Slater.

"I'll say it again," said Ken, again.

"Go ahead, then," said Slater. "Say it."

"You think I won't?" said Ken. "Because I will."

"Then go ahead and say it," said Slater.

"Don't think I won't," said Ken.

"Guys," said Kark, leaning between them to block the glarefest. "This is good energy. We can use it for the shoot tomorrow. A feeling of rising tension between you. But for now let's not worry about specific lines, OK? Let's ad-lib it during the shoot tomorrow. OK? Slater? Ken? OK?" He swiveled his head back and forth between them.

"Whatever," said Slater.

"Douchebag," said Ken, getting out of the truck.

"What'd you say?" said Slater. But before they could start another infinitely recursive macho-threat loop, Kark yanked the truck door shut.

"Asshole," said Slater. He gunned the engine, the tires spewing dirt as the truck shot out of the parking lot back onto the highway, headed back toward the cabin. He looked at Kark. "Right? You agree he's an asshole?"

"I guess," said Kark. "But we need him right now. Plus, he's kind of authentic, you know?"

"What do you mean?"

"I mean, we're selling a swamp show, and he really looks like he lives in the swamp."

"I live in the swamp."

"Yeah, but you look like a model in a men's-fragrance commercial, no offense."

"None taken," said Slater as the taillights disappeared. "But he's still an asshole."

* * *

Duck and Billy saw the truck headlights coming up the dirt road. They scuttled into some bushes, both men going into their backpacks and pulling out pistols.

After losing their Jeep they'd stolen a new vehicle—a Nissan Path-finder this time—and made their way back to their trailer, where they'd changed clothes and gathered supplies. Their plan—Duck's plan, really—was to resume their stakeout near the cabin. Duck was confident that sooner or later, Jesse would show up there, either going in or coming out. He intended to stay there and wait for her, however long it took.

As the truck drew close they peered from the darkness, trying to make out who was in the cab. Billy raised his pistol, aiming at the driver's side. Duck, seeing Slater and Kark, pulled his brother's arm down.

"No," he said.

The truck drove past, disappeared into the darkness.

Duck and Billy resumed walking. They came to the pickup, now parked in a little roadside clearing. Nearby was the stakeout spot they'd used before, hidden in the thick bushes across the road from the footpath to the cabin. They spread their sleeping bags on the ground and settled down to wait.

However long it took.

Chapter 39

Frank Wallner frowned at the photo on his computer screen: a clearing with a backdrop of sawgrass stretching toward a ruler-flat horizon dotted with the occasional clump of trees.

"This is it?" he said. "This is the site?"

"Yup," said Jacky Ramos. "It's in the Big Cypress preserve, maybe fifty or so miles west of Miami on Route 41. It's right off the highway. There's a short dirt road. Park Police checked it out. They say they can get the secretary's vehicle in there no problem."

"What about Skeeter?"

"He says he'll be there."

"Is he excited to meet the secretary?"

"Actually, no. Skeeter's not real big on authority in general. I'm not sure he recognizes the federal government. He's sort of his own one-man nation."

"The Republic of Skeeter."

"Exactly."

"But we can count on him to show?" said Frank. "You're in touch with him? Does he even have a phone?"

"Yup, and he says he'll be there."

"You trust him?"

"I do! He's actually kind of sweet, in a primitive swampy way. I think he likes me. He calls me 'darlin.'"

"Really? Are you saying Skeeter is potentially dating material?"

"Hey, I've dated worse. At least Skeeter doesn't live with his parents."

"OK, so we have Skeeter," said Frank. "Who do we have from the press?"

"Mostly local—the *Miami Herald,* the *Sun Sentinel,* AP, the TV stations. They love them some big snakes. Also a guy from the *New York Times,* named . . ."—she looked at her phone—"Anthony Evander Cornwall."

Frank frowned. "Is he the one who thinks everything is caused by global climate change?"

"That's all of them."

"No, but this guy, if a bird shits on him, he writes a ninety-inch front-page story about how global climate change is causing birds to shit on people."

"Yeah, I think that's him."

"Why's he want to go to a press event for the Python Challenge?"

"If I had to guess, he plans to connect it with global climate change."

"So we have Skeeter and the *Times* guy to deal with. Anything else we need to worry about?"

"Not really. Should be a pretty routine event."

Frank looked at her. "Routine? Seriously?"

Jacky laughed. "You're right," she said. "I need to remember this is Florida."

Chapter 40

Jesse was awakened by Willa, lying next to her, crying a hungry cry. Jesse looked at the phone Erik had given her, saw that it was midmorning, the latest she'd been awakened in a long time. She put Willa to her breast and closed her eyes, trying to steal a few more minutes' rest while her baby fed.

Two taps on the door. Jesse opened her eyes.

"Yes?" she said, pulling the covers up.

"It's me," said Brad. "Can I . . ."

"It's OK," she said. "Come in."

He opened the door and stuck his head in. "I heard the baby, so I figured you were up."

"We're up."

"I made some coffee, if you want." He stepped into the room, holding a chipped and stained white ceramic mug with a U-Haul logo. "It's old, so it's probably pretty bad."

"Sounds appetizing!" said Jesse.

"We don't have any milk or cream," he said, putting the mug on the nightstand next to her. "Or sugar. Or sweetener. So it's just like, stale old black coffee."

"You should definitely not go into marketing," she said, reaching for the mug. She took a sip, Brad watching her with a concerned look. "You're right," she said. "It's pretty bad."

"Sorry!" he said.

"I'm just kidding," she said. "It's fine."

"Honestly?"

"Well, it's honestly pretty bad. But it's the only coffee anybody's made for me for quite a while. So thank you. I appreciate it. Really."

"I was gonna make you breakfast," he said, "but we don't have anything you'd probably want to eat."

"What do you guys live on?" she said.

He smiled. "It's pretty disgusting. A lot of pizza. I mean, a *lot* of pizza."

"Including for breakfast?"

"Oh yes, many times. Also Skittles."

"You eat Skittles for *breakfast*?"

"I have. Also for lunch. And supper."

"Just Skittles?"

"Not *just* Skittles. Skittles and jerky. For protein. Also beer."

Jesse made a face.

"I told you it was disgusting," Brad said. "Anyway, since we don't have anything here, I was gonna go out and get you some breakfast, if you tell me what you'd like."

"That is so sweet," said Jesse. "But look, you don't have to keep doing things for me. You've done way too much for me already."

Brad had anticipated that Jesse would say something like this, and he had mentally prepared a response. It was basically an expanded version of the speech he'd planned to give her last night, the essential points being that he genuinely liked Jesse, and not just because she was beautiful, although of course, as a man, he was *aware* that she was beautiful, and he would not deny that her looks were what attracted him to her in the first place, but he had really enjoyed spending time with her and getting to know her, and he genuinely liked her as a person, a lot, and he also really liked Willa, and it seemed as though Willa also liked him, as much as a little baby could like a person, and so he did not feel—not at *all*—that Jesse was imposing on him, in fact he wanted to help her out any way he could with whatever was going on in her life, although he totally understood if she didn't want to tell him

188 • Dave Barry

what it was, but whatever it was, if there was anything he could do to help her with it, he wanted to.

Brad took a deep breath, preparing to begin his speech. "OK," he said. "The thing is—"

He was interrupted by a noise from the phone on the nightstand. Jesse looked at the screen, saw it was Erik calling.

"I'm sorry," she said to Brad. "I need to take this."

"No problem," said Brad. He left, closing the door behind him.

Jesse picked up the phone. "Hello?"

"Hey, Jess," said Erik. "It's me."

"Hi," said Jesse.

"You good? Everything good?"

"More or less," she said. "Other than guys trying to kill me."

"Right now?"

"No, not at the moment," said Jesse.

"OK, good," said Erik. "Listen, Jess, I'm calling about what we talked about yesterday in my office. About the . . . material."

"The material? You mean the gold?"

"Right, that material."

"Why can't you just say 'gold'?"

"I'm being careful, Jess."

"Why, are the Russians listening?"

"Jess, this isn't a joke. This is serious."

"I know it's serious, Erik. I'm the one people are trying to kill, remember?"

"Of course, and I'm trying to help you, Jess."

"OK, sorry. Go ahead."

"So I'm in contact with somebody, an associate of mine, who can help us."

"When you say 'help us,'" said Jess, "you mean . . ."

"I mean help us remove the material, and . . . convert it."

"You mean cash it in."

"Yes."

"And how much will your associate charge for doing this?"

"He's a reasonable guy, Jess. I've done a lot of business with him. I'll work out a satisfactory arrangement."

"Meaning what?"

"Meaning you'll get your money."

"And you'll take care of your associate? From your third?"

"Yes. He's my responsibility."

"And this is legal? I won't go to jail?"

"I'm confident we can do this without legal repercussions."

"That's what you said in your office. It sounds like a lawyer answer."

"That's because I'm a lawyer, Jess. But that's exactly what you need: a lawyer who is also your friend. You have to trust me on this, OK? I'm on your side here. And, if I'm being blunt, I'm the only person who can help you."

After a few seconds, Jesse said, "OK."

"That's my girl," said Erik.

"I'm not your girl," said Jesse, shifting Willa to her other breast.

"Right, of course not. So anyway, we need to discuss how we're going to make this work. You said you didn't want to lead anyone to the site."

"Correct."

"And you still feel that way."

"Yes. I'm not gonna risk showing the location to somebody who could steal the gold, or say they found it first."

"Even if I vouch for my associate?"

"I don't know him."

"But you know me."

"Exactly," said Jesse.

Erik sighed. "So you don't really trust me."

"I'm sorry, Erik, but like I told you in your office, this is the only leverage I have, and before I give it up I need to know for sure I'm protected. You told me you'd figure something out."

"Right, which is why I'm calling. I've been talking with my associate, and I think we have a proposal that'll be acceptable to you."

"I'm listening."

"OK, here's the deal. We'll give you a guaranteed advance of one hundred thousand dollars cash."

Jesse sat up, momentarily dislodging Willa.

"What do you mean, a guaranteed advance?"

"I mean we will give you one hundred thousand dollars, in cash, as an advance against your share. And you get to keep it no matter what."

"I keep it? No matter what?"

"Right. You can put it in a bank, give it to somebody to hold, whatever you want to do with it. It's yours to keep. It's your guarantee. And in return, you show my associate to the site."

"After I put the money someplace safe."

"Right. When you're absolutely sure your money is safe, then and only then you take him to the site. And no matter what happens, you keep that money. A hundred thousand cash. All yours, guaranteed, no matter what. OK? Is that enough protection for you?"

Jesse was thinking hard. She didn't really trust Erik, and she definitely didn't trust his "associate." She figured that once they knew where the gold was, there was a good chance they'd want it all, and the hundred thousand was all she would ever get. On the other hand, a hundred thousand dollars was more than enough to get her and Willa out of the hellish predicament she'd gotten them into. And she wasn't at all confident, no matter what Erik said, that she'd ever be able to legally possess the gold anyway. Cash in hand was better than nothing.

"OK," she said.

"Good girl!" said Erik.

"Call me that again and the deal is off."

"Sorry! Anyway, Jess, you're making the right decision. There's just one thing I need you to do."

Jesse frowned. "What one thing?"

"OK, you remember what you brought to my office?"

"Yes. A gold bar."

"OK, I need you to get me another one."

"What? No! I already gave you one!"

"Hear me out, Jess. My associate, like you, would like a little protection. He's concerned—and understand that this is him saying this, not me—he wants to make sure there really is a bunch of those bars out there."

"But why would—"

"Just listen, Jess. His concern is that you could have gotten that one bar from anywhere, like from some gold dealer or something, and that's all there is. So he wants to see another one like it, as proof that there's more."

"Seriously? He thinks I'd buy a gold bar and come to you with a fake story claiming I found it in the Everglades? Why would I do that?"

"Jess, I know it's ridiculous. I totally trust you, and I told my associate he could trust you. But he doesn't know you, and he's putting up the advance. So he wants proof, or it's no deal."

"I dunno . . ."

"Just do it, Jess. A hundred thousand dollars."

A long pause, then, "OK."

"Good gi— I mean, great! So listen, I think it's in everybody's best interests to get this thing done as soon as possible, you agree?"

"Yes."

"So how soon do you think you could go get the bar?"

Jesse thought about it. "I can do it today, I guess. This afternoon."

"Excellent! That's perfect."

"What do I do with it when I have it?"

"You call me immediately. You need to keep that phone with you, OK? So we can be in touch."

"And when I call you, what happens?"

"We arrange a meeting, where you turn over the bar and we give you your money. Then when both sides are satisfied, and your money is in a safe place, you lead my associate to the site."

"OK," said Jesse.

"Great. So I'll wait to hear from you this afternoon."

"Right."

"Make sure you take the phone, OK?"

"OK."

"So I guess that's it, then."

"Right."

"So just . . ." Erik hesitated.

"Yes?"

"Just . . . take care, Jess."

"Sure."

"Goodbye, Jess."

"Bye."

Jess ended the call, frowning, wondering why Erik had sounded so weird at the end there. But her thoughts quickly moved on. She needed to figure out how she was going to get to the gold, alone, without being seen—especially not by the two camo creeps, who were out there somewhere. And she needed to decide what to do about Willa.

She looked down at her daughter, still feeding contentedly. Willa looked up, their eyes meeting. Willa smiled a gummy baby smile; Jesse smiled back.

"Soon, baby girl," she whispered. "We're gonna get out of here real soon."

* * *

As soon as his call with Jesse ended, Erik pressed a speed-dial number.

"Yes?" said Kristov Berliuz.

"She bought it," said Erik. "She's going."

"When?"

"Today. This afternoon."

"Good."

"Listen, I, uh, I just want to make sure she'll be . . . she'll be OK, right? I mean there's no reason to . . . Hello?"

But Berliuz was gone.

Chapter 41

Channel 8 PeoplePower News reporter Patsy Hartmann and camera-man Bruce Morris climbed into their PeoplePower News van, which had been baking in an unshaded West Dade strip-mall parking lot for an hour, the result being that the interior was approximately the same temperature as an active volcano, but more humid.

Bruce immediately started the engine and cranked the climate control to MAX COOL, but they both knew that by the time the air-conditioning had any effect their clothes would be drenched with sweat. As longtime South Floridians, they did not bother to remark that it was hot, any more than a North African nomad would bother to remark that the Sahara was sandy.

"How am I going to edit this story?" said Patsy. "What in God's name am I going to put on the air without looking like a complete idiot?"

She was referring to the assignment they had just left, which had been dumped on Patsy by her news director and archenemy, Jennifer Taylor. It concerned a chiropractor/inventor named Rupert Malstroff, who claimed to have converted a tanning bed into a fully functioning time machine. Patsy had vehemently protested that this was a stupid story, even by PeoplePower News standards, but Jennifer had been ad-amant.

Thus Patsy and Bruce had spent an excruciatingly uncomfortable hour in Malstroff's "clinic"—a cramped and dingy storefront—listening to Malstroff, a small, pale, cadaverously thin, completely bald and pal-pably unbalanced man who wore a lab coat several sizes too large, like a Halloween mad-doctor costume from Party City. Malstroff had explained in incomprehensible detail how his invention worked—he used the word "algorithm" at least a dozen times—and then offered to demonstrate it. With Bruce recording video, Malstroff climbed into the tanning bed—which looked like an ordinary tanning bed with some extra wires attached—and closed the lid. Two minutes later he opened the lid and climbed out, at which point Patsy conducted an interview:

PATSY: OK, so, Mr. Malstroff, what just happened here?

MALSTROFF: *Dr.* Malstroff.

PATSY: Right, *Dr.* Malstroff, what just happened?

MALSTROFF: What happened was [*dramatic pause*] time travel.

PATSY: You're saying that while you were in there, you traveled through time?

MALSTROFF: That is correct.

PATSY: And where, or I guess I should say *when*, did you travel to?

MALSTROFF: The future.

PATSY: So just now, when you went into this . . . machine, you traveled to the future.

MALSTROFF: That is correct.

PATSY: And how far into the future did you go?

MALSTROFF: Approximately two weeks.

PATSY: You went two weeks into the future . . .

MALSTROFF: Approximately.

PATSY: . . . and then you came back.

MALSTROFF: Correct. As you can see, I am here now, in the present.

PATSY: I see.

MALSTROFF: Yes.

PATSY: And can you prove . . . I mean, is there any evidence you could show us to prove you were in the future? Like did you pick up, I don't know, maybe a future newspaper?

MALSTROFF: It would not have been possible for me to pick up a newspaper.

PATSY: Why is that?

MALSTROFF: Because I was inside the machine.

PATSY: So you stayed inside the machine the whole time you were in the future.

MALSTROFF: That is correct.

PATSY: So, what would you say to somebody who said that this is just a tanning bed with some wires attached to it?

MALSTROFF: I would say they are incorrect.

PATSY: Because ... ?

MALSTROFF (*patiently*): Because, as I have just demonstrated, this is a time machine.

"I can't put that on the air," Patsy was saying, back in the van. "I just can't."

"Maybe play it for laughs?" said Bruce. "Like, 'Here's a chiropractor who can cure your back pain *and* send you back to the future'. Get it? Back and back?"

"Not bad," said Patsy. "Do you have any idea what an algorithm is?"

"Not a clue. I failed trigonometry."

Patsy's phone beeped. "Uh-oh," she said, looking at the screen. "Jennifer." She read the text. "I don't believe this."

"What?"

"We're going back to the Everglades."

"Seriously? The swamp monster again?"

"Nope. The Python Challenge. They're holding a press conference to kick it off. The secretary of the interior's supposed to be there. Also the defending champion, whose name ..."—she looked at the screen—"is DeWayne 'Skeeter' Toobs."

"You're making that up."

"Nope. Says here last year Skeeter caught a sixteen-footer."

"That's a large snake."

"You don't think there'll be snakes at the press event, do you?"

"Well, if this is the kickoff, I'm guessing no. Because they haven't started catching them yet."

"That's good, because I hate snakes."

"On the other hand, it *is* the Everglades. There's definitely snakes out there."

Patsy sighed. "I am *way* too old for this," she said. "I'm supposed to be back in the studio, with air-conditioning, close to a bathroom, reading prompter and tossing to twenty-three-year-old school of communications grads out in the field doing these bullshit stories. I'm supposed to be sitting at the anchor desk and exchanging chuckles with my coanchor over the craziness of all these wacky South Floridians. I'm not supposed to be out here *interacting* with them."

Bruce heard her out, then put the van in gear. "So," he said. "On to Skeeter?"

Patsy sighed, grabbed a Kleenex from the console and wiped a smear of makeup off her sweating face.

"On to Skeeter," she said.

Chapter 42

Stu found Phil, as expected, at the bar of the Gallo Grande, in front of a Moscow mule. He was wearing the same ratty sweatpants and faded Duke sweatshirt he'd worn for the Melon Monster video. At his feet was the black garbage bag that held the head.

"You ready to go?" said Stu. The plan was for him to drive Phil out to the Everglades, pick up Ken at the store, then go to the cabin to meet up with Kark and Slater to shoot *Everglades Melon Monster Part II: The Sequel.*

"After I finish this," said Phil, pointing to the drink. "And the one after it."

"Phil, we need to talk about your drinking."

"You think I drink too much?"

"Yes."

"I agree. I drink too much. Good talk!" Phil drained his glass and signaled for a refill.

"Phil," said Stu, "I'm serious."

"I'm serious, too. I know I drink too much. I also know I'm about to go running around a fucking swamp on a fucked-up knee wearing a giant fucking head because this is currently my only source of income. Also my balls, in case you were wondering, still have not fully recovered from being hit with a fucking golf club. So if it's OK with you I'll address my alcoholism at a later date."

"You promise?"

"Absolutely not."

The bartender brought a new drink. Phil chugged it, set the glass down, burped.

"OK," he said, leaving some bills on the bar. "Let's go make video magic."

* * *

At that moment, right outside the Gallo Grande, a black Chevrolet Suburban drove past on the Tamiami Trail, westbound toward the Everglades. At the wheel was the massive form of Kristov Berliuz's top henchperson, Tenklo Jzerbak. Next to him, on the console, was Erik Turpake's iPad. Its screen displayed a map, at the center of which was a mobile-phone icon representing the iPhone Erik had given Jesse. The icon, which had not moved for a while, was sitting on Route 41, at the location of Bortle Brothers Bait & Beer.

Seated in the front passenger seat was a large man—not as large as Tenklo, but large by human standards. This was Kelmit Blüt, a veteran in the Berliuz organization. He had a bandage on his right forearm, covering a twenty-three-stitch wound that he'd recently sustained—this earned him much good-natured ribbing from the other henchpersons—throwing a client through a sixth-floor condominium window.

The Suburban was towing a flatbed trailer on which sat two brand-new, top-of-the-line Polaris Sportsman ATVs, one attached to a utility trailer.

The powerful Suburban sound system was blasting the 1980 hit "Super Trouper." Mixed in with the music was a discordant sound—a mournful rumbling, deep-pitched, off-key. It was the sound of Tenklo and Kelmit attempting to sing along. They were big ABBA fans.

Chapter 43

Jesse, holding Willa in her carrier, emerged from the Bortle brothers' house and entered the store through the back door. Brad was standing at the front counter, talking to four disappointed-looking teenage boys.

"Sorry, no T-shirts," he was saying. "We're supposed to get more tomorrow."

The boys left. As they opened the front door, Jesse saw more people milling around in the parking lot.

Brad, seeing Jesse, smiled, shaking his head.

"They've been coming in all morning long," he said. "We got nothing to sell 'em, but they keep coming. It's a freaking zoo out there."

"This is still because of that stupid video?"

"Yup," he said. "These kids are obsessed with it. Weird thing is, they know it's stupid. They know the whole monster thing is total bullshit. But they don't care. They tell me it's all over Instagram, TikTok, whatever, all these influencers and rap stars and whatnot making Melon Monster videos, dances, challenges, I don't know what. And it's all over the news. Supposably all these random people are calling the TV stations, claiming they also saw the Melon Monster. We had a bunch of reporters out here this morning. Get this: There was a guy here from the *New York Times*."

"Seriously? About the monster?"

"Well, he's out here because of some python thing, but he heard about the monster. He wanted to know if I thought it might be connected to climate change."

Jesse laughed. "Climate change?"

"Yup."

"What'd you say?"

"Well, what I *didn't* say was that it was connected to a drunk being paid by my brother to run around wearing a fake head."

"So what did you tell him?"

"I told him to talk to Ken. Speaking of which, they're gonna make another video, Ken and your Glades Man. They're very excited."

"Today?"

"Yup."

"Out at the cabin?"

"Around there somewhere, yeah."

Jesse hesitated, then said, "Speaking of the cabin, I have another favor to ask."

"Sure, no problem."

"I hate to do this, because you've already—"

Brad raised a hand, stopping her. "You don't need to keep apologizing. I'm happy to help."

"OK," said Jesse. "I need a ride out to the cabin."

"No problem."

"But that's not all."

Brad waited.

"OK, this is really a huge favor, but . . . would you be willing to watch Willa for a little while?"

"You mean, like, now?"

"No, when we're out there. I need to . . . to do something, and I was hoping you'd stay with Willa in the truck while I did it. Just for maybe twenty minutes or so."

Jesse had agonized over this plan. She hated the idea of leaving her baby, but she didn't want to be carrying Willa when she went to get the second gold bar; she wanted to be able to move fast in case she saw the camo creeps. She figured Willa would be safer with Brad than with her. She'd decided she had no choice but to trust him.

"No problem," said Brad.

Jesse put her hand on his forearm.

"Thank you," she said.

"No problem," said Brad, trying desperately to think—over the sound of his brain shrieking, *SHE'S TOUCHING ME*—of something more eloquent than "no problem," which he realized he was repeating over and over like a moron. Before he could come up with anything else, the door opened and in walked three hefty individuals of indeterminate gender with hair dyed the color of Easter eggs.

Jesse removed her hand, but Brad could still feel it, the warm place on his arm. As he was telling the disappointed trio there were no more T-shirts, he was thinking about Jesse's touch and feeling the warmth radiating from his arm throughout his body.

"You OK?" said Jesse after the trio left.

"Yeah, I'm good," said Brad.

"You sure? Your face is really red."

"Nah, it's just all the . . ." He made a vague waving motion, indicating the general situation.

"Right. Anyway, thanks again. For everything."

"No problem," said Brad.

Chapter 44

Duck was awakened by the sound of a car engine. He rose from his sleeping bag and peered out from the bushes where he and Billy had concealed themselves. He watched as a weather-worn Hyundai pulled off the dirt road and parked next to Slater's pickup. Stu, Ken and Phil got out and headed down the path toward the cabin. Phil was limping and carrying a black garbage bag.

Billy stirred, whispered, "Who is it?"

"Three guys," said Duck. "One of the bait-store guys. Not who we're looking for."

Billy yawned, scratching himself. "This shit is getting old, Duck. Where the fuck *is* that bitch?"

"She'll show up," said Duck. "Sooner or later."

"Better be sooner," said Billy.

* * *

Stu, Ken and Phil found Slater and Kark in front of the cabin sitting on folding chairs. Kark had his camera in his lap and a joint in his hand.

"We're just doing a little pregame here," he said, holding the joint out to Phil.

"Phil," said Stu, "I don't think that's a good idea."

"Absolutely," said Phil, accepting it.

They sat in a circle and passed the joint around, finished it, started another. On the second one Stu broke down and joined in.

"This is some good shit," he said, exhaling.

Kark nodded toward Ken. "You can thank him."

"Thank you," said Stu.

"You're welcome," said Ken, who had almost forgotten that only a few days ago, before he became an entrepreneur and producer of a worldwide viral megahit video, his primary source of income had been selling drugs. That recollection awakened a ghost of a thought in his brain, a vague sense that there was something he needed to do. He frowned, trying to pin it down . . .

"Holy shit, look," said Kark, pointing toward a tree at the edge of the clearing.

The others looked. Sitting on one of the lower tree branches, looking back at them, was a large owl.

"That's a barred owl," said Ken. "They live out here."

"In the daytime?" said Slater.

"Yes, in the daytime," said Ken. "Also the nighttime. What, you think they commute?"

"No, asshole," said Slater. "I meant, owls come out at night."

"Maybe you should tell that one," said Ken.

"You're thinking of bats," said Stu. "They fly around at night, by radar."

"Owls fly at night too," said Slater. "That's an expression, 'night owl.'"

Ken rolled his eyes.

Phil, looking at Stu, said, "Did you say bats fly by *radar*?"

"Yeah," said Stu. "I saw a documentary. They use radar to catch bugs."

"I saw that too," said Slater, nodding. "Animal Planet."

"It's *sonar*," said Phil.

"What is?" said Stu.

"Bats use sonar," said Phil. "Not radar."

"I think you're thinking of submarines," said Stu.

"I am not thinking of submarines," said Phil.

"Submarines use sonar," said Stu.

"He's right," said Slater.

"No, he is *not* right," said Phil.

"You're saying submarines *don't* use sonar?" said Slater.

"No," said Phil. "I mean, yes, submarines use sonar."

"Well that's what he said," said Slater.

"I KNOW THAT'S WHAT HE SAID," said Phil.

"You don't have to shout," said Slater.

Phil took a deep breath, exhaled. "OK," he said. "The point is, yes, submarines use sonar. But bats *also* use sonar. Bats do *not* use radar. *Airplanes* use radar."

"According to you," said Slater.

"No," said Phil. "According to science."

"You're telling me Animal Planet isn't science?" said Slater.

"Jesus H. Christ," said Phil.

"OK," said Stu, speaking unnaturally slowly. "Hear me out, Phil. Airplanes fly, right?"

"Yes," said Phil.

"And bats also fly, right?"

"Right," said Phil. "But—"

"But submarines do *not* fly, right?"

"Right, but what—"

"I rest my case," said Stu.

"He has you there," said Slater.

"HE DOESN'T HAVE SHIT," said Phil.

"Dude, you need to calm down," said Slater, handing Phil a third joint. "It's just a discussion."

"Yeah," said Phil, taking the joint, "but it's a *stupid* discussion."

"Maybe so, dude," said Slater. "But you're, like, half of it."

Phil, having no good answer to that, took a toke.

Kark, who had been watching the owl during the sonar/radar debate, said, "It just keeps *looking* at us."

They all looked over at the owl, which had not moved.

"What do those things eat?" said Stu.

"Mice, squirrels, rabbits," said Ken. "Frogs, snakes, whatever they catch. They're good hunters."

"I'm just glad I'm not a mouse," said Kark, staring at the owl. "I would *not* wanna see that thing coming after me."

"Oh, they'll attack people, too," said Ken.

"Seriously?" said Kark.

"Oh yes. You get too close to their nest, they'll swoop on you, cut up your face. They'll go for your eyeballs. You see those big old claws? Those claws are *sharp*."

They stared at the owl's long black talons, gripping the tree bark.

"You think it has a nest around here?" said Kark.

"Could be," said Ken. "Probably."

Kark turned to Slater. "I got an idea," he said. "For the *Glades Man* pilot. Let's get a shot of you with the owl."

"Now?" said Slater.

"The owl's here now," said Kark. "This'd be a nice little scene, Glades Man face-to-face with a possibly dangerous wildlife thing."

"I dunno," said Slater, looking at the owl.

"What's the matter?" said Ken. "Glades Man afraid of a bird?"

"I'm not afraid of it," said Slater.

"You sure?" said Ken.

"Just a quick scene," said Kark, picking up the camera. "Just go over and stand near the owl and, like, react to it."

"React how?" said Slater.

"Just, I dunno, a natural reaction," said Kark. "To an owl."

Slater rose, hesitantly, from his folding chair. He took a few tentative steps across the clearing in the direction of the owl, then turned toward Kark.

"How's this?" he said.

"You need to get closer," said Kark, looking through the camera.

"Yeah," said Ken, grinning. "Get closer."

Slater took two more reluctant steps owlward. He stopped and turned. "This is as close as I'm getting."

"OK," said Kark. "Now have some kind of reaction, a few words."

"Like what?" said Slater.

"Like 'Here I am with this dangerous owl.'"

"OK, hang on a sec," said Slater. He took off his T-shirt, tossed it aside.

"I don't fucking believe it," said Ken.

Ignoring him, Slater said, "OK, ready?"

"Ready," said Kark.

Slater, looking into the camera, adopted a serious expression, the expression of a man who does not flinch in the face of danger. A Glades Man.

"Right behind me," he said, "is—"

"It's taking off!" shouted Stu.

Slater spun around and saw that the owl had indeed unfurled its surprisingly wide wingspan. With one flap it was airborne, and so was Slater, who spun back around and launched himself away from the owl, landing facedown in the dirt, closing his eyes tight, covering the back of his head with his hands and emitting a high-pitched noise that sounded almost electronic.

As he lay there, the owl made a graceful, silent right turn, flapped its wings again and disappeared into the trees.

Phil, Stu and Ken were snickering. Kark was trying not to.

"Slater!" Kark called to the form on the ground. "It's gone! It flew away!"

Slater lowered his arms, opened his eyes and slowly raised his head. His face was smeared with dirt. He turned and saw that the owl was gone, then rose to his feet, picked up his T-shirt and walked back to the still-snickering chair circle. He sat down, turned to Ken.

"Not one fucking word," he said.

Ken, smiling hugely, held up his hands, palms out.

Slater turned to Kark and said, "You better delete that."

"Maybe we can use the first part," said Kark.

"Yeah," said Ken. "Just keep the part where he takes off his shirt."

Slater turned back toward Ken, about to say something, but Kark cut him off.

"We'll worry about that later, OK? Right now we gotta start thinking about the monster shoot."

"You don't think it's still too light out?" said Ken. He pointed to Phil, slumped in the chair in his Duke sweatshirt, his belly hanging out over the waistband of his ancient sweatpants. "I mean right now he don't look too scary, no offense."

"None taken," said Phil.

"I'll make it work," said Kark. "I'm gonna underexpose so it looks dark, it's called day for night. And I'm gonna dick around with it in post like last time. Trust me, he'll look scary."

"Where're we gonna do this?" said Phil. "Not far, I hope."

"No, it's close," said Kark. "I scouted a place this morning, on a path near where we did the last one."

"Good," said Phil. "Because my knee is killing me." He turned to Ken. "You got any more of those pills?"

"Phil," said Stu, "I don't think that's a good—"

"Shut up, Stu," said Phil, still looking at Ken.

"Not those exact ones," said Ken, "but I think I got something." He stood and dug into his right front jeans pocket. He pulled out two large white pills, flecked with lint. He handed them to Phil.

"What're these?" said Phil, frowning at them.

Ken shrugged. "Being honest, I got no idea."

"Phil," said Stu, "this is a bad idea."

Phil looked at him. "Are you gonna wear the head?"

"No," said Stu.

"Exactly," said Phil, tossing the pills into his mouth.

* * *

At the other end of the path to the cabin, Duck and Billy heard the sound of an engine approaching.

They pulled back into the bushes and looked down the road.

In a few seconds they saw the truck.

Saw Brad at the wheel.

Saw Jesse next to him.

"It's them," said Billy.

Duck smiled.

"Get the guns," he said.

Chapter 45

Frank ended the phone call and turned to Jacky.

"The secretary's two minutes out," he said. "Where the hell is Skeeter?"

Jacky held up her phone. "He's not answering. But he said he'd be here."

"He better be. Is he driving? Does he have a car?"

"I don't know."

"Well, he better get here."

They were at the end of a dirt road, a short drive off the Tamiami Trail, in a grassy clearing that had once been the site of a small wooden shack, long since rotted to dirt. In preparation for the Python Challenge press conference, Frank and Jacky had set up the secretary's official lectern, with the official seal of the Department of the Interior, in front of a scenic Everglades photo-op backdrop—a sea of sawgrass, rising out of dark water, stretching to the horizon. Scattered in the distance were clumps of bushes growing on patches of slightly higher ground. From the edge of the clearing, a barely-there footpath disappeared into the sawgrass stalks in the direction of a stand of gumbo-limbo trees.

In front of the lectern was the press corps—four TV crews, including Channel 8 PeoplePower News; two photographers; and five reporters, including Anthony Evander Cornwall of the *New York Times*. Chatting behind the lectern was a clot of local politicians and uniformed officials representing Everglades National Park, the Florida Fish and Wildlife Conservation Commission, the South Florida Water Management District and other agencies. Their function would be to stand behind the secretary and pretend to be interested in his remarks.

"That's exactly the visual he doesn't want," said Frank, looking at the officials. "All uniforms and suits."

"Well, it might be all he gets," said Jacky, nodding toward the road. "Because he's here."

Frank turned and saw a black Lincoln Navigator approaching.

"Shit," he said, hurrying over.

The Navigator stopped and Whitt Chastain emerged. He was a tall, blond, blue-eyed, trim, athletic man, handsome in a stereotypically WASP-y way. He wore his most casual attire: khaki pants, dress shoes, blue blazer, white shirt with top button unbuttoned, no tie. With him, also wearing khakis and blazers, was his security detail, two agents of the United States Park Police, both of whom had never worked with Chastain before but, after spending ninety minutes in the car with him, already hated him.

Chastain nodded to the reporters as Frank ushered him past them to the clot of officials. Chastain shook their hands with sincerely feigned warmth, then turned to Frank and, lowering his voice, said, "Where's the winner from last year? With the beard?"

"He's not here yet," said Frank.

"Well where is he?"

Frank shrugged. "We don't know. He said he'd be here."

Chastain smiled and put his hands on Frank's shoulders, the very picture of a caring, good-guy, father-figure boss. He leaned close to Frank's ear and, still smiling, said, "I ask you to do one simple thing, and you fuck it up. You don't think I can find ten other people who can do your fucking job?"

"No," said Frank. "I mean yes."

"So do your fucking job."

"Yes, sir."

Chastain dropped his hands. Frank shot Jacky a *Where is he?* look. She pointed at her phone and shrugged.

Chastain stepped up to the lectern, on which lay a binder with the remarks Frank had prepared for him. From somewhere in the sea of sawgrass behind him came the sound of a distant airboat. Chastain looked toward the cameras, forming his facial features into an expression of Leadership, and began reading.

"I want to thank everyone for coming out today," he said. "We are gathered here in a beautiful Florida setting, the Everglades, one of this great state's, and this great nation's, greatest treasures, and most vital natural resources." The airboat noise was getting louder, quite a bit louder. Chastain turned his head and shot an annoyed glance at Frank, then turned his Leadership face back to the cameras. "As secretary of the interior, I have devoted all my energy to preserving and protecting our precious ecosystems from their many threats. And among the most pressing threats to the Everglades is the Burmese python, an invasive species that since its introduction has—"

Chastain stopped, his voice overpowered by the roar of the now-much-closer airboat. He turned around to look back toward the sawgrass, as did the officials behind him. The sound was now overwhelming, like a prop plane about to land on top of them; they could see the tops of sawgrass stalks thrashing violently as the airboat approached at high speed. The group behind the lectern began to edge away from the water, moving tentatively at first but then fleeing in panic—with Chastain, in full sprint, leading the retreat—as the airboat burst into view, a fifty-mile-an-hour missile hurtling directly toward them.

Just before it reached the clearing, the driver cut the engine, but the momentum carried the airboat forward and up onto the bank, its flat-bottom hull sliding across the grass, the prow smashing into the lectern. The impact broke the binder and sent Chastain's prepared remarks fluttering into the sky. The official Department of the Interior seal, violently jarred loose, sailed, Frisbee-like, across the clearing and landed near Chastain, who had retreated behind the two Park Police officers, both of whom had drawn their pistols.

As the airboat skidded to a stop, a silence fell over the clearing. With every camera trained on him, the driver, DeWayne "Skeeter"

Toobs, rose to his feet. He was a thick, powerful-looking man wearing a ball cap with an image of a coiled snake over the words DON'T EVEN TREAD NEAR ME. His face was largely covered by a wild, thick beard, gray except for a brownish tobacco-stain ring around what was presumably his mouth. He wore a gray tank top and baggy gray shorts. His feet were bare.

Standing in the boat next to him was a 250-pound Everglades wild hog—bristly, tusked, feral—with a rope around its neck.

Skeeter peered over the airboat bow at the splintered remains of the secretary's official lectern and said, "Fucking throttle cable." He looked around at the crowd of press and public officials. "Which one's Jacky?"

"That's me," Jacky said, stepping forward. "Mr. Toobs?"

"Call me Skeeter, darlin'," said Skeeter. "Sorry I'm late. I brung you somethin'." He reached behind him and, with a grunt, lifted a large, bulging cloth sack.

"Is that a snake?" she said, stepping back.

"Fifteen-footer," he said, climbing out of the airboat, heaving the sack with him. "You want to see her?"

"Maybe later," said Jacky. "Right now I'd like you to meet the secretary."

She looked over at Frank, who escorted Chastain to the airboat, flanked by the Park Police officers, who had holstered their weapons. The press gathered around to watch as Chastain stuck out his hand and said, "So you're the famous Skeeter Toobs."

Skeeter set down the snake sack, shook his hand, and said, "So you're the . . . the . . ."

"Secretary of the interior," said Chastain. "It's a cabinet post."

"Good for you," said Skeeter. He nodded toward the demolished lectern. "Sorry about that," he said. "Fucking throttle cable."

Chastain waved it away. He pointed at the hog and said, "And what have we here?"

"That's Buddy," said Skeeter. "He's my emotional support boar."

Chastain started to laugh but stopped himself, unsure whether Skeeter was joking.

"C'mon, Buddy," said Skeeter, yanking on the rope. The boar clambered over the side of the airboat and began snuffling around in the dirt.

"He's smarter'n a dog," said Skeeter. "Finds his own food."

"In that case," said Chastain, "he's also smarter than a lot of— HEY!"

Chastain backpedaled frantically as Buddy launched a thick, powerful urine stream from his undercarriage, a gushing fire hose of rancid boar piss that soaked the legs of Chastain's khakis and splashed all over his dress shoes.

"You getting this?" said Channel 8 PeoplePower News reporter Patsy Hartmann.

"Oh yes," said cameraman Bruce Morris.

"Sorry 'bout that," Skeeter said to Chastain, not sounding sorry. "I trained him to hold it 'til he's out of the boat."

The crowd, keeping a safe distance, watched with growing respect as Buddy continued to urinate at high volume and pressure for a solid minute. Off to the side, Frank huddled with Chastain, who was looking down at his wet, reeking pants.

"What do you want to do?" said Frank.

"I want to have that fat retarded redneck fuck shot in the head," said Chastain, still looking down. "And then his fucking pig. And then you."

"Right," said Frank. "But I mean for right now, the press conference. You want to call it off?"

"No, I'd look like a pussy."

Chastain looked up, smiling, at the cameras, gesturing toward his pants and shaking his head to demonstrate that he was the kind of guy who could enjoy a joke at his own expense.

"Folks," said Frank, "if you can all gather around again, we're gonna continue with the press conference. Skeeter, if you'll stand over here . . ." He positioned Skeeter next to Chastain, with Buddy, who had finally finished voiding his bladder, on Skeeter's non-Chastain side. The officials lined up behind them; the press corps took its place in front. Jacky handed Chastain his prepared remarks, which she had collected and reassembled.

"As I was saying," Chastain began, "we're gathered here to launch the Python Challenge, although I'm thinking maybe we should expand it to include wild pigs."

He turned to Skeeter and smiled to indicate that he was being humorous. Skeeter, not smiling, said, "There's been pigs here for four hundred years."

"Right, of course," said Chastain, looking back at his prepared remarks.

As he forged ahead with his speech, Jacky and Frank moved away from the group to confer.

"So this is going well," she whispered, rolling her eyes.

"Yeah," said Frank. "Other than the secretary of the interior almost getting killed by an airboat and then literally getting pissed on by a pig."

"I just hope nothing else happens."

"What else *could* happen?" said Frank.

Jacky did not answer that.

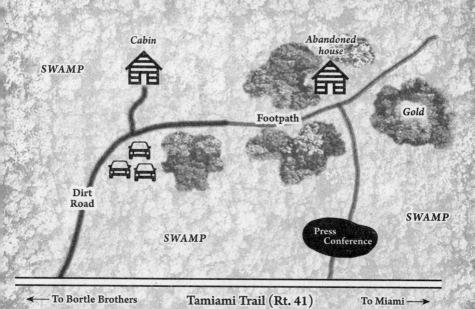

SWAMP

Cabin

Abandoned
house

Footpath

Gold

Dirt
Road

SWAMP

SWAMP

Press
Conference

← To Bortle Brothers Tamiami Trail (Rt. 41) To Miami →

Chapter 46

Brad stopped his truck and backed it off the dirt road, parking next to Stu's Hyundai and Slater's pickup near the thick clump of bushes.

"You sure you don't want me to go with you?"

"I'm sure," said Jesse. "I'll only be a few minutes. Maybe twenty minutes. Thirty at most. I'm not going far." She looked down at Willa, asleep on the seat between them in her car seat/carrier. She took a bottle out of her backpack and handed it to Brad. "In case she wakes up," she said. "I really, really appreciate you doing this."

"No problem," he said. He had given up on trying to be eloquent around her.

"OK," she said, putting her hand on the door handle. She took one last look at Willa, asking herself for the hundredth time if she should be doing this, leaving her baby with this man she barely knew. She decided for the hundredth time that she had no choice. "I'll be back soon," she said.

"Be careful," he said.

"Don't worry," she said, opening the truck door. "I'll be fine." She forced a smile to show she wasn't worried. It didn't fool either one of them.

* * *

Crouching back in the bushes, Duck and Billy watched as Jesse got out of the truck. They saw Brad still in the driver's seat, saw the baby carrier on the seat next to him.

Jesse closed the truck door and started walking on the road toward them.

Billy, gripping his pistol, began to stand. Duck put his hand on Billy's arm, stopping him. Billy looked at him, questioning. Duck held up his hand. *Wait.*

Jesse walked past the bushes, past the footpath leading down to the cabin, continuing on the road, heading toward the trees in the distance. Duck looked back at the truck. Brad was still there.

Billy was getting restless. "What're we doin', Duck?" he whispered.

Duck stared at Jesse's back. She was walking quickly, approaching the trees, where the dirt road turned into a footpath. Duck looked back at Brad. From where he'd parked the truck, the bushes blocked his view of the road, and of Jesse.

Duck made a decision.

"We're gonna follow the bitch," he whispered. "I think she's goin' to the gold. But either way, we got her."

"What about him?" whispered Billy, nodding toward the truck.

"We get him later. He ain't goin' noplace. He's waitin' for her. Her baby's in that truck."

They waited until Jesse disappeared into the trees. They grabbed their backpacks, took one last look back at Brad, then crept out of the bushes on the side opposite the truck. They started trotting on the road, Duck in front, heading for the trees, on Jesse's trail.

* * *

Ten minutes after Jesse left, Brad heard the snarl of engines. He looked up from the Candy Crush game on his phone and saw two approaching ATVs, both driven by large men, the second towing a utility trailer.

They passed in front of Brad's truck—neither man looking his way—and disappeared down the road, beyond the bushes.

Brad stared at the space where they had been, trying to figure out who they were.

They weren't locals, and they weren't hunters.

They definitely didn't look like tourists.

Who the hell were they?

Whoever they were, they were headed the same way Jesse had gone.

"Shit," said Brad. "Shit shit shit." He looked at Willa, who was watching him. "Sorry," he said.

He debated with himself for a few seconds, then made up his mind.

"C'mon, Willa," he said, unbuckling her carrier. "Let's go find your mom."

He got out of the truck and, carrying Willa's carrier by the handle, set off down the road.

As he passed the bushes, he saw that the ATVs were already out of sight, into the trees.

He broke into a trot, trying not to jostle the baby, but worrying with every step that wherever he was going, he would get there too late.

* * *

Thirty seconds after Brad disappeared into the trees, the members of the Everglades Melon Monster video crew, all five of them thoroughly baked, made their way up the path from the cabin.

Kark, camera in hand, was in front, followed by Ken and the shirt-less Slater. A few yards back were Stu and Phil. Phil was walking pretty well, as his knee was no longer bothering him. In fact, nothing was bothering him. Between the weed and whatever was in the pills Ken had given him, Phil was feeling pleasantly detached from the world and its worries. This feeling of detachment was enhanced by the fact that Phil was wearing the monster head. Kark had told him he didn't need to put it on yet, but Phil insisted: This was his happy place, inside the head, high as the sky. He couldn't see anything from in there, and he could barely hear, so Stu had to lead him by the arm. Phil was OK with that. He figured that was what agents were for.

They reached the road, and Kark led the group to the left, to where the road dwindled to a footpath, just before the trees.

Phil started to sing. Not the Beach Boys this time. This time, he went with "Summer Nights," from *Grease*. He had always loved that song; in fact he loved all the songs from *Grease*, which he first saw at age six, when his John Travolta–obsessed older sister took him with her to see it in a movie theater. She bought the soundtrack album and listened to it constantly in her bedroom; little Phil had learned all the lyrics by heart. But he had also learned not to sing them in public, because the older neighborhood boys—boys whose approval Phil craved; boys of ten and even eleven years—had declared that *Grease* was faggy.

And so Phil had kept the lyrics bottled up inside him, dormant. Until now.

Fuck those older boys. Phil was getting his *Grease* on.

"Summer lovin', had me a blast . . ."

Phil's voice sounded fantastic to Phil, inside the head, as he stumbled along on the road to wherever.

* * *

At that moment Pinky's Tesla rolled to a stop next to the pickup truck that Brad had vacated a few minutes before.

Pinky had gotten there by pure luck. He'd been westbound on the Tamiami Trail, headed to Bortle Brothers Bait & Beer, when he realized that the truck he'd just passed going the other way was the Bortles'. Pinky made a fast U-turn and headed back east, catching sight of the pickup just as it turned off the highway, onto a dirt road.

Pinky made the turn but quickly ran into a problem; the Tesla, sitting low on the deeply rutted road, got stuck on a rock, and it took Pinky several minutes to maneuver off it. His mood, already foul, was even worse by the time he found the pickup, parked and empty.

He pulled in next to it and heaved himself out of the Tesla. Seeing the path leading down to the cabin, he started across the road toward it. He glanced to his right and stopped, spotting a group of men in the distance, one of them wearing some kind of weird thing on his head. Pinky shaded his eyes and squinted, trying to get a better look.

As the men reached the trees, one of them turned his head partway, just enough for Pinky to see that it was Ken.

He immediately started walking toward them, moving with the gimpy gait of a big man with bad knees. Pinky couldn't move fast, but as more than one small-time drug dealer had learned, Pinky was relentless: If he was after you, sooner or later he would get you. And the harder you made him work, the worse it would go for you.

Right now, lumbering toward the trees, Pinky was working hard.

Chapter 47

Jesse kept up a brisk pace, eager to get to the gold and return to her baby. When she reached the spooky broken-down shack where she had once hidden the gold bar, she broke into a trot to get past it quicker. She looked back a few times but saw only the empty path behind her. Her mind was a dark swirl of worries: Were the camo creeps around? Was Willa OK? Had she done the right thing, making the deal with Erik? Would the gold still be there? *What if the gold wasn't there?*

She was breathing pretty hard by the time she got within sight of the mound of bushes with the lone gumbo tree that marked her destination. She stopped and took one last look around, checked for the dozenth time to make sure she still had her phone, then left the path. She sloshed as quickly as she could through warm, soupy swamp water up to her knees, at times to her thighs. She kept a nervous eye out for gators but saw none.

She reached the mound and stepped up onto it, dripping. She bent over and put her hands on her knees, panting, drained from exertion and tension. Then she pushed her way through the thick wall of bushes, into the clearing behind them. She took a few steps, her eyes anxiously scanning the ground, then exhaled in relief, almost crying out, when she saw a glint of bright yellow in the dark dirt, and beyond it a few more.

It was still here. *The gold was still here.*

She dropped to her knees next to the closest bar and plunged her shaking hands into the dirt. In a few seconds she'd cleared away enough to grab the bar and pull it free. She brushed the dirt off and put the bar into her backpack. Still on her knees, she thought about what to do next. Erik had told her to call him right away when she had the gold, but she decided to do that when she got back to the truck. She wanted to get out of here, wanted to get back to her baby.

She rose, turned and pushed her way back through the thick bushes. She felt the comforting weight of the bar in her backpack. With each step her spirits were rising. She dared to think about the money Erik had promised her, what she could do with $100,000, where she would go with Willa when she got out of this miserable swamp.

She stopped as she reached the edge of the bushes and peered through them, looking across the water toward the path, the way back. She saw no one. She stepped out of the bushes.

She didn't see it coming, the quick, hard, closed-fist punch to the right side of her face. She felt the shock, a stab of intense pain. She did not feel herself fall.

She did not, as she lay unconscious on the bank, feel the fat gob of Billy's saliva land on her shirt.

Did not hear Duck's voice, as he stood over her:

"Got you now, bitch."

Chapter 48

"How much farther?" said Slater.

"Almost there," said Kark.

They had reached a fork in the footpath. The path to the left was more heavily traveled; in fact, within just the past thirty minutes the left-hand path had been taken by Jesse, then by the Campbell brothers, then by Kristov Berliuz's henchpersons on ATVs, then by Brad. It was also the path that the Everglades Melon Monster crew had taken a few days earlier, when they shot their first video.

Today Kark went to the right. After a few steps he stopped and turned, waiting with Slater and Ken for Stu and Phil to catch up. Stu was still leading Phil, who was a bit wobbly on his feet but pain-free and in very, very high spirits. He was still singing his favorite tunes from the *Grease* soundtrack, currently performing "Look at Me, I'm Sandra Dee." It sounded great to Phil, inside the head, but to those on the outside it came across as a disturbing moan, like a man passing a kidney stone.

"Is he OK?" said Kark as Phil and Stu reached the others.

"To be honest," said Stu, "I don't know what's going on in there. Are we ready to do this?"

"A little farther," said Kark. "This path goes up toward the highway. What I'm thinking is, you guys"—pointing to Slater and Ken—"you're on this path, hunting for the monster, and then suddenly you turn around and see it coming after you from behind, and you start to run."

"But not like pussies," said Slater.

"Yeah," said Ken, "not like we saw an owl."

"Fuck you," said Slater.

"But seriously," said Ken, "we talked about this. We don't want to look like pussies."

"No," said Kark, "you won't. Like I said, the idea is, you're not afraid. You're . . . startled. The monster caught you by surprise, so your natural reaction is to, uh, regroup. So anyway, you're regrouping up the path, with the monster right behind you, and there's just this glimpse of the highway up ahead, maybe some cars on it, and then, boom, it ends, cliffhanger, we don't know what's gonna happen next. But the story arc is, this thing, this monster, is heading toward civilization, symbolized by the highway. So that way, when we do the third video, where you guys go after the monster, the message is, you're actually saving civilization."

"They're heroes," said Stu.

"Exactly," said Kark.

"I like it," said Stu.

Ken and Slater nodded, also liking the hero idea.

"OK, then," said Kark. "We'll start shooting up ahead, by those trees." He pointed up the path, toward a stand of trees.

"What about our lines?" said Slater.

"I think just ad-lib something, like last time," said Kark. "Keep it minimal. You're walking on the path, you're looking around, you hear a noise, you go, 'What's that?' You turn around, you see the monster, you go, 'There's the monster!' Then you . . . you regroup. The whole thing, we're talking like thirty seconds."

"We need to get Bortle Brothers Bait & Beer in there," said Ken.

"OK, sure," said Kark. "If you can work that in. So here's the deal. You guys"—pointing to Slater and Ken—"you'll be in front. I'll follow you, and, Stu, you bring the monster along behind me. When I give the sign, Slater and Ken, you start looking around like you're hunting, then you pretend to hear something, you turn around, you see the monster, you react."

"How about this," said Ken. "I'll say, 'What's that noise?' Then we turn around and see it, and he says, 'Uh-oh! There's the Everglades

Melon Monster!' And then I say, 'We better regroup back to Bortle Brothers Bait & Beer!' How does that sound?"

"It sounds like you get two lines and I only get one line," said Slater.

"It sounds like I'm paying for this," said Ken.

"I think something like that'll work," said Kark. "We can do a couple of takes if we need to. Main thing is, keep it short. As soon as you turn around and react, I'll turn the camera around and show the monster. Stu, when you see me start to turn, you need to duck behind a tree or something, OK? So you're not in the shot."

"Got it," said Stu.

"Good. So I'll get a shot of the monster coming toward the camera, then I'll turn back to Ken and Slater, and you guys take off, and I'll take off behind you, so the camera's bouncing, a handheld feel of urgency, and then we catch a glimpse of the highway. That sound good?"

Everyone nodded, except Phil, who had finished "Look at Me, I'm Sandra Dee" and had moved on to "Greased Lightnin'," the moaning sounding even more dire.

"You sure he's OK in there?" said Kark.

"I have no idea," said Stu. "But let's do this while he can still walk."

"Right, let's go," said Kark. He started up the path, the others following.

* * *

By the time he reached the fork in the footpath, Pinky was limping badly. This was the farthest he had walked in years, and both his knees were on fire. He stopped, looked around and spotted the men on the right-hand path, just before the trees.

He took a couple of steps in their direction, but a wave of pain throbbed through his legs, forcing him to stop. He needed to rest a few minutes. He stood impatiently, breathing hard, sweat pouring off his massive body. He stared at the men receding in the distance, his gaze focused on Ken.

Chapter 49

Jesse lay on the dirt in the clearing, on her back, eyes closed, the right side of her face starting to swell where Duck had hit her. Her bare arms and legs were scratched and bleeding from being dragged through the thick bushes. Her backpack lay next to her.

Duck and Billy, panting from the effort of carrying her, stood over her limp body.

"I wanna do her," said Billy.

Duck looked at the unconscious woman, then his brother. "Like this?" he said.

"I don't give a shit if she's awake or not."

Duck looked back down at Jesse, then over at the hole in the ground where Jesse had dug up the gold bar, and where parts of other bars were poking through the dirt. His plan was for them to carry the gold out in backpacks. It looked like it was going to be more than one trip, and he wanted to get started.

Billy, seeing his brother wavering, pressed the point. "We got the gold, Duck. It ain't goin' nowhere. We have a little fun with her first, we finish her off, then we worry about the gold. We earned this."

Duck looked back down at Jesse. Even beat up, she was a good-looking woman. And it had been a long time.

He looked up at Billy and smiled.

"Me first," he said.

Billy laughed. "You fucker. I knew you'd say that."

Duck started to unzip his camo pants, then stopped, turning his head.

"You hear that?" he said.

Billy listened, heard the engines.

"Shit," he said.

Duck rezipped his pants. He grabbed his gun from his backpack; Billy did the same. They went to the bushes and pushed partway through, keeping out of sight. They peered across the open water and saw the two ATVs on the footpath, moving slowly. The man driving the first one, a very big man, was looking in their direction, then down at something in his hand, then back toward them.

"The fuck is he looking for?" said Billy.

Duck, his eyes on the big man, said nothing.

The ATVs stopped. The big man was now looking directly toward the bushes where Duck and Billy were hiding.

"Mother*fucker*," said Billy.

Duck tightened his grip on his gun. "Get ready," he said.

* * *

Tenklo looked down at the iPad, looked across at the little island, looked at the iPad again. Assuming the woman still had the phone, she was over there, somewhere in the bushes, and she had not moved for a while.

Tenklo saw no sign of a boat, so he assumed the woman had waded across. He frowned at the water, wondering if it was too deep to drive the ATV across.

He looked back at Kelmit and motioned, *Wait*.

He turned the handlebars and nosed the ATV down into the water. The front tires found the bottom, then the rear tires. So far so good. He eased forward. The water got a little deeper, but the level stopped rising just before it reached the ATV's foot pegs.

Tenklo turned back and beckoned for Kelmit to follow. Then he resumed driving, slowly, toward the little island.

* * *

Duck and Billy, crouched in the bushes, watched them coming. Billy was breathing hard.

"They know it's here," he whispered. "How the fuck do they know?"

"I don't know," said Duck.

"What do we do?"

"Wait 'til they're close. You don't shoot 'til I shoot."

The first ATV was twenty-five yards away. Now twenty. Duck and Billy were getting a good look at Tenklo.

"That fucker is *huge*," whispered Billy.

Duck, thinking the same thing, decided he didn't want Tenklo to get any closer.

"Now," he said, rising. He pushed forward through the bushes, Billy right behind him, both men raising their pistols and firing.

The Campbells had surprise on their side, but not competence. To begin with, neither was a crack shot. Virtually all of their experience with handguns involved robbing unarmed victims or shooting at inanimate objects, including a microwave oven, several TV sets and countless vending machines, none of which fired back or took evasive action.

Their pistols were Glocks, holding seventeen rounds each. Billy, charging forward in an adrenaline-fueled frenzy, fired nine wildly off-target shots before he lost his footing and fell face-first off the bank, plunging into the water and losing his pistol in the muck.

Duck did better, firing twelve rounds and making more of an effort to aim them. But he was aiming at moving targets. Tenklo and Kelmit had both seen real combat, and they reacted instantly when the Campbells started shooting, swerving their ATVs as they reached for their guns.

The result was that most of Duck's shots missed. But not all of them. One struck Tenklo in his left shoulder. Bellowing in pain, he struggled to retain control of the ATV, in the process losing his grip on his gun, which fell into the water. He managed, barely, to get the ATV turned around. He gunned it back toward the footpath, zigzagging to make himself harder to hit.

Kelmit fared more poorly. He got off a single stray shot before Duck shot him three times, twice in his chest and once in his neck, the bullet severing an artery. Spurting blood, he fell sideways off the ATV and into the water. In ninety seconds he was dead.

Duck fired a few more shots at Tenklo, but he was now too far away. Duck and Billy watched as he reached the far edge of the water and drove up onto the footpath. Bent over in pain, he looked back briefly as he drove away, disappearing into the trees in the distance.

Billy, still on his knees in the water, started feeling around the bottom.

"What the fuck're you doing?" said Duck.

"I lost my gun."

"Forget it," said Duck. "We gotta get to work."

"I know we hit that big fucker," said Billy, climbing back onto the bank.

"We?" said Duck.

"OK, you hit him. I know you did."

"But he ain't dead," said Duck. "He could tell somebody."

"So what do we do?"

Duck looked at Kelmit's ATV, still running, the water next to it blooming red with blood. It was a gift, he realized. It even had a trailer.

"We put the gold in that ATV," he said, climbing down into the water. "Then we get the fuck out of here."

He dropped his gun on the bank and waded to the ATV. He kicked Kelmit's lifeless floating body aside, climbed into the saddle and drove back to the little island. There was just enough room for the ATV and trailer up on the bank, in front of the wall of bushes. Duck drove it there and turned the ignition key, shutting off the engine.

Billy looked into the trailer and smiled. "They even brought us shovels," he said.

Duck frowned. The shovels meant the ATV men had definitely, somehow, known about the gold. And that made it more likely that the one who got away would be coming back, maybe with help.

"We gotta move fast," he said.

They grabbed the shovels and pushed back through the bushes to the clearing. Jesse was lying where they'd left her, eyes still closed. The thought briefly crossed Duck's mind that maybe she wasn't going to regain consciousness. He decided it didn't matter; they were going to kill her anyway. Right now they needed to focus on moving the gold.

They plunged the shovels into the damp, sandy earth, and were rewarded immediately with the solid *clunk* of metal hitting metal. It seemed there were gold bars everywhere, dozens of them, most just beneath the surface. They dug in a fury, fueled by adrenaline and greed, stacking the bars at the edge of the bushes. Billy counted them, calling out the number as each new ingot clanked onto the stack. In minutes they had thirty, and were finding more.

* * *

Brad had heard the gunshots, many gunshots. He was frantic now, running as fast as he could without jouncing Willa out of her carrier. He was grateful she wasn't crying; in fact for some reason she seemed to actually enjoy the bouncing around, smiling and occasionally emitting little baby giggles.

As he neared a bend in the path he heard an ATV coming toward him. He quickly moved off the path, stepping down into the sawgrass, out of sight. The ATV, driven by the huge man he'd seen before, blasted past without slowing down. As he flashed by, Brad saw that he was hurt, his face white, blood seeping through his shirt.

As soon as he was past, Brad was running again.

* * *

It took Duck and Billy a little less than ten minutes to dig up the bars, at least the easily accessible ones. Billy's count stood at seventy-four. Duck, increasingly edgy, jabbed the blade of his shovel into the ground around the perimeter of the area where they'd been digging, but he hit nothing.

He looked at the stack, guessing at the weight of the bars and doing a rough calculation of their value.

He decided they had at least two million dollars' worth of gold.

"Let's go," he said.

He hefted a stack of three bars, then plunged through the bushes. He dropped the bars with a loud *clang* into the ATV trailer. Billy was right behind with another three bars.

They fell into a rhythm, going back and forth through the bushes, loading their treasure.

Jesse's eyes were still closed.

* * *

Brad, holding Willa, crouched in the grass next to the footpath, looking across the water. He caught his breath when he saw the body floating faceup. He exhaled when he saw that it wasn't Jesse.

His focus shifted to the two men, the scumbags who'd been chasing Jesse. They were busy with a repetitive task—emerging from the bushes, dropping something heavy into the ATV trailer, going back into the bushes, coming back out with more.

Brad didn't see Jesse. But he knew she had to be in there somewhere.

He wished he had a gun.

He watched as the brothers made more round trips. He tried to gauge how long they were out of sight on each trip, wondering if he could make it across to the little island unseen, carrying a baby.

The other thing he wondered was what the hell he was going to do when he got there.

Chapter 50

The video shoot for *Everglades Melon Monster Part II: The Sequel,* was not going well. The principal actors, Ken and Slater, were having major creative differences about the dialogue. Also Stu, the monster wrangler, was getting into the shot; he had blown the first two takes.

Kark, the director, was trying to remain patient.

"Stu," he was saying, "you gotta move away before I turn the camera around, OK? You need to let go of Phil sooner."

"OK," said Stu, who was standing behind Kark on the footpath, holding Phil's arm. "But I don't know what he's gonna do."

Phil, inside the head, was continuing to work his way through *Grease,* currently performing "You're the One That I Want," although outside the head it still sounded like anguished moaning.

Kark turned to Ken and Slater, ahead of him on the path. "OK, let's try another one. You guys ready?"

Ken and Slater glared at each other.

"I *been* ready," said Ken. "He's the one keeps trying to get more lines."

"I'm trying to give it a more natural flow," said Slater.

"A *flow?*" said Ken. "We're running away from a fucking monster. It's not supposed to *flow.*"

Slater, appealing to Kark, said, "It should flow, right? The dialogue?"

Kark sighed. "Listen, guys, you're overthinking it. This is really mostly about the visuals. You don't need to say a whole lot. You're hunting, you hear something, you turn around, you go, basically, 'Hey, there's a monster!' Then we show the monster, and cut. That's the scene. Just keep it simple, OK?"

Ken and Slater continued to glare at each other, saying nothing.

"Great!" said Kark. "Let's do another one." He looked back at Stu. "Remember, when I start to turn, you need to be out of the shot, OK?"

"OK," said Stu, over the moaning emanating from the head, inside which Phil had moved on to "Beauty School Dropout."

Kark looked back at the principal actors. "OK, we pick it up with you guys hunting." He raised the camera to his eye, hit the record button. "And . . . action."

Slater and Ken started walking ahead, the two of them turning their heads from side to side, trying to look like men who were hunting but overdoing their head motions, so in fact they looked like men watching two different tennis matches.

After a few steps Ken stopped and turned around dramatically, attempting to appear concerned.

"What's that noise?" he said.

Slater turned around, also dramatically, biceps flexed. He pointed into the distance and said, "Uh-oh! There's the monster, over there!"

Ken, pretending to see the monster, said, "That's the Everglades Melon Monster! We better regroup back to Bortle Brothers Bait & Beer!"

"Yeah!" said Slater, still flexing. "We better get out of here right away!"

"That's what I just said!" said Ken, mainly as an appeal to Kark, but Kark was already turning the camera to get the shot of the monster.

Stu, seeing Kark's movement, released Phil's hand and lunged sideways to get out of the shot, but he stumbled and fell, sprawling in the dirt. Phil took a couple of wandering steps and tripped over Stu, going facedown on the path, the monster head coming off and rolling away.

"Fuck," said Kark. "Cut!"

"Sorry!" said Stu, getting to his feet and helping Phil up.

Phil, blinking at the daylight, said, "Is it over?"

"Not yet," said Stu.

"Where's my head?" said Phil.

Stu picked it up and handed it to him. Phil put it on and resumed his rendition of "Beauty School Dropout."

"All right," said Kark. "Let's try it again. And, Stu . . ."

"I know, I know," said Stu.

Kark turned to Ken and Slater. "You guys ready?"

They glared at each other.

"OK," said Kark, raising the camera. "And . . . action."

Ken and Slater started walking, resuming their tennis-spectator hunting motion. After a few steps Ken turned around, dramatically, and said, "What's that noise?"

Slater, flexing, turned around and said, "Uh-oh! There's the monster, over there!"

Ken peered into the distance, and suddenly the pretend concern on his face morphed into genuine fear.

"Oh fuck," he said.

Slater looked at him and said, "That's not your line."

"Yeah," said Kark, "you're supposed to—"

"*Fuck*," said Ken. He was staring down the path, past Stu and Phil. Slater and Kark, following Ken's gaze, saw it then, maybe fifty yards away—the massive, menacing form of Pinky, lumbering toward them, slowly but doggedly.

"Who the fuck is that?" said Slater.

Without answering, Ken turned and started walking briskly away on the path.

"Where're you going?" said Kark. "Ken! Hey!"

Ken, not looking back, broke into a trot.

"Do you know who that is?" Kark asked Slater, pointing at Pinky.

"No," said Slater, "and I don't wanna know."

"What's happening?" said Stu, still holding Phil's arm. "What're we doing?" He saw Kark and Slater looking at something behind him. He turned and saw Pinky coming toward him, saw the look on Pinky's face.

"Who is *that*?" said Stu.

Nobody answered. Stu turned and saw that Slater and Kark were now also moving briskly up the path, after Ken.

"Hey!" said Stu. "Wait up!"

They did not wait up.

Stu, glancing back at Pinky, pulled Phil's arm and said, "C'mon, Phil." He started dragging Phil up the path after the others.

Phil was now singing "Rock and Roll Is Here to Stay." He was feeling good. He was even trying a few dance moves. They were not artistic moves—Phil was a clumsy dancer even when he was not drunk and high on multiple drugs—but they were heartfelt, putting a swivel in Phil's hips as Stu towed him up the path, following the other members of the cast and crew of *Everglades Melon Monster Part II: The Sequel,* as they fled, in an unforeseen plot twist, from an entity far scarier than the one in their video.

Chapter 51

The Campbells, having finished loading the gold into the trailer, stood in the clearing, looking down at Jesse. Her eyes were still closed.

"Maybe she's dead," said Billy.

Duck nudged Jesse's head with his foot. She groaned, though her eyes remained closed.

"She ain't dead," he said. "Yet."

"So what do we do?"

"We make sure," Duck said. "Go get my gun. It's by the ATV."

"You got any bullets left?"

"Some. Enough."

Billy pushed his way back through the wall of bushes. Emerging on the other side, he scanned the ground, saw Duck's Glock next to the ATV trailer. He was reaching down to pick it up when he heard a sound coming from the other side of the trailer.

A baby's cry.

Billy grabbed the gun and rose just as Brad came sprinting around the trailer. Billy, shouting, "Hey!," tried to get off a shot, but Brad was on him, taking him down with a hard tackle.

They wrestled desperately in the dirt, rolling over and over to the edge of the bank, grunting as they tried to hit each other, gouge each other's eyes, knee each other in the balls, gain any kind of advantage as they grappled furiously for control of the gun. Billy had been in plenty of fights, including a few in prison, where the penalty for losing could be death, or worse. But Brad had also been in some serious fights, and he was in better shape than Billy. He also had a higher IQ, which is why, when the opportunity presented itself, he had the presence of mind to bite down hard on Billy's hand, breaking the skin, forcing a scream from Billy as he involuntarily loosened his hold on the Glock.

Brad yanked the pistol from Billy's grasp, bashed Billy in the face with it and quickly rolled back and out of reach. He scrambled to his feet, gasping for breath. From behind him he heard Willa crying—he'd set her carrier down by the ATV trailer—but he didn't want to turn his back on Billy, who was on the ground at the edge of the bank, breathing hard, holding his bleeding hand.

Brad aimed the pistol at Billy's face and said, "Where is she?"

"Fuck you," said Billy.

Brad took a step closer, pointed the gun at Billy's knee.

"Where is she?" he said again.

"I said fuck you, asshole," said Billy, suddenly sounding more confident. Brad saw that Billy was looking past him, seeing something behind him.

Brad turned and saw what it was.

Duck was standing by the trailer.

In his right hand he was holding a gold bar.

In his left hand he was holding Willa's carrier. She was crying harder now.

"Put the gun down," Duck said. He raised the gold bar. "Or I kill the baby."

Brad aimed the pistol at Duck and said, "Put the baby down, or I kill you."

Duck smiled, moved the bar so it was right over Willa's face. "You sure, asshole? You sure you could hit me from there, before I smash the baby's face in? You sure you're that good with a gun?"

Brad said nothing, but Duck saw the doubt in his eyes.

Duck nodded, his smile broadening. "That's right," he said. "You ain't sure. I know your girlfriend wouldn't like it, her baby dead on account of you."

Brad still said nothing.

"I'll count to three," Duck said, clenching the bar, raising it a little. Willa was screaming now.

"One . . . ," said Duck. "Two . . ."

Brad dropped the gun.

"There you go," said Duck. "Now move away from—"

"Behind you!" shouted Billy.

Duck turned, instinctively raising the arm that held the bar, but not fast enough to protect himself as Jesse, a look of burning hatred distorting her battered face, burst from the bushes swinging a shovel with all her strength, as well as excellent form grooved into her neurons from years of softball. The metal head hit Duck full in the face with a loud *clang*. He grunted in pain and staggered backward, dropping the gold bar and the baby carrier, which landed upright, Willa screaming. Duck lunged toward Jesse, raising his hands to protect his face. Jesse countered by switching to an overhand swing, turning the shovel edgewise and bringing it down like an axe on top of Duck's head. Duck cried in pain and toppled sideways onto the grass, groaning, blood pouring from his nose and scalp, curling into a ball as he tried to protect himself from the shovel blows, which kept coming. Jesse was nowhere near done with the man who had threatened to kill her child.

Brad was halfway across the clearing toward them when he remembered the gun. He turned and ran back just as Billy, crawling toward the Glock, reached for it with his nonbitten hand. Brad stomped on the hand hard, felt bones crunch. Billy yelped in pain, rolling away. As Brad picked up the gun, Billy rose and stumbled toward the bushes, holding the broken hand with the bit hand. Brad, letting him go for now, turned back toward Jesse, who was standing over the curled-up form of Duck, hitting him with the shovel, again and again.

Brad reached her as she was raising the shovel to strike again. He put his arms around her, pulling her away. Duck lay motionless, his head covered with blood.

"It's OK," Brad said. "It's OK."

"I want to kill him," she said, sobbing.

"I know," he said, holding her tight. He felt her slump against him, then gently took the shovel from her shaking hands. She dropped to her knees next to the baby carrier, tears streaming from her face and dripping onto Willa as Jesse unclipped her and lifted her out.

"I'm sorry, baby," she sobbed, hugging Willa to her chest, rocking from side to side. "I'm so sorry, Willa. Mommy's so sorry." She looked up at Brad. Her face was a mess, streaked with dirt and tears, the right side swelling and turning purple, her right eye swollen almost shut.

"I'm sorry," she said.

"It's OK," he said.

"It's not OK," she said, turning back to Willa. "Nothing's OK." She rocked some more, gradually calming her baby and herself. Then she looked at Brad again and said, "How'd you get here?"

"Followed some guys," he said.

"These guys?" she said, nodding toward Duck.

"No. Two different guys, on ATVs. These guys shot 'em. Killed one." He pointed at the body floating in the water.

"Oh God," said Jesse. "He's dead?"

"Yup."

"Oh God," she said again.

"They shot the other one, too," said Brad. "But he got away." He stepped over to the trailer, looked down at the gold, then back at Jesse. "So that's what all this was about?"

Jesse, holding Willa, walked over and looked into the trailer. She stared at the gold for a few seconds, then back at the floating body.

"What did I get myself into?" she said, shaking her head. "I almost got my baby killed. And you . . . I got you into this, too. This is all my fault. I thought I could . . . Jesus, I was so *stupid*. I screwed everything up. I am so sorry."

"It's OK," said Brad. Then, after a pause: "Any idea who the gold belongs to?"

She shook her head. "None. Do you?"

"No," said Brad. "I mean, I heard stories, ever since I was a kid, old guys and Miccosukees talking about gold out here. But I always thought it was just stories." He looked at the gold again. "I guess it's not."

"I just found it out here one day," said Jesse. She nodded toward Duck. "These creeps were looking for it, too. They knew I knew where it was. That's why they were after me. They must've followed me here."

"What about the other guys?"

She shook her head again. "I have no idea who they are."

"Seems like they knew about the gold. They came out here with a trailer. They knew where to go."

"I don't know how they knew," said Jesse. "I never told anybody."

"What about your lawyer friend?"

"No," said Jesse. "He wanted to know, but I didn't tell him. I was supposed to call him when I . . ." She paused, frowning.

"What?" said Brad.

"That *scumbag*," said Jesse. "Erik. That slimy piece of *shit*."

"What?" said Brad.

"The iPhone!" said Jesse. She pulled it from her pocket, showed it to Brad. "He gave me this when I was in his office. He made a big point of how I should keep it with me when I came out here."

"Find my phone," said Brad.

Jesse nodded. "That *bastard*. I *trusted* him."

"Turn it off," said Brad. "They could still be tracking you."

Jesse turned off the phone, shoved it back in her pocket. "I'm gonna kill him."

"Listen," said Brad, "we need to get out of here, like, now."

"Shouldn't we call the police?" said Jesse.

"Technically, yes," he said. "But . . ."

"But what?"

"For one thing, there's a dead body floating out there."

"We had nothing to do with that."

"Yeah, but the police don't know that. They're gonna have questions." He pointed to Duck. "They're gonna have questions about him, too."

"He was going to kill Willa!"

"I know that. But they're still gonna have questions."

As if on cue, Duck moaned.

"He's not dead," said Jesse.

"Which is a shame, because he's the kind of scumbag who'll tell the cops he's the victim here, and you're the bad guy."

"But who'd believe him?"

Brad shook his head. "The way things are, he gets a lawyer, he tells everybody how bad you beat him, his face is all messed up . . . who knows what'll happen. You really want to find out?"

Jesse looked at the shovel. "Maybe I should finish him."

Brad shook his head. "Remind me never to piss you off."

"So you're saying we just leave?"

"Yeah. We leave, and we never come back here, ever."

"What about him?" she said, nodding toward Duck.

"What about him?"

"Shouldn't we tell somebody he's here?"

"Thirty seconds ago you wanted to kill him."

"I don't know what I want."

"Don't worry about this one," said Brad, pointing to Duck. "His friend's back there in the bushes somewhere. Let him deal with this scumbag. We need to go."

"OK," said Jesse.

Brad pointed to the ATV. "I'll drive. You and Willa can ride in the trailer."

Jesse hesitated. "So we're taking the gold?"

"Why not?" he said. "You found it. You wanted it, right?"

"I did. I thought I did. But it seems like all it does is make everything worse."

"OK, we'll figure out what to do with it later. But right now we really need to leave."

Jesse clipped Willa back into her carrier. Brad helped her climb into the trailer. She sat down, holding her baby, on top of the pile of gold. Brad started the ATV, nosed it slowly down into the swamp and drove through the shallow water.

He had reached the other bank and was maneuvering the ATV back up onto the footpath when Billy stumbled out from the bushes, where he'd been hiding. He looked over at Brad and Jesse, then went and crouched next to his brother.

"Duck," he said, shaking him by the shoulder. "Wake up."

No reaction. Billy shook Duck again, harder.

"You gotta wake up," he said. "Those fuckers're getting away with the gold."

Duck moaned and opened his eyes.

Chapter 52

The Python Challenge launch event was winding down. After the rocky start, it had gone smoothly, much to the relief of Frank and Jacky. Secretary Chastain and several other functionaries had delivered their remarks without further incident, after which Skeeter Toobs had opened his sack and revealed its occupant: Zelda, a pregnant fifteen-foot female Burmese python.

Zelda then participated, reluctantly, in a photo opportunity, with Skeeter gripping her head while the rest of Zelda was held, in order, by the secretary of the interior, the superintendent of Everglades National Park, the commissioner of the Florida Fish and Wildlife Conservation Commission and, down at Zelda's tail, the chairman of the South Florida Water Management District, all of these officials trying, with varying degrees of success, to appear as though holding a large unhappy snake was a totally natural and fun thing to do.

The event had attracted a growing crowd of members of the actual public. These were mostly Everglades Melon Monster fans who'd been on their way to, or coming back from, Bortle Brothers Bait & Beer when they saw the TV satellite trucks just off the highway. They stopped because they thought there might be breaking monster news; they stayed because there were cameras, and some supposedly important politicians, and—best of all, for social media purposes—an authentic swamp redneck with a snake AND a pig.

Thus a decent-sized audience was on hand for the final part of the Python Challenge event, which was a press Q & A with the secretary of the interior and Skeeter, who had Zelda draped around his neck and Buddy the emotional support boar snuffling around his feet. Most of

244 • Dave Barry

the questions were being asked by Anthony Evander Cornwall of the *New York Times*, and all of those involved climate change. The premise of these questions was that before long the entire state of Florida was going to be underwater, and that Florida pretty much deserved it.

Chastain handled the Cornwall interrogation with the smooth professionalism of the experienced, principle-free politician, emitting a dense, billowing cloud of words suggesting, without explicitly saying it, that he either was or was not deeply concerned about climate change, and as such was taking all necessary steps.

Cornwall eventually gave up on Chastain and turned his attention to Skeeter.

"Mr. Toobs," he said, "in your view, how has the python infestation been exacerbated by global climate change?"

Skeeter frowned thoughtfully for a moment, then said, "I think it's the pythons fucking."

This got a big laugh from everyone except Anthony Evander Cornwall. He was about to ask a follow-up question when Frank, prompted by a look from Chastain, stepped forward and said, "OK, folks, we're gonna have to wrap it up here. The secretary needs to get back to work."

Frank, Jacky and the two Park Police officers began trying to usher Chastain back to the Lincoln Navigator. But they managed only a few steps before they were surrounded by the crowd. Chastain, reluctantly, began posing for selfies, which only attracted more people to the clot surrounding him. Chastain hated selfies and the idiots who wanted him to pose for them, but he believed they were good for his image as a regular guy who enjoyed hanging around with the common person. So he stood there, grinning outwardly, seething inwardly.

A few yards away, Skeeter had returned Zelda the python to her snake sack and was trying to figure out how to get his airboat back into the water. Sticking close by Skeeter was Buddy the emotional support boar, who was acting jittery. Buddy had good reason. He had detected something very disturbing, to a swamp creature: A dozen yards away, just breaking the surface of the dark murky water, were two large eyeballs, each under a scaly green dome.

No doubt somebody in the crowd would soon have noticed the lurking eyeballs, but suddenly there was an exciting new distraction. A young woman in the crowd spotted it first: Emerging from the swamp, on the barely-there footpath threading through the sawgrass, were two figures, one shirtless, running toward the clearing. The woman aimed her phone at them and zoomed in on the screen image.

"Hey!" she shouted. "It's the guys from the monster video!"

Heads turned, and there were more shouts as people recognized the Internet celebrities Ken and Slater. Dozens of phones pointed their way as they approached the crowd.

Chastain, turning to Frank and Jacky, said, "Who the hell is that?"

"No idea," said Frank.

Jacky said, "I think it's those guys from the Everglades Melon Monster video."

"The Everglades what?" said Chastain.

"Melon Monster," said Jacky. "It's a social media thing. A fad. It's stupid, but it's gotten pretty big."

It was getting bigger as they spoke. Word was spreading through the Melon Monster community at the speed of TikTok: *Something was happening right now in the swamp.* Immediately the Bortle Brothers parking lot began to empty as a stream of vehicles, a nerdcade, poured onto the highway and raced the few miles to the site of the Python Challenge event. They turned into the little dirt access road and quickly filled it up, forcing the overflow vehicles to park haphazardly along the highway, which soon swarmed with people jumping out of their cars and running toward the action. Traffic began to back up as drivers slowed to gawk; in minutes the clog of cars and the swarm of running people had stopped traffic altogether. The Tamiami Trail was now completely blocked. And more cars, many more, were on the way.

Meanwhile Ken and Slater, panting hard, reached the clearing and were quickly surrounded by monster fans. Slater was relieved; he hadn't really known why they were running from Pinky in the first place, but he figured he was safe now, with all these people around. He began posing and flexing, a Glades Man graciously accepting the adoration of his public.

Ken, who knew exactly what he was running from, was not reassured. He tried to smile, but he kept looking back toward the swamp as the fans thronged around him and Slater.

Meanwhile Secretary Chastain continued to pose for selfies, but after a few minutes it became clear, as the new arrivals rushed past him, that he was not the center of attention. He decided he wanted out of there. He turned to the two Park Police officers, hovering nearby, and said, "Let's go."

The senior officer looked uncomfortable. "Sir," he said, "there's a problem."

"What?" said Chastain.

"We can't get out right now," said the officer. He pointed in the direction of the Lincoln Navigator. "The road's blocked. There's cars parked all over the place, all the way out to the highway. We called the Florida Highway Patrol, and they're sending some—"

"I'm not waiting for the Florida Highway Patrol," said Chastain. "I want those cars out of here now. Order them to move."

The junior Park Police officer, a brave man, spoke up. "Sir, the thing is, right now there's nobody in the cars that we could ask to move." He gestured at the crowd. "They're somewhere in this mess."

"Then *find* them," said Chastain.

The officers looked at each other for a moment, then turned and plunged into the crowd, which now numbered in the hundreds, with more arriving every minute.

As the two officers departed on their clearly impossible errand, Chastain turned to Frank. He was smiling, because somebody in the crowd could have been recording video. He put a hand on Frank's shoulder in a fatherly manner.

"This is completely fucking unacceptable," he said.

"Yes, sir," said Frank.

"This whole fucking mess has been a fucking disaster from start to finish."

"Yes, sir," said Frank.

"I can't have this level of staff incompetence."

"No, sir," said Frank.

Chastain, still smiling hugely, the Good-Guy Boss just hanging out with his staff, turned to Jacky.

"That goes for you, too," he said.

"Sir," said Frank, "I'm the one who's responsible for—"

"Shut the fuck up," said Chastain, still looking at Jacky. "Don't think I've forgotten about that fucking pig."

"No, sir," said Jacky.

"These fucking pants are ruined."

"Yes, sir," said Jacky.

"That's coming out of your fucking salary."

"Yes, sir," said Jacky.

"When we get back to Washington, if we ever get back to Washington, I am going to formally reevaluate both of you, your pathetic performance here. You understand what I'm saying?"

They both nodded.

"I cannot have this level of incompetence on my staff."

They both nodded. Chastain took his fatherly hand off Frank's shoulder and looked around at the crowd, which was still growing. The Park Police officers were not visible. Chastain looked back at Frank and said, "Get me a helicopter."

"Sir," said Frank, "I don't know if a helicopter could land with all these—"

"GET ME A FUCKING HELICOPTER RIGHT FUCKING NOW," said Chastain, starting to lose it.

"Yes, sir," said Frank, pulling out his phone, although he had no earthly idea who he was supposed to call to summon a helicopter.

A roar went up from the crowd, followed by a surge toward the edge of the clearing as the Melon Monster fans caught sight of more figures appearing on the footpath, emerging, one by one, from the sawgrass.

The first figure was Kark, walking briskly, carrying his camera but no longer recording, glancing back frequently.

The second figure was Stu, looking hot and harried, dragging the third figure by the arm.

The third figure was Phil, still wearing the head.

The sight of Phil sent the crowd into a frenzy of speculation—was *that* the Melon Monster? Some porky guy wearing a weird head and a Duke sweatshirt? Was the whole Melon Monster thing a fake? Or were these guys making some kind of parody video? *What was going on?*

And then a fourth figure appeared, the hulking, sweating form of Pinky, his wide, flat face a mask of dead-eyed determination. He moved slowly, laboriously, swinging his massive body sumolike to advance each plodding, painful step.

The sight of him—this huge, scary, pissed-off dude—sent the monster fans to a new level of frenzied speculation. Who was he? Was he chasing the video guys? If not, what was he doing? Did *he* have something to do with the Melon Monster?

The crowd was thick along the water's edge as people pushed forward to get a better view of the strange procession heading toward them.

In the heart of that crowd stood Ken. He'd thought about running but decided his best bet was to stay hidden in the mob, at least for now. He shrunk back, peering through the forest of upraised phones, watching Pinky's slow, dogged advance.

A few feet away stood Channel 8 PeoplePower News reporter Patsy Hartmann and cameraman Bruce Morris.

"Are you getting this?" Patsy asked, nodding toward the odd procession emerging from the sawgrass.

"I am," said Bruce, watching his viewfinder. "Whatever it is."

"Should I maybe call the station?"

"What're you gonna tell them?"

"I dunno," said Patsy, looking around at the crowd. "But this seems to be getting kind of—"

She was interrupted by a chirp from her phone. She looked at the screen, made a face and said, "Jennifer." She held the phone to her ear. "Hello? Yeah, we're still here . . . Yeah. Right. Yeah. Yeah. OK." She ended the call, looked at Bruce.

"What?" he said.

"So apparently the Tamiami Trail is totally closed."

"By this?"

"Yup. Big, big mess out there. Caused by this. They want us to go live."

"OK."

"I don't know what the hell to say. I mean, what's going on here? Is this about the Python Challenge? Is it about the monster thing? Or something else? What am I gonna say, Bruce?"

Bruce shrugged. "Florida," he said. "Just say it's Florida."

Chapter 53

Brad nosed the ATV along the path, trying to avoid ruts, looking back every few seconds to make sure Jesse and Willa were OK in the jouncing trailer. A few times he shouted, "You OK?" Each time Jesse answered with a thumbs-up, although she looked pretty bad, her face swollen and bruised. Willa was crying hard.

Brad's plan was to drive the ATV back to the pickup. He wasn't sure what Jesse wanted to do about the gold. He figured he could shift it to the truck if she decided to hang on to it. He'd worry about that later. For now he wanted to get them as far as possible from the dead body and the two scumbags.

They were approaching the fork where their path was joined, from the left, by the lesser-used path—the one that veered off toward the highway; the one that had been taken a little while earlier by the video crew, followed by Pinky. Brad intended to go straight here, staying on the main path leading to where he'd left the truck.

He had almost reached the fork when he saw it.

The other ATV. With the big man driving. He was coming straight at them, fast. It looked to Brad like he was planning to ram them.

"Hang on!" he yelled back to Jesse. He yanked the ATV into a sharp left-hand turn, onto the smaller path. For a second he thought the trailer was going to tip over; he felt the heavy gold cargo shift, dragging the rear of the ATV with it, spinning it almost sideways. He looked back and saw Jesse struggling to stay upright, gripping the side of the trailer with one hand and Willa's carrier with the other. He wrestled the skidding ATV onto the new path, got it straightened out and gunned it.

He took another look back.

The other ATV was right behind him, the big man grimacing, obviously in pain, but coming hard.

* * *

Tenklo was driving one-handed. His left arm was almost useless, the oozing bullet wound in his shoulder radiating searing spasms of pain each time the ATV hit a bump. But he hung on, grimly twisting the throttle, motivated by an emotion more powerful than the agony racking his body, which was fear of disappointing his boss, Kristov Berliuz.

After fleeing the gunfire, Tenklo had raced about a quarter mile down the path before stopping to call Berliuz. Speaking in the language of their homeland, he reported that they'd been ambushed, and he'd been wounded, and Kelmit might be dead.

Berliuz had expressed no concern about either of his men.

"Who ambushed you?" he said.

"Two men. I don't know them."

"And the gold?"

"I don't know," said Tenklo. "We didn't get close."

"And the woman?"

Tenklo looked at the iPad. "She was there," he said. "But now the icon is gone."

"Where are you?"

"Not far."

"Go back," said Berliuz. "Do not let them leave. I will send Lokias and Premi. Keep your phone on so they can track you."

Tenklo didn't want to go back; he wanted to get out of there and do something about his throbbing, bleeding shoulder. He felt dizzy and weak; he was unarmed, having dropped his weapon into the swamp. But he knew better than to tell any of this to Berliuz.

"Yes," he said.

"Do not let them leave," repeated Berliuz, ending the call.

Tenklo had just one-handedly wrestled the ATV into a U-turn when he heard the other ATV coming toward him. The driver was a man, but not one of the men who had shot at him; riding in the trailer was a woman, presumably the woman Tenklo had been tracking.

Whoever they were, Tenklo decided he had to stop them, so he gunned the ATV forward. When the other driver swerved onto the side path, Tenklo swerved after him. He wanted to call Berliuz, but with only one working arm he couldn't call and drive at the same time. For now all he could do was follow the man and the woman, and find some way to stop them.

Chapter 54

The Python Challenge launch event was now the epicenter of a scene of utter chaos. The traffic jam on the Tamiami Trail stretched for miles. A dozen harried Florida Highway Patrol troopers were doing their best to unjam it, but they were overwhelmed by the number of cars, mostly out of Miami, filled with people, mostly young, who drove as far as they could, then, blocked by the mass of immobile vehicles, parked wherever and started running toward this . . . this *thing* that was happening out in the swamp.

Nobody knew exactly what the thing was, or if it was in fact many things. Social media was exploding with images and video—of Ken and the shirtless Slater (especially the shirtless Slater); of Skeeter with Buddy the boar and Zelda the snake; of secretary of the interior and presumed presidential aspirant Whitt Chastain getting peed on by a giant pig; of Phil in his weird, battered head; of the menacing figure of Pinky; of excited Melon Monster fans running alongside an endless line of cars. These images were instantly sucked into the vast, incomprehensibly complex content vortex that is TikTok, which immediately spewed them back out mixed, mashed, memed and mutated into a myriad of parodies, duets, dances, songs, riffs, rants, challenges, these new creations colliding and interacting with each other in a fission reaction that spewed out still more creations, and more, and more. Within minutes there was virtually no phone-owning young person in America who was not aware that something huge was happening out there in the middle of the Florida swamp, something too big to be random—a concert maybe (there were rumors of celebrity sightings, including DJ Marshmello) or something even bigger, some kind of reveal of the true

254 • Dave Barry

story behind the Everglades Melon Monster. Or something even bigger than that, like some Bitcoin thing, or a new Kardashian fragrance. After all, a freaking *cabinet member* was there.

Whatever it was, it was big. Everyone could see that.

The people who were actually in it, who were part of the dense, non-virtual crowd now overflowing the clearing, were as confused as everyone else; nobody knew what was going on more than a few feet away. The mob swirled and surged this way and that, phones held aloft, everybody trying to see whatever it was that everybody else was trying to see.

A large crowd had formed around Phil, who had been led into the clearing by Stu. Phil was no longer singing, having completed the *Grease* soundtrack, but he was still very high. He had briefly lifted off his monster head, but, seeing the mass of people aiming their phones at him, he immediately put the head back on. Nevertheless in the few moments his face was visible, he was recognized.

"It's the guy from the YouTube video!" shouted a young man. "Who got hit in the balls by the little girl! And fell in the cake!"

Instantly word went out worldwide that Golf Club to the Balls Guy was here, wearing a weird, funky head. Speculation raged about what it meant, with the predominant theory being that it was a pathetic attempt by GCTTB Guy, having already had his fifteen minutes of fame, to cash in on the celebrity of the real Melon Monster. The crowd around Phil and Stu badgered them with questions, but Phil remained cloistered inside the head, and Stu would say only that the two of them were "tourists."

Another part of the crowd was warily watching Pinky, who was lumbering around the clearing, his massive head turning slowly from side to side, scanning the faces around him. People quickly moved out of his path, as they would avoid an irate rhinoceros. Nobody asked Pinky any questions.

Pinky's quarry, Ken, was watching the big man from behind, lurking inside the mass of gawkers, trying to decide whether he should make a run for it or remain hidden in the crowd.

Meanwhile at the edge of the clearing, Skeeter Toobs, with the help of some young men, was dragging his airboat back to the water. He still had Zelda the python in her sack and Buddy the boar on his rope.

Buddy was increasingly skittish. The two big eyeballs poking out of the murk were now a dozen feet closer to shore. As yet they had not been noticed by any of the excited, distracted humans. But Buddy was acutely aware of them. Buddy was very close to freaking out.

A few yards away, so was the secretary of the interior.

"Where is my fucking helicopter?" Chastain was asking Frank, for the fifth time. He was still smiling, so that onlookers wouldn't know he was furious. But the smile was wearing thin.

Frank, holding a phone to his ear, said, "Sir, I'm talking to the Florida Highway Patrol, and they're saying they can't land a chopper in here. It's just too dangerous, all these people . . ."

"Then what am I supposed to do?"

"They're saying if we can get back to the highway, they can maybe get a trooper to pick you up."

"I'm supposed to walk through this?" Chastain gestured at the crowd.

"I'm afraid so," said Frank.

Chastain was about to say something unpleasant when Skeeter, still holding Zelda's sack and towing Buddy, walked up.

"You folks need a ride outta here?" he asked. "I got the airboat back in the water."

"No," said Chastain. "And keep the pig away from me."

As Chastain spoke, Buddy was moving behind him, pressing close to his legs. But this time it wasn't because Buddy intended to pee on Chastain. This time Buddy was trying to hide.

What happened next was captured not only by dozens of onlookers' phones, but also by Channel 8 PeoplePower News cameraman Bruce Morris, who happened to be standing in exactly the right spot to shoot the video that would soon be seen, in hi-def and slo-mo, by many millions of people.

It began with a scream, as a young woman standing at the water's edge was the first person to spot the gator, a big fella, fourteen-footer, as it lunged out of the water and sprinted—oh yes, gators can sprint—directly toward Chastain.

The gator was not after Chastain. It had seen a few humans in its day, but it had never tasted one. No, the gator was after Buddy. Over the years it had eaten plenty of critters along the lines of Buddy. Buddy definitely qualified as gator chow.

It happened fast, but in hi-def slo-mo the sequence was clear:

Alerted by the scream, everyone looked toward the gator. Secretary Chastain saw this terrifying thing coming right at him, very fast, its massive jaws opening to reveal two long, ugly rows of gnarly, jagged teeth. Chastain assumed—who could blame him?—that the gator was coming for him. Chastain wanted to protect himself. It was a natural instinct.

So without thinking he grabbed the thing that was closest at hand, and he threw it at the advancing gator.

The thing closest at hand was Jacky.

Chastain was a strong and fit man—he benched 180—and Jacky was a slight woman, caught completely off guard. She was literally lifted off her feet and tossed through the air, landing, stunned, on her back, no more than a yard from the gator's gaping jaws. The gator was not going for her, but she was right in its path; it seemed certain that she was going to get chomped.

And she surely would have been, if not for the astonishingly quick, decisive action of an unlikely hero.

Frank.

He launched himself before Jacky hit the ground, diving Superman-style, his arms outstretched, glasses flying off his face, phone flying from his hands. He reached Jacky a nanosecond before the gator did, getting his arms around her and rolling sideways hard, taking them both out of the way just as the jaws slammed shut, the two of them tumbling together for two full revolutions, winding up several feet away with Jacky on top, looking down at Frank, while he looked up at her, the two of them barely comprehending what had just happened.

Now the air was filled with screams and shouts. The gator was still charging toward Chastain, who lurched back, tripping over Buddy and emitting a distinctly un-Leadership-like shriek as he fell backward, arms flailing. Now he and Buddy were both on the ground, and the gator was upon them, jaws opening again. Chastain, attempting to shield himself, grabbed Buddy the way a drowning man would grab a life preserver, his face contorted by a look of terror that contracted into a violent flinch at the sudden *BANG!* from two feet away as the .357 Magnum revolver that had suddenly appeared in Skeeter's hand fired a bullet into the gator's skull, dead center, a few inches behind the eyes, perfect placement for an instant kill. The gator abruptly collapsed, lifeless. Skeeter calmly lifted his tank top and holstered his gun. He had done this before.

"You OK?" he said to Chastain.

Chastain did not respond. He remained lying on the ground, curled fetally, still clinging to Buddy, who had also been traumatized and who seemed to feel comforted by Chastain's embrace.

A few feet away, Jacky and Frank were still in each other's arms, looking into each other's eyes.

"Thank you," said Jacky.

"I love you," said Frank.

"I love you, too," said Jacky.

Meanwhile all around them panic was spreading, surging outward through the crowd, powered by screams and shouts, gaining intensity as the news spread and mutated—*There's a giant alligator attacking people! There's an active shooter! Some politician was shot! It might be the secretary of state!*

In moments the mob had gone batshit crazy, people running in all directions, some trying to get away from the threat, some trying to get closer, nobody sure what or where the threat was. People were being knocked down, trampled, shoved into the water. It was a maelstrom of panic, a soccer riot on steroids.

It was about to get crazier.

* * *

Brad heard the crowd before he saw it, the screams coming from up ahead audible over the roar of the ATV engine. He was driving as fast as he dared, but the footpath was rough, and he was towing a heavy, jouncing trailer containing Jesse and her baby and a shitload of gold.

He glanced back, as he had every few seconds since the chase began. Jesse was still hanging on grimly, her left arm wrapped around her screaming baby, her right hand gripping the side of the trailer.

Less than ten feet behind her was the pursuing ATV, driven by Tenklo, his face pale and pain-twisted but determined, his shirt drenched in blood. He had accelerated a few times, bumping the trailer, trying to knock it off course or tip it over. So far Brad had been able to regain control. So far.

He looked forward again just as the ATV emerged from the tall sawgrass, and saw the source of the screams: a huge crowd overflowing the clearing. He frantically scanned the wall of people ahead, but he saw no opening, no way through. He felt a jolt as the pursuing ATV rammed the trailer again.

"OUT OF THE WAY!" he shouted as he reached the edge of the crowd. "GET OUT OF THE WAY!" The people immediately in front of him skittered out of the ATV's path, but behind them were more people, and more. Brad saw that unless he was willing to kill somebody, he was going to have to slow way down. He eased up on the throttle and immediately felt another jolt, a harder one. And then another, this one knocking the trailer almost sideways.

They were in the crowd now, people getting out of their way but not fast enough. Another big jolt, and now, with Brad fighting for control, Tenklo was coming up along the right side, passing the trailer, and Brad realized he was planning to ram his ATV into Brad's.

As Tenklo pulled alongside, Brad looked to his left, but there was nowhere to go without hitting people. Tenklo cranked the throttle and swerved toward Brad. Brad winced, bracing for the collision.

It didn't come. The instant before the two ATVs met, Tenklo swerved violently away, ducking as he did to avoid the gold bar sailing past his head, missing by a few inches. Brad whipped his head around and saw that Jesse, still holding tight to Willa with her left arm, was leaning down to pick up another bar, and Brad realized what was happening.

She's throwing the gold at him.

Tenklo was coming back their way, his eyes flicking from Brad to Jesse and back. Seeing that Jesse was still bent over, he swerved toward them again, apparently assuming he had enough time to ram them before she could launch again.

This assumption proved to be incorrect. Jesse had been captain of her high school girls' softball team and an all-county shortstop. She had turned many a double play. She had a quick and accurate release.

The second bar caught Tenklo directly in the forehead. It wasn't enough to kill him, but it was more than enough to stun him, causing him to lose control and tumble off the ATV, landing on the dirt with a hard *WHUMP*.

Brad kept going, dodging the people in his path. He slowed for a moment to look back. He saw the other ATV, now stopped, with Tenklo lying on the ground behind it. A few feet away a skinny bearded man was holding a gold bar over his head and yelling something; nearby two more men were fighting over the other bar. People were shouting and running toward them.

Brad shifted his glance for a second to Jesse. She gave him what passed, on her battered face, for a smile. He smiled back, then turned and resumed dodging people, weaving left and right, determined to keep moving, to not get stuck in the seemingly endless sea of people.

"BRAD!"

Brad turned his head toward the sound, saw Ken pushing frantically toward him through the mob, a desperate look on his face. A second later Brad saw the reason for his brother's terror: Several yards behind him, in grim pursuit, was Pinky. And Pinky was making better progress, because he was literally picking up the people in his path and throwing them out of the way.

"BRAD, WAIT!" yelled Ken, after glancing back over his shoulder.

Brad swerved right. This enabled Ken to get close enough to grab the trailer and clamber into it, next to Jesse and Willa. But it also brought them closer to Pinky, who had summoned up a burst of speed and was almost on them.

Brad looked back, caught Jesse's eye, and nodded toward Pinky.

"THROW ONE TO HIM," he yelled.

Jesse understood instantly, reaching down for another bar. *God bless this woman*, thought Brad. Jesse heaved the bar to Pinky, who was surprised but caught it cleanly, an athlete's reflexes. He stopped, looked at the bar, frowned, then started lumbering after the ATV again.

"ANOTHER ONE," shouted Brad.

Jesse tossed Pinky a second bar. He caught it one-handed, then, looking at Brad, held up four fingers.

"TWO MORE," shouted Brad.

Jesse tossed two more. Pinky caught the first, then lurched forward and picked up the second, which had landed in the dirt. He straightened up, nodded at Brad, then turned and started lumbering away through the crowd, which was now converging alarmingly on the ATV.

"THROW OUT SOME MORE," said Brad, gunning the throttle and swerving hard, narrowly missing a clot of people.

Behind him Jesse tossed out a bar, then another, then another, then another, then three more. A chorus of shouts arose behind the ATV. Brad saw an opening in the crowd ahead and shot forward, picking up speed, finding a lane that took him around the outside of the clearing. Ahead he could see the dirt road leading out to the highway. It was clogged with cars, but there was room for the ATV to blast through the tall weeds on the side and reach the highway.

He glanced back. Everyone in the crowd seemed to be surging toward the area where Jesse had flung out the bars. He looked ahead again, toward the highway, the way out of this lunacy.

Behind him, in the jouncing trailer, Ken was staring down at the gold, then at Jesse, then down at the gold again, then at Jesse again.

Finally, he said, "Is this gold?"

Jesse nodded.

Ken looked at the gold again and said, "Holy fuck."

Jesse said nothing.

"It's gold," said Ken.

"Yes, it is," said Jesse.

"This is gold."

"Correct."

"We're sitting on a pile of gold."

"Yes, we are."

"Where did it . . . I mean, how did it . . . I mean, what the fuck?"

"Not now," said Jesse, tending to the squalling Willa.

Ken nodded, then looked down.

"We're sitting on a pile of gold," he said again.

* * *

At the other end of the clearing, by the water's edge, Frank and Jacky were climbing into Skeeter's airboat. They had accepted his offer to give them a lift out of the insanity. Already in the boat was Buddy the boar, who had finally been pried from the arms of Interior Secretary Chastain.

The secretary was standing nearby, brushing the dirt off his sport coat and pants, trying to regain his dignity while the two Park Police officers shielded him from the crowd as best they could. Chastain was not making eye contact with Jacky or Frank. Nor was he asking why they were leaving. He knew why they were leaving.

As Skeeter prepared to shove off in the airboat, he remembered Zelda the python. He'd dropped her sack when he pulled his gun to shoot the gator. He scanned the ground, saw the sack, went over and picked it up.

The sack was empty. During the excitement Zelda had escaped and made her way back into the swamp, where, in a week or so, she would lay somewhere between fifty and one hundred Burmese python eggs, thereby pretty much negating whatever ecological benefits would accrue from the Python Challenge—which, although few would remember it, was the reason for this gathering in the first place.

Chapter 55

Kim Miklos: *Good evening, I'm Kim Miklos.*

Michael Tescotti: *And I'm Michael Tescotti. We're interrupting our regular programming to bring you a live report on a major story that's happening right now out in the Everglades. The aerial shot you're seeing right now is from the Channel 8 PeoplePower News Chopper, showing Route 41, the Tamiami Trail, which is completely blocked by a huge crowd of people about fifty miles west of Miami.*

Kim Miklos: *We go now to PeoplePower News's own Patsy Hartmann, who has been on the ground out there all day. Patsy, can you tell us what's going on?*

Patsy Hartmann: *Kim, Michael, I've been covering South Florida for over twenty years, and I can honestly say I've never seen anything like this. As you can see behind me, there's still a huge crowd here. I understand FHP is out here in force trying to clear the Tamiami Trail and get people to go home, but with night falling it's still a complete mess.*

Michael Tescotti: *Patsy, can you give us some kind of overview of what happened out there today? Because the station has been flooded with calls, and we're getting all kinds of wild rumors, including some really crazy stuff on social media.*

Patsy Hartmann: *Well, to be honest I'm still a little confused myself. I think the best way to understand this is if I take you through the events of the day, with the help of some video clips shot by my cameraman, Bruce Morris. It started with a press conference to launch the Python Challenge, which was fairly routine until this happened.*

Michael Tescotti: *Whoa! Is that an airboat?*

Patsy Hartmann: *Yes. It was driven by a man named DeWayne Toobs, who won the challenge last year. He apparently lost control of the boat, and as you can see it went right into the press conference being held by Secretary of the Interior Whitt Chastain. It was a pretty scary moment, but fortunately nobody was hurt.*

Kim Miklos: *Patsy, we've gotten many reports saying the secretary was attacked by an alligator. So you're saying it was actually an airboat?*

Patsy Hartmann: *No, it's true, the secretary was attacked by an alligator.*

Kim Miklos: *OK, so there WAS an alligator?*

Patsy Hartmann: *Right, but that came after the airboat. And the boar.*

Michael Tescotti: *The boar? Like a pig?*

Patsy Hartmann: *Right, a wild boar. It arrived on the airboat.*

Kim Miklos: *So wait, are you saying a wild boar attacked the interior secretary?*

Patsy Hartmann: *Not attacked, exactly. It . . . OK, here's the clip.*

Kim Miklos: *Oh my gosh.*

Michael Tescotti: *Is the boar . . . is that the secretary?*

Patsy Hartmann: *Yes. Those are the secretary's khakis.*

Kim Miklos (laughing): *That's disgusting.*

Michael Tescotti (laughing): *It is.*

Kim Miklos: *OK, but I'm still confused. When did the alligator show up?*

Patsy Hartmann: *That was later. Before that happened—and this is when it started to get weird—these men were coming out of the swamp. That's when the really big crowds started showing up, because some of these are the same men who were in the Everglades Melon Monster video.*

Michael Tescotti: *And just so our viewers know, the Everglades Melon Monster is . . .*

Patsy Hartmann: *It's this alleged mythical creature out in the Everglades. It's huge on social media.*

Kim Miklos: *I understand from my daughter that Lemons Rockwell did a TikTok video about it.*

Patsy Hartmann: *Who?*

Kim Miklos: *Lemons Rockwell, the DJ.*

Patsy Hartmann: *Right, there's been many, many social media videos. It's everywhere. It's super viral. So all these monster fans were already out in the Everglades, and when word got around that the men who were in the original Melon Monster video showed up, all these people swarmed to this location.*

Kim Miklos: *Did these monster guys have anything to do with the press conference?*

Patsy Hartmann: *I don't think so, but I honestly don't know.*

Michael Tescotti: *What's that thing that man is wearing on his head?*

Patsy Hartmann: *I don't know that, either. I was trying to get some answers when the alligator attacked. We're going to show you this video in slow motion, and I want to warn our viewers that it's pretty graphic. OK, here you see the interior secretary is talking with two of his press aides, and all of a sudden this very large alligator came running out of the water.*

Kim Miklos: *Oh my God.*

Patsy Hartmann: *Yes. So watch . . .*

Kim Miklos: *Oh. My. God.*

Patsy Hartmann: *Yes.*

Kim Miklos: *OH MY GOD.*

Patsy Hartmann: *Yes.*

Michael Tescotti: *So the young woman...*

Patsy Hartmann: *She's on Secretary Chastain's press staff.*

Kim Miklos: *And she's OK?*

Patsy Hartmann: *Everyone was OK. Except the alligator.*

Michael Tescotti: *Patsy, the boar that Chastain is hugging there, is that the same one that...*

Patsy Hartmann: *The one that relieved itself on him. Yes.*

Michael Tescotti: *Wow. That's... that's quite an image.*

Patsy Hartmann: *Yes.*

Kim Miklos: *OK, Patsy, so if I understand this, basically what you're saying happened out there was this press conference started to get out of hand when these Melon Monster people showed up, and then there was this alligator attack? Is that basically what happened? Because we've been hearing all these crazy rumors...*

Michael Tescotti: *Right, like people are saying they were finding gold out there.*

Patsy Hartmann: *No, that's true.*

Michael Tescotti: *What?*

Patsy Hartmann: *There was gold.*

Michael Tescotti: *There was actual gold?*

Patsy Hartmann: *It appears that there was. Gold bars. We don't have great video on this, because the crowd was ... I mean, at this point it was basically a riot. But, OK, in this video you can see that man waving around what appears to be a gold bar. And here's some people fighting over gold bars on the ground.*

Kim Miklos: *Where did the gold come from?*

Patsy Hartmann: *I've been trying to find that out, but there's a lot of confusion about this. Supposedly people saw somebody throwing bars of gold out of an ATV. People are saying somebody must have located this legendary lost treasure from the Civil War that is supposedly in the*

Everglades. Some people told me they saw a large man walking around carrying a bunch of gold bars. There's all kinds of rumors, but I can't verify any of this because we couldn't get close to where it was happening. Like I said, it was basically a riot, and the people who managed to get hold of the gold bars all took off. But as far as I can tell, there was definitely gold. People are still showing up here because they heard about the gold.

Michael Tescotti: *Do you have any idea why anybody would be throwing gold bars out of an ATV?*

Patsy Hartmann: *I do not.*

Kim Miklos: *OK, I've just been handed this . . . We have a statement from the office of the secretary of the interior, concerning the video we showed a few moments ago.*

Patsy Hartmann: *Really? That was fast.*

Kim Miklos: *Right, it's just a brief statement. It says the video we showed was—and this is a quote—"taken out of context."*

Patsy Hartmann: *Excuse me, it was what?*

Kim Miklos: *Taken out of context.*

Patsy Hartmann: *Taken out of context? Seriously?*

Michael Tescotti: *Well, we're just reading the statement.*

Patsy Hartmann: *I know, but for God's sake, why are we even repeating this ridiculous cr—*

Kim Miklos: *Patsy, it's just a—*

Patsy Hartmann: *WHAT context? You SAW it! The secretary of the interior threw a woman at an alligator! What fucking context do you need for THAT?*

Michael Tescotti: *OK, we're . . . Apparently, we lost our feed from Patsy.*

Kim Miklos: *She's had a very long day out there.*

* * *

Brad turned off the TV and looked at Jesse. "Did you hear what that reporter said, at the end there?"

Jesse nodded. "The f-bomb."

"That's gotta hurt her career."

"Not as much as that video's gonna hurt that politician's career."

Brad smiled. "Yeah, that was not a good look."

They were back in the little house behind Bortle Brothers. Brad had driven the ATV on an off-road route to the store. When they arrived night was falling and the parking lot was empty, all the monster fans having joined the mob down the road.

Jesse was sitting cross-legged on the living room sofa, nursing Willa, a towel draped across her and her baby. The side of Jesse's face was still swollen and had turned an ugly purple.

"So," she said, "I guess the word is out, about the gold."

"At least they didn't show any video of us," said Brad.

"But a lot of people saw us."

"Yeah."

"What'd you do with the ATV?" she said.

"It's out in back, under a tarp."

"People will be looking for it," she said. "That big guy who was after us. And all those idiots back there. And everybody who watched the TV news. They're all gonna be looking for the gold."

"Yup."

"What about your brother?"

"What about him?"

"I mean, he knows about it, and he doesn't seem too trustworthy, no offense."

"Don't worry about Ken. He can be an idiot, but he's not gonna give us away. For one thing, he's my brother. For another thing, I told him I'd kill him."

Jesse smiled, then grimaced at the pain of smiling.

"You want some more aspirin?" Brad asked.

"Maybe in a little while," she said. "So where's your brother now?"

"He went back to your cabin, to get the truck and connect with the rest of the crew. He's all excited about the Melon Monster."

"Still?"

"More than ever." Brad waved at the TV. "He thinks all this is great publicity. Thinks he's gonna get rich."

"So he doesn't know about the men who're after the gold."

"No. He knew that one guy, Pinky, the big guy you threw the bars to. Ken owed him money. But he thinks it's over now. He doesn't know about the other stuff, the bad guys."

Jesse was quiet for a few seconds, then said, "I'm really sorry."

"About what?"

"About getting you into all this. I know I keep apologizing to you, but I mean it. I'm really, really sorry."

"It's OK."

"You keep saying that, but it's *not* OK. It's bad, and it keeps getting worse, and it's totally my fault. You had *nothing* to do with this, any of it, and you could . . . I mean you *should* just tell me to . . ." She looked away, tears streaming down her face, dripping onto the towel. "I'm sorry," she said, her voice choked. "I'm not trying for pity here, I swear."

Brad went over to the sofa, sat down next to her. Tentatively, very tentatively, he put a hand on her shoulder.

"Jesse, listen to me," he said.

She looked at him. Her face, in addition to being swollen, was now beet red where it wasn't purple, her eyes puffy and bloodshot.

"What?" she said.

What Brad intended to say here was along the lines of: *Until a few days ago, my life was boring and pointless. And then I met you. And since then I have not been bored for one single second. I'm not sure what the point of all this is, but it's a whole lot better than Candy Crush, and I really want to stick around and see how it comes out. I know you think I'm just another guy who's after you for your looks, but I actually think you're a really interesting person. Maybe a little crazy, but interesting. I also think you're amazingly tough and brave. And you're a good mom, and even though I never thought of myself as a family man, when I'm around you and Willa I can sort of see why people start families. So you don't have to feel sorry. I'm really, really glad I met you. You make me happy.*

That was what Brad intended to say.

What he actually said, to his great surprise, was "I love you."

Jesse blinked, sniffling.

"What?" she said.

"I love you."

"Brad, you don't even know me."

"I *do* know you," he said. "I mean, I don't know a lot *about* you, but I think I know *you*."

Jesse sighed. Brad was not the first man to have declared his love for her after only a brief acquaintance.

"That's sweet, and I appreciate it, really," she said. "But I think you're confusing love with physical attraction."

Brad smiled. "Have you looked in a mirror lately?"

Jesse laughed, then grimaced in pain. "I guess I don't look so physically attractive, huh?"

"No offense."

"None taken," she said.

"But you're right, you're beautiful, and that's what I noticed first, like every other guy in the world. But that's not what this is about. Or it's not *only* what this is about. I really like being with you. I can't stop thinking about you. You make me happy. So you don't have to keep telling me you're sorry. Because I'm not sorry about anything. I love you. You don't have to love me back. I don't expect you to. But please stop apologizing, OK?"

Jesse put her hand on the hand Brad had rested on her shoulder.

"OK," she said. "I'll stop apologizing."

She left her hand on his for a few more seconds. These were without question the best seconds of Brad's life to date.

Then she pulled her hand away and said, "So what do we do now?"

"About . . ."

"About the ATV and the trailerful of gold that everybody in the world is looking for. If we leave it here, sooner or later somebody's gonna find it."

"I can drive out into the swamp," he said. "Sink it somewhere nobody'd ever find it."

"What about the gold?"

"You tell me," said Brad. "What about the gold?"

Jesse stared at the floor for a while.

"I don't know," she said.

"It's a lot of money," said Brad.

She nodded. "Yeah, which is why all these people want it so bad."

"You found it."

"I don't want to die for it."

"So what do you want to do?"

"You think it's safe for now?"

"For tonight, yeah."

"Then if it's OK with you, I'd like to decide in the morning. Right now I just want to get some sleep."

"Sure. I'll just—"

Brad was interrupted by somebody knocking on the front door, the knocking quickly turning into impatient pounding.

Brad went to the door and opened it a crack. He stepped back, shaking his head disgustedly.

Slater walked into the living room. He was still shirtless. He looked at Jesse and said, "I thought I'd find you here."

"And you were right," said Jesse.

Slater was staring at her face. "Jesus," he said. "You look like shit, Jess."

"Thank you," she said. "Will there be anything else?"

Slater looked at Brad, then back at Jesse. "You shacking up with him now?"

"Yes," she said. "Yes, I am. I'm shacking up with him. We are shack-

ing our brains out, and it's great, because he actually notices which specific person it is that he's shacking with."

Brad snorted. Slater whirled to face him. "You think that's funny?"
he said.

"I do," said Brad.

"Well, fuck you," said Slater.

"Good one," said Brad.

Slater stared at Brad for several seconds to let him know he was not
done with him. Then he turned back to Jesse.

"I'm here about the gold," he said.

"What are you talking about?" she said.

"You know exactly what I'm talking about. I saw you back there,
throwing gold bars. I saw you. Everyone knows there's gold. So don't
say you don't know about it."

Jesse nodded. "And your point is . . ."

"My point," said Slater, "is that you have gold, and half of it right-
fully belongs to me."

Jesse frowned. "How do you figure that?"

"Because I'm legally entitled to half. As your common-law husband. Under Florida law."

"Seriously? Did Kark tell you this? Is he your legal authority?"

"No," said Slater, in such a way as to leave no doubt that Kark was
in fact his legal authority.

Jesse sighed. "OK, first, you don't know where the gold came from.
You don't know who it legally belongs to. You don't know where it is.
You don't even know if it really exists."

"I know I saw you—"

"Shut up and listen to me, Slater. Even if it does exist, and I have it,
you're the last person on Earth I would give *any* of it to, let alone half
of it. I'd dump it all into the ocean before I'd give you one ounce of it."

Slater nodded, thinking, strategizing. Then he smiled at Jesse. It was
his most winning smile, the smile that never failed him with women,
the smile that had won Jesse's heart when they first met.

"Jess," he said. "I know you're mad at me. I get it. I've made some mistakes, and I'm sorry. Really. But you're being unfair here. I've been taking care of you for, like, over a year now, with the cabin and food and— HEY!"

He ducked to avoid the iPhone Jesse had pulled from her pocket and thrown, with all-county shortstop accuracy, at his head.

"What the fuck, Jess!" he said.

"You bought that cabin with *my money*," she said. "You also spent *my money* on your girlfriends and God knows what else. You spent *all* of my money, Slater. I don't owe you anything. *None* of what I have is yours."

Slater's smile was gone. "That's not true, Jess. You have one thing that's half mine."

"What?"

"The baby."

Jesse involuntarily drew Willa closer. "You're not getting near her."

"We'll see about that," said Slater. "I'm the father. I can prove I'm the father. I got rights. I'll get a lawyer. We'll see how the courts feel about it. How they feel about a mother taking the baby away from its father, carrying the baby into a crazy mob of people, throwing gold around. Seems dangerous, you know? Reckless. Like you're an unfit mother. You could lose custody, Jess."

"You wouldn't do that."

"I might have to, Jess, if I don't get my half."

Jesse stared at him. "Get out," she said.

"Jess, come on, you—"

"Get out!"

Brad stepped between them, facing Slater. "Time to go," he said.

"You gonna make me?" said Slater.

Brad shrugged. "Sure," he said.

Slater gave him a hard stare, letting him know that he was a hard starer. Then he turned and went to the front door. He opened it and looked back at Jesse.

"I'm serious, Jess," he said. "Give me half, or I'm coming for the baby."

He left, slamming the door.

"God," said Jesse. "How did I ever think I was in love with that asshole?"

"No comment," said Brad. He picked up the phone she'd thrown at Slater, the phone Erik had given her.

"You want this back?" he said.

"Did I break it?"

"Looks OK."

"Yeah, I want it. I need a phone."

"If you turn it on, they'll know where you are."

"I'll reset it, wipe out the settings. I need a phone."

"OK," he said, handing it to her.

"Do you think he's right?" she said.

"The asshole? Right about what?"

"About Willa. Do you think he could take her away?"

Brad shook his head. "I mean, obviously it'd be wrong, but you never know, when lawyers get involved . . ."

"He *is* the biological father."

"He is."

"I could just give him half the gold."

"You could."

"But he's a complete piece of shit."

"There's that."

She sighed. "This is such a mess."

"It is."

"And here you were, just minding your own business until I dragged you into it."

"No apologies, remember?"

"You're right, I'm sorry."

"That sounded like an apology."

She smiled, then winced. "I need some sleep."

"OK."

She rose, carefully lifting the now-sleeping Willa, and went to the hallway, Brad following. She stopped at the door to the bedroom that once belonged to Brad's parents. Brad stopped at the door to his room. They looked at each other.

"Thanks," she said. "For everything. You're a good guy."

He frowned. "You mean like a friend? Are you friend-zoning me?"

She smiled again, winced again, then got the smile back on. "No," she said, opening the door. "You're not in the friend zone."

"Whew," said Brad. "What zone am I in?"

"Good night," said Jesse, closing the door.

"Good night," said Brad.

He fell asleep happy.

Chapter 56

Jesse awoke to the smell of man-stink and the feel of a cold, sharp blade against her throat. A callused hand was gripping her face, covering her mouth.

"Don't scream," whispered Duck. "I'm gonna take my hand off your face. You make any noise, I cut your fucking throat. You understand?"

Jesse nodded.

Duck removed his hand from her face. He switched on the bedside lamp and stood. Billy was next to the window, which was open. Billy's broken hand was wrapped in duct tape.

Jesse turned to check on Willa, sleeping peacefully next to her. Then she sat up, grateful that she'd slept with her clothes on.

"Look at me," said Duck.

She looked. Duck was wearing a hoodie, the hood pulled forward and down, covering most of his face. He yanked the hood back, and Jesse gasped. Duck's face was something from a horror movie—a half-dozen big oozing wounds where the shovel blade had sliced the skin, an eye swollen shut, the lower lip split in two. A curtain of blood from his scalp was seeping down his forehead.

"Thought you finished me, didn't you, bitch?" he said.

Jesse said nothing.

"We figured your boyfriend would bring you back to his store. You made it easy. First window we tried, it's not even locked, and here you are."

Jesse said nothing.

"I should kill you right now," he said.

Jesse said nothing.

"Only one thing keeping you alive," he said. "You know what it is."

Jesse nodded.

"So where is it?" said Duck.

"It's here," she said.

"Where?"

"I don't know exactly."

Jesse flinched as Duck jerked the knife toward her face.

"What does that mean?" he said.

"It's out back somewhere, I don't know exactly where. Brad hid it out there."

"The boyfriend," said Billy.

"Where is he?" said Duck.

Jesse hesitated. Duck moved the knife again, this time toward the sleeping Willa.

"No, please," said Jesse.

"Where is he?" said Duck.

"He's here," she said. "In the next room."

Duck thought for a few seconds.

"OK," he said. "Here's what we do. You're gonna pick up your kid and hand it to me."

"No," said Jesse. "Please."

Duck jerked the knife again, this time toward Willa.

"No, please, no," said Jesse. "I'll do what you say."

"Fucking right you will," said Duck. "Now give me the kid."

Jesse, struggling to hold back tears, gently picked up Willa and held her out to Duck.

"Please, please be careful," she said.

Duck, holding the knife in his right hand, cradled the sleeping baby in his left arm.

"You do exactly what I tell you," he said. "Understand?"

"Yes," said Jesse, her eyes on Willa.

"Let's go wake up your boyfriend."

They went into the hall. Duck nodded toward the door to the other bedroom. Jesse knocked three times.

"Brad," she said. "Brad, please wake up."

Thirty seconds later the door opened. Brad, pulling up his jeans, said, "Is everything—"

He stopped, seeing Duck and Billy.

"Hello, asshole," said Duck.

"I'm sorry," said Jesse. "They have Willa."

Brad nodded. He looked at Duck.

"Let them go," he said. "I'll show you where the ATV is."

"Yes, you will, asshole."

"So let them go."

"You don't give the orders, asshole. You take the orders, understand?" He held the knife near Willa's sleeping face.

"Please, Brad," said Jesse, her voice wavering. "Please just do what he says."

"Yeah, asshole," said Billy. "Do what she says."

Brad nodded. "OK if I put my shoes on?"

"No," said Duck. He nodded toward the living room. "Take us to the ATV. Walk in front where I can see you, and don't get too close to me, understand?"

Brad nodded.

"Go," said Duck.

Brad led the way, followed by Billy. Jesse, also barefoot, stayed near Duck, and her baby. They went out the front door, then around to the back of the little house, past a jumble of random junk—tires, a couple of skeletal airboats, a battered canoe, many cans and bottles, some piles of rotted garbage. Brad set off across a weed-infested lot with scattered patches of dirt, illuminated by a full moon in a cloudless sky. Thirty yards out the lot ended and the swamp began, the water's edge marked by a line of cypress trees.

Tucked between two of these trees was the dark shape of the ATV and trailer, covered by a blue plastic tarp, the kind Floridians put on their roofs to stop leaks after a hurricane blows through.

Brad grabbed the edge of the tarp and pulled it off.

Duck, keeping his distance from Brad, nodded toward the trailer and said to Billy: "Take a look."

Billy, favoring his broken hand, climbed into the trailer and bent down. He came up holding a gold bar in his nonbroken hand, showed it to Duck.

"It's here," he said, climbing back out. "Looks like most of it."

"OK," said Brad. "Now give her the baby, and you can go."

Jesse held her hands out for Willa.

Duck shook his head.

"Nuh-uh," he said.

"Please," said Jesse. "You have the gold."

"That's right," said Duck, "and we got the baby, too. That's our insurance. We keep the baby 'til we're out of here."

"No!" said Jesse. "We won't do anything, I swear it. You can take the gold! Brad, tell him."

"Give her the baby," said Brad. "I won't do anything."

"Like we would ever trust you," said Billy.

"My brother's right, asshole," said Duck. "Soon as I hand over the baby, I got no way to know what you're gonna do. The baby stays with us."

"No!" cried Jesse. Willa, startled awake by her mother's voice, started crying. "*Please*," said Jesse, sobbing. "I'm begging you. *Please*." She fell to her knees in front of Duck.

A leer formed on Duck's hideously marred face. "Maybe while you're down there, you should give me a blow job."

Billy laughed, Duck joining him. They stopped when Brad took a step toward them.

"Watch it, asshole," said Duck, waving the knife. Brad stopped.

Willa was crying harder now.

Jesse looked up at Duck. "If you take her," she said, struggling to control her voice, "how do I get her back?"

"We'll work something out," said Duck, smiling.

"Please, God, no," Jesse wailed, grabbing at Duck's legs.

He kicked her away, his look warning Brad to keep back. She put her face in her hands, sobbing. Duck went to the trailer, threw a leg over and climbed in. Willa was bawling.

"Billy," said Duck. "Time to go."

Billy climbed onto the ATV seat. He looked at the console, frowned, looked back at Duck.

"There's no key," he said.

"What the fuck," said Duck. He looked at Brad. "Where's the fucking key?"

Brad waited a couple of beats, then dug his hand into his jeans pocket. He pulled out a large, flat, silver-colored key and held it up. It glinted in the moonlight.

"Give it to Billy," said Duck.

"Give her the baby," said Brad.

"We done this once already, asshole," said Duck. "Last time you dropped the gun. This time you're gonna give us the key."

Brad shook his head. "No."

Jesse was staring at him.

"If you don't drop it," said Duck, "I'm gonna hurt this fucking baby."

"You do *anything* to the baby," said Brad, "and I throw this key into the swamp."

"How do I know you won't do that anyway, if I give up the baby?"

"Because then it'll be me here with a woman and a baby against two pissed-off guys with a knife. I *want* you to leave."

Duck frowned. "You don't want the gold?"

"Not as much as I want to keep the three of us alive."

Duck nodded slowly. "So how do we do this?"

"Duck," said Billy, "we can't—"

"Shut the fuck up, Billy," said Duck. He looked back at Brad. "How do we do this?"

"I set the key on the ground and walk away from it, let's say ten steps. Your brother does not move. You hand the baby to Jesse. When she has the baby, she comes to me and your brother goes to the key. Then you leave. With the gold."

A long silence from Duck, then: "OK."

"OK," said Brad. He bent over and set the key down on the ground. He straightened, looking at Billy, then Duck.

"Billy," said Duck, "don't move."

Brad walked away from the key, ten steps exactly. He looked at Jesse.

Jesse rose and went to the trailer. As she leaned over the side and reached for her baby, she lost her balance and almost fell in, her legs waving in the air. After a few seconds she pushed herself back upright and again reached out toward Duck. He handed Willa to her. Jesse turned and ran to Brad, hugging her crying baby. Brad put his arm around her, pulled her close. She sobbed into his shoulder, her body shaking as she comforted Willa.

Billy went over to the key and picked it up. He went back to the ATV, inserted the key into the ignition and turned it. The engine started.

Duck was staring at Brad, standing with Jesse twenty feet away.

Raising his voice over the sound of the ATV, Duck said, "We ain't done, asshole."

Brad said nothing.

"We're coming back for you," said Duck. He pointed to Jesse. "You too, sweetheart. We are *definitely* not done with you. We got money now, and we'll be back." He turned to Billy. "Let's go."

Billy cranked the throttle and the ATV rolled forward, pulling the trailer with the gold and Duck, who was still staring at Brad and Jesse. The ATV crossed the weeded lot, swerved around the side of the little house. Duck was still staring back at them as the trailer disappeared.

Brad and Jesse watched it go, his arm around her, her arms around

Willa. Willa was calming down, soothed by her mother's voice and touch. Jesse was still shaking a little but no longer sobbing.

"I'm sorry," said Brad, finally.

"Sorry for what?"

"Well for one thing, they got the gold."

"I don't care. I'm glad it's gone. All I care is about is you got Willa back."

"I wasn't sure how you'd feel about . . . I mean, when I told him I wasn't gonna give him the key, I was taking a chance."

"Yeah, but you were right. It was the only way. If we'd let him take Willa . . . I can't even think about it. You have nothing to be sorry about."

"I'm sorry about one thing."

"Which is?"

"They're still alive. What he said at the end there . . . I believe him. He's not gonna let it go. They'll come back."

"Maybe not."

Brad looked at her. "What do you mean?"

"Remember when I went to get Willa from the creep, and I lost my balance and fell into the trailer?"

"Yes."

"I didn't lose my balance. I did that on purpose."

Brad frowned. "Why'd you do that?"

"So I could put the phone in the trailer."

"Holy shit. You . . . you *did* that?"

"Yup. When I was on the ground, I felt it in my pocket. And when you were talking to the creep, I turned it on. I stuck it down the side of the gold pile, where it won't show."

"So if somebody is still tracking it . . ."

"Yeah. They'll find the creeps."

"Holy shit, Jesse. That was really, really smart."

"Thank you."

"Remind me never to piss you off."

"You better not."

He still had his arm around her, and this seemed like a natural time to give her a squeeze. Feeling it, she lifted her face toward his, gave him a little smooch on the cheek. Then they walked together back to the little house, still touching. Brad wanted that walk to go on forever.

Chapter 57

As the sun rose over the Atlantic the next morning, Tenklo was back on South Beach, at his post outside Kristov Berliuz's office in the hotel behind the Bongo Mongo.

Tenklo's head was bandaged where the gold bar had hit him. Also bandaged, more heavily, was his shoulder, which had been treated by the extremely discreet physician employed to tend to members of the Berliuz organization.

Tenklo did not feel great, but his main concession to his injuries was that instead of standing in front of the office door, he was sitting on a folding chair. In his hand was the phone he was using to keep in touch with the rest of Berliuz's crew, who were out searching for the gold. Kristov Berliuz had not given up on the gold. Kristov Berliuz never gave up on anything.

At Tenklo's feet, its charger plugged into a wall outlet, lay the iPad. It had been retrieved, along with the ATV, by the Berliuz henchpersons who had rescued the semiconscious Tenklo from the mob out in the Everglades. Tenklo had spent the night in a hazy, painkiller-induced stupor, so he hadn't checked the iPad until early this morning, when he found that the battery had died.

Now he picked it up and pressed the power button. As the iPad came to life, he wasn't expecting much: The last time he'd looked, out in the swamp, the icon indicating the location of the iPhone had not appeared. But he knew he had to check, because Berliuz would expect him to. Berliuz was a very thorough man.

The iPad powered up. Tenklo navigated to the Find My app.

And there it was.

Tenklo stared at the icon.

It was back. It had moved, but it was still in the Everglades.

Tenklo stood, grunting in pain. He knocked on the door.

"Come in," said Berliuz.

Tenklo entered the office. Berliuz, behind his desk, shot him a questioning look. Tenklo set the iPad down on the desk. He pointed to the icon.

"The phone," he said, speaking in the language of their homeland. "It's back."

Berliuz looked at the icon. "Where are Lokias and Premi?"

"Not far from there. A few miles."

"Send them."

Tenklo nodded. "I will go, too."

Berliuz raised a questioning eyebrow, pointedly looking at the bandage on Tenklo's forehead. This was the closest Tenklo had ever seen his boss come to expressing concern for his welfare.

"I will go," Tenklo repeated. Then, in English, he added: "It's personal."

Berliuz nodded.

Tenklo picked up the iPad, turned and left.

Chapter 58

Brad was awakened midmorning by pounding on his bedroom door. It was Ken, his eyes bloodshot. He'd spent most of the night at the cabin smoking weed with Kark and Slater.

"What?" said Brad.

"Need you in the store, bro," said Ken. "We got a UPS delivery, T-shirts and some other shit. A LOT of people out there wanna buy Melon Monster merch. We're all over the news. Also huge on social media. *Huge.*" He lowered his voice. "Also there's a lotta people looking for the gold. Which, FYI, Slater also knows about it. Says half of it's his. So wherever you got it hid, make sure it's hid good."

"It's gone," said Brad.

"You mean, like, you took it somewhere?"

Brad shook his head. "It's gone. There is no more gold."

Ken arched his eyebrows. "OK, then. No more gold. Anyway, I need you in the store, like, now."

"I'll be right there."

A few minutes later Brad entered the store through the rear door and pushed through the crowd to the front. Ken was behind the counter, selling T-shirts out of cardboard boxes on the floor next to him. They were going fast; people were literally throwing twenties at Ken (Bortle Brothers was cash only). Brad went behind the counter, picked up a shirt.

"Ken," he said, "you know 'melon' has only one 'L,' right?"

"These people don't care," said Ken, accepting a wad of bills.

Brad looked out the window. The parking lot was overflowing, a jumbled mass of vehicles and people, many of whom had slept there in their cars. Hundreds of people were wandering around, some carrying metal detectors, some wearing monster costumes. Brad counted four TV-news trucks.

"Jesus," he said.

"I know," said Ken. "Give me a hand here, OK?"

In less than an hour they sold everything they had. People kept coming in; Ken told them he was expecting another T-shirt delivery any minute. They all decided to wait. Meanwhile, outside, more people were showing up, and still more.

"I don't get it," said Brad when he and Ken had a quiet moment. "Why are these people here?"

Ken held up his phone. "Because it's on here. Go to TikTok. Every other video is about this. There's videos with celebrities, influencers ... OK, look at this one."

Brad looked at Ken's phone, which displayed a video of a man in a white robe, standing in front of a huge crowd. The man held up a Melon Monster head that looked a lot like the one Phil wore in the videos. The man put it on. The crowd went wild.

"Is that ... ," said Brad. "Is that the *pope*?"

"Yup," said Ken. "CGI. You can't even tell it's not real. Look how many views it has. And there's thousands of videos like that."

"But *why*? I mean, no offense, but this whole thing—the monster, the video you made—it's stupid. And it's obviously fake. Everybody can see it's stupid and fake."

Ken shrugged. "So?"

Brad gestured at the parking lot. "So why are all these people here?"

"Because everybody else is here."

"But it's *bullshit*."

"Yeah, but it's *their* bullshit. To these kids, *everything* is bullshit, but at least this is bullshit they can be part of." He pointed out the window to a young woman holding a crude homemade version of the Melon Monster head. As they watched, she put it on and took a selfie in front of the Bortle Brothers sign.

"See?" said Ken. "She's part of the same thing as Cardi B. And the pope!"

"Who's Cardi B?" said Brad.

"Never mind," said Ken. "The point is, this isn't really about the thing it's supposably about. It's about them." He pointed at the parking-lot crowd.

"You think it'll last?"

"Probably not. I say we cash in while it's here."

Brad nodded, looking at the Bortle Brothers sign, and said, "Know what I think?"

"What?"

"I think Dad and Uncle Canaan would've loved this."

"Really?"

"Absolutely. This was their whole business model. Taking money from tourists for complete bullshit."

Ken laughed. "True." He looked at Brad. "So you're saying I was right? My idea? That you said was so stupid?"

"I still think it's stupid," said Brad. "But I guess, these days, stupid is what works."

Ken nodded. "I'll take that as an apology."

As he spoke Jesse entered the store, holding Willa in her carrier. They both looked better than they had the previous night; Willa had just been fed, and Jesse's face was less swollen, though still deeply bruised.

"Morning," she said.

"Morning," said Brad and Ken.

"I apologize for how I look," said Jesse. "I don't have any—"

"You look beautiful," said Brad, getting a look from Ken.

"Well, I don't, but thank you," said Jesse. "Looks like you've been busy out here."

"We've sold a lot of T-shirts," said Ken, pointing to a customer sporting one.

"You know there's only one 'L' in 'melon,' right?" said Jesse.

"I need to write that down," said Ken.

"Anything I can do to help? I worked retail a couple of summers in college."

"At the moment," said Brad, "we got nothing to sell."

"That's about to change," said Ken. He nodded toward the parking lot. A UPS van was pulling off the highway. The crowd, seeing it, was already heading toward the store.

"I'll go help the driver," said Ken, hurrying out the door.

Jesse set Willa's carrier down behind the counter. "So," she said. "What do you need me to do?"

"You don't need to help, really," said Brad. "We can handle it ourselves."

"I want to help," she said. "And judging from the condition of your store bathroom, you can't handle it yourselves."

Brad laughed. "Seriously, you don't need to—"

"Brad," she said, putting her hand on his forearm. "I need to make myself useful around here. I'm not rich anymore. I need a job."

"So you're planning to . . . I mean, you want to stay?"

"Do you want me to stay?" She kept her hand on his forearm.

"Hell yes, I want you to stay," he said.

"Then I want to stay," she said.

They were looking into each other's eyes.

"If this was a movie," said Brad, "we'd kiss each other now."

"Not in front of Willa," said Jesse. "Maybe later."

"It's a date," said Brad.

"OK," she said. "Now let's sell these people some misspelled shirts."

Chapter 59

Phil awoke with a fierce headache, a throbbing knee and a bursting bladder.

Somebody was rapping at the door to his apartment.

"WAIT A MINUTE," he said, limping to the bathroom. He relieved himself for what felt like a solid five minutes, then looked at himself in the mirror. He was still wearing the Duke sweatshirt, having fallen asleep in his clothes when Stu finally, after hours stuck in the Tamiami Trail traffic mess, got him home. His hair was a tangled, oily mess; he had massive bags under his bloodshot eyes; his skin, beneath three days' worth of gray beard stubble, had a distinctly yellowish cast, with some red splotches. He looked like a homeless person, which he realized was what he would be pretty soon.

More rapping on the door.

"I'M COMING."

He limped to the door, opened it.

Stella stared at his face.

"Ohmigod, Daddy," she said. "You look horrible."

"I'm OK," he said. "Just a little tired."

She shook her head. "You're not OK."

"How'd you get here?"

"I drove."

"Alone?"

"Yes."

"Your mom let you drive all the way out here?"

"She thinks I went to Dadeland."

"Baby girl, you shouldn't have done that."

"We need to talk."

He nodded, then winced from the pain bomb that the movement detonated in his forehead.

"OK," he said. He led her into the living room, which was also the dining area and kitchen. He cleared some old *Miami Herald*s off the sofa, which was rented and was about to be repossessed, as Phil had not made any payments for five months.

They sat down.

"OK," he said. "What are we talking about?"

Stella took a breath, let it out, then said: "Your drinking."

Phil sat up. "Stella, I really don't think my drinking is your business."

"Really?" She took her phone out of her pocket, tapped the screen, handed it to Phil. It displayed a slo-mo video of him during the mob scene in the Everglades. In it he lifted the monster head briefly, revealing his face, beet red and glistening with sweat, his jaw slack, his eyes glassy and unfocused.

Phil turned his head, but Stella moved her phone so it stayed in front of him.

"Do you know how many views that has?" she said. "You know how many of my friends have sent me that and said, 'Is that your dad?' Do you know how big of a joke you are?"

"Stella, you're not being fair here. You don't know the whole story."

"What's the whole story, Dad?"

"OK, I was . . . first of all, I hurt my knee, so I was on painkillers."

"So you took pills *and* got drunk?"

"I wasn't drunk."

"Really, Dad? You didn't have anything to drink?"

"I didn't say I didn't have anything to drink. I said I wasn't drunk."

"How much did you drink?"

Phil was getting angry. "Stella, you don't get to ask me these questions. I don't answer to you. I'm your father."

"Yeah, and I'm your daughter, which is why I'm asking you these questions."

Phil sighed. "OK, you're right. Maybe I've been drinking too much. But, baby girl, I'm under a lot of pressure."

It was Stella's turn to sigh. "You were also under a lot of pressure when Mom got sick."

"Stella, that's not—"

"Let me finish. You were under pressure when Mom got sick. Before that you were under pressure because of your job. Now you're under pressure because you don't have a job. And the way you handle the pressure is always to drink. It's how you handle everything. Because you're an alcoholic, Daddy."

"I'm not an alcoholic."

"Yeah you are."

"What, did you google alcoholism? Is that how you know this?"

"Yes."

"Fucking Google," said Phil.

"You need help," said Stella.

"Let me guess," said Phil. "You think I should go to a meeting, sit around with a bunch of drunks, tell everybody I have a problem."

"Yes," said Stella. "I think you should do that."

"I'm not going to a meeting."

Stella leaned forward. "Daddy, one of my girlfriends' fathers had a drinking problem, and he got help, and now things are much better. He's a really nice guy. You could talk to him."

Phil, bristling, said, "Did you tell him about me?"

"Not him, no. I talked to my girlfriend. She said her dad has done this before, talked to people who . . . who're like you."

Phil thought for a moment, then shook his head.

"I'm sorry," he said. "I don't want to talk to some guy I don't even know."

"Daddy, please—"

"But listen," he said. "I'll tell you what I will do."

"What?"

"I'll stop drinking."

She stared at him. "What do you mean?"

"I'll stop drinking."

"For how long?"

"For as long as it takes to convince my daughter I don't have a drinking problem."

"You mean it?"

"Yes."

"You won't drink at all?"

"I won't drink at all, until you're convinced I'm OK."

"You swear?"

"I swear."

"You really really swear?"

Phil smiled. "I really really swear."

"You swear on my life?"

Phil hesitated, then said, "I swear on your life."

"Thank you, Daddy," said Stella. "Thank you." She started sobbing. Phil hugged her, Stella saying thank you over and over, Phil patting her back, his little girl, telling her it was OK, he loved her, everything was going to be OK.

After they hugged for a while, Stella dried her tears, composing herself. Phil asked her a few questions about school, just so they could be talking about something else. Then he walked her to the door. Stella hugged him again.

"Thank you, Daddy," she said.

"No, thank you," he said. "I know it was hard for you to do this."

She kissed him on the cheek and left.

Phil went back to the living room and sat down on the rented sofa. He spent several minutes staring straight ahead, looking at nothing.

Then he rose, got his keys and wallet, and went outside. He lowered his head against the glare of the Florida sun as he limped across the parking lot.

He opened the door of the Gallo Grande, welcoming the dim light, the air-conditioning, the familiar smell of fried food and stale beer. He took his usual seat at the bar and signaled to the bartender, who nodded and began making a Moscow mule.

Phil looked up at the TV monitor, which was showing a rerun of an international curling match, Sweden vs. Scotland, apparently a classic. He heard the door open behind him. The bartender set his drink down in front of him. He picked it up, anticipating the smell, the taste, the warm, comforting feeling of the alcohol seeping into his body.

Then he felt the gaze on his back.

He turned and saw her standing in the doorway.

"Stella," he said.

She turned and left.

Phil looked at the drink, still in his hand. He brought it almost to his mouth. He could smell it now.

Then, slowly, he set it down. He stood, put a bill on the bar and left.

Outside he saw Stella across the parking lot, walking toward her car.

"Stella!" he called to her back.

She kept walking.

Phil started limping after her. "Stella, wait!"

She kept walking.

"Stella, please!" Phil broke into an ugly trot, his knee throbbing. He managed four steps before he stumbled and fell, his hands barely breaking his fall, his face almost hitting the hot asphalt. He struggled clumsily to rise, managed to get himself into a kneeling position. He looked up and saw that Stella had stopped. She was looking back at him. Her face was red and streaked with tears.

"Please," he said. "Please."

Slowly, slowly, she started walking back toward him.

Phil, still on his knees, put his face in his hands, sobbing. Through his fingers, he saw her standing in front of him. He couldn't bring himself to look up at her. He tried to stop crying, but he could not.

"C'mon, Dad," she said softly. "I'll help you."

He looked up, blinking. Stella was holding her hands out to him.

He reached out for his daughter's hands, the way a drowning man reaches for a life preserver.

Chapter 60

When Duck and Billy got back to their campsite, towing the gold they'd been seeking for so long, they celebrated by fondling some ingots and consuming an entire bottle of Everclear. It was a fairly brief celebration, progressing from giddiness to unconsciousness in a little over an hour. Now they lay passed out in the dirt in front of their camper, Billy with his head on a gold bar he was using as a pillow, Duck sleeping with a bar in each cargo pocket of his camo pants. The rest of the gold was still in the ATV trailer.

Their campsite was in a clearing next to a weed-choked stream miles from the paved road. Somebody had once planned to build a home here, but that plan had apparently been abandoned long ago. The clearing was the end of what was left of a long, winding dirt road that had been almost entirely reclaimed by swamp vegetation. They had barely been able to tow their little camper in there, dragging it through the thick bushes closing in from both sides.

The Campbells had never seen anybody else on this property, or even near it. They felt safe here, safe and hidden, and had passed out unconcerned about being found.

Duck awoke suddenly, hearing the snarl of ATV engines, definitely more than one. He rolled over and stood, cocking his head. The engines were getting louder.

"Billy!" he said, kicking his brother. Billy groaned and rolled away. Duck kicked him again, harder. "Get up!"

Billy opened his eyes and sat up. "What the fuck?"

Duck was staring at the road. "Somebody's coming."

Billy scrambled to his feet, heard the engines. "How the fuck do they know—"

"Get the shotgun," said Duck.

The shotgun, a Remington 870, was the Campbells' lone remaining firearm, as they had both lost their pistols back at the original gold site.

Billy ran into the camper, grabbed the shotgun. When he came back outside Duck had climbed onto the seat of the ATV and started the engine.

"What're we doing?" said Billy.

Duck pointed to the overgrown road, which curved sharply just before the clearing. "When they come around the curve, shoot 'em."

Billy looked puzzled. "What're you gonna do? I mean how're we—"

"LISTEN to me, Billy. You empty the shotgun at them, understand? You got seven shells in there and you keep pumping 'til that fucker is empty. Then you jump into this trailer and we get the fuck out of here."

The engines sounded very close. Billy looked toward the road, then back at Duck, his face pale. "Duck, are you sure this—"

"DO NOT FUCKING PUSSY OUT ON ME," shouted Duck.

Billy turned back toward the road and racked the shotgun. As he did, the first ATV appeared, Tenklo driving it. Right behind were two more men on ATVs.

"SHOOT!" yelled Duck.

Billy pulled the trigger. His broken hand made it difficult for him to aim. The blast of buckshot went mostly wide, but a few pellets caught Tenklo's left leg, making him swerve violently.

"SHOOT!" yelled Duck again, but Billy had already racked the shotgun and was firing. This time he missed everything, but he got lucky: Tenklo, swerving again to evade the shot, yanked the handlebars too hard and rolled his ATV. The second ATV, following close, smashed into Tenklo's, and the third smashed into the second, a chain-reaction collision that sent all three riders flying.

That was the end of Billy's luck. Before he could rack the shotgun again, Tenklo, on the ground, drew and fired twice, both shots hitting Billy in the chest. Billy staggered backward, dropping the shotgun, then fell to his knees. He looked down at the two holes in his shirt, then turned to look at his brother.

But Duck was already gone. Duck had taken off the instant he saw Tenklo draw his gun. Duck had anticipated this outcome; he knew he and Billy would probably be outgunned by whoever was coming down the road. That was why he had given Billy the shotgun job. Duck figured that even if that tactic didn't work, it might delay the attackers long enough to provide a chance to escape. At least for Duck.

Duck did not look back at his brother, lying in the dirt, staring in his direction, taking his last breaths. Duck's attention was focused ahead of him as he fought to maneuver the ATV through the underbrush, its engine screaming, the trailer jouncing. He veered right, toward the shallow stream, hoping to follow it to some kind of more manageable terrain. He looked back over his shoulder, trying to get a glimpse through the bushes, to see if the men were after him. So far they weren't, but he knew they'd be coming.

Duck kept blasting ahead, wrestling the handlebars. The landscape was opening up, the thick bushes giving way to sawgrass. The terrain was getting wetter, the ATV splashing through shallow water, Duck struggling to steer between clumps of vegetation. Again and again he looked back; still no sign of the men. There was an open stretch of water ahead; easier going, it looked like. Duck cranked the throttle all the way to full. The engine was screaming now, the ATV going close to forty miles per hour. Duck took another look back over his shoulder.

That was when he hit the sinkhole.

It was filled with water, so it was indistinguishable from the rest of the swamp. But the rest of the swamp was only two or three feet deep. The sinkhole, its walls starkly vertical, went seventy feet straight down.

The ATV tilted suddenly backward, pulled by the heavily laden trailer, then plunged toward the bottom. The handlebars caught on

Duck's hoodie and yanked him beneath the surface. He had no time to react, no time to take a breath before he found himself being dragged relentlessly down in the murky water, toward the blackness below.

Struggling frantically, he managed to free himself from the handlebars and began desperately trying to get back to the surface, kicking with his heavy boots, flailing his arms wildly, his lungs burning. But he made no upward progress. He sensed that something was still dragging him down and suddenly remembered: *He had gold bars in his pockets.* He stopped flailing his arms and reached down, frantically searching for the pocket flaps. But the instant he stopped flailing he felt himself sinking fast, and as panic flooded his brain he started flailing again, but not enough, nothing he could do was enough, and as each agonizing second passed his efforts became more feeble, until finally Duck could make no effort at all.

His body came to rest on the trailer, which had overturned and dumped its precious load onto the bottom. The gold had already begun to sink back into the Everglades soil, where it had rested for many years, and where it would rest again forever.

Epilogue

Jesse and Brad—but you knew this already—got married. For a while they lived and worked at Bortle Brothers Bait & Beer, which continued to be the epicenter of the ongoing phenomenon that was Everglades Melon Monster mania.

Eventually Jesse and Brad moved to Miami, seeking better schools for their kids (they wound up with three, producing a brother and sister for Willa). Jesse became a middle school teacher and highly successful softball coach. Brad started a contracting business, which was also highly successful because he showed up when he said he would and finished jobs on time; in Miami these were viewed as revolutionary business practices.

Jesse reestablished relations with her parents, who initially disliked Brad on principle but warmed up to him when he repaired a persistent second-floor bathtub leak in their home using $38 worth of materials after Jesse's parents had obtained an estimate, from a reputable plumber, of $11,000.

Ken stayed at Bortle Brothers, making good money selling Melon Monster merchandise, much of it with "melon" spelled correctly. (Although the original double-"L" T-shirts were worth far more, fetching insane prices from collectors on eBay.) Ken continued to be a big *Shark Tank* fan and continued to have ideas for making money. All of these ideas were terrible, but Ken was making enough from his one profitable idea that he could afford to continue happily having them.

That idea, the Everglades Melon Monster, continued, inexplicably, to resonate in the popular culture. The original iconic video, featuring

Slater, Ken and Phil, passed ten *billion* YouTube views, with no sign of stopping, inspiring a seemingly endless stream of social media content.

While most people viewed the Melon Monster as comic entertainment, there were those who believed it was real. Reinforcing this belief was the fact that almost every day people claimed to have seen the monster. Often these people produced photos or videos as evidence, although for some reason the images were always blurry.

Tourists flocked to the Everglades to take Melon Monster tours, led by professional (in the sense of getting paid) cryptozoologists. The highlight of each tour was a stop at Bortle Brothers Bait & Beer, which was now billing itself as the official Melon Monster Scientific Research Institute. Ken always made time to meet with the tour groups, dramatically recounting his harrowing encounter with the monster, answering the tourists' questions and stressing the importance of purchasing authentic Melon Monster merchandise, because proceeds from the fake knockoff crap did not go toward the ongoing scientific research being carried out by the institute.

Slater also tried to cash in on his celebrity, although less successfully. He got his reality show, *Glades Man*, with Kark as executive producer, but it was canceled after one season because of poor ratings and withering reviews. As one critic put it: "Mr. Slater is certainly pleasant enough to look at. But after watching him spend episode after episode doing little except preen and flex amid the Everglades vegetation, the viewer begins to suspect that the vegetation has a higher IQ than Mr. Slater does." Eventually Slater found his way to the porn industry, where he starred in a series of moderately successful videos, all directed by Kark, and all with titles containing the word "melons."

Phil quit drinking and started faithfully attending Alcoholics Anonymous meetings. Through his AA sponsor he got a job as a researcher for a public-interest law firm. He proved to be very good at this and played a critical role in winning a landmark $27 million discrimination lawsuit against Andrew Pletzger, the developer whose daughter whacked him in the balls with a five iron. In time Phil was able to pay off his debts, move to a decent place, catch up on child support and—best of all—buy nice things for Stella. He also became involved in community theater, getting excellent reviews in the local press for his portrayal of Coach Calhoun in *Grease*. He still had the Dora/monster head, which he kept in a garbage bag under his bed, but he never put it on.

Stu, seeking to capitalize on his connection with the Melon Monster, started a consulting business, describing himself as a "digital marketing specialist." He was not good at it, and he ended up with just one client: Bortle Brothers Bait & Beer. Stu would drive out to the store once or twice a week and take notes while Ken explained whatever terrible moneymaking idea he'd had most recently. Then they would smoke some weed and forget the whole thing. It was a solid business model.

Whitt Chastain was forced to resign as secretary of the interior amid widespread public outrage sparked by the video of his actions in the Everglades. Most people were appalled that Chastain had endangered the life of a staff member, although members of PETA were more upset about what happened to the alligator. In any event, Chastain's presidential hopes were dashed. He tried, several times, to make a political comeback but gave up because his public appearances were inevitably disrupted by audience members making oinking noises.

Things worked out better for Jacky Ramos and Frank Wallner, who started dating and eventually got married. They invited DeWayne "Skeeter" Toobs to their wedding, but he did not attend, as the wedding was held outside of the Everglades. He did, however, send the couple, as his wedding gift, a rare two-headed turtle.

Bob "Pinky" Kearful retired from drug sales and found a successful second career dealing in non-fungible tokens.

Patsy Hartmann was fired from Channel 8 PeoplePower News by her nemesis, Jennifer Taylor, for dropping the f-bomb on-air. Patsy considered retiring, then decided, like roughly two-thirds of the US population, to start a podcast. It was called *What Fucking Context?* and it consisted of Patsy drinking wine while watching, and commenting upon, the Channel 8 evening news broadcast. She was profane, snarky and vicious; she was also an instant hit. Before long the number of people listening to Patsy's commentary far exceeded the number of people actually watching Channel 8 News. Patsy never again had to wait for a table at Joe's Stone Crab.

Anthony Evander Cornwall won the Pulitzer Prize in the explanatory reporting category for a twenty-one-thousand-word story whose central thesis—supported by more than a dozen impressively credentialed academicians—was that mass disturbances such as the one that erupted at the Everglades press conference were increasing in both frequency and intensity because of widespread public anxiety about global climate change.

The nude, headless body of attorney Erik Turpake was discovered on Miami Beach in what the authorities ultimately ruled was a freak windsurfing accident.

Rupert Malstroff, the chiropractor/inventor, mysteriously disappeared from his office one afternoon and was not seen again, at least not for a while. It turned out that Malstroff's converted tanning bed really was a working time machine, and he had traveled to the year 2073. Upon arrival he was immediately arrested and imprisoned, as chiropractic is strictly banned in the future.

Kristov Berliuz never found the rest of the gold, although his henchpersons searched for days, trying to find the trail of the ATV that had managed to escape from them into the trackless swamp. They were not the only ones looking. Everyone had seen it, on the videos—people holding gold bars, people fighting over gold bars. It wasn't some phony legend. The gold was real. It had to be somewhere.

And so they came to the Everglades, day after day, people with metal detectors, and maps, and theories, looking for the gold, obsessed with the gold, certain that if they found it—if they could just get their hands on the gold—their lives would be changed forever.

Acknowledgments

Novel-writing is a solitary job, consisting mostly—in my case, anyway—of staring at a screen and thinking, *What the* hell *did I get myself into?*

But even though you write alone, there are times when you need other people—for advice, for moral support and, above all, for information about snakes. For that I turned to my old friend Carl Hiaasen, who is not only a brilliantly funny writer but also an expert on Florida wildlife. I thank Carl for his guidance on some snake questions I had while writing this book. He also helped me out on boar urination.

Another great writer I want to thank is my buddy, bandmate and sometime coauthor Ridley Pearson, who patiently tutored me in using Scrivener, a kind of writing software designed by and for people who are clearly a lot smarter than I am. Ridley is also always willing to take time to talk to me about computers, monitors, keyboards and other technical things that we writers love to discuss because that way we can avoid actually writing.

Two other writers of my acquaintance, Alan Zweibel and Adam Mansbach, did not help me at all in writing this book. Forget I even brought them up.

I thank attorneys George Pallas, Manuel Valdes and Michelle Otero-Valdes for their guidance on some legal questions. They were very helpful, although I probably got everything wrong anyway. This is totally my fault, so please don't sue them. Please don't sue me, either. Please don't sue anybody. It's just a novel.

Thanks to two veteran Florida news pros—Mary Ellen Klas, the *Miami Herald*'s Tallahassee bureau chief, and Ari Odzer, longtime reporter for NBC 6 in South Florida—for answering some technical questions. I hope the fact that I am mentioning them here does not ruin their careers.

Thanks to my two wonderful children, Rob and Sophie Barry, and my daughter-in-law, Laura Barry, for trying to educate me in the deep mysteries of social media, such as what, exactly, is the difference between TikTok and Instagram. I also want to mention my grandsons, Dylan and Kyle Barry, because they like to see their names in a book.

I thank my agent, Amy Berkower, and my editor at Simon & Schuster, Priscilla Painton, for their wise guidance and steadfast support. Without them I might have to find meaningful employment.

Finally, I thank my smart, funny, beautiful and incredibly hardworking wife, Michelle Kaufman, who, when I point at the writing on my computer screen and ask her if it's funny, always declares that it is, even though she's sitting too far away to read the words.